D1785136

OUT OF THE
GREY

SPARX LUMINARY BOOK I

OUT OF THE
GREY

SPARX LUMINARY BOOK I

K.B. SPRAGUE

GaleWind BOOKS An imprint of Whisperwood Publishing | Canada

OUT OF THE GREY, SPARX Luminary Book I by K.B. Sprague

© 2021 by Kevin Sprague. All rights reserved

ISBN: 978-1-988363-10-3 (paperback)
ISBN: 978-1-988363-11-0 (epub)

Cover designed by Damonza
Maps by Josephe Vandel of MapForge
Valkyrie sketch and illustrated half-title page by Josephe Vandel

Published in Canada by GaleWind Books,
an imprint of Whisperwood Publishing, Ottawa.

All of the characters and events in this book are fictitious.
Any resemblance to actual persons, alive or dead, is purely coincidental.

No part of this publication may be reproduced, distributed, or transmitted
in any form or by any means, including photocopying, recording, or other
electronic or mechanical methods, without the prior written permission
of the publisher, except in the case of brief quotations embodied in critical
reviews and certain other non-commercial uses permitted by copyright law.

Please purchase only authorized electronic editions, and do not
participate in or encourage the electronic piracy of copyrighted
materials. Your support of the author's rights is appreciated.

www.galewindbooks.com

For Gena, for believing.

Dancing blades…

CONTENTS

MAP OF
THEIA

DRAMATIS PERSONAE

LUMEN HADAMARD, a luminary who walks the line between enforcing the anti-tech treaty and dabbling in banned arts. How else can he protect the archives and his people against constant threat and aggression? But is he unleashing a greater destructive power?

AKRYLLA, a demented old shaman scarred by experimentation in the Star Sands and haunted by her past. She is intent on regaining her rightful place as a spiritual leader – no matter what the costs.

VEY LANCER, a promising young diplomat summoned to Fort Abandon to discuss treaty compliance and new alliances – and if a little romance is to be had along the way, all the better. But a chance encounter with Akrylla leaves her abducted, drugged, and set on a twisted path of darkness.

HERSH TEHAN, the vice-regent of Fort Abandon, is at a crossroads: comply with the treaty and continue to live in the dark ages, or forsake it and allow his people to prosper like their elite neighbors. But can he abandon his allegiance and live with the greater consequences?

GALEWIND, a knightmaiden tormented by the recent tragedy to befall her wind-riding sisters in Order Valkyrie. She struggles to conquer her guilt. With demands rising for air-surveillance and special operations, Hadamard's new 'striker' weapons could be a force-multiplier. Can Galewind overcome her remorse and secure one for her elite sisterhood?

BERENDT GARONDI, a commander in the Kith Quarter who knows what it means to have the odds stacked against him. His men are rough and wild, but they sure know how to improvise.

AMOT RIXIN, a true wild-card, the young scout has been chosen to partake in Hadamard's latest training exercise to determine who will wield the luminary's advanced weaponry. Will he rise to the expectations of his Kith brothers, or will the effort end in yet another disaster for the impulsive Wilder?

ERIFF HAULIK, a champion duelist, radiance channeler, and true-hearted queensman. He has the best of everything. Why shouldn't he and his elite Queen's Guard possess the strikers?

OUT OF THE GREY

GaleWind BOOKS AN IMPRINT OF WHISPERWOOD PUBLISHING | CANADA

The Essence persists
For the One outside all things
Devours
And the One outside all things
Remembers
And the One outside all things
Brings renewal upon the Void.

—The Diviner

AKEDAN RUINS

(Berendt, Hadamard)

THAT'S WHERE THE altar must've been. Crouched and hidden from view, Berendt surveyed the grounds of the imminent treaty bust. To what leviathan the temple had been devoted to, he couldn't be sure. *A majestic beast, no doubt.* The ceiling had long since collapsed. Above, the evening sky darkened fast. The smell of the sea hung heavy in the air, with sharp hints of dulse exposed by the low tide. Waves broke upon the sandy bay in regular succession.

Persons unknown had cleared debris from the ruined shell of the fallen temple—that was the first tip-off something was amiss. Stubby remnants of support columns cast long, crooked shadows over the stone floor, the stacked cylinders they were made of having slid out of line. Each stood merely a few segments high, arranged in two neat rows along the length of the former grand hall. Along the middle of the hall ran a sunken throughway where water pooled. At the head of the ruined chamber, wide steps led to a stone dais, raised by sturdy blocks and backed by a curved recessed area—the apse. Its domed top was fractured and flakes of color still clung to the stonework there, dominated by dark hues of blue and green.

A fringe cult back then, Berendt reminded himself, *the roots of Harrow.* Historians held that the congregation knelt in water during sermons and ceremonies, draped in seaweed. Berendt's eyes drifted to the crumbled temple walls where fractured scenes, etched onto heavily pitted limestone panels, hinted of a whale-like deity with the tentacles of a kraken protruding from its massive forebody. The Kith commander scratched at his bearded chin, wondered if such a beast ever existed. Then something caught his eye.

Berendt lowered his gaze to a section of the floor where the rough-cut tiles were oddly stained, pitted and tarred. *Someone's been experimenting, measuring*, he thought, *the way treaty breakers do. And illegally,* he was sure. Fort Abandoners had reported strange flashes coming from the ruins at night. That was the second tip-off. Berendt had thoroughly investigated the claims. The guilds were silent on all counts, the oligarchs wouldn't admit to any unsavory deeds, and none of the administrative offices carried any record of official activity in the area.

The third tip-off was an informant. Berendt smirked to himself. *There's always an informant, an insider.* In this case a former luminary, 2nd Institute. *I hope to hell she got the message and I hope to hell she stayed away.*

Berendt looked to the spotter lying prone beside him, whispered, "Seen enough, Rix?"

Rix nodded, his features lost in the cowl of the hood he wore. He whispered back, "The low walls in front of the two doors…" His bow was out and ready, one arrow notched and two more in hand.

"I know," Berendt replied, keeping his voice low. Rix was referring to a small section of the temple that hadn't collapsed, extending out from the dais. Steps led down left and right to sunken doors, wholly intact. "Keep watch on those portals while I confer with our friend from the Order. It's his job to let us in on what the hell we're up against. He should have arrived with Amot by now." Berendt paused, eyed the portals closely. "I suspect at least one opens to an underground facility. Don't shoot anybody if you don't have to. New directive states at least half are to be taken alive."

Rix scoffed. "Is the other half suddenly going to surrender themselves? That's just stupid." He could hide his red hair under his hood, but he couldn't hide his equally fiery attitude.

Berendt grimaced in response. "We've been accused of heavy-handedness."

The spotter scoffed again. "Is there a limit on how many of *us* they can kill? I don't think so."

Berendt shrugged. "Don't let it get in the way, Quick. Think of it as a guideline."

Rix nodded, then sniffed at the air. "Do you smell that?"

Now that he thought of it, Berendt had caught a strange odor in wafts now and again. Unrecognizable, but with a distinct, manufactured tinge to it. "Probably something from the lab. They can't hide everything—a vent maybe? Or a leak of some kind? The luminary should be able to fill us in on the details."

"Hope so. Don't like it."

"Never mind the smell. Just keep an eye on those doors."

The hood nodded.

With barely a sound, Berendt crept back through the rubble towards the rendezvous point. Halfway there, he halted. He remained still for a long moment, ears perked and eyes slowly scanning the ruined city around him. *I'm alone,* he concluded. Then he ducked behind a partial wall.

Just one for focus, he promised himself. Berendt slipped his hand into his belt pouch, pulled out his pewter flask of whiskey and downed a swig. The golden liquid felt like fire going down his throat, and just enough to set his mind straight. He wiped his lips. *Tough friggin' op.*

After a subdued sigh, the Kith commander put the flask away, set aside his trepidations and continued on his way to where he'd meet up with his latest "project": Amot. The young scout—only a couple of years older than Rix—was an aggressive, risk-taking scrapper. *He'll grow out of that eventually,* Berendt hoped, as he crept around the last shattered alley to his destination. *It's all about keeping him under control in the meantime, so he doesn't get himself killed.* Sometimes though, it seemed like the scout was trying to do just that.

The meeting place—the crumbled statue of an Akedan general

overlooking the bay—appeared vacant, until the young scout stepped out of the shadows to greet the commander. Amot was outfitted for close combat, Wilder style of course. That meant light, tribal armor and no helmet. Getting a Wilder to wear headgear was like convincing a cat to wear a beret. Amot's straight, dark hair draped over his sturdy shoulder pauldrons. A thin braid dangled to one side, tied with a single bead.

A quick glance to the man behind Amot confirmed that the scout had brought an enforcer in from Gan. The tall, bearded man wore dark red armor with a charcoal-colored cloak. He was younger than others Berendt had met from his order, perhaps in his late thirties. He carried a straight, wooden staff, with what Berendt perceived to be a caged luminary gemstone on the top end, sheathed in black leather. *That's different,* he thought. The usual custom was to wear the fire amber on an iron chain around the neck or, rarely, encrusted onto a helm.

"Commander," the scout said quietly, "this is our enforcer, Lumen Hadamard."

Berendt regarded the luminary, addressed him in hushed tones. "Do you have authority in this matter?"

"Commander Garondi," Hadamard replied, "I've heard a great many things about you." He reached into an inner pocket.

Berendt grunted. "Any of 'em good?"

"No," he replied. From the man's flat tone, Berendt couldn't tell if he was serious or joking.

Hadamard's gloved hand produced a rolled document. He unraveled it in front of the Kith commander's eyes. "Signed by Forsetti at the urging of the Hidden City, backed by the Grand Overseer and… Lady Apsarla."

Berendt raised an eyebrow as he examined the document. "Lady Apsarla?"

Amot interjected, "We had need of her mounts."

Berendt accepted with a nod, still fixated on the wording of the third section.

"Alchemical? Again? Shroud's Well. I have two on the mend from last time."

Hadamard sighed. "That was a small lab. *This* is the big one."

Amot addressed his commander, "Lady Apsarla agreed to fly in an assault team from Gan."

Berendt grumbled back, "One assault team, that's it? Are they any good?" *Better not be newbies, shoved into harm's way just for experience sake.*

Amot nodded. "Some of the best. A kithblade, Hallman, plus two Stout trackers... and—"

"I know Hallman," Berendt broke in. "Good choices all around. We'll need the muscle. How did you and Lumen Hadamard get here?"

"Horseback."

"Hmph." Berendt rubbed his beard, regarded the enforcer. "Lady Apsarla couldn't spare another gryphon, could she?"

The man half-shrugged.

Berendt shifted his gaze to Amot. "Well, I pulled up a deadeye from training to help out. He's younger than you even, but a damn good shot. You know him."

"Rix Caledon?" Amot said.

"That's him."

"And there's another that flew in," Amot said. "One Taint."

"Blade or bow?"

"Blade. We're short on bows again."

"I'll fill in." Berendt patted the hand crossbow hanging at his side. "I was a deadeye once too, y'know." He couldn't think of a single Taint in the Kith brotherhood. "A Taint, eh? What mix is he?"

"She," Amot corrected. "Baruush."

Berendt grunted. "Hmph. Strong as a bear then, I'll bet. But still not enough." He regarded the luminary. "What about the gryphons that brought the assault team here?"

Hadamard shook his head. "They crammed everyone onto a single Gold and it can't be risked. Not for this."

But our lives sure can, thought Berendt.

"On top of that," Hadamard continued, "Lady Apsarla was short-handed. She had to call on a classroom flight trainer to fly the beast. The woman hasn't been on ops for a decade."

Berendt growled in displeasure. "No end to the troubles. All right then, we'll make do." He wondered if the luminary was referring to the knightmaiden he'd once worked with on deep patrols. *Galewind. It'd be good to see her again. Really good.* He'd never even learned her true name. Berendt dismissed the notion, turned to Amot. He updated the scout on the situation, then gave him his orders. "Amot, give the assault team the layout. Set them up to breach the doors."

Amot shook his head. "No, we should keep waiting. Follow the hostiles as they depart and ambush them farther away from the facility, out in the open. Easy to subdue that way—50/50 rule, you know."

Berendt gruffed, "That won't do."

Amot offered a second alternative. "Or Rix can pluck them off one by one as they exit."

The Kith commander grimaced, shaking his head. "That won't go over well either, trust me." He swung his gaze to the luminary in their midst. "Enforcer?"

Lumen Hadamard spoke with a firm, imploring voice. "No waiting. We need to go in fast, hit hard. A wind rider tracked a full company of Scarsanders incoming. Due by nightfall and it's already getting dark."

"We can't hold *that* off." *Why am I just hearing about this now?* Berendt rubbed his forehead. "And if they get dug in, get ready for a long standoff."

"Precisely." Hadamard looked the Kith commander in the eye. "Shroud only knows what the treaty breakers might concoct in the meantime, having had access to one of our own. The answer is NO. Like I told you: go in fast, hit hard."

Berendt said, "Tell me, then, how do we approach this? What do these treaty breakers have at their disposal? How do they fight?"

The enforcer didn't answer.

"Don't get tight-lipped on me now." Berendt knew he was crossing into protected territory, the "grey-zone" of knowledge, so to speak. But he had to know *something*. Lives depended on it.

"They're alchemists, not fighters," Hadamard said. "Without Scarsanders in the way, we should be able to subdue most of them. We'll start with the doors, just like you said, but one at a time." Hadamard made a passing glance over Berendt's armor, then Amot's. He made a sour face. "Neither of you are outfitted for this kind of fight. Hang back and let the assault team go in. Provide overwatch and cover fire, and keep an eye out for those damn Scarsanders. If they arrive early, it'll be up to you to keep them busy until we're done what we need to do. Valkyries are in the area. We might be able to get that wind rider tracking the Scarsanders to airlift us out, in a pinch."

Well, some of us. Berendt kept the snide remark to himself.

"Roger that," he said, but his mind had become preoccupied. *Can this possibly work out well?* His gut felt sick with the thought of it. Berendt hadn't known what he was up against the last time he'd encountered alchemists and wasn't fully prepared for what came at them. *My men had gotten off lucky—just a few minor acid burns.* The Kith commander drew a deep breath. *None of that matters,* he convinced himself. He would do what he had to do.

✧

It happened fast.

Letzi, the Baruush, breached the left door. She reeled away, grunting in pain, holding her face.

Acid trap. How did nobody see it?

A ball-projectile flew out of the same doorway, the thrower shrouded in darkness. It smacked the stone temple floor with a deafening bang. While Berendt's ears rang, a short stick spun through the air, spewing smoke. *Cover. For what?*

The second door opened, on the right. Three alchemists in robes stepped out, hurled vials of liquid at the assault team. More screams. Vapor rose. *They're no better protected than we are.*

"Shoot!" Berendt commanded. He'd barely heard the sound of his own voice, but Rix shot anyway. In a split second, the young spotter thrummed off three arrows. One of the three defenders fell. Another ducked behind the wall just in time, while the third stood firm, defiance in her stance and in her hardened gaze. The Kith commander drew his own ranged weapon, a hand crossbow, cocked and loaded.

Amot sprung up, drew his sword and let out a battle cry so piercing it cut through Berendt's dulled hearing. The Wilder charged through the central pool towards the alchemists, splashing up water as he sped. Hadamard, taking cover beside Berendt, tore the wrapping from the stone set on his staff. The unsheathed gem sparked a fiery light.

From behind the partial wall, the defiant alchemist lobbed a vial, sent it soaring into the dark heights. Then with a swift motion, she flung a bag straight at the oncoming scout. Berendt took careful aim through the rising smoke, triggered off a shot and plunged the bolt into her throwing arm. She whirled at the impact, stumbled back, dropped behind cover. By then the assault team was down, moaning and writhing on the steps. Two alchemists spilled out of the breach virtually on top of them. One looked to Amot, sparked a torch. The other hurled a vial Rix's way.

Shroud's Well, that smell…

An image flared up in Berendt's mind—the pool bursting into flames around Amot. "TORCH!" he yelled. The commander fumbled to load another bolt, but the attempt was hopeless. He heard a muted twang—Rix felled the torchbearer almost instantly. The man's fiery stave hit the stairway, erupting in flames, while the vial hurled towards Rix smashed into a column and exploded before reaching him.

The bag whipped at the charging Wilder had missed by a wide margin, leaving a mound of black, sticky tar in the shallow pool. Amot easily dodged the trap.

What? Immobilize and burn? Buggers. To hell with 50/50.

Amot barreled through the flammable liquid into the billowing smoke, unhindered and unburnt.

Berendt had lost track of the second vial, lobbed high, until it came crashing down onto the rubble beside him. Hadamard swung around as it shattered, exposing his back. Berendt barely lifted his arm to shield himself from the exploding vial. Shards of glass blasted into him; liquid splashed over him. Something sliced at his eye. The side of his face burned. He couldn't help but to cry out, roll, cup his face in his hands.

The enforcer cursed the Nine. Berendt felt a firm, gloved grip wrench his hands from his face. Then a second splash. The hand let go. The liquid soothed the burn. A searing flash of bright light erupted above him. *The staff,* he thought, as he spiraled out of consciousness.

≈

The tarnished plaque on the door read:

CUSTODIANS OF OLD-WORLD KNOWLEDGE.
PRESERVERS OF THEIA THROUGH ENFORCEMENT
OF THE TREATY OF NATURE.

Hadamard must've read the words a hundred times and thought little of them. Lately he wondered how far they could be stretched and twisted, yet remain intact. He caught a whiff of pine-scented candles as he stood in the doorway to the First Office of Order Lumen. Inside the chamber, the Crimson Tower's number one sage sat at his desk, head down, eyes pouring over a document, one hand stroking his smooth beard. The luminary had a perfect view of the man's bald spot and the white, wispy hair encircling it. He was garbed in his usual grey and red robe. "Prime Lumen Forsetti, you sent for me?"

The sage finished his read, signed the document, then motioned with his hand to a plush chair on the other side of his desk. "You may take a seat, Lumen Hadamard."

The luminary stepped inside. "I'll stand, if it's fine with you."

Forsetti grunted. "Suit yourself. Stand, then."

"This is about my proposal, I take it?"

Forsetti grimaced. "*This*," he enunciated, "… is about many things, not the least of which being that disastrous raid in the Akedan ruins."

Hadamard met the sage's antagonistic gaze. He knew full well that hawkish stare was meant to make him feel small, unworthy, inferior. But he didn't let it get to him. He held steady, kept his calm and appealed to the greybeard's sensibilities. "We're getting pummeled out there. Our numbers are dwindling. The constraints on how we operate are getting more and more complicated—50% survival rate? Really? We have no resources… and treaty breakers are becoming more sophisticated. They have small armies of thugs, you know… Scarsands… Bitterhelm…"

Forsetti leaned back in his chair and clasped his hands together, eyes hard as stone. "Lumen Adur Kaazik also has a proposal. He's made the same… observations. He claims the only way to combat the rise in treaty violations is to dip into the archives."

"Forbidden technology?" Hadamard didn't have much patience for Kaazik. *Reckless, self-serving fool.* "Kaazik shouldn't even have access to the archives. He's being alarmist."

Forsetti raised an eyebrow. "And yet, you advocated that your good friend Feleg gain access—a grig, no less."

Damn right I did, Hadamard thought, but out of respect for his superior—the head of all nine luminary institutes—he held his tongue. Feleg had poured over the archives to teach himself the intricacies of managing a dangerously fragile, old-world technology, and only to keep it from poisoning most of what was left of the human race. Kaazik, on the other hand, would access the archives for his own gains.

Forsetti prodded on, "Fight fire with fire, Lumen Kaazik says."

Hadamard scoffed. "Imagine that, coming from Harrow." The place hosted a den of treaty breakers enabled by its masterful slaves—the kingdom's best kept secret.

The Prime Lumen's shoulders stiffened. His black, bushy eyebrows twitched up. "Are you saying I shouldn't trust him? What about the other luminaries posted there? Spies, every one?"

Hadamard considered carefully his evidence. *Sometimes I wonder.* After a long pause, he answered: "No, I'm not saying that."

Forsetti relaxed in his chair, nodded slowly. "Good." He raised a hand and patted a closed booklet on his desk. Hadamard recognized it—the latest project idea he'd submitted. "Now tell me, Hadamard, how is what you are proposing any different from Kaazik?"

Hadamard folded his arms across his chest. "My experiments don't violate the treaty, for one."

"No, of course not," Forsetti said, sarcasm building in his voice. "They circumvent it entirely. Many would say, Hadamard, that your dabbling goes against the *spirit* of the treaty. When it was written—"

"When it was written, no one foresaw *elemental stones*," Hadamard pointed out, "and yet we've justified using *them* in the name of enforcing the treaty. And what about rejuvenation?"

"There is such a thing as going too far," Forsetti stated firmly.

"How else are we to counter Harrow? How else are we to… enforce the treaty?"

Forsetti gave Hadamard a long and measuring look. "Lord Ralador is already breathing down my neck about your dancing swords—the strikers. Wasn't *that* supposed to be your force multiplier?"

Hadamard shook his head. "Not if Ralador gets his hands on them."

"Hmph." Forsetti did not look impressed. "The man argues that rangers already have the best ranged attacks—their archers, of course—and they have no need of your 'dancing swords.' But in the hands of his queensmen—"

"We need a backup plan."

Forsetti sharpened his tone. "Which is exactly what Lumen Kaazik has proposed."

Hadamard raised his voice in response. "Then what separates us from Harrow? From the treaty breakers?"

Forsetti let out a heavy sigh. "Shut the door."

Hadamard did as his superior bade.

The Prime Lumen casually flipped through a notebook on his desk, found the page he was looking for and scanned it quickly. Then he raised his eyes to Hadamard, met his gaze. He spoke softly. "Tell me again about your proposal, or should I say obsession."

This will take some convincing, thought Hadamard as he took a seat on the chair offered previously. He rested one elbow on Forsetti's desk, spoke matter-of-factly. "The strikers are what we need for defense. Lord Ralador is right about that. Having them in our arsenal will cast doubts in the minds of our enemies and maybe even curb the ill plans of would-be treaty breakers. But in the long run, they won't be enough to uphold enforcement. We can't suppress knowledge forever: spies are accessing the archives, Harrow is developing an invasion weapon, unrest is stirring in the Outlands, Fort Abandon is about to break out, and the Jhinyari are preparing to respond with force. Leviathans and behemoths in every major center are redefining their alliances."

Forsetti grunted. "I've seen the reporting. The Grey Tower is scrambling to stall the coming power shifts on all fronts."

Hadamard scoffed. "An interim solution to a greater problem. You know as well as I do the greater purpose, above and beyond the treaty, is to understand the line that was crossed when humankind was nearly annihilated. We need to think beyond enforcement to find another way out when everything goes to hell again. We need to get *inside* the projections that power the dancing swords; explore time and dimensionality, see where it brings us."

"Inside?" Forsetti's eyebrows shot up again. "And how, exactly, will your project accomplish that?"

Hadamard paused. Forsetti had hit on the crux of the matter. In the conduct of his most recent experiments, Hadamard believed he'd stumbled upon a greater and more fundamental power than anything he'd ever borne witness to, even in the archives. And he knew that it could be harnessed, bent to his will… somehow. But he didn't have the specifics.

"I don't know," he said, finally. "That's what I intend to find out."

The Prime Lumen frowned. "Do you have any evidence?"

"Two observations," Hadamard offered, with a mind to keep the narrative of his experiments simple. "A Jhin temporal effect and a Hurlorn memory effect."

"Speculation," Forsetti stated flatly.

Hadamard shrugged.

Forsetti asked, "And what if that which you find is beyond humanity's ability to comprehend?"

Hadamard leaned forward. "Actually, I'm counting on exactly that."

Forsetti shook his head. "Hmm… You are one of a kind, Lumen Hadamard." He jotted something down in the notebook on his desk, then flipped through to another page. Without raising his eyes, he continued. "Don't overwork yourself supporting the 4th while they wait for someone to backfill your old position, you're an enforcer now." He snapped the book shut and met Hadamard's gaze. "Let me know how it turns out. Now on to other business, about those dwindling luminary numbers…"

CHAPTER I
HADAMARD'S GAME
(Hadamard)

NEKENEZITTER'S VOICE SOUNDED small and hollow in the Netherdome. With his round little mouth, he looked like an owl about to hoot. An ugly owl. But he didn't hoot; he clicked. He clicked and he clacked and he chirped all day and all night like some half-crazed cricket.

"The advantage <click> was obvious from the very beginning <chirr>. We didn't need to do this."

Hadamard glanced down at his diminutive companion. Annoyance bled through his temples like forked veins of wild fire. *I damn well know that.* He wanted to raise his hand. He wanted to smack the little snitch in the head so hard it would make him fall over. He'd scramble for his bent-up glasses, so thick his face was all eyes when he wore them. Hadamard would make him admit he was a spy.

The luminary just shook his head, let the anger pass. Why he ever agreed to let this buggy little imp shadow his every move was beyond him. Luminaries don't need to be watched and don't want to be watched, especially by some piss-ant Gloom. Hadamard was a private person.

Patience.

"It's by *how much* that matters," Hadamard told him, giving in to his gentler side, the side that tolerates and perseveres. "To say this little rain dance will make rain is one thing, but to say that it will cause a flood is quite another."

Hadamard half-expected the naïve courtier to ask how a dance could make rain. He was *that* dense at times. The analogy might be lost on him. The luminary felt the need to explain himself before more senseless questions about tribal rituals cropped up.

"By measuring how the 'strikers' perform in battle compared to conventional weaponry, I can make informed judgements about how best to use them and how many are needed. Then I can weigh the consequences against the extraordinary effort required to create each and every one." *And then I can make my recommendations—to be ignored by fools in high places. But not this time. No, this time they will have to put their personal agendas aside and listen.*

The gargoyle-like Gloom bobbed his ugly head and said nothing. That silent nod was his token response unless some other inane question yet lingered, fizzing on the tip of his twisty tongue, ready to pop.

What Queen Xara saw in Nekenezitter was a mystery to Hadamard. She seemed to like having unusual things at her side—her would-be husband, for instance. But asking one of the most prominent luminaries in her service to babysit such an annoying, quizzical little twit—forever prodding on with distracting questions—was nothing less than insulting.

The luminary and the annoying crown advisor turned their attention back to the scene playing out.

"Keep mechanical track of the timing this run," Hadamard told Nekenezitter. He didn't fully trust the Gloom's mental timekeeping. The measurements never seemed to quite add up. Nekenezitter reached into his vest pocket and pulled out a timepiece.

"This <click> thing is off by thirteen <tic> seconds since yesterday," he complained.

The same line of giants charged the same hilltop overlooking Harrow and Dim Lake—summer daylight conditions—trampling through the same charred remnants of a failed Hurlorn line. The arborescent defenders stood rooted where they'd fought, tall and black like a burnt-out forest. *Alchemist's fire always gets them.*

The giants' charge was painfully slow. As always, the Queen's Guard drew their prototype strikers and began hacking away at the giants as they advanced, projecting out to nearly a hundred feet. Three dancing swords to one foe seemed to be a fair rule of thumb and all that could be spared. Hadamard had witnessed the scenario play out a hundred times before. Well, ninety-nine to be exact.

Only Hadamard and the Gloom were present for this test cycle, and that meant less observations. Vey Lancer, a substitute apprentice for the one he'd driven mad, had been called back to the Grey Tower and would be off to Fort Abandon by week's end. He'd be lucky to get her back at all, from what he was hearing. On top of that, his good friend Feleg and his worthy apprentice Vil'nyan apparently had better things to do. That meant cutting back on data collection. No matter. If Hadamard had learned anything in his long years in the Order, it was how to extrapolate. Everyone wanted results—answers. No one cared how he got them. Sure, there would be questions and half-baked criticisms, but the simple fact of the matter was that no one but Hadamard really knew what the hell was going on. Well, except maybe the Lord of the March. But with solid footing and some convincing arguments, Hadamard could handle Ralador.

Just like the last run, most of the giants advanced to the top of the hill, unscathed. For the eightieth time, they went on to slaughter the Queen's Guard as though butchering lambs. *Eat that, Ralador.*

When the battle was done, everything disassembled. The giants, the Queen's Guard, the Hurlorns… everything. The terrain flattened underfoot. A hollow silence filled the Netherdome again, until the damn bug opened his trap.

"That <click> makes an eighty <tic> percent failure rate," noted Nekenezitter.

"On the dot?" said the luminary.

"On the <click> dot <trill>," repeated the imp.

This was Hadamard's conundrum: proving his point to the Lord of the March was a good thing, but the Royal Quarter losing by so much was a bad thing. The numbers were already maxed out, the formation optimal.

Range. I need more range.

CHAPTER II
TO ABANDON
(Vey)

VEY DIDN'T CARE if she left Fort Abandon a virgin, or not. Vice-regent Hersh Tehan was more than eligible, he came recommended. It was Srylla who'd told her the Tor Lord daughters were taking their turns with the young steward, passing him around like some kind of play toy, for pleasure's sake. Srylla was an easy bed and she knew such things. According to her, Hersh wasn't complaining though. Vey would change that. She would be different. Vey would show the oversized brute the wonders of Gan and offer him *rejuvenation*. All the sisters of Harrow could ever offer were their scantily clad bodies, skin wrapped over skeletons from what she could tell, and the promise of an equally corpse-like body of his own to share with them some day. Yes, he would live on, but destined to steadily decay with the rest of the withering vamps. That kind of so-called "life" wasn't for Hersh. He needed to keep the meat on his bones.

She also didn't care that he wasn't Elderkin—foreigners had become more accepted in recent years. The older generation behaved like toddlers, sucking their thumbs and clinging to prejudice like some kind of geriatric baby blanket. But anyone under age twenty knew better. Some said the newcomers threatened to ruin Elderkin society, but that was nonsense—the original populace was in decline due to a "lack of diversity." That much came straight from a Tower study. Besides, the Elderkin had learned to adapt. Practically anyone could become a member of Gan now. The queen reserved the final word though. And Vey knew the queen—sort of.

Officially, Vey was a special assistant to the Grey Clerk, on secondment to the lower levels of the Crimson Tower. Unofficially, she was the favored protégé of a madman. Vey had a gift for organization that the influential luminary knew exactly how to exploit—and he did just that. It had been an especially grueling week, with Lumen Hadamard's all-consuming obsessions driving experiments day and night. He kept her on post late, compiling results and mulling over endless theories. All this before she had even graduated.

The travel duty to Fort Abandon had been a gift from the Grey Clerk, whose office had handled all of the arrangements. It was an important assignment and she had to stay focused; but, if there was a little fun to be had along the way, all the better.

The forested road out of Gan had been tolerable despite the early morning rain. As bumpy as it was, with all its stubborn roots and muddy potholes, the swampy edge near the Mire Trail proved far worse. Vey could always tell when it was near, by the smell of rot in the air. The going was slow over the mushy ground and unduly midge infested for September.

Keeping one eye to the road, the coach driver passed a sideways glance at Vey back in the cabin, tipping her off that another one of his "wonderful insights" would be forthcoming. They typically came in the form of short, crass observations. Wisps of his patchy white hair frolicked with the wind as he spoke.

"Worse than a skunk's arse," he told her. The man was not wrong. He was not exactly charming either.

"What a wonderful insight," Vey repeated, just like the last time. *Will he ever get the message?*

Wyatt was rough-skinned, wiry and cynical. He called himself an ex-bogger which, from what Vey could gather, meant he used to work as a guide throughout the swampy areas west of Deepweald Forest. He grew up in that smell.

Vey was glad Wyatt didn't talk much, and even more glad he didn't look at her much either. His eyes tended to wander up and down her body for long moments when he did gaze her way.

Once the tree line was breached, the calming sight of open, rolling hills to the south was enough to set Vey's mind straight. The view would persist all the way to Turnsby Corners, and it was all she needed to compose herself before meeting Hersh. That, and a magnifying mirror, some makeup brushes, sponges, and every powder, cream and eye shadow a young woman is apt to have in her possession.

Vey set her mind to applying a few finishing touches.

She ran a finger along her hairline and felt the bump she knew was there. *Ugh! Damn monstrosity.* Vey sighed. *There's still time to shrink it.* Her skin was otherwise flawless. The abomination had made its debut appearance when she first woke up early that morning and looked in the mirror. It had stared back at her like a witch's evil eye, red and winking. Vey had nodded off again at her desk at work, and spent the night.

She huffed. *There's no air flow in that damned, dank tower.* The weather hadn't helped much either, nor had sleeping on one side of her face, pressed against an open book. *I'm glad that job's over with.*

She raised her mirror and held it away from her face. *And what will I ever do with my hair?* The water in the air had drawn out the split ends and stood them straight up. She smoothed them out with a few strokes of her free hand.

"Miss," Wyatt interrupted, "we're a little behind schedule and my mares have been work'n hard all morning. Would you like to stay the night at Turnsby? I know a great—"

"It's not going to happen," Vey retorted with a sharp tongue. She decided to leave out the "thank you for offering" part. Vey had to make herself unmistakably clear about such matters. Wyatt recommended staying over in Turnsby to nearly all of his passengers of the female persuasion. The town was a crossroads and a center for commerce, and a comfortable day's ride from just about anywhere in the region—village, town, or city. Maybe he thought women would be pushovers and he could slip in a business trip, or maybe he had friends or family there. Vey had her own suspicions though.

Pushing them aside, she thought ahead to her meeting with Hersh. In her mind, the young protégé immediately put herself at the Fort's administrative hall, with clerks all around. She imagined how she would make the half-giant squirm. After less than two years in office, the fort steward was already making a mess of things. She would control the conversation and start off ruthless about pressing treaty matters, following up firm but fair, and then charitable in the end once he'd given up and expected nothing. Hersh would begin civil, but confrontational. Once he realized his mistakes, his naivety would shine through and his demeanor would change to politely apologetic, more than willing to accept whatever concessions she put on the table.

Vey sighed. His only demand would be a candlelit dinner for two in his most luxuriant meeting chambers... to clarify a few "subtle points"—a late night exchange of the utmost diplomatic importance. Vey smiled to herself at the thought of it all. She liked the sound of it so much she mouthed the words: "late night exchange."

She'd packed her favorite evening gown. It was red, like her hair, and form fitting, with one bare shoulder and a diagonal cut on the skirt that showed one bare leg. The dress hung protected in its own special place on a hook in the back of the carriage, ready and waiting for her to slip into.

The *Treaty of Nature* was a finicky agreement to have to deal with. The Fort had long abandoned recognizing or enforcing its articles, favoring instead to indulge in the advantages that came with noncompliance—increased industry, production, quality of life, commerce and trade. It was time to take a serious look at the conditions for renewal and the price of noncompliance. To that end, Vey would arrive armed with grim advice from the Grey Clerk. The situation was getting out of hand and negotiations with Harrow were impossible while Fort Abandon carried on with its rhetoric that the treaty is outdated, flawed, prejudiced against them, and based on supernatural nonsense. Something had to be done. Technology was springing up everywhere.

CHAPTER III

WOLF'N STEIN
(Hadamard)

"TETHERPORT IS AS beautiful as it is a dive."

Feleg nursed his *Wolf'N Stein* pint for a long moment to drown the words, then set the potion down on the bar. The Wilder's droopy eyes had a far-off look to them. The hair on top of his head seemed to have thinned since they entered only an hour earlier. *Damn lighting in here*, thought Hadamard, so dim and yellowy. *Sucks the life right out of you.* Feleg knocked the ashes out of his pipe and patted his shirt pockets for a light.

Hadamard slouched on the barstool beside him, savoring the buzz of his mediocre ale. The luminary knew what the port town meant to his friend, how he loved the place and how he hated it just the same. Located on the dark side of Seventh Kaeda, it was barren and grim with terrible winds. Yet elegant towers, translucent grey and swaying, rose against the backdrop of Kaeda's Temper—a never-ceasing storm—and the ghostly outline of the Elderkin Conduit.

It was at that moment, with Hadamard still lost in thought, that the owner of the establishment chose to amble by. He hummed to himself inaudibly. The man was dressed in the same filthy barkeep clothes he always wore. With a soft, damp cloth, he wiped a stale beer smell all over the counter in front of the two patrons, smearing Feleg's ash into a long, black streak.

"Wulfe" was lousy at his job. He was lousy at everything Hadamard could think of, including conversation. Yet, the man insisted on pushing his way into every discussion within earshot.

"And getting to Tetherport is treacherous," Wulfe butted in, nodding with eyes wide and the air of an expert about him, as though he were the first to come up with the well-known fact. He ducked under the bar, fat hands fumbling their way through odds and ends underneath.

Intolerant Feleg made a pained expression, shook his head. He called out over the bar. "What would you know?" he said, with a biting tone. No breaks. No leniency. "You never set foot on Seventh Kaeda, *stupid arse*, and you wouldn't. Not to save your hide, not to save your flee-bitten inn, not to save all of Theia."

The barkeep gasped and sputtered incoherently. Like a trapper's snare, the throttling had twisted his tongue into submission. Wulfe was a dolt.

Hadamard leaned sideways to his friend, lowering his voice so no one else could hear. "Shit Feleg, I have to eat here."

Wulfe huffed at his unsuccessful search. He broke surface from behind the bar, scowled at them both, then scuffled to the back room.

Feleg scoffed, changed the subject. He addressed Hadamard.

"How's that prospect of yours, out there on the other side?"

Hadamard gulped down the ale sloshing in his mouth. "He's perfect," he replied, then rested his cup on the bar. "Doesn't have a clue I'm scouting him out, or that he's being evaluated."

The Wilder narrowed his eyes. "How did you manage that?"

"I took your advice," Hadamard explained. "I showed him an elemental stone, the big one, and led him on about *shaping*. He suggested we set up a joint project," Hadamard smirked, "to explore exactly what I wanted him to explore."

"That's not what I meant. How did you manage to get it past Prime?"

"Oh." Hadamard groaned. "Forsetti agreed to the trials as long as they were on the sly, but said unless my prospect works miracles, there's no way he'll be sworn in. Then he got to thinking, and before long I was to bring in a whole new batch of luminary wannabees for a damn tour and evaluate them on the sly too. He wants six confirmed Member Prospects by the end of the month. I can think of one. Maybe."

Feleg chuckled. "Translation: three by the end of the year. I don't know why you luminaries always recruit in frantic batches. Take your time, why don't 'cha." He shook his head—a pitiful shake, like he felt sorry for Hadamard nearly as much as for himself. "My friend, it's all because of that crazy pipe dream of yours, isn't it? To combine *Hurlorn* and *Jhin* thaumaturgies? Don't you have enough troubles?"

"I have to think big or it's an automatic fail. Besides, one more pipe dream gone sour isn't going to kill me. I have to spend the royal allotment before I lose it. Ralador's already clawing back. And that damn imp he sicced on me almost blew everything the last time I went to the dome. The little turd told my unconfirmed prospect that the Jhin projections and the Hurlorn network functioned on totally different levels, and were incompatible."

"He's probably right."

"I don't think so."

"Any success?"

"No… but it's early."

"What's his name—the prospect?"

"It's a long one. No sense telling you, you'd never remember."

Feleg nodded in acknowledgement. "They're all long on the other side."

Hadamard snickered. "I had to write his name down for my proposal. I hate all the damn paperwork. I shortened it to 'Crusher.' He doesn't seem to mind, so let's just call him that."

Feleg nodded in agreement. "Doesn't read, does he?"

"Nope. None of them do. Clever though, learns fast. Talk always centers around Jhin though—gets a bit weird sometimes… Jhin this, Jhin that."

With a flick of his head, Feleg gestured to a bottle on the shelf behind the bar. "There's nothing weird about centering your conversations around *gin*."

Hadamard rolled his eyes, drew in a deep breath. Feleg snorted beer and wiped it with his sleeve, then raised his cup and downed another swig of ale.

A boisterous group behind them burst out laughing at something else entirely. Hadamard and his old friend swung their gazes to the booth where it came from—a rough looking bunch of heavily-inked Wilders, all in ranging gear and just out of the woods by the looks of them. Drinks all around before the clock even struck noon.

The pair turned back to the bar.

"Brings me back," was all the grig said. He stared through the glass at the little swill that remained. It was getting near to the bottom. He would stretch it out though. He always did.

Hadamard pulled one back. For a long moment he let the ale soak into his synapses.

"Jhinyari presence?" Feleg said, changing the topic yet again.

"Hope to hell not. Nothing reported. It's Abandoners doing the scouting though."

"Crazy bastards." Feleg leaned back on his chair just as Wulfe reappeared from the back room with a shiny green-colored ashtray. The barkeep slammed it onto the beer-soaked wood beside Feleg, where the finish had worn off, and then leaned over the bar. He glared at the aging Wilder with cold eyes. A decade's worth of food stains decorated his once-white apron, including a wide and smeary yellow line where the top of his bulging gut pressed against the lip of the bar.

Feleg remained calm while in "the Wolf's" sights. In his usual laid-back way, he struck a match and lit up. Lips pursed, the grig breathed in a long drag until the weed caught, then followed through with a few quick puffs at Wulfe's face.

The barkeep jerked away, flapping his cloth in the air and wincing. "Treacherous," he reiterated. "Wait 'til they come for you, muck'n around in their stomping grounds. And *they* will."

"The Jhinyari?" Feleg said.

"No," Wulfe retorted, sarcasm bleeding into his voice. "The cursed Windswept, swooping in to peck your cheeks." He rolled his eyes. "Of course, the Jhinyari! You're supposed to have some smarts. Not luminary smarts, maybe... but some, at least. Smart my ass, I say. Damn grigs. How can you be smart when you don't know a damn thing about common sense?"

"We're still accepting applications, if you'd like to try out," Feleg said.

Wulfe sneered at the suggestion. "Not on yer life!" He left in a huff again, this time down along the bar to a younger patron with swindler looks who'd just walked in off the street. He addressed the man in his usual way: "What can I do ya fer?"

Feleg laughed foully at Wulfe, drink trembling in his hands as he did so. He sipped his ale, all lips to catch the spillover. The bemused look on his face did little to disguise his age. Deep wrinkles had long hardened onto Feleg's forehead, and the complex ink lines that ran across his face, once sharp and fresh, had become stretched and blurred and wrinkled over time. Undoubtably fearsome to behold when newly inked, the Kith badge of honor had become more like weathered graffiti on a crumbling wall. It must've added twenty years.

"Grig," Feleg muttered to himself, shaking his head, repeating the common name for a druid of his order.

Sometimes the term could be construed as derogatory and other times friendly, depending on the context and the company. *From Wulfe, it's a slight,* thought Hadamard.

For the most part, members of the Kith such as Feleg worked themselves into early graves for their chance at life eternal, or fought like berserkers and fell into them. Few received the fullness of longevity sought, and those that did found only more servitude in it as incarnated beasts. Many would have been better off as complete outsiders, waltzing in through the gates of Gan with some grandiose idea or impractical talent able to draw in respectable sponsors. *Hail Queen Xara for that. He looks worse every time I see him.*

The drooping bags that hung beneath Feleg's sunken eyes spoke to sleeplessness. The roundness in his build spoke to how busy he was all the time—no opportunity to take care of himself. Constant smoking didn't help either, yellowing his teeth and a strip of his speckled beard, not to mention the stringy tufts of hair sprouting above his forehead.

Wulfe, on the other hand, had more thick hair circling his bearded face than a real wolf could ever stand, silky and silvery grey. The barkeep's plumpness gave him a soft, pampered look, and supplied him with unbounded energy. His eyes were quick to meet those of a gentleman patron in need, and just as quick to stray to his lady friend. The man was useless and empty in most ways that counted, but he was Elderkin, and for that he would still be useless and empty a hundred years from now, barring ill-fortune. On the other hand, Gan could not function a single day without the likes of Feleg. He was indispensable and yet might never live to see one-fifty.

Hadamard emptied the last of the backwash from his own tankard and swished it around in his mouth. It tasted warm and sour, but somehow it mixed well with the smoky residue coating his palate. After swallowing, he banged on his chest to compose himself. Bleary eyed, the luminary made his decision. His voice was solemn.

"Dive or not, Tetherport is still my best option… the only real option."

Feleg took a drag from his pipe and only partially exhaled before responding. Smoke puffed out of his mouth as he spoke. "That means rejigging Diamond Saber top to bottom. The exercise was supposed to be at Brillyerd's. Moving it to Seventh Kaeda on such short notice will be damn near impossible."

Hadamard stared into his empty glass and nodded. Feleg was right. Nature tended to misbehave in the Otherworldly Realm, and Seventh Kaeda was no exception. The move could introduce spurious effects impossible to predict with their current knowledge. *But what choice do I have?*

Hadamard kept silent.

Feleg kept silent.

Unfortunately, Wulfe did not keep silent.

"A fool's option, whatever yer scheming," the Wolf barked out of the side of his mouth, from five seats down the counter. The barkeep nodded to the half-stoned patron he'd been serving—coaching, more like, in his unique blend of idiocy. Wulfe spoke in low tones to the man, then swiveled his gaze to where Hadamard and his friend were sitting. The patron followed suit, clenching an over-sized cigar in his snarling lips as he turned his head to stare. He leaned forward and muttered something back to Wulfe and they both laughed.

Feleg leaned in towards Hadamard, his voice a low grumble. "We shouldn't be talking about this shit here."

Through the late-morning haze of the smoke-filled Wolf'N Stein, the luminary discreetly scanned the room. *Mostly regulars*, he thought, *and mostly buzzed. Wulfe will forget this entire conversation by closing, if he hasn't already.*

Tilla Closhorne sat alone at a table near a boarded-up window. Hadamard had gone out with her when they were both too young not to be stupid. His eyes met hers for a brief moment. A shy smile formed on her lips. He pretended not to notice and quickly turned away.

Feleg caught him in the sly act. The grig sucked on his pipe and took a long, measuring look at Hadamard. Eyes steady, the smoke puffed back out through his nostrils. Then he glanced over his shoulder to Tilla, then back to Hadamard. Instead of commenting, he lifted his cup and took another swig of ale. Then he commented anyway.

"You're thirty-nine now, aren't you?"

Hadamard nodded with a smirk.

"So, when does your dick fall off?"

Hadamard snorted, shook his head. "Next June, asshole."

"Still thinking about marriage, kids and all that before the big day?"

Hadamard didn't answer. He peered into his empty tankard and contemplated whether he had time for another.

Feleg patted him on the shoulder twice. "Trust me. They're not worth it."

"How would you know?"

"I'm an uncle. Uncles have it made. Play dad for a day or two, then you get to give them back. Buy them a present once in a while and give them some bullshit advice. It's easy and they'll love you for it. Trust me. Be an uncle."

"You're not even a real uncle."

"Even better."

Hadamard shrugged. "I don't know."

Feleg drew a heavy sigh. "Don't delay then, or you'll end up like me."

Hadamard quipped, "Overworked and in desperate need of a woman?"

"Hmph. You're already there, pal." Feleg swung his gaze to Tilla Closhorne, lingered too long, and then swung it back. "Maybe that sort of thing just isn't in the cards for people like us."

As though on cue, the swindler strutted past them with two drinks in hand. He sat down at the table with Tilla. They started talking. The man smiled at her and she smiled back.

"Yep," was all Hadamard said.

Feleg finished the swill at the bottom of his cup, then tapped his pipe. They both sat in silence at the bar, slouched over their empty tankards. Wulfe didn't offer them another.

The barkeep's comments about traveling to Seventh Kaeda bothered the luminary. He didn't want to admit it, but the rude, simple-minded dolt had a point—the journey's treacherous, and in more ways than one. Any vessel passing into Jhin's Cave risked running aground and a hull breach. The currents were fast and the mists hung thick where the river ran wild, dampening the yellow glow of even the brightest fore lanterns. And where the mist was thickest, somewhere, somehow, the crossing would be made; the crossing of the Great Barrier into the Otherworldly Realm—the ancestral home of the rival Djinxarai and Jhinyari tribes.

The grig slapped the bar. "I'm done."

Hadamard pushed himself up from his chair. "Read my mind."

෴

Wulfe scoffed at the pair on their way out of his tavern. "Please come again." The barkeep waved them off. "Cheap bastards." Under his breath, Hadamard heard him muttering "<something>… screwball …<something>… pointy-heads."

"I'll be back the day you stop serving piss," Feleg retorted.

"I'll stop right now," snapped the Wolf, "and start up again the next time I see your ugly mugs around here."

A discomforting thought. Like always, Hadamard had left exact change for his brew and that of his old friend Feleg. He shut the solid oak door firmly behind them. After exiting the gloomy confines of the shuttered Wolf'N Stein, the bright of day seemed unnatural, as though it didn't belong in the streets of the Shroom district. Indeed, direct sunlight only peeked into the narrow rift at the bottom of the gorge for a brief stint around noon on your average day. Hadamard glanced up to the sign above the door, like he always did, and the painted wolf-man there, in muted colors, raising a frothy stein of ale, about to proclaim a toast.

"I can't go with you to find a charter." Feleg winced as he spoke the words, as though internalizing great pain. The ink lines on his face warped and twisted with the contortion. "I have to catch up with that damn contraption underground—you know the one I mean. The pressure was… a little unsteady when I left, and Nahm's a good worker, but… he's a bit of an idiot with the dials. Let me know how it goes." The grig patted Hadamard on the back. The two parted ways, each with a wave and a smile.

Feleg got on his way first. "Same time tomorrow?" he called back, without turning around.

"Same time tomorrow," Hadamard repeated, still standing there.

The luminary watched as Feleg hobbled along the mushroom-choked alley and then hung a left towards the docks. Hadamard took a brief moment to remind himself of all the times he'd crossed over to Seventh Kaeda, weighing each voyage there and back again in his mind. *I know the perfect vessel,* he thought, *and the perfect captain.* Later that day, he had them both commissioned.

Chapter IV
Kith Rangers
(Vey)

Without warning, the carriage jerked violently. Vey jolted out of her slumber. An ear-piercing whinny cut through the air.

"Whoa!" Wyatt called, as the horse kicked out, bolted sideways. "WHOA!"

Vey struggled to process. The carriage veered. Her heart raced. Off the trail. Down the hill. Vey bounced in her seat, tilted sideways. She screeched, braced herself. Hooves thudded. A loud crack. The carriage buckled. Another loud crack. She flew. A loud crunch.

In a blur, the carriage had turned over. Stuff was everywhere. Vey lay in a tangle in the overturned cabin, muscles frozen. Gathering her senses, she put a hand to her chest and gasped.

"Shroud's Well!" Wyatt cursed, from outside. He'd been thrown off his seat.

Vey turned her head to peer through the cabin's front window. Wyatt was there, pushing himself up off the ground. Covered in sludge, he brushed clumps of goop off his clothes, turned his gaze to her. His eyes went wide as he took in the disaster. The ex-bogger hurried over, limping. He squatted to peer inside the cabin.

"Miss?" He extended a hand. "Are you all right?"

Vey bit her lip, took the hand and allowed herself to be hauled out.

≺

"It's hopeless."

The special assistant stood at the side of the trail, shaking the dirt off her red evening dress, heels sunken in mud. Like everything else she owned, the prized garment was a mess. Her chin quivered ever so slightly. The incident had jarred her. She caught herself welling up…

I will not cry like some sobbing schoolgirl, she insisted. *No.* Instead, Vey allowed the anger to well up inside. Jaw still quivering, she narrowed her eyes, pursed her lips. *It's Wyatt's fault. What kind of respectable carriage driver would let this happen?* The grizzled old coot scratched his head as he stared down the slope at the overturned carriage. It'd run off the trail among the rolling hills and scrublands nearing Doncaster, a farming hamlet.

"Well, I'll be. Never, never, never… Are you sure yer all right, Miss?"

Out of nowhere, one of the horses had whinnied, upset the other, and both had bounded towards the trail edge. Wyatt explained that a wheel must have cut into soft ground and caused the carriage to slide downhill, bouncing over exposed roots and half buried stones. Then the rollover. Inside the cabin was a mess. Wyatt apologized profusely and said he'd never seen anything like it.

"Spooked is all," was the only explanation he could offer after unhitching the mares—lying on their sides. He'd led them to higher ground, complaining that the white, spotted one was acting funny. *Trying to pass the blame,* thought Vey. It wouldn't be the first time Wyatt had leaned on a lame excuse.

"Well, at least my brown mare's no worse for the rollover," he conceded, still eyeing the white one suspiciously.

The special assistant held the dress up in front of her and examined it carefully. *It's not working.* With a huff, she snatched her canteen and splotched water on the soiled garment. Frantically, she scrubbed at the grime left behind. Some just wouldn't brush off. *What a disaster.*

Frog-faced Wyatt begged for an insult. Yes, he had a face like a frog, an old and wrinkly one, and she just might say it this time.

"Turnsby's just a hop, skip'n jump… less than an hour's ride. We could be there by dinner. I know the perfect—"

"No! I don't want to backtrack." *Idiot.* "I have plans. Keep trying… please," she forced the last word. It was a stern "please." More like "do it, or else." At least she didn't call him "Frogface." Vey prided herself on her show of restraint.

Wyatt navigated the slope and inspected the underside of the carriage. He cursed when he saw the damage. Vey didn't pay much attention to his profanity, at first. She had her own problems to deal with.

I knew I should have wrapped the dress up before I left. Everything hinged on that garment. Vey didn't care so much that her business attire had suffered a worse fate. Her carrying bag had landed and popped open on the only wet patch of an otherwise dried-up pond. And she wasn't overly concerned that her makeup bag had taken a tumble and become soiled, its contents largely spilled. The little left inside, spattered in mud. Better pigments and finer lotions could be found at the Abandon seaside market anyway. *But not the red dress…* There would be no replacing that in a day.

There was never enough time to do anything right, it seemed. And whenever Vey let one thing slide, however small, or let her guard down for half a minute, or counted on someone for one small favor, she paid for it dearly.

"I got two buckled wheels and only one spare," Wyatt reported. "Broken spokes on the one… can replace 'em with right-sized sticks. I got a cracked felloe there, too. I can reinforce 'er…"

Vey huffed with impatience. "Can you fix it?"

The handler rubbed his bristly chin, then nodded his amphibian-looking head.

"Yep."

Wyatt rambled on about a clearing crew he'd seen in the area the previous fall, and then went off to gather what deadwood he could find lying about to prop up the carriage. Vey gathered her things together, brought them to dry ground, and tidied them up as best she could.

Eventually, she helped the handler right the tipped carriage. He'd fastened the brown mare to one side, and as Vey coaxed the horse to pull, the carriage tilted up just enough for Wyatt to slide some old logs underneath. The handler then proceeded with the repairs using a rusty saw, some rivets, and various tools he kept in a wooden box. He'd searched through the carriage three times for his hammer, until he finally gave up on finding it.

"Someone must've stole it," he grumbled.

Vey knew better. No one steals in Gan.

The front wheel—the worst one—took only a few minutes for Wyatt to replace. At least that made for three good wheels. With a self-gratifying sigh, he started working on the rear wheel. The metal tyre, which formed the outer rim of the wheel, had come completely off the felloes. Wyatt grunted. "Once a circle's bent out of shape, you can't never get it back the same again."

The ex-bogger picked up a conveniently sized rock to use as a hammer, and started the wheel repair by reshaping the metal rim. He cursed when he banged and cut his thumb, cursed when the leather strap he was using to secure the rim snapped, and cursed for just about anything else that happened, good or bad. The worst of the "bad" curses came after Wyatt realized that, the whole time, he could have used the butt end of his hand axe as a hammer. That was apparently the fault of the colossi and they were all against him. The "good" curses took an entirely different tone from the "bad" ones, framing his progress by describing explicit ways in which some woman was finally yielding to his will. Cold shivers of disgust coursed through Vey's body at the words, and she tried to push the things she'd heard out of her mind.

Wyatt soldiered on as he cursed, and cursed as he soldiered on, red-faced and irritated in the swampy conditions. Not much was going his way. Every few seconds, his hand whipped up to swat a fly or wipe the sweat stinging at his eyes.

Vey stared at her salvage and wondered how the losses might impact her official meeting with Hersh. "Unbelievable," she said out loud to herself, shaking her head.

Wyatt paused his task. "Don't worry miss, I'll be fine," mistaking her comment as a show of empathy for his own struggles.

Vey puffed, then snickered silently. It wasn't that she didn't care, Wyatt was just… different. She gazed at her makeup bag and business apparel. *I've done all I can with it*, she admitted to herself, then shifted her gaze to the dress. *I'll think of something once it's fully dried. Clever accessorizing might help with the remaining watermarks. The bottom will be tricky though…* She expected at least some of the discoloration to linger there. *At worst, I could hike it up a bit to hide a stain or two near the hemline. I'm sure Hersh won't complain.* The thought made her giggle.

Despite all that had happened, Vey stared blankly into the wildwoods on the river side of the trail and mused about the relaxed evening get-together to come. It was inevitable. There would be no stopping it. Not even this catastrophe. Vey lost herself in the dream of it all again. Long minutes fell like light rain, tingling her skin. Tingling her mind.

Late night exchange…

⤜

A stick crunched somewhere in the woods. Vey jolted out of her daze. She glanced at Wyatt. He'd nearly finished re-hitching the brown mare to the carriage and was adjusting the harness. *It wasn't him.* Another stick snapped, definitely behind her. She swung her gaze to the white, spotted horse, feeding on roadside grasses. *Looks docile enough.* Then her eyes scanned the scrublands beyond. *Nothing.*

Somewhere off the trail, rocks clapped and knocked. *Kicked?* Then silence. She gasped. Her pulse quickened. She turned back to Wyatt.

The ex-bogger stood hunched over, scratching his head as he eyed the repaired wheel, fretting over it not being incredibly sturdy. "She'd better not turn ov—"

"Wyatt," Vey said in a hushed tone.

He didn't even look her way. "Miss, can you come take the reins so's I can muscle her out."

"No. Shush!"

Another crunch sounded off the trail—a loud one—followed by

the mushing sound of what could've been boots over leaf litter. Vey frantically waved her hands at the oblivious handler to get his attention.

Wyatt flicked his eyes to her for an instant, then double-checked the harness. He pulled tight on the strap, stretched the leather and hooked in the prong. Then he swiveled his head her way, stared blankly.

Vey lifted a finger to her lips, "Shhh." She pointed to where the noises seemed to be coming from—the opposite side of the trail. Wyatt nodded once. His eyes traced her stare through the thinned-out bush to a hillock, a short walk off the road. Its base was obscured by waist-high thickets. He rose to the tips of his toes, stretched his neck up. They both watched and waited in silence.

The quiet was broken by the sound of hooves clopping, filtering in from an entirely different direction—south.

"Aha." Wyatt relaxed his stance. "Riders is what yer hearing." He immediately resumed his task, firming up the breaststrap harness. "Sound's just reflecting," he went on. "Happens in the Bearded Hills sometimes too, and it's damn right eerie when it happens on the Mire Trail at night, I'll tell ya."

Vey scrunched her brow. "No," she insisted, still whispering. "It was snapping twigs I heard, not horses."

Wyatt spoke much louder than a whisper; louder than normal, even. "Whatever it was, sharp ears on ya m'lady. I'll give ya that. We'll have visitors soon, you'll see—from the Fort. Too much trot for a Stout wagon. That'd be a stroke of good luck right about now, wouldn't it? A Stout wagon from Doncaster? They're handy folk and their horses are fer haulin'. Just the same, 'tis good to have some company out here. Maybe not for long though. Most'll just pass us by, traders 'n all gabbing on about their wares and business. But maybe one will have the heart to help pull us back onto the road." He glanced to where he'd tied the other horse. "I don't know about that spotted mare though."

The presumption of goodwill notwithstanding, Wyatt casually wandered to the trail side of the wagon where his crossbow hung. He cocked and loaded it, then hung it back, unfastened. It would take half a second to level the device and send a quarrel flying. Then the handler produced a sheathed knife from under his riding seat and slipped it behind his back, tucking it into his pants. He flopped his shirt loosely over it.

A slight shiver crept over Vey. She moved behind the carriage, near to where Wyatt kept his axe handy, and pretended to fuss with her makeup bag. She glanced at the axe. She'd never used one, but she would grab it if she had to. *Do I swing down or sideways?* She imagined the impact both ways. *Down.* Vey lowered her head slightly—the natural position to view the contents of her bag—but kept her eyes fixed to the trail ahead.

Around the bend emerged the first rider on a spotted horse, grey over white. He looked tall and broad-shouldered, and he carried a bow slung across his back. His long locks of straight, dark hair flopped along with the steed's canter. The leather armor he wore was cured in dark browns and reddish browns, with overlapping bands on his shoulders to make them appear even wider. Overlapping scales formed the vest and tassets, while vambraces covered his forearms from wrist to elbow. Sleek pads protected his shins and knees.

"Whoa," he called out, a hint of the unexpected in his voice. He reined back his horse. As the steed came to a halt, the rider's gaze shifted from her, to Wyatt, to the handicapped carriage. Vey spotted markings along his brow that swirled into intricate traces around the eyes.

Wilder ink.

She'd crossed paths with many sorts of Wilders on the streets of Gan over the years. They rode in from the surrounding woodlands to fetch supplies, carry out official business, and inevitably pay a visit to the Shroom district. Some were rowdy and weathered, others shady as rogues. This one looked to be neither: too young for a ruffian—about her age or a shy younger—and there was nothing shady about him.

"Howdy there!" cried the handler. "Whew." Wyatt wiped his forehead with his shirtsleeve. "Sure glad to see… uh… glad to see a friendly face, and able-bodied at that. Could you maybe give us a hand? Wyatt's the name. I'm due in Abandon by evening and, well, as you can see…"

Vey eyed the Wilder carefully. *"Friendly" is not quite the word I would use to describe him*, she thought, and tried to come up with a single word that suited him better. *Not simply "handsome" or "strong" either, both are too plain. "Dashing" was ridiculous—too rugged for that. He's not a queensmen, after all. "Daring" maybe? No… venturesome.* Vey smirked to herself for having come up with it. *Yes, venturesome.*

The rider backed his horse up a few steps and signaled to those following with a shrill whistle. His eyes met Vey's for a long moment. There was something dangerous about his wide-faced stare, almost predatory. She shot a glance to the handler. *Wyatt, whatever you do, don't mess with this one.* She could see the indecision on his face. His hand rested casually on the crossbow. Ever so gently, Wyatt slid his finger to the trigger.

As the other riders were about to round the bend, a gruff voice carried over the trampling hooves of horses breaking their speed. "We're late already, we don't have time for any nonsense…" The accent placed him as a fort man, reminding Vey of a prospector her father once knew. He stopped talking as soon as he came upon the scene—a bearded man in his late thirties or early forties with sandy brown hair, an eyepatch, and not a trace of ink. He wore all tans and beiges, with a cloak to match. Either he wasn't wearing armor or it was made to appear like regular clothing, crisscrossed with leather straps and their buckles. His horse was dark brown. Two younger men on dark horses rode alongside him. They were the cleanest cut of the group, cloaked in forest green, leathers crisp and unscuffed. No ink again. They could have been brothers. One had badly wrinkled skin along the side of his face and neck, like a healed burn. The two of them and the bearded one all looked to be fort men, just as Wyatt had suspected. The handler passed them shooting glances.

That's right, Wyatt, keep your cool. Too many to take on at once.

The bearded rider brought his horse next to the Wilder's. He cleared his throat and addressed the stranded travelers.

"We're with the Kith Quarter. I'm in command here." He glanced at the scuffed carriage, the impression it had made in the ground, the repaired wheel, and then the cocked crossbow. He looked Wyatt in the eyes. His voice was calming. "You have nothing to fear. What happened? You on the bottle?"

"A boozin'?" Wyatt shook his head vigorously. "No, 'course not.

I'm on the clock." He casually removed his hand from the crossbow, pointed with his finger. "No, no. My white mare over there, she got spooked is what happened." The commander swung his gaze to the horse, eyed it carefully.

Vey stole a quiet breath and tried to hide any sign that she might have thought the horsemen were anything but honorable. Kith do not wear uniforms. Like the Wilders that make up much of their ranks, they can appear as rough as raiders or as ragged as vagabonds.

The special assistant stepped out from her partial concealment behind the carriage and into the open. She fastened shut her makeup bag and tossed it into the cabin. The rider on the spotted horse chose that same moment to dismount.

Before his feet even hit the ground, a patchy brown and white dog crossed into view from the trailside, tongue hanging out. It scuttled along half sideways and panted heavily. Vey didn't know much about dogs, but she could see this one was harmless. This canine was medium-sized with a bit of a silly, happy demeanor to it. The dog stopped to sniff something on the ground on the way over to the Wilder, then jerked its head back.

Stroking his horse's mane, the commander regarded Wyatt again. "Give me a moment to tie my horse. I'll take a look at the damage." He shifted slightly forward on the gelding's back. "Walk," he said, into its ear.

"STOP!" the young Wilder shouted. He lunged for the bearded man's reins, yanked them back. The horse resisted, snorting defiance.

"Damnit Amot!" the commander spat, as he struggled to bring his horse under control. "What the hell?" The gelding backed up a step when the young Kith let it some slack.

The Wilder, named Amot, plopped his own horse's reins into the hands of the bearded man. "Hold these." He raised a palm to his comrades farther back. "No one move." Uneasy glances passed between the riders.

With careful steps, Amot made his way over to the dog, scanning the ground as he went. He hunkered down and scruffed the canine behind its floppy ears.

"What do you have there, Howler?" The Kith ranger picked up a metal contraption with spikes jutting out of it. As he examined it closely, a subtle change came over him, a darkening. The curves of his Wilder ink thickened, while new lines began to appear on his face. Dramatic red lines formed under his eyes.

Vey marveled at the sight. A pulse of excitement ran through her. She'd never actually witnessed the transformation before, although she knew it was triggered by emotion. The markings that began to show reminded her of ones she'd seen on a grig friend of Lumen Hadamard's—except that man's were old, stretched and faded. This Wilder's markings were artful and vibrant, with sharp curves and edges.

The dog sniffed at the contraption in Amot's hand. Its head shot back before the Wilder could pull the device away in time. "Nasty, isn't it Howler." Amot gave the dog a rough, consolatory rub.

"Crow's feet?" called one of the two fort men behind him—the one with the burn mark.

"Here." Amot tossed him the device. "See for yourself." The man snatched it out of the air, then winced as he juggled it from hand to hand. His brotherly companion chuckled.

"Crow's feet?" Vey asked.

The Wilder rose and regarded Vey. "Caltrops, m'lady. They stab into the tender flesh of a horse's hoof and cause excruciating pain. Your driver's white mare stepped on one and ran you both off the road." Amot broke eye contact to scan the tree line and the hills. Beneath his eyes, red gashes bled through stronger than ever. He slowly drew his short bow and notched an arrow, tip to the ground. While Amot kept watch, the Kith commander dismounted. He sauntered over to Vey and Wyatt, horses in tow, kicking debris aside on the ground in front of him before each step.

"Berendt Garondi," he gruffed when he reached them, sounding like a lifetime smoker. Rough as his voice was, it carried a polite and respectful tone. On the rougher side in appearances as well, the commander had a nasty scar down his brow that disappeared under the patch then reappeared below, near the cheekbone. The surrounding skin was mutilated. Yet, he was otherwise unmarred, and Vey could see the skin elsewhere was smooth and youthful.

"My rangers here are all treaty enforcers, returning to Gan for… special training." The commander extended his hand to Wyatt, who introduced himself before shaking it vigorously.

"Wyatt Earthrin," he stated. "And this here fine lady is Vey Lancer." Wyatt gestured to his passenger. "She's a… one of them'a… y'know…"

Vey cut in. "Special Assistant to the Grey Clerk."

Berendt offered her a polite nod, holding to the usual custom. "Lady," he said. He swiveled his gaze to the Wilder, who relaxed the bend on the bow he carried.

Vey instinctively rolled her shoulders back, setting her posture upright with a slight arc to her back.

"M'lady," started the young ranger, duplicating Berendt's nod. His eyes met Vey's as he spoke. "As you've heard my commander say many times, my name is Amot."

His stare…

Vey felt a surge of energy as her own eyes widened. She felt flush in his gaze. His were grey-green with a splash of something feral. But the manner in which the Wilder regarded her did not deter Vey from locking eyes with him in return.

Intense.

"Yes, I suppose I have heard it, Amot. Please, call me Vey." She purposely toned down the smile that wanted to unleash itself.

When Amot shifted his gaze to address Wyatt, Vey stole a deep breath. She exhaled slowly.

"Your white mare won't hold a rider, not for days," Amot said.

Berendt added, "Looks like someone has designs on you and your belongings."

"Yes," Vey said. *I knew it.* She pointed to the hillock. "We heard something over there. Right Wyatt?"

The handler only shrugged. "Maybe it was just the dog."

Amot stepped forward, kicking something out of his path as he did so. It bounced towards Berendt. "No. Howler was well behind. I'm betting there are Outlanders in the hills."

"I wouldn't jump to conclusions," Berendt said. He paused for a long moment, then let out a sigh. "But we've had trouble with Baruush slavers lately. And a brigand of Scarsanders not too long ago."

Vey gasped, put her hand to her chest. "Scarsanders? In these parts?"

"Never spotted this close to Turnsby, at least not yet," Berendt said. "We think they were passing through to the East. Smugglers, maybe." The commander stooped over and picked up what Amot had kicked aside—a second crow's foot. He examined it closely, rotating the metal device as Wyatt looked on. It had four metal spikes arranged so that one pointed up no matter how it fell.

"Nasty things," Wyatt said.

Berendt grunted. "But don't worry," he assured Vey. "Whoever put those contraptions here won't bother us. We have the best spotters and archers in all of Theia. Speaking of which…" He handed the caltrop to Amot, then barked out orders. "Carlyle, Hem, check the white mare, and then check the road for caltrops." The two fort riders slid off their coursers.

"Outlanders could be watching," said the Wilder. "It only takes one stray arrow…"

Berendt drew a heavy sigh. Stroking his beard, he eyed Amot with a measuring look.

"All right," he said, half-convinced. "Go then, but make it quick."

Amot quivered the arrow, slung the bow over his shoulder and led Howler off the trail. For a long moment, he squatted and let the dog smell the crow's foot in his closed hand. He offered the animal words of encouragement to sniff out the shrubs and grasses just off the trail. The dog seemed to understand. He sniffed at everything, meandering one way along the trailside and then the other before moving farther from the road and repeating the process. Suddenly, he stopped, ears pricked, facing just right of the hillock. The canine let out an excited bark.

Amot made his way through the understory, squatted down beside the dog. The scout whispered something into its ear. Howler stiffened his stance, then bounded off into the bushes. The Wilder leapt to his feet. At a hurried pace, he swept through the ground cover with long strides, in pursuit.

Wyatt snickered, leaned towards Berendt. "A lively pair, those two."

Berendt snorted. "You don't know the half of it." The Kith commander motioned to the carriage. "So, what happened here?"

Wyatt proceeded to tell him a colorful and exaggerated account of all that had transpired.

◈

Hem found two caltrops jammed into a single hoof of the white mare. Wyatt yanked them out with pliers, then harnessed her in. Carlyle—with the burn mark—cleared the crow's feet from the road. The carriage was ready to roll.

"It'll be a long, slow road to Abandon with that mare the way she is," Wyatt proclaimed.

Atop his horse, the commander pulled two fast swigs from a shiny metal flask he carried. He tucked it into the saddlebag, then stuffed and lit the pipe he kept in his shirt pocket. A minute later he was calmly blowing smoke.

The Wilder returned, rested his hands on his knees and drew deep breaths. He then straightened up to lean against a bare-leafed tree. The dog flopped down beside his master, onto its belly with its tongue hanging out.

The Kith commander regarded Amot, waited for him to report.

"Yep… Baruush," puffed Amot, addressing his commander. "Two or three, by the tracks. On the small side. And something else… a large wolf or dog. Really large. This was meant to be an ambush."

Berendt removed his pipe from his mouth. "I doubt they were waiting around—they'd have been here sooner. More likely they plan to loop back every so often and check in on their trap."

"That's what I heard, then," Vey said. Her thoughts raced at the realization. She put her hand to her chest. "If you hadn't come…"

"Slavers?" Wyatt asked.

Berendt nodded slowly. "More than likely."

Wyatt rubbed his face with his hands, leaving it clean with worry. "How do I spot the next trap? My eyes aren't what they used to be."

The commander took a long draw from his pipe, slowly blew the smoke out. "Shouldn't be any behind us, unless they're right fresh out of Bitterhelm."

Amot pushed himself upright, ran his fingers through his hair, then strode over to his horse. "I found their camp in a deep hollow a quarter league off the road." He untied the reins and positioned himself near the front of the horse, left hand resting on the leather pommel of the saddle. He addressed Berendt directly. "The Outlanders can't be far—I poked through the ashes and there were still hot coals in it. There's a trail—rough—but if they kept to it, we can catch them on horseback." The Wilder fit his left foot in the stirrup and swung his body onto the courser.

"No, no," Berendt said. His voice had the inflection of one who does not want to bother with something arduous. "Stand down. That isn't our duty. They're not breaking any treaties and we're already late for orientation."

Amot's expression changed from one of focus to one of disgust. "What? What good is a fake exercise if we ignore a real problem?"

The commander's eyes narrowed on Amot. He bit down on his pipe. "Diamond Saber is the priority," he stated flatly, teeth clenched. Smoke puffed out of his nostrils.

Amot scoffed. "The exercise is days away. These Outlanders could have captives already."

"You can't go alone and I can't spare a man. I don't want surprises. There's no telling—"

"I don't need—"

Berendt jerked the pipe from his mouth. "Enough, Scout!"

Vey cringed at the commander's harsh voice.

Amot kept silent, his brow slightly furrowed.

The commander glanced at Vey. "Sorry you had to hear that, Miss." Then he countered his scout's words with a firm, decisive tone. "You probably chased them off, Amot. For now, at least. The Fort can handle this from here. Send a raven to Abandon from the outpost when we get there. Give them the location and bearing—a couple of leagues south of Turnsby. Got it? Ask them to dispatch a few good—"

"The Outlanders will be long gone by the time anyone gets here,"

Amot said, defiance in his voice. Coppery tones flared in his ink, just above the cheekbones.

He wants to hunt them down, thought Vey. An uncomfortable choking sensation welled up in her throat, constricting. Although she bore no sympathy for those who would abduct for ransom or slavery, this sort of problem was getting out of hand. *The trail needs to be safe. But hunting them down can't be the best answer.*

"Stand down," Berendt commanded. He glared at the Wilder and Amot glared right back. Howler raised his head, glanced from one to the other.

Berendt pushed on. "Are you ready to stand down or not?"

Amot's silence and restraint provided enough of an answer to satisfy the commander.

"Good then," Berendt said. "We're leaving." He called out to his men. "Rangers, pack up. I don't want to hear a single word from any of you the rest of the way."

Hem's shoulders slumped.

The Kith commander turned to regard Wyatt and Vey. The special assistant had already reclaimed her seat in the carriage, while the handler held the reins, ready to go. Berendt wished them a safe journey. "I'm sending one of my scouts to escort you to Doncaster. After that, you're on your own."

Amot wasn't done after all. "But you said—"

Berendt shot him a slicing glance. The Wilder kept his mouth shut, this time. His compliance was stiff and sour, but compliance nonetheless. The commander regarded his fort men. "Hem, you're up, then double time it back to Gan."

"Yes sir!" was the ranger's prompt reply.

Amot clenched his jaw, shook his head, and then in a flurry set his horse to gallop north, onwards to Gan. With tired eyes, the dog watched him go. He didn't get up right away.

Berendt sighed a lung full of smoke as he watched the departing horseman. "Too much energy for us, pooch."

"He'll be all right," Wyatt said. "Just let'im burn it off."

"I know," Berendt responded. After a moment of silence, one of the remaining fort men spoke up.

"Sir."

"Yes, Carlyle."

He held up the sack of caltrops. "What do I do with these, Sir?"

Berendt drew another long drag from his pipe, then answered. "Keep them. They might come in handy if we're ever pursued." He leaned low on his horse, whispered gruffly to Wyatt and Vey. "Someday, that Amot will make the best damn kithblade anybody ever saw." He winked to the two of them, then sat tall again upon his horse. He called back to his men.

"Hem."

"Yes, Sir."

"Make that *all* the way to the gates of Abandon, then high-tail it back to Gan."

"Yes, Sir!"

"Carlyle."

"Yes, Sir!"

"Don't let that bag get away from you."

"Yes, Sir!"

The commander swung his gaze to Wyatt. "Safe journey," he said.

The handler gave a six-tooth grin in reply, thanked Berendt and the fort men as well.

Berendt turned to Vey. The kind expression on his face seemed to erase the scar altogether. He offered her another polite nod. "Special Assistant."

"And safe journey to you too, Kith Commander Berendt Garondi… and thank you kindly. We are in your debt. Please pass on my gratitude to Amot. He was brave to do what he did."

Berendt grunted. "I will. He'll appreciate that."

Before heading off, Vey stole a moment to examine her dress, back hanging in its protected place where it belonged. It didn't look so bad after all.

CHAPTER V
THE LEGEND OF JHIN

*I*N THE AFTERGLOW *of the Deception of Enormity, a limb of humankind was left stranded. Amidst the chaos, a passage opened to them, to a place outside all things.*

Jhin was a colossal Hurlorn root who had taken to a purely subterranean existence. He drew sustenance from a rich vein of minerals that he'd tracked deep underground, and he drank from the pristine waters of a turbulent river that plunged into the forgotten depths from a great gorge in the world above. Jhin had a canopy once, but the cave was so dark and so windy that he'd shed his leaves, of use no longer. That river would later be named the Elderkin River, and that gorge would later host the three noble towers of the Hidden City. But none of those names yet existed.

Jhin was a creator who knew the One's ways. He used his knowledge to build a grand cavern around him, in the dark depths, at the top of the tallest subterranean waterfall. The place he fashioned became a marvel of texture and sound. It held everything he needed within its water-hewn walls. Everything, except one thing…

Companionship.

Then one day, when the winds in his cavern suddenly shifted to become a great wind, Jhin sensed the opening of The Passage. A hidden passage, to the eyes, but Jhin never knew that, for he was blind. Curious, and possess-

ing the heartwood of an explorer, Jhin extended his longest vine past the waterfall and felt into that passage.

Beyond was an airy and turbulent place, lacking firm ground. But he sensed sustenance in the air and mists therein, and he felt how solid objects floated about like leaves in a breeze. Feeling heavy and waterlogged and desiring freedom, Jhin leapt through the passage and into a new world, where everything drifted on currents of air. He felt elated to have discovered such a place, until he found the dead things that floated about with him. Small creatures, curious feeling, like none he'd ever known. They were not animals of the normal sort. They had very little fur—mostly just on their heads—and instead draped their bodies in materials as thin as leaves, with many interesting textures and cuts to them.

Over time, Jhin the Root began to find some that were alive. He collected the living in his great roots, which they clung to. He had no water to offer them, but they drank from pools where globs of mist collected. He had no food to offer them either, but they feasted on fungi that grew in the furrows of his rough bark.

The displaced people called themselves Abindohns. Through vibrations of thin branches and roots, Jhin learned to hear their words and whisper back to them. And after learning their sad story, a great pity surged in his heart. He believed such delicate life would not survive the world above, so harsh and unforgiving and full of behemoths. And so Jhin allowed the Abindohns to continue living amongst his roots, while he worked to fashion a more favorable environment using all he'd learned in creating his great cavern. But it wasn't enough. It wasn't enough until he changed himself to provide better shelter and conveniences for his people.

Jhin knew the Abindohns would have need of light; light he craved for himself as well. And although he himself could not see, the Root was aware that light came from heat. And so he began collecting the many rocks floating about. Some had strange minerals in them, easily shaped to his will. Reaching into the mind of the One Outside All Things, Jhin created the Starshine and set it to spin. He tangled his longest vines around that spinning ball, and spun along with it.

Many good years passed in orbit about the Starshine, during which Jhin taught his people the secrets of the One's design. And he continued to *shape a limited pocket of existence for them, tuned to their every need. Jhin was generous with his knowledge. Too generous.*

A faction desiring ultimate power—calling themselves the Jhinyari—learned the secrets of the strange metals Jhin had discovered in the floating rocks. With that knowledge, they fashioned a silvery sword and cut out Jhin's heart before his work was complete. "Jhinyari" was Abindohn for "those in opposition to Jhin."

The other Abindohns were appalled. Some fled immediately and eventually found a passage out. After many travels, they made their way to the surface of the world above and settled in a bay which they named after themselves.

The Abindohns that did not agree with the Jhinyari, and did not flee, were oppressed, enslaved, and forced to live out their lives in fear and servitude. They never stopped whispering Jhin's words among themselves, and they trained in secret to overthrow the Jhinyari. One day, with their bare hands, the oppressed fought the Jhinyari and drove them away. These heroes called themselves the Djinxarai, which means "Avengers of Jhin."

—The Diviner

Chapter VI
TETHERPORT
(Hadamard)

E VEN WITH THE windows wide open, the main floor of the Crimson Tower smelt like freshly treated wood. After three years on order, the new furniture had finally arrived, completely unannounced and on the morning of Hadamard's whirlwind preparations.

"Nothing like injecting a little chaos into a rush," Hadamard grumbled to himself as he collected his things, trying to get organized before a half-dozen or so brawny men barged into his office. A single guard wandered amongst them, keeping watch over the rock-delved chambers while the movers heaved out the old and carried in the new. And as they banged around in the foyer and the commons area, Hadamard double-checked that he had everything: In his traveling bag, three neatly-folded changes of clothing and personal effects. In his satchel, reference guides, scenario notes, writing supplies, and sundries. And in his inner pockets, important keys, his diplomatic colors, a list of the unconfirmed prospects, a summary of their entrance exam results, and…

What am I missing? It was hard to grasp a thought with all of the distractions—the cursing, the thumping, the ruckus. Hadamard tilted his head up to clear his mind, stared at the rock dome ceiling for a long minute.

"Of course!" he muttered to himself, then looked to his desk. "The chain. I'll need it for the kinship stone." The luminary made his way to the rickety old piece of furniture, hunkered down, and rummaged through the rightmost bottom drawer. He hadn't worn the simple iron chain with its custom oversized locket in years, not since the deepwood staff had come to him from the 8th. Yet, the chain and hollow pendant were right where he'd left them. Hadamard grasped the chain, ducked his head down and slipped it around his neck. He paused to think again, scanning the office as he did so. *Hmm… what else? Food and lodging will be taken care of by the host… and the Djinxarai don't have currency to speak of.* But it felt wrong to go traveling without any money at all. *A dozen griffs can't hurt, plus a few royal notes in case something big comes up. I have to get into the safebox anyway.*

The luminary pushed himself to his feet, strode to the wide book-shelf against the wall and swiped an assortment of handwritten tomes aside. He dug the key out his pocket and plunked it into the hidden keyhole. After a quarter turn to the left, the lock clicked and he swung the safebox door open.

Front and left in the compartment lay several stacks of twelve griffs and an envelope stuffed with royal notes. Hadamard scooped up a stack of coins, slid them into his satchel. Then he counted out one hundred and fifty griffs worth of notes, neatly folded them, and added them to the other thirty already in his money clip. He slid the notes into an inner pocket. The precious elemental stones were also in the safe, tucked to the right in a long, wooden box. When he lifted the lid, the glow of Order Lumen's most prized possessions spilled out. They flickered erratically: red and green; on again, off again.

Stroking his beard, Hadamard stared at the collection, trying to decide what to do with each one. A good assortment they were, con-sisting of three of the six fundamental types: a transmuter charm, a kinship stone, and a shadow stone. Missing were the slider charms needed for the strikers; the mysterious dual charm waiting for him in Seventh Kaeda; and lastly the seeker stones on loan for a variety of uses, not the least of which to locate more of the rare gems.

The chamber door creaked open. Hadamard jolted at the sound.

Dragging footsteps followed. He swatted the safe door. It slammed shut.

Shit, too loud.

With deft hands, the luminary grabbed a book and spun around, just as a mover barged in. The chamber door thudded on the doorstop. The footsteps ceased. With his eyes lowered to the cracked-opened tome, Hadamard calmly flipped a page. After a measured moment, he slammed the book shut as though it were his habit, then casually returned it to the shelf. He placed it in front of the brassy key that stuck out of the wall.

Double-shit.

Putting on a plain face just the same, Hadamard turned his gaze to the man standing in the doorway. He was medium-built and scruffy, balding on top with light brown hair. He sported a solid pot belly that peeked out beneath a loose-fitting shirt. His arms were short and thick, and his shoulders well-rounded.

The mover kept his eyes lowered to the clipboard he held. He glanced at the number on the door—137—then down to the clipboard again. He spoke without looking up.

"Lumenship," he said, followed by a long pause.

"Yes," Hadamard replied. The pause persisted. In the silence that followed, Hadamard found himself inexplicably wondering whether or not this man had children—a family to take care of, a family that took up all his free time. Then he wondered what it would be like to worry about moving stuff instead of—

"Room's next, Lumenship." The mover flipped to another page of his clipboard and read quickly from a list. "New desk, new cabinet, new chairs, new deep…" He scrunched his brow. "…de-jinx-er spere?" Then he scoffed. "Ekkon's Wheel, whatever that is."

Djinxar sphere.

"It's a custom piece," the luminary explained, unsure exactly how the device became lumped in with everything else being delivered that day. He'd sent the specs to the 8th Institute only three weeks ago. "Pronounced 'gin-zar sphere,'" Hadamard went on. He gestured to a highly cluttered area of his chamber. "It goes in the corner with all of the other instruments. Just find a clear space and set it down gently."

"Well, change is good for the soul." The mover sniffed at the air. "Getting rid of the furniture won't get rid of that smell though." He tilted his gaze down to the Kel Samu carpet covering the floor, then sideways to the shelf. He sniffed at the air again. "It's them dusty old books."

"I need another minute before I can get out of your hair," the luminary told the man, hoping the mover would get the hint and afford him some privacy before turning the room upside down.

With quick glances, the intruder assessed the chamber's contents. "Bah." He curled his upper lip. "Don't bother me none you're here." The man gestured to his younger helper who'd slouched into the room behind him, hands in his pockets.

Hadamard sighed, then nodded to the man with the clipboard. "Leave the bookshelf for last. I need to find a particular book before everything's in a big, disorganized pile."

"Easy," the man replied. A few seconds later the movers were pulling drawers from Hadamard's desk.

"Be sure to swap the contents with the new furniture," Hadamard added. "Everything."

The pot-bellied man grunted his compliance.

As the pair worked, the luminary recalled another item he'd need. He wandered over to his locker, pulled out his protective gear and laid it on the floor to put on later. Hadamard didn't normally wear the robe armor outside of actual missions—too showy and unnecessary in his opinion. The attire was dark crimson and leathery, with an alchemical-resistant coating from the 2nd Institute that gave it a slight sheen. The worst part was that the gear clearly identified the wearer as a luminary. With the uptick in treaty violations in Fort Abandon and the recent triple-slaying of luminaries stationed in Harrow, the Grey Quarter had made it official policy for all members of the Order— especially enforcers—to wear protective gear while abroad. It was a policy Hadamard largely ignored. *I can't get away with not having it this time though,* he reasoned, given the visibility of the upcoming exercise and the presence of notable higher-ups. *Someone will complain. Lord Ralador, for one.*

After stacking the drawers in neat piles, the two movers each grabbed an end of the old hardwood desk, heaved it up and whisked it out of the office.

The moment they left the room, Hadamard hurried back to the safebox and reopened it. His eyes fell upon the three elemental stones he'd been mulling over before being interrupted. The oblong one flared up immediately.

"Yes… I'll bring you for sure," he said in low tones, speaking to the gem as though sentient. "Someone has to keep Forsetti honest."

He grasped the piece, polished and translucent. Its rich, golden brown color was nearly a dead ringer for amber. Only the tiny dot of green light confined within hinted at its unique origins, flickering wildly at Hadamard's presence.

The luminary clamped the kinship stone into the cage-like setting dangling from his neck. Then he snapped the blocker shut. No matter how brilliant a luminary prospect might be, failure to resonate with the kinship stone meant failure of the trials, and possible redirection to Alchemy, Book Inspection, or some other more mundane institute. *Well… not quite,* Hadamard reminded himself, as he tucked the chain under his shirt. *There's always the 7th Institute, Special Projects.*

Even for those who passed the trials, finding a suitable elemental stone could be impossible. Unlike Jhin thaumaturgy where every Djinx-arai is born to master its ways, the tree-like Hurlorns pick and choose their own. Hadamard knew the game. For the Jhin it was simple—heritage. The Hurlorns took a more complex approach though, focused on bringing new blood into their ranks: kindred spirits and fresh minds to join in their shared consciousness, talent foreseen as mandatory for the future. Hadamard could identify with that right now, in his own much clunkier search for prospects. *Kinship stone resonances are tuned to the desired personal attributes of a prospect and, as proven by a handful of autopsies, a certain rare condition as well…*

Hadamard tried not to think of the fungus likely to have implanted itself somewhere on his skull, following an insect bite he could've only received near the bog lands. *The fever.* And he tried not to think of how that organism must've since expanded in small patches to either side of the bone, connected by thin-filaments that bored through it. He tried not to think of the tiny invader, but try as he might, he could still almost feel the fungi's parasitic presence. The skin of his cranium crawled with it.

Hadamard swung his gaze to the doorway. *Still clear.* The grunting and cursing beyond it placed the movers at the outside stairs, likely struggling to carry his new desk up from the street and into the foyer. He turned his attention back to the secret compartment, eyed the remaining elemental stones. One was still in the rough: the dull shadow gem or "dud"—a stone that by all appearances had the right composition, yet no known purpose. *You're staying,* he decided.

The last stone was dear to Hadamard and sadly in need of a new owner. That stone was the transmuter charm he'd called his own for nearly a decade, before his newly assigned dual charm had been unearthed. As he watched, it sparked up in its usual way, familiar and inviting. The fiery point of light within flashed and danced. Seeing it again imparted peaceful sensations to his mind. Warmth. Relief. He thought back to his training. *All those years.* Charms share a bond with their evokers. It had been a deep and personal experience. The path of discovery easily can take a lifetime and is only complete when one sheds their mortal form, at which time the Hurlorn seed finally takes root and the two—charm and owner—merge into a single being. *We'll never get that far,* he thought solemnly, *you are meant for another.*

Hadamard sighed. A hollow, empty feeling filled his gut. But he knew what he must do. *With luck, I'll find you a worthy and compatible master in no time,* he thought. The luminary withdrew the charm and squirreled it away in a black, hand-sized pouch he carried. For no apparent reason, he made a snap decision and took the dud too. *You never know.* Then he pulled the drawstring tight and tucked the pouch away in his satchel. He shut and locked the safe, and had just started donning his armor when the movers entered with his new desk. It was more refined than the old one, with a deep red stain that ran rich and even over the wood's close-knit grain. Once Hadamard clasped his last buckle, he strode over to the newly placed piece of furniture and ran his finger along the top's beveled edge.

"Good and solid," he told the movers, paving the way for a conversation about the desk—its history, the wood, crafting methods… anything. Such narratives made for good small talk when visitors showed up.

The pair offered no response.

Hadamard shrugged. *Obviously not carpenters. A carpenter would have talked my ear off.* There was no reason to linger. "Well, I must be going now," he announced to deaf ears. The luminary picked up his traveling bag, slung it over one shoulder, then grabbed his satchel. "Don't forget to transfer *all* the contents."

Before leaving his office, Hadamard took one last look around. Then he was out the door, through the hall and down the basalt steps. Standing on the cobbled Elgar's Way, he glanced up at Icy Blue fronting the falls, hoping for a morning gryphon sighting. Icy Blue was the second of Gan's three monolithic towers and the only one to have a gryphon aerie at its summit. Hadamard scanned the jagged crown of the volcanic plug, the cascading torrent behind it, and the grey sky above. *Not today.* Feeling slightly ripped, Hadamard turned around and strode towards three heavy carriages filled with furniture. He spotted his Djinxar armillary sphere in one of them, polished brass shimmering in the early morning light. *Magnificent,* he thought, and approached for a closer look. It had turned out better than he'd ever imagined. Once there, he began rotating the outer rim. It spun smoothly, like a gyroscope.

I absolutely have to bring this along. I have to show Nydar. The glideboat captain and shipwright had helped Hadamard draw up the specifications, to the best of his abilities. No one actually knew the full architecture of the vast Otherworldly Realm the luminary was traveling to that day, so only those regions the captain had sailed were represented, and only in approximate terms. Outside the model, surrounding it, Nydar had referred to the existence of a grand structure known only as the Great Barrier, which he and others described as a massive rock wall blocking passage in every direction. Only three outlets from the realm were known to the captain: Jhin's Cave, the Dim Sea, and a well of sorts in the Star Sands—but the latter only before the desert kingdom had fallen into ruins.

The luminary pushed an inner rim of the model. It, too, spun smooth and easy. He turned to his tower and spotted a guard in the nearest open window. Hadamard cupped his hands around his mouth, called out, "Watchman." The man poked his head out, homed his gaze on Hadamard.

The luminary pointed to the metallic Djinxar sphere beside him. "I'm taking this. Tell the man with the clipboard I have it." *It'll be cumbersome, but worth the haul.*

The guard hollered back, "What is it, exactly?"

"Just say the 'de-jinx-er spere.'" Hadamard smirked despite himself.

The guard nodded and pulled back from view.

Hadamard turned back to his prize. He stooped, clamped the sphere to his stomach with one arm, and then, as he straightened, slowly rolled it up to his chest. Fully cradling the unwieldy astrolabe, he continued along Elgar's Way towards the royal wharf, located behind palace walls at the mouth of the river cave. As he walked the cobblestone street, the luminary eyed the Starshine at the core of the replica, then bent his thoughts toward getting there.

Tetherport…

⌘

A daring half-Djinxarai glideboat captain and a capable crew would get him and his unconfirmed prospects to Tetherport unscathed. The trying harbor was the only known way onto or off of Seventh Kaeda—the cradle of the reclusive Djinxarai tribe. Most importantly to Hadamard, "the Rock" was also home to the proving grounds for a rapidly evolving capability that Gan needed desperately. The revelation had come out of nowhere, it seemed. And unwelcome to all but a handful of misfits and dreamers. Academicians disbelieved the notion, discredited it, and mocked those who embraced it. Their resistance helped to validate the coverup and the veil of secrecy that followed.

As much as Hadamard could grasp, "remote kinetic psionica,"

the pet name eventually adopted by academia, appeared to be a fully natural phenomenon. Despite claims to the contrary, the luminary's assessment was that no one in the secretive Grey Quarter understood the underlying mechanism at work. Others did though, on some level. In a sense, he'd reasoned, the Hurlorns had a feel for it all along—they had to. Their creations made his work possible. Historical records also alluded to Jhinyari knowledge of the phenomenon and perhaps some guarded use.

Hadamard suspected the Djinxarai invoked some variant of remote psionica, perhaps a distant cousin. Lived by it, even. But, until recently, Djinxar—the decision-making core of Seventh Kaeda—had been completely silent on the matter. At the same time, the Djinxarai suddenly became far more engaged in their dealings with the monarchy and aristocrats of Gan's Hidden City.

It's because they know we know, Hadamard suspected.

Within Gan itself, a grossly overeducated toymaker, of all people, had been the first to unravel the mysteries of remote kinetic psionica. Prime Lumen Forsetti quickly invited him to join the Crimson Tower's prestigious 4th Institute. Soon after, in secret, of course, the toymaker proposed the leading theory. It was wholly bizarre and unreal. *Let the academicians have their fun trying to figure that one out.*

Hadamard shook his head. That was years ago. His life had been chaos ever since. And now, he had trouble believing that only two days had passed since his discussion with Feleg over a beer. Only two days had passed and already he was about to dip oars on a major new mission to Tetherport.

More like juggling a fistful of missions, he lamented. *And Forsetti threw a wrench into things by nominating half of the unconfirmed prospects himself. Always everything at once.* In his mind, he ran through all that he had coming. *Prep and then conduct Diamond Saber, evaluate Crusher's workmanship, evaluate a batch of luminary hopefuls, give them a tour, and test out the new dual-charm staff.* A tall order indeed.

As he passed through the palace entrance, Hadamard made the final turn on his way to the wharf barely noticing the gatehouse and the majestic Grey Tower. The guards, in turn, barely gave *him* notice.

Hadamard rarely had to produce his diplomatic colors for them to inspect. And this time, they seemed more interested in the bulky astrolabe he carried than in him. The luminary shifted the metal sphere to his other hand.

Hadamard shot a glance at the Grey Tower banner as he passed, like he always did: an amber cat's eye in a pale moon, fronting a night sky. The banner spanned two high stories of that third and final monolithic structure of Gan.

Before reaching the secured area where the Djinxarai vessels pushed off, Hadamard played out in his mind how the coming exercise would unfold. If all went according to plan, boatloads of rangers and queensmen would join him in the Netherdome. Diamond Saber would begin and Hadamard's own theories would be put to a live test. Normally, that would be a good thing. But his work was incomplete and Lord Ralador had it in for him. Hadamard knew it, Feleg knew it, even the damn ugly gargoyle knew it. And that made the preparations especially grueling. *There can be no mistakes.*

CHAPTER VII
SAILORS AND SAGES
(Vey)

AN UNFAMILIAR SCENT rode the breeze as the carriage crested the final hill and wobbled towards the gatehouse. Not the salty sea air Vey remembered from her childhood, whirring off the bay, nor the farm-fresh air blowing in from the Doncaster Flats behind her. The closest sensation she could come up with was a taste, from a time she'd been out celebrating and, without looking, had taken a drink from a cup that her friend Tara'd made an ashtray out of. The breeze carried the bitter, ash taste of industrialization. Ahead, the lights of the city gleamed in full display.

Hem said his goodbyes and bid the two travelers farewell before galloping ahead to the gatehouse to report the incident on the road. Afterwards, he would head back to Gan on a fresh horse to join his detachment. A new day would dawn by the time he got there; noon or later if he took a layover in Turnsby.

Wyatt's repairs had held up well and Vey's room lay in waiting only minutes away, with its over-soft bed and private powder room. She sighed at the thought. Only the affluent could afford the security of Abandon's limestone curtain—oligarchs and guild masters, higher-ups in government, Stonebones clergy and successful merchants or entrepreneurs, to name a few. They lived well, and their indulgences gave rise to the Spa District. Vey's thoughts drifted to the promise of relaxation and pampering, her well-deserved rewards after such a stressful, arduous journey.

Vey felt small when the carriage passed beneath the imposing Fairwind's Arch, its ornate etchings of those lost in battle or at sea gleaming in the torchlight. The feeling reminded her of the time she'd first met the vice-regent, just over a year ago, while merely an apprentice at the Grey Tower. He'd seemed so proud of the fort he commanded and its heritage. The vice-regent had stumbled upon her, working hard at her desk over a jumbled pile of water-stained documents, crinkled and torn and smelling of mold. It was a sweltering hot summer day and the Tower was uncomfortable and stuffy. The young half-giant had stopped by on his way to a meeting with the Grey Clerk herself. Vey had felt small then too, with Hersh standing at the arched doorway of her workspace, tall and dark and blocking all light from the adjoining hallway. She couldn't blame him for getting lost—the lower levels were a rat maze. He'd asked for directions and they'd gotten to talking. Vice-regent Hersh Tehan was an interesting man and a good conversationalist. They talked for an hour and he missed his meeting entirely. "No worries," he told her in parting. "I'll blame it on my sense of direction."

Such a stark looking place though, pondered the young protégé as she glimpsed the fort city's interior, *for all its underlying lavishness.* Wyatt's tired horses limped past the gates. Vey's gaze wandered over the scene. The stronghold's outer wall and fortifications loomed high above the two travelers, sturdy and unembellished. Like the original construction, it was a product of pure function. There were no grand halls or elaborate towers within the age-old walled city. And curvature, quite prominent in Gan architecture, was so entirely absent in Fort Abandon one might have thought it'd been outlawed. Every structure was simple and rectangular, and taken together they all lined up perfectly in well-ordered rows, brightly lit in the night. Buildings had walls of quarried stone, were plank roofed, low ceilinged and squat. They were well maintained and easy to heat over the long winters. Townsfolk and business owners had made practical efforts to add decor, like stuffing small, windowsill garden pots with bright, cheery flowers popping out in full bloom. But in simple truth, the artful arrangements looked cheerfully out of place.

Most of the bay's working inhabitants lived outside the walls in small villages with forgettable names. The routine for many was to enter by day and exit by nightfall. A single church atop a small hill appeased those who still clung to the old religions, shared amongst the various denominations, small as they were and ever dwindling. At least they'd stopped fighting one another. The Stonebones temples were all underground, centered around the lair of the withdrawn colossus himself.

In their conversation that day back in the Grey Tower, Hersh had seemed eager to share his version of what had happened to the Akedans—his forebearers—so long ago. He'd spoken with great reverence about their heroism and sacrifices. Vey knew that historians hotly disputed the events he described: the descent of the Jhinyari on Akeda, the darkness that fell like an instant plague, and the holding of the fort she'd just entered by mere scores of brave defenders.

Such debates are better left to sailors and sages, she'd thought at the time. And Vey was neither. So rather than contest, the young protégé just sat back in her seat and allowed herself to be lulled by Hersh's deep, rolling voice as the words poured out of him, and the sweat poured out of both of them.

None of that history mattered now, at least not to Vey. What mattered now was that, until recently, only Akeda had dared to experiment with technical manufacturing, and that was back in the days before Jhinyari descended upon the bay to snuff it out. Less than a decade ago, Hersh's father had resurrected power generation machinery and equipment for small labs from the ruins. At first, he'd stated it was for archaeological purposes; then later, after it had been activated, to revitalize an ailing economy—depleted fishing grounds, crop failures, leviathan attacks and vessel pirating had all but wiped out trade.

When presented with viable alternatives in the Meeting of the Six, and when pressed by Gan and the Tri-towns to cease and desist his technological pursuits, the former vice-regent had slapped the table, stood up from his chair and, chest puffed, had famously declared: "You would make me a beggar? A bottom feeder? I don't need your hand-outs, and I don't want them either." Before storming off, he'd gone on to say living off Gan's throwaways was no way to feed their growing population or revive a dying economy, and swinging steel was no way to secure the Fort's walls or confront the Fort's enemies at sea. "We can do better than that, and we will."

Since that day, the relationship between Abandon Bay and Gan has deteriorated, while illicit trade and cooperation between Harrow at Dim Lake and the bay's fort has flourished. Caught in the middle, as usual, were the Tri-towns: Turnsby, Webfoot, and the Bearded Hills. Hersh could change all of that. Instead of following in his father's reckless footsteps, he could turn over a new leaf for the fort—cease all old-world technological pursuits and redirect innovation towards embracing markets allowed for by the treaty. *But would he? And even if he did, would it be in time?* The consequences of noncompliance could be devastating: a second Jhinyari invasion, or worse—detection by the entity that destroyed the old world in the first place and nearly all of humanity along with it. *Is there a nice way to tell him his father's naïve and dangerous views need to die with him?*

Wyatt navigated through the market district's narrow and busy streets to the waterfront, where the grounds opened up. Smells of fish and sea air mingled with the ash, growing stronger on approach. Moored ships lined the shore along the open wharf, together with a market, stone-block inns, well-stocked taverns and buildings of various sorts devoted to shipping and fishing enterprises. Most merchants had already packed up their wares for the night, while the local watering holes were gaining patrons.

The coach came to a stop alongside Vey's prearranged lodgings: the *Seaside Rendezvous*. Wyatt swiveled in his driver's seat to face her in the cabin. "I'll wait if you like. I have a good many repairs to make properly..." He tilted his head and grimaced. "And see about that mare too. That'll take me... maybe—"

"No need, Wyatt," Vey cut in, waving him off. She handed him a fistful of royal notes. "Accept the first charter you can. And thank you." She felt terrible for how she'd treated Wyatt. She'd been judgmental and intolerant, when really, he'd handled a difficult situation quite well, all things considered. Vey could see the regret on his face though, like after swearing in the presence of young children. She dispelled his expression in an instant with an over-generous smile. The equally generous gratuity couldn't have hurt either. Wyatt stared at the notes in hand. A wide grin crossed his face and his eyes sparkled.

He's a simple man. A slight sense of elation welled up in Vey.

"Maybe you can get yourself a new hammer," she said.

"If you ever need a driver—"

"I'll be sure to ask for you," Vey said, rising from her seat.

Wyatt made to get up. "Your bags," he offered.

"I can handle them," Vey replied. She'd already began collecting her things. Fully laden, she headed for the front desk of the inn. The special assistant to the Grey Clerk had early morning plans, her clothes were a mess, and it was too late to find a seamstress.

Tomorrow, she thought, *after a good long session at the spa.*

CHAPTER VIII
BEING AKRYLLA
(Akrylla)

THE EVENING WAS warm for September, but nonetheless Akrylla packed her sleeveless shirt in her satchel and donned a new, long-sleeved tunic to wear to the seaside market. It wasn't really new, but it was new to her, having spotted it blowing in the wind on someone's dry-line earlier that day.

The predominantly dark-red garment made her feel special, almost pretty, and she liked the way the embroidered vines ran along its length on either side. The tunic was long, but not long enough for Akrylla to wear without a skirt, so she acquired one of those as well. The skirt she "found" was a nice and simple charcoal grey and it nearly fell to her ankles. So, along with her sleeveless shirt, she rolled up her robe nice and tight and packed that away too.

Akrylla's dark brown cincture went well with the skirt. She used it to draw the tunic around her waist. A bright green ribbon kept the long locks of her hair tied back, grey-streaked and grizzled as they were. The green was a dead-ringer for the vine and leaf pattern on her garment. In her mind, she was suddenly elegant.

~Pretty

Elegance was not the only reason Akrylla chose that particular tunic over the others, hanging on lines in the outlying village. For one, it was easy pickings—some lovely housewife had been down the road gabbing to her neighbor, oblivious to the world around her. Another reason was more personal. Something about the owner had set her off.

"That woman should have shut up and kept a better eye on things," Akrylla muttered to herself, "and she's lucky I left her the child."

Akrylla had two more reasons: First, the long sleeves covered her unsightly arms. Second, it was a sign. She'd chosen the red garment because it symbolized the river of blood that would be shed in the coming days. The green vine, she postulated, symbolized new life springing up from the blood-soaked earth. Recognizing signs was the most important thing about being Akrylla.

Dumb, gabby woman, the hag mused as she entered the walled city. She huffed, uttered a minor curse, and then took in the sights.

~My fort

Abindohn, she called it, as her ancestors had. Akrylla mouthed the name as she turned onto Fargoer Road. Spite and pride kept her from ever calling the place "Fort Abandon"—that would be blasphemy to the land and disrespectful to the memory of her ancestors, whose bones the fort was raised upon. A name like that isn't something you just toss away on a whim blown in from the sea. Most in the fort had no idea. *Soon, the name will be reborn*, she prophesized. While breathing in the toxic air of the industrial district, Akrylla imagined the walls in rubble. Just the thought of it curled her lips into a smile, long and thin.

~Teeth

Don't show your teeth, Akrylla scolded herself. *They'll sniff you out right away if you show your teeth.*

The cobblestone felt warmer underfoot than the bare earth had been. Lined with shops, Fargoer Road ran south to the docks. *I should have taken some shoes as well.* Had she thought of shoes earlier, she would have.

~Satchel

Akrylla undid the flap, felt for her coin purse. She found it and counted the skull-shaped coins inside by feeling their edges. Thirty-nine, along with seven griffs.

~Thieves

No thieves had gotten ahold of her money. It was all there. But it still might not be enough. Some merchants refused to deal with anyone bearing the swirling, spider-veined scars typical of a Scarsander.

~Blackmailers

Other vendors would charge steep prices if they found out—a fee just for agreeing to associate with such an ingrate; this despite the fact everyone knew money was terribly hard to come by in the Scarsands. Akrylla had borrowed, cheated, stolen and sold anything she could sell, in order to get what she needed. *Stock up now, I will, while the shops still stand. One shop in particular...*

Akrylla let out a huge breath as the most important shop came into view, tucked into the bottom level of a wooden three-story building. The level above jutted out overtop it. *My first stop,* she decided. The shopkeeper was a renter, she knew, and renters were unreliable, likely to close down or move on. Before embarking on her journey, she'd had many visions about the *Fargoer Apothecary* and they all carried the same theme. But visions cannot be trusted fully, and it disturbed her to have had so many foretellings of such a mundane thing.

~Soul sister

Someone else was there: a redheaded miss.

Akrylla approached the apothecary, but she had to wait her turn. The girl behind the counter was new, young and fresh. *Good. That one will be easy to dicker with.* Her ash brown hair was neat and tied back, and she wore a tan coat with supple, white gloves. She smiled often as she conversed; an easy, tight-lipped smile.

Akrylla gave the redheaded customer a sidelong glance, held back a scoff.

Who's this? And why won't she leave us be? Rich little hussy looks like she just stepped out of the spa.

Akrylla sniffed the air. *Lavender, honeysuckle, fruits… scents of perfumed cleanliness.*

"Hmph." *She did just step out of the spa.*

Unabashed, the shaman looked the girl up and down. Everything about the redhead was well manicured, well put together. *Yessums. The spa.*

And the young woman was taller than she'd seemed from afar. It was her thin build that made her look that way. Akrylla glanced at the shopping bags she carried, held back another scoff.

Doesn't know where money comes from either. Useless things.

~My time

Yes, she's wasting valuable time. Akrylla tapped the redhead on the shoulder. She used her "pleasant" speaking voice. Between words, a big round grin arced over her face. She was careful not to show her teeth as she spoke.

"Did-you-enjoy-it?"

The red-haired "hussy" put a stop to her conversation with the new teller, mid-sentence. She and the girl behind the counter both turned their heads to Akrylla. The expressions that painted the young women's faces were all too familiar, all too unflattering. The redhead met Akrylla's gaze, nearly at eye level.

"Pardon?" she responded. Her tone was polite, yet suggestive in some inexplicable fashion of rudeness on the part of the interrupter.

"Did you enjoy the spa?" Akrylla repeated.

"Why, yes, I did, very much. Have you ever… been?" The redhead's voice faltered near the end of her question. She probably regretted asking it.

"Who me? Nosomes, call me a simple country girl, my sweet." Akrylla put her hand over her mouth and giggled girlishly.

The hussy gave her an examining look. "Oh my, you must be so tired. Are you here for medicines?"

No, pretty.

"Medicine for a wolf, maybe," Akrylla replied. Her throat felt rough. She wasn't used to talking much. She hadn't drank much either.

Thirsty. Need water.

"Oh my. Wolfsbane then?"

"Yes." Akrylla cleared her throat. "And something for my dreams."

"Valerian?"

"Nosomes. I sleep just fine."

"Bittergrass or moonwort?"

"Nosomes."

"You don't mean belladonna, do you? Ingestion could kill you."

"Are you an herbalist?" The question came out scratchy. Akrylla rubbed her throat, then shifted her gaze to the teller. "A drink dear, if you please." The girl offered an accommodating smile, then ducked down behind the counter.

"No," the redhead shook her head, "I'm afraid not. But I did spend a summer in the queen's solarium."

"Ahem… Excuse me… Do you still go there?"

"Not to work, only to lose myself in my thoughts. I'm at the Grey Tower now."

~Secrets

So naïve, so open, Akrylla observed. She cleared her throat again, and sawed out another question.

"The Grey Tower? You must know a lot of secrets." The red-haired miss shifted from one foot to the next, then glanced at her shoes.

Discomfort.

"Not really. Nothing I ever see looks very secret at all. Quite mundane really, the bulk of it."

The teller reappeared with a wooden cup and handed it to Akrylla. The shaman accepted with a pleasant grin, raised the cup to her mouth, instinctively gave it a quick sniff. *Water.* Satisfied, she downed the contents. The tepid liquid soothed her throat. There was a slight aftertaste though—something medicinal. When she finished, she wiped her mouth with her sleeve and swung her gaze back to the redhead.

"Why does the queen need a solarium?"

"Oh." The redhead's expression lightened. Her voice jumped up an octave.

Fond memory, thought Akrylla.

"She loves to wander the winding paths," said the redhead.

"Alone?"

"Sometimes. And she is interested in… natural beauty enhancements."

"Of course," Akrylla said, keeping to a tight-lipped grin, "a woman wants to look her best on her wedding day. It fast approaches. I absolutely love a fall wedding."

The redhead hesitated. Her good posture deflated slightly.

~Sympathy

Akrylla leaned in, attentive.

But the pampered young hussy simply continued on, as though she hadn't been stirred by emotion. "I studied herbs all summer just so I could strike up conversations with her. She is very nice. In fact, I'm picking up a small gift for her right now—belladonna drops for her eyes. This place has the very best." She giggled, then lowered her voice to a whisper. "Even better than the 'Upgrace Beauty Shop.'" The redhead smiled at the girl behind the counter, and the girl behind the counter smiled back, casually. On the surface, the exchange seemed rather innocent. But something in the way they held each other's gaze suggested to Akrylla that more than just words had passed between them.

~Conspiracy

Heat flushed high on Akrylla's cheeks and behind her eyes. *They're ridiculing me.* Biting her lip, she put the indignity aside and finally introduced herself, sort of.

"My name is Milla." Akrylla considered offering her hand, but thought better of it. *Too risky.* "Such a pleasure to meet you," she added.

The redhead's response seemed awkward. "And I am Vey. It is… nice to meet you too, Milla." She sighed, feigned a sorry expression. "Please excuse, but I must be going now. I have to get to Upgrace before it closes."

Indeed, thought Akrylla. *They never stay long to chitchat with me.*

The redhead turned to the teller. "Unfortunately, the Fargoer doesn't have everything." She smiled at the girl. "By mid-morning, tomorrow then?"

"Everything will be ready," the teller replied. The pair exchanged partings and Vey went on her way, smiling politely as she passed. She strode with the awkward grace of a fawn.

Akrylla huffed. The moment Vey was out of earshot, she addressed the girl behind the counter. She forgot herself and was blunt.

"Wolfsbane, like the redhead said, and I'm nearly out of poppy extract."

"So," said the girl, removing one glove. "Long journey?"

She knows.

The teller leaned forward on her elbows, cupping her chin in her hands. She whispered: "Do you need something to soothe your aching bones? Soften your skin?"

No. Pretty today.

With her bare hand, the girl reached out, pinched a tress of Akrylla's grey-streaked hair and twirled it around one finger. "Something to wash the *sand* out of your hair perhaps, and darken it a little? I suggest Upgrace for that." She withdrew the hand and left the tress to dangle.

Akrylla just glared at the girl.

"I love your tunic," she added. "Wherever did you get it?"

Smug little…

Akrylla scoffed. "Where is Dugon?" *Real men never notice such things.*

The teller gave Akrylla a measuring look, then sighed.

Done with your little game, girl?

"Dugon got himself sick," she responded, "… very sick. He just lies in bed."

"His son, what's his name?"

"Darren. Darren is scouring a mountainside north of the Bearded Hills for some rare herb."

"Hmph." Akrylla gave up on her ruse. "I have money." She knocked her coins on the counter and proceeded to provide the teller with a long list of medicinal herbs, poisons and hallucinogens. The list was shorter than what she'd originally intended. The full list would make her look even more suspicious. *Could get me a lovely chat with the Wall Guard.*

The girl behind the counter barely glanced at the list, then asked, "Anything else?"

~Use her

"Vey is a capable girl, and so pretty, isn't she?"

Unhindered by the sudden change in topic, the girl nodded in agreement. "She seems very much that way. I've only just met her today though."

Save the redhead, I will, from what is to come.

"So, is that everything then?" the girl asked again.

Akrylla gave her a measured look. *She'll suspect, but she won't tell.* The shaman reached into her satchel, felt her way to a hidden pocket, then pulled out her last coins. She placed them on the counter in a neat stack. Then she added a few extra-special items to her list.

"Three more," she replied. "Night shade, as much as you have; chroniker leaf… and a packet of your best smelling salts. And I need them before the late bell rings."

The girl winced slightly. "Can you come back in the morning instead? I'm new at this and it'll take me half the night to sort through everything… unless Darren returns." Her shoulders dropped; her chest deflated slightly. "Who am I kidding? He won't."

~Opportunity

Yes, a sign: Dugon sick and Darren fetching medicinal herbs can't be a coincidence. Two big orders to fill and no one to help… there's a chance.

"Hmm… not so sure," Akrylla replied. "I just wasn't planning to stay overnight. I've spent every last skull and every last griff right here at your shop."

"Oh." The girl lowered her gaze to the shaman's order and scanned the list carefully, shifting her jaw and biting one side of her lower lip as she did so. She obviously needed a helping hand and surely was reluctant to lose good business. After all, Akrylla had just spent a minor fortune at the apothecary.

Akrylla seized the moment. "Can I stay with you?"

The teller withdrew slightly, stiffened. But before she could say "no," Akrylla added, "I'll pay with work. Quality work. I have a lot of experience, I do. I once ran an apothecary too, of sorts."

The girl behind the counter opened her mouth as if to speak, but hesitated.

Akrylla kept on. "I'll sleep in your garden shed," she added, "if you haven't a spare room. I just love the fresh air." She tried hard not to gag.

Her reassurances seemed to put the girl at ease.

"Can you clean?" she asked. "I have baking to do."

"Yessums, and I love baking."

The girl lowered her gaze, resting her forefinger on her chin. She paused, then sighed.

"Very well," she said at last, followed by a nervous smile. The girl extended the gloved hand to Akrylla. "Clea is my name."

Careful not to let her sleeve ride up, Akrylla took the hand in both of hers and held it like something dear to her. "So nice to meet you, Clea."

Save the pretty clever girl, I will, and teach her to veil her words. Maybe this one too. Hmm… not so pretty. Not so clever. But business savvy, impressionable, and willing to take a risk to learn a thing or two.

CHAPTER IX
WICKED DREAMS
(Vey)

VEY STILL ACHED from the bumpy ride the evening prior, and her feet were sore from shopping the cobbled streets of the fort's market district. The muscles in her arms trembled when she finally stumbled into her room at the end of the day, tired from all the bags she'd lugged around—clothes mostly, and nearly as many beauty products.

But her time at the spa had left every pore in her body feeling clean and refreshed, open to the air. Vey retrieved a small packet of moonwort from the apothecary's stocks. With the hot water delivered to her door, she made tea to soothe her throat. And as the wind whistled outside, the special assistant settled down on the room's lush armchair and began sipping. She stared out the framed window, past her reflection to the dark streets beyond. The strange old woman occupied her thoughts, the one she'd met at the apothecary. Vey hadn't thought much of their conversation, really, but the one comment about Queen Xara's upcoming wedding had stuck in her mind. *Curious her name would come up like that,* she thought, *Xara being the main reason putting me there in the first place.*

Vey deflated in her chair, then covered her eyes with her hand. *I messed up.* The hour was late, her resistance was low, and the whole situation with Xara made her feel foolish. *Did I offend her?* The uprooted memory, the casual observation she'd made in the solarium that day, continued to tug at her conscience; a casual observation made while discussing the harmless topic of a new line of rouge from Fort Abandon. "You will drive King Taeglin mad with lust," was all Vey had said to Queen Xara, in a playful, girlish tone. They used to talk that way.

But I overstepped, Vey thought. *Yes, I definitely overstepped.* She knew that now. It wasn't like she'd been chumming around with one of her socialite friends. No, not in the least. Xara was practically the leader of the free world.

The queen had paused at the remark, eyes suddenly vacant. She'd politely excused Vey, citing the need to reflect on crown business in private. It was the last they'd spoken.

Since then, Vey had learned the fall wedding had become a winter wedding. Knowing Xara's strong sense of duty, the special assistant suspected she might not be marrying the Harrowian King for love after all, and that somehow rolled into the affair was the queen's belief that she had to protect her people—and all of Theia—from Harrow's blatant and dangerous violations of the Treaty of Nature. Vey hoped the belladonna drops she'd just purchased would smooth over their next chance encounter in the solarium, and open the door to reconnecting.

Vey sighed. *Maybe I'm reading too much into this,* she thought. *It wouldn't be the first time.* But the dullness in her chest suggested otherwise. She sighed again and let her mind drift elsewhere. Her thoughts flowed to the next day's affairs and the official purpose of her visit. The special assistant knew the task would not be easy. The outcomes the Grey Clerk was looking for were lofty: limiting Harrow's influence and investments in the region, reinforcing the treaty, or, at the very least, delaying the fort's plans to abandon it. The assignment had been important enough to pull Vey away from a key exercise by the Crimson Tower that wasn't anywhere near ready to go. She almost felt sorry for Lumen Hadamard.

I learned a lot under him in a short time, she admitted to herself. And the knowledge she'd gained would help her in the coming negotiations. Hadamard understood something of the line that was crossed by

Theia's predecessors when their world was destroyed, and he understood why Gan wouldn't be able to hold that line if Abandon continued on its course. He'd told her once that if all went to hell, the Hidden City's only choice would be to delve into the archives and take their chances on old world tech. She repeated aloud the luminary's words to her: "… adding catastrophe to catastrophe."

Vey sighed again. *Too heavy,* she told herself. *And my brain is too tired to mull over such heaviness now.*

Resting her cup and saucer on the end table beside her, the special assistant pushed herself to her feet. She drew the curtains and readied herself for a good night's sleep.

Her bed was soft and comfortable when she finally lay down, and when she pulled the blankets over her body, they felt heavy and warm. And as she lay there, exhausted, in the scant, satiny nightclothes she'd just purchased, the young protégé bathed in the relief that her red dress had been saved. Vey's head sank deep into the pool of down that was her pillow, and she soon drifted off to sleep. Her dreams were dark and technological.

CHAPTER X

A THIN VEIL
BETWEEN WORLDS

(Hadamard)

WHEN HADAMARD REACHED the wharf, his beaming entourage of luminary prospects were there waiting for him. *An odd-looking bunch,* he thought, as he surveyed the group, so awkwardly loitering alongside the glideboat he'd commissioned. The vessel itself was a curious blend of schooner and freighter, sleekness and functionality, elegance and complexity; its hull a hybrid of two worlds—a strong wooden frame wrapped in durable glace.

The luminary retrieved his master list of tower-approved prospects and immediately executed a quick roll call, pausing to match names to faces for later recollection.

"Goremann Smat? There you are—check." Smat was a known quantity to Hadamard. He stood easily as wide as any two other prospects, the only Taint of the group, visibly part Outlander. His clothes were loose-fitting and wrinkled, and his shirt food-stained. Overall, he bore the look of a slob who'd just rolled out of bed. *Typical Smat.* He'd come a long way since being plucked out of the ruins of Akeda, where a camp of Outlanders had taken up residence to escape a brutal Ironeagle warlord. Gan had welcomed each and every escapee into the gorge.

"Sorral?"

"Here," called out a young teen with a mass of orange hair on top. A run of dark freckles stretched from cheek to cheek, crossing over his nose. He towered a head above the rest. And although Sorral stood tall, his skinny build and terrible slouch lessened his stature. Hadamard sized up the teen's attire and shook his head—*pants too short, boots too big, jersey too green.*

"Vil'nyan—check." Another known quantity. Vil'nyan stood casually in sandals and wore a simple, earth-toned dress of a durable material with a fall theme to it. The rugged Abindohn had worked for Hadamard on several occasions. *Capable.*

"Nana and Ogmund Rese," he called next. A thick-limbed female raised her hand, so did her scrawny younger brother. *Abandoners,* he could tell by the way they dressed. Both donned thick glasses, wore baggy clothing of neutral colors and had shaggy, sandy-brown hair.

"Seddner Pawl?"

"Here," responded a rather jolly-looking male. Soft-skinned, shorter in height, he came well-dressed in sharp tans and greys. *Might be part Webfooter, this one.* A former mayor of the boggish village of Webfoot went by the same surname years ago. Seddner bore some resemblance in build and facial features to the townsfolk there. *A rare mix, if he is.* Webfooters were known for their keen memories and made for fantastic record keepers, diplomatic aides, curators and librarians. *Might be worth a try… almost certainly has the fungus if he's kept up family ties.* Hadamard immediately placed a glimmer of hope on this prospect.

The luminary looked about. "All present… and then some." He turned to address a newcomer. "And who are you?"

"Yuri Haulik," replied the youth: medium build, stocky and blond, wearing greys and off-whites with gold trim.

Hadamard recognized the surname. *A Horse Lord brat. Looks more like a queensman than a luminary.*

The last-minute addition produced a recommendation letter signed by Forsetti himself. Hadamard patted his clothes for a pencil, found one, and scrawled the new name onto his list. Hadamard regarded the group. "Anyone else?"

Heads turned; shoulders shrugged.

"Good, then. Done." The luminary had prepared introductory remarks, inspiring words for the sendoff. But all he had time to blurt out was "welcome to the trials" before a Grey crewman began ushering the passengers aboard, citing delays to the schedule. *Must be Kaeda's Temper on the other side flaring up again.* Hadamard knew the captain of the vessel to be as calm and steady as one could be, and that the only thing that got him rattled was an inclement Temper. The luminary shrugged off his rushed introduction, moved aside to let his prospects shuffle past.

I won't clutter their minds with details until we're at Seventh Kaeda, he decided. *Let them focus on the wonders of the voyage into the Otherworldly Realm. It'll be a most memorable experience.* But there were a few things he absolutely had to tell them.

"Prospects," he called out. "There's a belt and harness for everyone. Grab a seat and hook in, or you'll find yourself floating in the nether. Secure all personal items or place them in the hold." Hadamard watched as they proceeded up the gangway to board the vessel. He didn't want to get his hopes up about the prospects' chances. As clever as they might be, he had his doubts that those vying for a place on his projects would have what it takes to become a luminary. Apart from Seddner, maybe, the only exceptions were the two known quantities: Vil'nyan, on loan and currently Feleg's assistant, and Smat, who already worked under Hadamard in the tower. Indoctrinating the former meant stealing from his best friend, and the latter he'd tried to confirm secretively already, without success. *Well, maybe that last trip to the bog did him some good.*

A minute before push off, and with all on board, out of nowhere the crown advisor appeared at the wharf. The captain gave the order to hold departure until the Gloom hobbled up the ramp to join them. Feeling charitable, Hadamard addressed him in a less than critical tone.

"Hello, Nek, glad you could join us."

Nekenezitter greeted Hadamard with a click and a chirr, then took a seat next to him. The Gloom donned his restraints, hooked in for the ride.

Hadamard sighed. *Damn near got off without him for a change.*

Moments later, the crewmen pushed off. Oars extended and dipped into the cool river waters. The vessel swung in line with the waterway as the current gently pulled them past the canal that led to the Dim Sea locks, and then put them on course. The glideboat drifted under a great tree root, gnarled and twisted, that marked entry into Jhin's Cave. The flow picked up as they entered the gloom and the roar of faster moving waters gained strength. On a roll, the vessel plummeted towards the spattering wall of water known as the Elderkin Veil, dead ahead. They burst through to the other side.

⋘

Beyond the Veil, narrow, winding channels cut through the living rock. Lanterns lit the way. The tributaries were many and visibility at a minimum from all the rocky obstructions and tight turns. The glideboat crew kept the vessel tight to the middle course, steered clear of rock piles, and skirted the edge of a whirlpool.

Once through the treacherous waters of the underground rapids, the river ran smooth and fast. The *Hyperion's* hull creaked and groaned as her bowsprit dipped and she tilted into the final slide, speeding towards the wall of river mists that lingered at the brink of the great plunge. The rush of acceleration filled Hadamard.

Working free of tethers and with uncanny speed, the Grey crew retracted the oars and poles that had brought the vessel safely through the raging river. At the last possible instant, they raised the rudder and locked the steering mechanism to the aft fins, for later navigation in the nether.

The *Hyperion* punched through the rolling mists, effortlessly. A long moment after, the sounds of rushing water broke. With a silent push, she lurched forward.

Carried by her forward inertia, the glideboat emerged suspended in a grey expanse of empty space. A pressure wave arose from beneath the hull, engulfing the vessel and its occupants in a blast of warm, moist air. The *Hyperion* swayed and rolled in response, buffeted by the gusting winds of Kaeda's Temper. Jostling this way and that way, Hadamard's feet lifted from the deck during the first stretch of zero-gravity. Throughout the turbulence, his harness kept him secure.

In tandem, the nethership's main sails unfurled and ballooned with air. The crew hurried to ready the glide blades and stabilizer poles. Without a Djinxarai-blooded captain and a seasoned crew, the vessel surely would have crashed onto the rocks at the bottom of the great plunge in Jhin's Cave, a plummet known to have sent many unwary cave boaters to watery graves.

On the other side, it was not a plain or tired grey that painted the omnidirectional skies of Kaeda's Temper. Dark swirls of bulky matter rotated about, illuminated by dull flashes that pulsed like lightning, shrouded by clouds. Lively and ever churning, the patchy nether mists were set aglow by the flicker of the incubating Starshine in the far-off distance. Its unpredictable radiance was the closest thing the Djinxarai tribe had to sunlight. But the Starshine was no star, and its light brought little warmth above that of the howling winds. Djinxarai of the metaphysical sort claimed to have touched its flickering surface with their minds. Luminaries took a more sensible approach and likened the phenomenon to an extra-dimensional rotational anomaly.

The light-giving enigma and the perpetual storm would soon be exterior considerations: the *Hyperion* was about to enter the Elderkin Conduit. And as long as she remained within its confines, no harm would come to her. At least, not from the Temper.

As the vessel flew through the giant tube's outer rim, the glide blades extended. Hadamard felt a jolt as the aft-starboard blade bit into the glacé surface of the structure. Following that, through clever manipulation of the sails, the hull slowly descended, in as much as "down" was down, pressed by the winds. The blade supports flexed as the metal made firm contact. A gusty tailwind nearly plucked the glideboat off the surface at that point, but the crew quickly extended the stabilizer braces and waited for the perturbations to balance out. Only a practiced navigator of the nether could traverse the portal.

Captain Nydar cleared his throat and shouted from the stern, one hand gripping the ball handle of his steering sweep. The voice of the heavily bearded man was smooth and sonorous, as was common among the netherfaring Greys. It stemmed from his Djinxarai heritage.

"All-clear!" he boomed.

The Elderkin Conduit was basically a wind tunnel—a flexible, ever-changing umbilical cord that connected Seventh Kaeda to the outside world. With a few adjustments to the sails the vessel began to pick up speed. And when the track began to curve into the first spiral of a much larger helix, Hadamard felt the draw of inertia forcing him towards the deck. A heartbeat later Nydar bellowed out.

"Casual on deck!"

His first mate followed up. "Stretch yer legs, landlubbers, but be mindful of light feet."

Hadamard interjected, "That means no acrobatics and no jumping around," he explained to his prospects, "or you'll launch yourself straight off the deck. I don't want to see any of you bouncing along in tow." The luminary earned a few scattered laughs for his remark, while others retched up their breakfasts. He winced at the disgorging heaves and gulps.

The first mate added, "Mind your tethers and keep a hand ready at the rails. For getting around obstacles, you'll notice two lines from your belt that are clipped to the middle rail. Unclip one at a time; never both at once."

He neglected to explain why none of the crew bothered to tie in. *They never do.*

The sounds of metallic snaps and tings filled the air as passengers undid their harnesses. Nekenezitter was one of the first to get moving, on towards the raised quarterdeck before the way became clogged. Those prospects who weren't queasy took to strolling about the decks, keeping the weak "pseudo-gravity" in check. For some, exploring the sensations of near freefall would be the highlight of the trip. For those with weak stomachs, it would be unbearable.

Goremann Smat ambled Hadamard's way, hair tousled by the wind, one hand gliding over the rail and the other holding a dangling tether. To accommodate his girth, the luminary flattened himself against the rail as the prospect passed. Even so, he barely squeezed by, hitching and unhitching as he did so.

Hadamard patted the Outlander's shoulder. "Smat," he said, "a quick word before you run off and start doing backflips off the bowsprit."

The prospect glanced over his shoulder, chuckling, "How did you know?" He shuffled over, fidgeting with his tethers, then made himself comfortable leaning against the rail. Smat regarded his superior. "What is it, boss?"

"When we get to the dome, I'd appreciate it if you kept quiet while I address the group and ask them questions. I already know your willingness to find answers to everything asked of you. I need to hear the voices of the others in attendance." With the Order Lumen trials imminent, Hadamard had put Smat on an unofficial path to Member Prospect, so long as Hurlorn affinity could be confirmed through the kinship stone… eventually. The same was true with Vil'nyan, and perhaps Vey—if the Grey Clerk would ever agree to letting her go.

Smat shrugged his indifference. "Sure thing." He paused, then raised an index finger. "I do have one question for you, though."

"Shoot," Hadamard said.

"It's about the last hundred runs you gave me. There has to be a mistake."

"Why?"

"The timings are off."

Hadamard shook his head. "No. Nekenezitter keeps perfect time—I double-checked with a mechanical timepiece. The recorded scenario or 'game' events that you analyzed are labelled by precise time and position, thanks to his uncanny timekeeping and ranging abilities."

Smat scratched one of his small horns. "But when you add up the durations back-to-back, the total is longer than the entire time you were away. And that doesn't even factor in travel time."

"Well, Smat," Hadamard said, strengthening his grip on the rail as the glideboat ripped around a tight curve, "Two things: first, one has to understand that scenario time has a certain… multiplicity in the Netherdome. Overlap, from our perspective."

Smat grimaced. "What does that even mean?"

Hadamard paused to gather his thoughts. "For all practical purposes, Smat, what we observe in different runs appear to be multiple realizations of the same battle, happening in parallel. Each data stream you analyze literally describes the same mimics at the same time—

giants and warlorns and queensmen and the like—all faced with the same scenario, under the single-minded control of a Djinxarai projectionist. This is the heart of Jhin thaumaturgy—the splitting of the mind that projectionists are able to accomplish in that special place. It allows them to simultaneously follow all possible paths that branch out from a single event. When we watch them do it, all we see is a blur."

Smat furrowed his heavy brow. "What's the second thing?"

"Nek and I conducted the runs differently last time." Hadamard glanced to the Gloom, then back to his prospect. "What's even more amazing than what I just told you is what happens when they bind us—bring us in—to their projections… when we watch the runs play out one-by-one instead. We're still trying to sort that part out." The luminary paused again. He had more to explain but Smat interjected.

"Weird." The understudy gazed at Hadamard as though the man were crazy, blew his cheeks full of air, then released. "If you say so." Bracing himself with his legs, Smat put his hands in his pockets, shrugged his shoulders. "Makes no difference to me as long as the results are all straightened out by the time I get them."

"They always are," Hadamard said. "We'll talk more, later."

"I'm really glad I asked that question," Smat said.

Hadamard doubted his sincerity but didn't fault him for it. *He'll come around.* The Outlander nodded and continued on his way without another word. *Nimbler than he looks,* thought the luminary, as he watched Smat amble towards the bow. Despite the high winds and shifting underfoot, the portly prospect made his way casually and with a well-balanced step.

The luminary turned his gaze to the wall of the tube they were racing through. Beyond the glace barrier, muted lights flashed in rapid succession, putting on display the internal workings of the swirling storm outside. They went dark for a stretch before starting up again.

Out of the corner of his eye, Hadamard spotted Nekenezitter hobbling down the steps of the quarterdeck to intercept Smat. *Better him than me,* Hadamard thought, and chuckled to himself. Then he took a moment to observe how his prospects had paired off. Vil'nyan proved to be a natural center of attention, drawing talk from crew members and Yuri Haulik. Nana Rese lingered on the outside of the conversation, while her younger brother eyed the rigging. But when Nana broke in, she did so with impressive maritime lingo. Hadamard raised an eyebrow. *She knows ships. They both know ships.* Sorral and Seddner, on the other hand, were out of the game: green-faced, hunched over, and keeping to themselves.

Hadamard spent the next twenty minutes reviewing the results of the prospects' entrance exams, then turned his attention to the glide-boat captain at the *Hyperion's* helm. He watched as the Grey carefully skated the vessel along the gentle bend of the conduit, translucent and winding. A practical dresser, Nydar wore a knitted white sweater over a drake-leather vest. His white hair was barely visible under the blue cap tight to his scalp. The sword at his side was of the cutlass variety, more for show than for dueling. His first mate stood next to him, calling to the crew in his booming voice whenever there was an order to be had. *Sounds ready for his own command,* thought Hadamard.

Nydar took notice of Hadamard's attention. The Grey waved him over to the steering sweep. Acknowledging with a nod, the luminary left his place to join the captain. He stopped at the hold along the way to retrieve his brass model of the realm they were in, then climbed the stairs.

"Oh, look at that," Nydar said, eyes smiling as the luminary approached. By all appearances he was genuinely impressed with the creation. Hadamard plunked the astrolabe down at the captain's feet and fastened it with a deck tether. Nydar toyed with the flexible tube mechanism representing the conduit, wiggling it freely between the contraption's rotating rings. "Amazing," he remarked, shaking his head. Over the next few minutes, the two of them discussed the model's inner workings. But that was not the reason the captain had called the luminary over.

Nydar always had a story to tell, eager to share his adventures with interested and interesting passengers. The luminary was one of those few who happened to qualify as both. Sometimes the good captain repeated a story, but Hadamard never complained...

CHAPTER XI
WINDSWEPT
(Hadamard)

NYDAR SPOUTED THE words of his Windswept encounter with reverence. Hadamard had heard the inevitable tale to come, or some variant of it, twice before. Yet, the thought of dissuading the captain from retelling it didn't dawn on him. Nor did such a notion seem to dawn on the crew, who must have heard the same narrative dozens of times over. They simply stayed on task. They kept the vessel stable as it glided along the steady bend of the conduit, fully engaged in the delicate act of maximizing forward thrust while maintaining optimal contact with the glace surface and balancing off-trajectory forces. The trick was, so Hadamard was told, to keep the glideboat going fast enough that the sails were barely needed, and to give the vessel the right "twist" every so often along its corkscrew path.

With a rolling rumble, the captain cleared his throat. He glanced to Hadamard to confirm that the luminary was attentive, then swung his gaze back to the usual vector: dead ahead, straight over the *Hyperion's* bow.

"I once followed a flight of the Windswept," he began. "You've heard of them?"

"I have," Hadamard responded. "Vaguely human-like flying creatures that dwell in the nether. They find one another through some form of bioluminescence."

Nydar nodded slowly, eyes slightly squinted, still staring ahead. "Oh, but they're much more than that. I've seen their ways and I've seen the desperate looks on those glowing faces... like the sum of human suffering. It was nigh one year ago when I first met the Windswept in the open nether... so graceful and bright they were..."

The glideboat captain trailed off. Hadamard couldn't tell if he was focused on something oncoming or just lapsing. Seeing nothing of concern himself on the path ahead, the luminary waited patiently for Nydar to continue. *Whatever latitude he needs to get his story straight,* thought Hadamard. Long pauses were the captain's way of stringing all the disparate elements of his tall tales together. The experienced Grey was an interesting character who'd been through a lot. Hadamard could appreciate that.

"Some ways off, they were," he continued, finally, "the Windswept. Dozens. Thin as sheets... silent... flowing... a flock will move through the nether as one body and one mind, y'know."

"Is that so?" Hadamard pictured a swarm of them, flying in close formation and banking to the winds in unison, like starlings.

The captain adjusted his grip on the steering knob. "I had the good *Hyperion* here, and she was just rising out of Tetherport when the Windswept appeared, a whole flock of 'em streaking across the Starshine. It was an off day in the nether if I've ever seen one. The vessel was becalmed. One of those rare cycles when the winds are just about nonexistent. I can't say why Kaeda was in such a fine mood that cycle. I'm not sure what I like better—a foul mood or a fair one. They can be equally deadly."

From what Hadamard had pieced together in his studies of the Otherworldly Realm, the drag of some unseen mass created the tourbillions and fueled the disturbances of Kaeda's Temper. In turn, the disturbances fueled winds, and those winds mixed with other winds of the nether to continually drive the motion of the realm in unpredictably ways.

"She must have blown herself out," remarked the first mate, who stood squarely nearby monitoring the crew, feet planted solid on the quarterdeck.

"Aye, Neeran." With a slow and steady hand, the captain slid the steering sweep a few degrees to the left. "So anyways, I ordered the crew to give'em chase." He snorted at the thought of his next words, shook his head slightly. "The *Hyperion* here was as slow going as a sprouting mushroom, but so were the Windswept. They mostly swoop and glide, y'see, on currents of air, and thus I was able to keep them in my sights. Their strange bodies—unnatural I say—drifted far from the Starshine and the Conduit. Just when I thought I'd lost them, they decided to stay put and I caught up again. They just halted out there in the nether, in the middle of nowhere I say, of their own accord. The Windswept didn't seem to notice or mind my presence. I worried though, that Kaeda's winds would blow up strong and I wouldn't be able to make my way back."

"Any idea what they were doing?" Hadamard said.

"Well, sure I have an idea," Nydar replied. "They made patterns in the nether, for starters."

"Patterns?" *This is new.* The last time the captain had spoken of the Windswept, one had landed on the *Hyperion's* bow and then flew off, leaving behind a polished stone, black and cool to the touch.

Nydar went on. "Glowing, streaming patterns, y'know, a blur to distinguish them from flashes and other sorts of light. Me'thinks they had to perform some special ritual. Me'thinks they had a message to send."

"What kind of message?" Hadamard asked.

"Well." He paused. "Don't know what they were signaling, with all that circling about and swirling in and out of one another's streams like they was tying a knot. But I do have an idea *who* they were signaling too. They have a belief, y'see."

"A belief?"

"A prayer and dance, I say, for the return of the winds that propel them through the nether."

A viable alternative came to the luminary's mind. "Couldn't it be a signal to another flock?"

Nydar pressed his lips together, nodded. "Could be," he replied, "but I scanned the nether and saw naught of another flock. It seems like more of a belief to me."

"Really… a belief." Hadamard was not convinced. It would indicate a higher level of sophistication than was previously thought. "What makes you so certain?"

Nydar hesitated, swung his gaze to Hadamard and looked him square in the eye. His amber irises stood out against the splotchy grey of his wind-weathered skin, and the white hair against the gold trim of his blue cap. "Along the lines of what you asked. It's exactly 'cause I didn't see any others flashing back. They wouldn't go through the motions without a reason. Me'thinks they worship the Temper."

"As a god?"

The captain returned his attention to the view straight ahead. "As a leviathan." Nydar paused, squinting at what he saw as he peered ahead into the grey distance. He glanced over his shoulder to his first mate.

"I see it too," Neeran said before he was spoken to. The first mate shouted out, "Crew, man the stabilizers! Passengers, hold on tight! We're about to lose gription."

"Gription" was the crew's word for what would normally be gravity, that is, the sensation counter to one's feet lifting off the floorboards of the vessel.

As the *Hyperion* sped through the conduit, Hadamard began to make out the cause for concern—a section of the tube had unwound. Travel distances could double or half in a day's span due to the conduit's occasional unraveling in certain sections because of shifting winds. At any rate, the sensation of gravity might be lost. Worse, the glideboat could lift from the glace and become unstable. She'd have only the tailwind to keep her pressed against the tube's inner surface.

Sure enough, Hadamard's heels lifted slightly, he felt a pull starboard. He quickly pushed off towards the nearest rail to grab on. The ship wobbled, and the sounds of whisking blades eased as one side tilted up. But the captain and crew had her pressed back down in no time. They maintained tight control, kept the blades in firm contact with the glace after that.

Nydar never returned to his story, his full attention devoted now to the delicate journey ahead. With gription restored, the luminary quietly slipped away and left him to his duties. Keeping to the quarterdeck, Hadamard gazed off the starboard side, through the translucent walls of the glace tube to the nether beyond.

Nekenezitter, having eventually been abandoned by Smat, shuffled up the stairs and along the rail towards Hadamard. "<click> <chirr>," the Gloom began, coming up squat beside the luminary. They both looked out over the rail. "The ritual <click> of the Windswept is not so far-fetched <tic> as it might sound."

Damn bat ears; he hears everything. Nekenezitter gladly proceeded to fill in a few details.

"The Djinxarai believe that their land <clack> is the carcass of the dead god of the Abindohns, and that one day he will awaken <click> and lead the tribe across time and space <chirr> to their ancestral home among the stars <tic-tic>."

Hadamard scoffed. "And that isn't far-fetched?" As well-versed as he was in Djinxarai beliefs, this part seemed a bit much. "What do *they* even know about *real* stars anyway, stuck in this shell all the time, confined within the Great Barrier?"

"<click> The Djinxarai know of stars," Nekenezitter replied. "Besides their presence in Gan, <tic> they have historical ties to the desert and appear in many legends, under many names."

"The desert? You mean the Scarsands?"

"Back then <click>, they were called the *Star* Sands."

He's got me there, little turd. "Well, when is this dead god supposed to wake up?"

"No one knows," admitted the Gloom. "But legends and myths <click> are often rooted in seeds of truth <chirr>. The Windswept may have somehow inherited that same belief."

Hadamard let out a heavy sigh. He didn't answer. He didn't answer because he had trouble believing in the influence of dead leviathans on the living, and he lacked the fortitude to argue the point. Not now, at least. He swiveled his gaze to the ship's bow and peered ahead. The tube branched. They'd reached their exit.

Nekenezitter followed Hadamard's gaze, sent out a high-pitched, fast-tempo chirr.

"Keeping to starboard!" Nydar called, as the glideboat shifted in that direction. The crew maintained the ship's bearing afterwards, steady ahead.

"Ready the sails for flight," bellowed the first mate. "Harnesses, land-lubbers!"

The passengers scurried to their seats, clicked in. Moments later, the *Hyperion* shot into the rightmost tunnel. The nose dipped slightly as she shunted off the Elderkin Conduit and into open space. The glideboat captain shouted orders to his crew to retract the blades and orient the pivoting mast. Working the crew with a dozen more such commands, he skillfully wove a safe path through the Temper's tourbillions. And through utter patience and expertise, he closed in on the Starshine, a pulsing bright patch veiled in mist.

In the grey-lit distance, the swirling haze suddenly parted. Seventh Kaeda came into view—an entire city built on an irregular clump of mountain-sized matter. It rotated in a wide arc about the light-giving Starshine, bound to it by a forest of vine-like tendrils stretching tens of miles. *The Tangles.*

After chasing the rock five times in a row and circling back—two or three misses being normal—on the sixth pass Nydar found his entry vector above the dark side of Seventh Kaeda. He set her on course to dock. And in the time it took to draw a sigh of relief, a humble quay materialized off the starboard side, carved into the cliff at the back of the giant maw that defined Tetherport. A narrow glace tube fronted the cliff face, shooting down from the overhang to the quay's rocky surface, and then through it.

Hadamard gazed at the incoming structures. Most of Tetherport resided in the shadows of a sizable chunk of overhanging rock. Rows of freestanding piers extended from the cliff face that held the quay, with a network of massive chains fixed to their ends to moor the nether-ships. Towed vessels bobbed in midair like tied balloons, swaying gently with the nether winds in the wake of Seventh Kaeda's wide rotation.

Haunting sounds of chains clinking and wood creaking welled up as the *Hyperion* closed in.

Captain Nydar hollered out orders to sharpen the glideboat's approach vector. A good captain perfected the port approach to an art. All Grey captains were good captains, and Nydar was no exception.

Chapter XII
The Treaty of Nature
(Vey)

WITH HER NEW sash and a sharp coat from the market, not to mention a sleek, imported handbag that she simply could not resist, Vey was able to wear her red dress and still present herself as one ready to discuss important matters of state. Her matching black pearl necklace and earrings seemed appropriate for the occasion, black on silverleaf.

Abandoners stole sideways glances at the young woman in red as she passed by on the cobbled streets of District 24. Her stride was smooth with a deliberate sway of the hips. She held her head high with confident expectation. Vey was Elderkin, and many would say the fire of that eternal race shone through in her presence. She could forego rejuvenation and not even begin to fade out of youth for thirty years.

The morning was grey and windy, stricken with sporadic episodes of light rain. The cobblestone in the streets and alleyways was grey and even. It dried quickly and seemed to soak up more than its fair share of the moisture. Passersby on foot carried furled umbrellas and wore long coats over business attire. The clip-clop of horse drawn coaches echoed off the buildings.

The meeting location was easy to find—Fort Abandon was nothing if not orderly. The walled city's administrative machinery was nearly all contained within District 24. Gridded with narrow streets, it formed the southwest quadrant of the fort. Every building was stone block and numbered, but void of other markings. Even office labels were absent. The streets were officially nameless, but unofficially the populace assigned colorful names to some: Crooked Lane held the tax collection office. It was one of the few streets with a kink in it, made that way to accommodate a natural rock formation that looked very much like a sail, veined in red and white. The builders—all seafarers—didn't have the heart to shatter it. Beggar's Lane was where the Reestablishment Office resided, and Gown Town held the courthouse and legal firms.

Vey did not know of any special name given to the street she was headed for. She just followed the sequence of numbers until she came at last to Building 144. Inside the foyer, she showed her colors to the building's commissioners, gentlemanly and in their seventies. And as she waited for her name and colors to be cross-referenced and verified, the special assistant admired the modest tapestry hanging on the wall next to the staircase leading up. It depicted the coming of the Jhinyari. The caption on the tapestry simply read: "They shall not pass."

Suddenly, the gravity of the situation hit her. Like vertigo. All that was happening felt surreal to Vey, as though she'd been drawn into something much larger than herself. A world thing. The Grey Clerk had pointed out two good reasons for selecting her—a novice diplomat—for this important mission. Two good reasons out of three that Vey could think of. For one, she'd proved nigh impossible to defeat in debate or argument. The fort's tactic of coming up with excuse after excuse would not fare well under her scrutiny. Secondly, technology soon would become Vey's area of surveillance and she had to eventually learn the file, the sooner the better. Getting involved at a high level would firmly establish her as vital to the function of the Grey Clerk's office, and keep the other offices—desperate for bright talent and resources—from laying claim to her for their projects.

And then came the third reason, a reason shrouded in plausible denial that would never be written down or admitted to in any way. The Grey Clerk was not wholly naïve as to the reasons behind Hersh's tardiness that day in the tower. Hersh's reputation as a lady's man was well documented, and there was little doubt in Vey's mind that the Grey Clerk wanted her injected into Gan's dealings with Abandon as a resource to help smooth over relations, and to effect whatever strategies the Head Office might devise using that new degree of freedom. *Use the time to unwind*, she recalled the Grey Clerk saying. *Consider it a gift and a vacation from that crazy luminary.* Vey was fully prepared to play that role, whatever it might lead to, and perhaps she would even revel in it.

A commissioner politely interrupted the young woman-in-red's daydreaming. After a minute flipping through a thick book of names on his desk, he handed Vey her diplomatic colors, then turned his gaze to his comrade. "I'll take this one," he told him.

The pair shared knowing looks. "Beat me to it," the other replied, with a chuckle. Promptly, the commissioner escorted Vey to the meeting room, opened the door quietly, and beckoned her in.

Hersh had chosen a wide, third story chamber with a view open to the sea. It was airy and full of light. Three men of vastly different shapes and sizes sat discussing business. As they carried on, Vey's eyes were drawn to the picture window and the view across the water. Swollen waves rolled and crashed against the rocky shores and the fort's seaward wall. The sun seemed almost lost in the grey luminescence above. Darker clouds loomed on the horizon.

The meeting room held a slab table, long and wide, made of thick limestone with a smooth surface and rough edges. Vey approached the table and stood for a moment, resting a hand on it. It was cool to the touch. The wooden chairs around it were nondescript. The men stopped talking. Heads turned and she met their gazes, one after the other.

"The view is beautiful," Vey remarked, glancing again to the window. Two tall ships and a dory braved the rough waters. Two tall men and a Webfooter rose up from their seats at the table to welcome her. The Webfooter was Hersh's aide, nearest to where Vey entered. He stood about the same height as shriveled old Wyatt. She wondered who the tall, thin bespectacled man beside him could be. *Minister? Oligarch?* Hersh stood at the very far end of the table, his presence broad and looming.

Hersh's aide made a move towards the chair nearest Vey, at the head of the table.

"Oap," Hersh boomed. The Webfooter froze at the sound as the half-giant strode across the room. The ground he covered seemed astonishing, from one end to the other in little more than two long strides. Hersh pulled out a different chair for Vey instead, the next one over that faced the window. "For the best view," he offered, with a graceful smile. Vey took the seat, while Hersh took the head chair that would otherwise have been hers. They sat close.

"Leave us," Hersh bellowed to his aide and the man wearing glasses. They seemed to have expected the dismissal. And if they were annoyed at not being introduced, they didn't show it.

"See you shortly," said the bespectacled man to Vey before nodding and turning to go. He left a black notebook and a pen at the table. Hersh's aide simply nodded politely, smiled and followed. The half-giant watched until the door to the room was firmly shut behind them.

"Now we are even," he said to Vey. "One-on-one."

Vey responded with a half-hearted protest. "This should go on record."

"Not everything, not yet," Hersh said, his voice deep and sonorous. "If you would like our formal meeting to commence, I can call back Olerik and Rush in an instant. They will recite Abandon's official position on the Treaty to you *verbatim* and *ad nauseam*. But that is not what you are really here for, is it?"

Vey shook her head in agreement, doing her best to hide a girlish smile. "No, it isn't." The butterflies were back. "I suppose you are correct." *He has a gentle way of forcing things*, she mused. *I like that.*

Hersh dressed simply. He wore a long, buttoned down suit jacket and matching pants, a shade darker than the gloomy skies. The fabric was light and the cut slimming. His black shoes had a dull sheen to them, unmarred by creases.

Vey prided herself on being ready for anything. If need be, over dinner she could lose the new coat, let down her hair and transform herself into an elegant consort. *No sense holding back*, she surmised. Vey knew that she appeared nothing less than stunning.

"Thank you for agreeing to meet with me, Vice-regent Tehan," she began.

"Please call me Hersh," he replied. "We are happy to have a visitor from the Grey Clerk. It has been too long—since my father…"

"Indeed," Vey said. "You do know why the Grey Clerk sent me?"

Hersh shifted in his chair. "The Grey Clerk has only one reason to send anybody anywhere," he replied.

"You've been cheating, Hersh." She raised an eyebrow, waited for an explanation.

Straightaway, he put on an abashed look. "I wouldn't go that far," he countered.

Vey frowned. "Your little devices and mysterious products have been showing up everywhere—even in Gan."

"There is nothing illegal about any 'little devices' coming out of Abandon," he rebuked.

"How are you making them? Ionics are forbidden under Article I. Shall I recite it for you?"

"No, no," he replied, "that won't be necessary. I am familiar with Article I. And by the way, 'I' don't personally make anything of the sort. Industry does what it does, sometimes in ingenious ways. I only see the end results. An awful lot can be accomplished with heat, pressure vessels, and the clever application of spin."

"Like turbines?"

Hersh said nothing.

"Hmm…" Vey felt like adding *tsk tsk*. His lack of response only added to her suspicions. She moved on. "Someone has been excavating the Akedan ruins. If you are digging up things best left buried—"

"Stop right there," Hersh cut in. "It is Abandon policy to neither confirm nor deny such accusations."

"Oh, how convenient." She passed him a stern look. "This is a serious matter, Hersh. Treaty violations under Article IV—"

"Article IV is unenforceable. There is no consistent way to monitor all of Theia for violations. How do I know that Harrow is not violating the treaty right now, as we speak?"

They probably are, Vey thought, but she held her tongue.

"Or Gan for that matter. Are you telling me all your dabbling in bioengineering is treaty-friendly? That kind of activity violates the spirit of the treaty, if nothing else. Circumvents it, I say."

Vey attempted to get a word in, but Hersh overspoke her.

"And Irongate… now *there* is a beehive of illegal activity, from everything I have heard, and I have heard plenty. Now tell me, Special Assistant, what the hell happened to the Star Sands? That disaster has Gan bio-meddling written all over it."

That's his father speaking. Vey pushed aside her knowledge of what she considered to be an actual example of treaty circumvention. That is to say, Hadamard's strikers. She pursed her lips. "I admit there is a fine line," she countered, adopting a firm tone, "but Gan walks it. As for Harrow and the others… the Grey Clerk has her concerns as well, but that doesn't make it acceptable for Fort Abandon to break the agreement."

Hersh sat back on his chair, balanced it on two legs. His eyes shifted to the picture window, to the sea, and then back to meet hers. "The Treaty of Nature is basically a gentleman's agreement," he said, teetering. Vey thought he might tip over, but the giant man steadied himself. The shrugged expression he ended on could not be mistaken.

Vey responded bluntly, "Are you not a gentleman?"

The half-giant swallowed a deep breath. "Well…"

He paused.

Vey raised an eyebrow. "Hmm?"

Hersh dropped his chair back to all fours. He shook his head slowly, eyes closed for only a moment. Then he folded his hands in front of him on the table, looked the special assistant in the eyes. "You have to understand, Vey," he started, in a convincing tone, "that Gan's access to old-world knowledge creates a huge divide between our two societies. And we're neighbors—a day's ride with a swift horse. You might not use the technology in the archives itself, but you certainly use your knowledge of it. I don't mean you personally… 'Gan' uses it to push the boundaries, extend the lifespans of its citizens five-fold, while we in Fort Abandon grovel in darkness and die young. Everyone wants to be a part of the Hidden City's vision… our youth, our best minds. What does anyone in Gan have to worry about? No famine, no drought, knowledge beyond compare. Only now is that beginning to change in Fort Abandon. Only now are we beginning to prosper… and you want to put an end to it? What does Gan have to worry about?"

"Gan has to worry about the end of humankind."

Hersh hesitated.

Vey leaned towards him. "Vice-regent," she implored, "the Grey Clerk is seeking advice on information sharing arrangements with Fort Abandon. It will help to even the playing field."

"She is?"

"Yes. Who would you rather work with? Gan or Harrow? Look at how Dim Lake treats its citizens versus how we treat ours—slavery, corruption among the Tor Lords, incarceration to any who speak out against the King… they're heavy-handed and brutal."

Vey waited patiently as the vice-regent swiveled his gaze to the window and stared out to the sea. In the distance, another ship had entered the scene, bearing in from the West. He took a deep breath, sighed.

"Abandon needs a boost," he started. "The economy is stagnating and the lost bones of Akeda can help turn that around."

That's his father again, Vey thought. *Stubborn.*

He continued. "The Fort City's 'little devices' and 'mysterious products', as you call them, are creating new markets in the West. And when the Scarsands quarantine is lifted, our industries will be poised to supply aid and profit greatly, once society there starts to rebuild itself. It has already begun—we have joint labor contracts with the Bearded Hills. We can help the Scarsanders regain their dignity and help ourselves at the same time. Gan should join us; there is enough prosperity to spread around… for a change."

"It isn't the 'little devices' themselves so much that worry the Grey Clerk," Vey replied, "or the 'mysterious products.'" He was coming around. All she had to do now was lure him in. "Her office can work with your industries to find alternative ways to manufacture them. It's the *other* technologies she is worried about… you know what I mean, don't you? It all starts with power generation."

Hersh didn't answer. *It is Abandon policy to neither confirm nor deny such accusations,* she reminded herself. Vey's next words came out as an accusation, although she was not sure of them. "Fort Abandon has been dabbling."

At that moment, Hersh locked eyes with Vey, and she could see the truth hidden within, bubbling to the surface. He *wanted* to share something with her. But his answer was not the one she was hoping for.

"I am afraid I must excuse myself. I have another meeting to attend. Olerik, my Technology Advisor, will answer any further questions."

He stood up to take his leave, looming tall. "It appears the Grey Clerk and I have much to discuss before this misunderstanding gets out of hand."

Vey rose beside him. "Yes. You should have words with her soon," she agreed, "before any actions are taken."

"Actions?"

"Well, yes, actions."

"It hasn't come to that yet, has it?"

"I am not at liberty to confirm or deny," Vey stated. She relished in the delivery of the dose of his own medicine. Hersh grimaced, while Vey continued. "All I can say is that *action* could be closer than you might think."

The half-giant nodded slowly, as a man just sentenced for a crime that had been eating him up from the inside. "We are on the brink, then?"

Vey nodded. "Much hangs in the balance. It is the Jhinyari that the Grey Clerk is most concerned about, for the present. The indicators are indirect, but you know what happened the last time technology gained a foothold in the Bay…"

Hersh went silent at the grim news, his expression blank. In a solemn tone, he finally spoke.

"The Council will be dead set against me." He rubbed his clean-shaven chin. His eyebrows gathered in. "But I have waited too long. You have convinced me, Special Assistant. I shall meet with the Grey Clerk tomorrow. I need assurances from her to make this work, and I need them fast: something I can offer to the oligarchs and the guild masters; something more than an empty promise. I will commission an early coach and…"

Vey winced slightly. "I'm afraid the Grey Clerk will be gone by mid-morning, to Harrow. We lost a few luminaries in the treaty office there recently, under suspicious circumstances."

"I am so sorry to hear that." Hersh rested his hands on the back of his chair and stared out the window at the wind whipping across the dark waters, rippling them. Vey didn't want to have to strong-arm the vice-regent the way she did, but she had no other choice. *The more he knows now, the better,* she thought.

He sighed a giant's sigh, then swung his gaze back to Vey. Out of nowhere, the whole conversation took an unexpected turn. "Do you think it would be prudent for me to accompany you back to Gan then, this evening?" His voice was soft and polite. "I could have a raven sent tonight so the Grey Clerk knows I'm on the way, and meet with her before she departs."

"Oh," Vey said. "A night coach?" Although she'd anticipated some form of polite advance on Hersh's part, she was thinking more along the lines of a romantic, seaside dinner.

"An important matter like this can't wait," he said. "I simply must see it through. I won't be able to sleep a wink otherwise. The Council has a midnight vote coming up to allow… I can't get into the details, but it involves Harrow and this very topic. They won't postpone—the day after next when the clock strikes. Your visit is quite timely, Vey. I can *just* make it to Gan and back again in a fast coach. I'll need something in writing from the Grey Clerk… Olerik can advise Rush how to draw up the documents."

"My lodgings…"

"I'll take care of any commitments you have to break, and I'll bring dinner."

Vey hesitated to think Hersh's offer through. She'd obviously hit a nerve, but Hersh didn't actually need her in order to meet with the Grey Clerk. *Quite the career move for me, though.* The special assistant imagined the look on the Grey Clerk's face upon presenting the vice-regent to her, eager to negotiate treaty reinforcement, eager to stave off

Harrow's encroachment on the Bay's industrial sector. Everything she wanted. And there was more…

Vey put one finger to her lips as she considered *all* her options. *This could make for an interesting evening,* she mused: *dinner on the run, talking and laughing until the wee hours of the morning, carrying on.* She knew she could tease out of him the purpose of the secret Council vote. *He'll need good advice on how to handle them, and Olerik and Rush won't be there for him.*

And when the late-night chill sets in, Vey would break out the blankets. They'd both be drowsy. Unable to stay awake, her head would fall to rest on his shoulder. His arm would draw her in close to share his warmth.

The proposition fell short of the evening out she was hoping for, but the notion of traveling to Gan overnight with Hersh had potential. He would also need lodgings on the other side. *And if there were no inns available at five in the morning…*

"Yes, I would like that," Vey said. *That sounded too eager.* She backtracked slightly. "I mean, I do think it would be prudent. The Grey Clerk will be most pleased that you are taking her concerns seriously."

"Indeed," Hersh said, "what could be more serious?"

With official matters out of the way, the gracious host in Hersh took over. "I will have a handler stop by this evening."

Vey nodded. "And I will pack my things."

"Splendid! No need to bore yourself with dinner at the wharf. We'll have our meal on the way, a fine 'coach dinner' at that. And no talking business. You won't be sorry. Trust me."

Vey smiled with polite anticipation. "That sounds… exciting."

"And you are staying at the Seaside Rendezvous?"

Vey nodded.

When Hersh did take his leave, and she was alone for a moment, Vey finally let out her girlish smile and the quiet giggle that had been hiding with it. Everything had gone just the way she'd imagined it… sort of.

After a few hushed words with the steward at the doorway, Olerik and Rush entered. They took their seats a safe distance from Vey, one beside the other. The special assistant suddenly felt as though her red dress was wasted on such company, and found herself wishing she could change back into her business attire, mud or no mud. *Better yet, wrapped in my grandmother's shawl.*

In long drawn-out sentences and monotone words, the soft-spoken technology advisor informed Vey of Fort Abandon's official stance on recent developments with respect to the treaty. He explained, for one, that his cadre of 'technosages,' as he called them, were only studying technology to learn about the threats it could pose to Abandon and how to defend against those threats. He also mentioned that it might be possible to "unsign" the treaty in the event that it no longer serves the fort's interests. By an overarching rule of thumb, a treaty can be dispensed with by a member if it can be shown to be obsolete, or little more than superstition, or an unnecessary barrier to future prosperity, or just about any other reason that can be justified.

Everything Olerik said confirmed the reservations Hersh had expressed. What he went on and on about wasn't really that important though. *In the end, Hersh will do what he wants to do.* The trick was to get him to want to do the right things—he could convince the councilors, he could convince the oligarchs, and he could convince the guild masters. Everything would fall into place. Vice-regent Tehan was the key.

҈

The rain had come and let up by the time the meeting ended, and a cool breeze blew in from the waters when Vey finally stepped out onto the street. On the way back to her room, she made a stop at the Fargoer to pick up her goods. The haggard woman from the Scarsands, the one she'd met the previous day, greeted her from behind the counter. A false kindness lurked behind her wide grin. *Odd.*

"Milla? Where is…" The name of the girl who managed the apothecary lingered on the tip of Vey's tongue. She was mentally exhausted.

"Sleeping, poor thing," Milla said, still grinning. "Up all night, Clea was. Asked me to fill in for her this morning."

Vey took note of the bags under Milla's eyes and her drawn face. "Oh, I didn't realize…"

"No bother." The woman sniffled. "That's just how things happen. Everything at once, it seems, and nothing in between. Pardon me." The haggard woman stooped down behind the counter, shuffled things around, then reappeared a minute later. Any discomfort Vey might have felt about Milla replacing Clea quickly dispelled with one look at the decorated basket the woman produced. It was overstuffed with fresh flowers, cut-out animals, and bright ribbons.

Vey's eyes went wide. "That looks wonderful," she said, picking through the contents. *Clea must have put this together.* She reached into the basket and drew out a thin wooden box with a sliding lid. "Did I order this? It looks special."

"It is special. A special treat from Clea," Milla said. "Green Dragons. A kind of chocolate flatcake with herbs mixed in… from the West. Sinful and invigorating all at once. I'm sure you'll just love it."

"Would you like a piece?" Vey asked.

"Oh no, my dear," Milla replied, rubbing her belly. "The food in this district is too rich for my taste buds…"

Vey smiled, slid the lid open and peeked inside at the cut squares of gooey cake. They were greenish brown and smelled like a mixture of chocolate and fresh-baked bread. She savored the sweet air. *Decadent.*

Vey smiled graciously. "Thank you."

"Don't thank me," the haggard woman said. "Thank Clea. I'm about to break for tea at the wharf. Would you like to join me? I have my own special blend, I do. Special for you."

"No," Vey said abruptly, then caught herself and spoke with sincerity. "I have to pack and go." She shut the wooden box and tucked it back into the basket. "I'm due to leave for Gan very soon and I simply cannot miss my ride."

A flash of anger might have crossed Milla's face at that moment, but if it really was anger, it passed quickly, before fully taking form. Still, an uneasy feeling crept over Vey as she reached for the basket handle.

"Perhaps some other time," the woman said, nudging the basket towards Vey. "Perhaps some other time…" Milla smiled a broken smile.

"Yes," she continued, "some other time, before you even know it." Vey grabbed the handle, again sensing something false behind that smile.

Their parting was awkward and uneasy. Basket in arm, Vey backed away slowly, smiling nervously and shrugging. She turned and departed at a brisk pace, eager to put some distance between herself and that woman.

Chapter XIII
Schemer
(Akrylla)

~Take

The moment the red-haired hussy was out of sight, Akrylla stuffed her satchel with all the herbs, roots and compounds she could fit into it. She left the Fargoer Apothecary without locking up.

~Home

She made her way to Clea's terrace house—a modest home in a modest neighborhood.

~Horse

Akrylla took the money hidden in Clea's mattress, then lifted the girl who worked behind the counter into her bed. On the shaman's way out of the room, she glanced back at Clea, lying motionless. The girl's color wasn't good. *Poor thing might never come to.* Akrylla shrugged. *Most do though, eventually.*

~Choose

"The redhead was supposed to drink tea and come home," she complained to herself. Her other self. *No choosing.*

~Choose

Akrylla knew that if she hurried, she could find a way to bring Vey back to the house and still have both. *My Vey seemed to be in such a rush though…*

~Choose

My ak'la. Akrylla mulled over the decision for a moment, but it wasn't really close. She returned to the bedroom, bound Clea's hands and feet, then gagged her. *I can't have anyone following me.*

~Horse

Akrylla took a long cloak to wear from Clea's wardrobe, snatched a pair of sandals while she was at it. She rolled up a blanket, locked the front door and left by the back door. Then she hastened to the Travel District and searched the narrow streets and alleyways until she found a suitably shabby, run down set of stables. There, with Clea's money, Akrylla purchased a horse and cart. The horse was old and the cart rickety. She didn't haggle. There wasn't time to haggle—she'd never find Vey amongst the inns in time, not alone, not vulnerable, not without ten pairs of suspicious eyes tracking Akrylla's every move. *But there is only one road to Gan…*

The shaman packed the blanket and her satchel into the cart. She grabbed the old horse's reins, seated herself comfortably on the blanket, and then headed for the gates.

Hurlorns are far more than trees; that much is obvious. The sages of Gan have studied the most common sorts extensively: 'Sleepers' they are called. A holdover from the days when behemoths walked these lands and hunted them for food, it is generally accepted that early Hurlorns were more like giant bugs than trees: slow moving terrestrial invertebrates that fed on swarms of insects and vegetation. They had no hope of outrunning or outsmarting the crafty predators that pursued them. However, over the course of eons, the species adapted, and nonetheless developed some interesting defenses…

—Fyorn the Wilder,
on the Origins of the Kith

Chapter XIV
VOICES IN THE TREES
(Elu)

ELU AWOKE, FACE pressed against the earthen floor of the dugout cave. He had no idea how long he'd been lying there. He lifted his head. Gelled blood tore away from his flesh, breaking its bonds with the clump of blood-soaked earth beneath him. He rubbed his gritty, stinging face, then scanned his surroundings—darkness and shadows everywhere, even with his superior vision.

The air was dank and smelled of surface animal. A growling form of speech, muffled and gruff, issued from the cave's exterior. All Elu knew about the beasts that had captured him was that they were fur-bearers with strong jaws and dangerous claws, and that usually, but not always, they walked on all fours. Other captives referred to them as "Wulvers."

Is anyone still with me? Markine?

A dozen had been captured with Elu, but only three originated from the Dim Sea caves he called home. He knew his grandmother had been taken elsewhere—all of the female slaves had been taken elsewhere. Elu felt his wrists, still bound and chafed. He pulled one foot away from the other. There was no resistance. *They've untied my ankles. Must've needed the rope for some other unlucky wretch.*

Elu stretched out his leg, searched with his foot until it bumped into something. Someone's limb jerked away from the unexpected touch. He narrowed his eyes, trying to discern the shape in the dark.

"Markine, is that you," Elu whispered. He sat upright, leaned sideways against the wall of the Wulver dugout. The two had stuck together throughout the ordeal. They told each other they'd stick it out to the bitter end. *How many days now?*

"I'm here, Elu," a voice whispered back, but from another direction. It was him all right: Markine. That meant he'd bumped his foot into the only other youth around, that boy who wouldn't give his name.

"Are you bound?" Elu asked Markine.

"Just my arms."

"We could run."

An older man's voice cut in. "Don't be fools," he gruffed. "Those dogs'll run you's down and tear you's to shreds."

"You don't know Elu," Markine jibed. "He's 'Elu the Elusive.'"

The two friends shared a chuckle. Markine had started calling him that soon after they were captured, for it had been Elu who'd chosen the hiding spot for all of them. "I couldn't hide your smell though," had been Elu's retort. No matter how bad things got, there always seemed to be a laugh worth sharing with his oldest friend.

"What's this?" gruffed the older man, accusing. "Sniggling at such a time as this… shameful. I know you, Elu. Think of the slaves *not* among us. Think of Elise, your grandmother. Does that make you want to laugh?"

Elu's gut suddenly felt rotten. Rotten to the pit. He wanted to punch the old man in the head. After all, it wasn't the old man's family.

Markine huffed in the dark. *He's pissed too.* But Elu and Markine otherwise ignored the comment. They knew when to hold their tongues to keep out of trouble. A scuffle with the old man would only attract attention. Unwanted attention. *All attention is unwanted in this place.*

"Who else is here?" Elu called into the darkness. The boy with no name answered.

"Only me," said the boy. He sounded about thirteen.

"Who's me?" Elu said, hoping he'd provide a proper answer this time.

The older man grunted. "Just keep calling him 'Boy.'"

The boy didn't correct him.

Elu heard Markine shuffling about. "What are you doing, Mark? Going somewhere?"

Markine responded with an over-dramatized groan, but not so over-dramatized that the old man would complain. "I was just about ready to save your ass... AGAIN, when you interrupted." He grunted and scratched along the dirt floor in his struggle to free himself. "Give me a minute."

"I can help," Elu said.

"You's 'ill just get yourselves eaten," the man said, his voice cutting. "Roasted on a spit. Best bide yer time 'til they sell us off... caused enough trouble for the rest of us already." He started to grumble. "Bide yer time... nowhere's worse than here."

No signs of fire in this place, Old Man. Elu kept the thought to himself though. He wasn't about to correct the crusty bugger—it might set him off. The man was probably right about the rest though. Any show of resistance from a prisoner was dealt with swiftly and harshly by their brutish captors. And the violence always seemed to spill over to whichever unfortunate bystander happened to be near. Biting and scratching were the usual punishments, but serious flesh tearing and beatings with a club were becoming more popular. Elu rubbed his hand over the swollen wound on the side of his face. That's what happened the last time he'd decided to make a run for it.

"It must be dark outside," Elu commented.

The boy responded. "Unless they've blocked up the hole. I heard some..." He hesitated.

"Some what?" gruffed the older man.

"Shush," the boy replied.

That just raised the ire of the man. "Don't you dare hush me, you little shit."

"Stop talking," Elu snapped. "He has keen ears compared to yours."

The man grunted in protest, but remained silent.

"I hear them again," the boy said. "Those new voices."

"Maybe they're dinner guests," the older man said. "And we're on the menu. Who do you think they'll eat first, Boy? Tough old meat like me, or a soft, tender morsel like yourself?"

"We told you to shut-up," Markine said.

The man didn't stop. "I think they'll go for the morsel, myself." He let out a soft chuckle.

Markine scoffed. "*That's* what's worth laughing about to you?"

"Shush." Elu tuned his ears to the voices. "No. Those aren't Wulvers."

"I heard them before, when you's were sleeping," the boy said. "They sound like Outlanders."

"Outlanders?" Elu said.

"That's right. Baruush accent. From Bitterhelm way. My father runs a work camp—"

The old man cut in. "Shut yer trap, Boy. Gonna get us all tortured and killed."

Markine shuffled over to Elu in the dark. Elu felt his friend's hand grip his shoulder tight. "Let's get you out of those."

Elu bared his wrists. "How'd you get free?"

"Their rope is crap," Markine replied. He proceeded to loosen Elu's bonds. "Just a few pulls and they come apart." A second later, Markine tossed the rope aside. Then he shuffled over to the youngest among them.

"Boy, your next. Old man, you can go screw yourself. Stick it out with the dogs, if you're so afraid to do anything."

The man let out another soft chuckle. "They didn't bother to tie me."

~

The stick barricade that blocked the cave entrance wasn't much of a barricade at all—a poorly woven bundle of branches set on a lean, reinforced with more of the same crude ropes. The real barricade was the guard Elu knew would be out there. The older man had followed the three younger captives closer to the entrance. He hung back though, far enough to scurry deep into the tunnel if need be. The coward didn't want to be anywhere near if something went wrong.

Dim light filtered through the stick barricade. Elu knew it wasn't the sun, which would be much brighter. He had an idea, though, what it might be. He'd never seen the moon before, but he'd listened to his grandmother speak of it, so casually, as though hanging bright in the dark sky were no great feat at all. And she'd spoken as though the endless sky itself was not something to marvel over, but something rather commonplace. He wondered if the moon was full that night.

The barricade didn't even completely cover the cave entrance. A small gap remained at the left bottom corner. Markine regarded the boy.

"Boy, you're the smallest, and the hardest to spot…"

The boy didn't hesitate. "I'll look." He got down to crawling on his hands and knees, squeezed part-way through the tight space. He stopped suddenly, wriggled back.

"What is—" Markine started, but the boy put his hand over Markine's mouth before he could finish.

The boy uttered a low whisper into Markine's ear, so quiet that Elu had to inch his own ear close to Markine's, just to hear it.

"… right in the way."

Markine responded just as softly. "Any others?"

The boy shrugged. "Dunno."

Markine nudged him towards the entrance. "Then look again," he whispered.

The boy resisted. "But—"

"Never mind 'but.' You said you'd look, now look. Do your part. Then I'll do my part and figure a way to get us out of here."

The boy huffed. "Okay," he said, then crouched before the entrance. Eyes about level with the top of the stick barricade, he drew a deep breath, then tugged it aside ever so slightly. He peeked out. Wide-eyed, he swung his gaze back to Markine.

"This one's just lazing," he whispered, excitement in his voice, he spoke rapidly, "but I saw his ears twitch some."

"How the hell are we going to get around him?" Elu muttered.

The boy turned away, popped his head out again, then withdrew. He backed into Elu, forced him deeper into the den.

Markine scrambled over and addressed the boy. "What?" he whispered.

The boy whispered back. "Th-Th-There's two of 'em at the edge of the clearing. Straight ahead." Then he pointed to the right side of the barricade. "And an Outlander, that-a-way."

"What about the other slaves?" Elu said, in hushed tones. "Did you see the women and girls?"

"No, not there," the boy said.

"You didn't look hard enough," Markine said.

"Did so," the boy retorted. His voice began to crackle. "My sister's one of them." He started to whimper. "I'd know if I seen my sister."

Elu sighed. "Stay here. Let me look." He swapped places with the boy. Without a sound, Elu inched the barricade aside a tad more, enough to gain a clear view of the outside. A curved sliver of light shone in the sky above. It hung just above the treetops. Around it, tiny dots of light. Elu stared, mesmerized. Someone poked him from behind. He knew that poke. It was Markine.

"What do you see?" Markine whispered.

"Trees," Elu whispered back. Tall like spears with jagged tops, they stabbed up at the sky. The scent of the forest had a purifying quality.

"And the moon," he added. *Magnificent.*

Markine's impatience erupted. "I don't care about the damn trees and the stupid moon. Where are the girls? The women?"

Elu peered into the darkness between the trees. His senses sharpened: a faint rustling, a blur of movement. His instincts ignited. *Follow.*

A soft voice called to him from the woods, "Elu." It seemed to surround him. "Elu, come."

Lanaora.

He'd met the girl briefly. She'd spoken kind words to him before they were separated.

Elu whispered back to the others: "I hear her voice. It's Lanaora." He cupped his hands in front of his mouth, whispered loudly out to the trees. "Lanaora."

The boy cuffed Elu in the back of the head. "Shush! You'll wake the guard." His voice wavered. "Something's off about those trees."

Markine tugged on Elu's shirt. "Boy's right. Hang back a bit."

The Wulver guard stirred, then sawed out a warning growl.

Elu froze. A chill shot up his spine.

The boy scampered back into the dark.

Markine's reaction was the exact opposite. Grunting with the effort, he pushed past Elu, seized the stick barricade in his wiry grip and rushed it forward, out of the den. With all his scrawny might, he slammed the sorry contraption down on the Wulver guard. Markine knocked him right flat; the guard yelped. Markine whipped his gaze back to Elu.

"Fly!" he shouted, bobbing up and down on the stick-and-twine platform. The Wulver struggled to turn over and gain its footing.

The boy paused, glanced back to the older man behind him.

"Don't go, Boy," the man called, desperation in his voice.

"Come on," Elu cried. He scrambled over to the boy and yanked him out.

Growling and baring its long, yellow fangs, the trapped Wulver twisted free, flinging his attacker. Markine crashed into Elu and the boy.

A heartbeat later, the old man charged out of the den. Grunting and cursing, he threw his weight at the Wulver guard, grappled the beast to the ground. A second Wulver dashed to the fight. To their right, a short and stocky Outlander drew a wicked, curved blade.

Elu, Markine, and the boy exchanged knowing glances. They all broke left and bounded past the scuffle, out of the clearing and into the woods.

The old man shouted gargled curses behind them as he fought on against two Wulvers, tearing him apart. *He's done for,* thought Elu, as he raced through the forest. A whisper came to his ears.

"I hear her voice," Elu called to Markine, through the bush. "I hear it in the trees. And another… wait…" Elu called forward to the boy. "Is that your sister?"

Markine veered right to meet up with Elu. The third Wulver, and maybe more, joined in the chase, crashing through the bushes behind them.

"The whole pack is after us!" Markine cried. "Faster!" He huffed. "Faster!"

The boy's arms flailed in front of him as he trampled through the understory, swiping at branches and pushing them aside. He huffed words between breaths, his voice still a whimper.

"I heard my sister's voice," he huffed. "But she's not really there. These trees, they… lie. They play with the echoes." He hesitated. "Are the Wulvers gaining on us?"

They had to be gaining.

In his peripheral, Elu saw Markine hazard a glance back. Then came a loud snap. Markine stumbled. A swooshing sound came out of nowhere.

"Markine?" Elu glanced back. His friend was gone; whipped away.

"Markine!" he yelled again.

Branches whipped at Elu as he tore through the woods, ducking limbs and leaping over deadwood. There was no answer.

"I'm going to climb a tree," the boy said.

"No. Keep running!" Elu said. "They'll catch you."

A voice called out: "Lanaora!" It was Markine.

Suddenly, without warning, the entire forest erupted with voices. The sounds filtered in from all directions. Some faint; some near. "Lanaora… I'm over here," called a voice like Markine's, but from another direction entirely. Elu's gaze darted this way and that way, but he could not see his friend or Lanaora. When he peered ahead, the boy was gone.

"Sam?" called a young girl's voice, in the distance.

The boy's sister?

Elu cried out, "Boy, where are you? Stick with me."

A sultry-sounding woman called out next. "Elu. Come to me. I'll show you the moon."

More voices joined in, twisted and taunting.

"Go back, Lanaora."

"No, come here."

"I need you, Lanaora."

"We all need you. Elu needs you too."

Elu slowed to a halt, spun around. Everyone was gone. The boy.

Markine. Lanaora. Even the Wulvers. Everyone. *Only trees. Voices in the trees.* He was lost in the forest, all alone. *Trees everywhere.*

Until he heard a sharp growl.

Elu's leg erupted in pain.

CHAPTER XV
DJINXAR LANDING
(Hadamard)

THE LUMINARY BRACED himself. He knew what was coming.

Nydar shouted the approach order to his crew. The *Hyperion* dipped sharply. Her main mast skimmed the tips of the inverted towers above them. Thin and translucent, they hung like ghostly teeth from the roof of the great maw of Tetherport.

Hadamard's innards lifted in the opposite direction, and as the glideboat was about to squeeze between two closely tethered ships, he leaned towards the Gloom beside him.

"Utter madness," he remarked. "One rogue gust and we're done for."

Nekenezitter peered out over the rail, one finger pressed to the rim of his glasses to keep them in place. He watched as the free pier tilted into view. The Gloom swiveled his buggish gaze to the luminary, shrugged. "<click> As involved <tic> as the entire process might seem <chirr>, accidents are extremely rare <clack><clack>."

Hadamard glanced over the side, gestured to the base of the maw where the remnants of wrecked vessels lay, snagged on the jutting terrain. The place was a ship graveyard and littered with broken rock and stray debris.

"Perhaps not as rare as you think," he said.

Nekenezitter let out a sorry chirr.

The vessel sailed past the first nethership unscathed, a bulging water collector tethered to one of the longest piers, then veered hard to starboard. The Gloom re-doubled his grip on the rail as they floated past the second ship, an older transport vessel that swayed wildly. But not Hadamard. Over his many voyages, the luminary had become quite familiar with the strange balance of forces at work on Seventh Kaeda. And he had confidence in Nydar's abilities.

A well-timed miss, it turned out. Captain Nydar barked out a complaint that the early-model stabilizers on that transport needed refitting.

Everything about the Djinxarai realm seemed to be a delicate balance of sorts, fraught with precariousness and near misses: Were it not for the tendril forest, the Rock and the Starshine surely would go their separate ways. Were it not for the even dispersal of air throughout the seemingly boundless Otherworldly Realm, the Rock would not hold an atmosphere and life would suffocate. And as much as the Djinxarai insisted that their homeland was self-sustaining and fully independent of Hadamard's world, the luminary knew there had to be a multitude of connections, if for no other reason than to equalize pressure and replenish the atmosphere. The average Djinxarai, however, lacked even a basic understanding of such concepts. The air was *just there* to them, like the rock, or the ever-flickering light, or the ever-changing winds.

Relying on the silent but heavy exertion of his crew, Captain Nydar maneuvered his vessel to a vacant tie line, a light but strong rope harvested from the Tangles. Hookmen with long poles swiped at the heavy ring-link at its end until one snagged it, then drew it in. That's when the shouting began, as a crewwoman snapped the wooden loop to the fastener on the bow. Next, the captain let the glideboat drift gently, until she swung about and the slack ran out on the cord. The tether tensed. The *Hyperion* creaked in protest.

Over the few long moments that followed, the crew rushed to adjust her aerial stabilizers while a team of dockworkers cranked a winch to draw her to the pier. Only a careful alignment of sails kept the glideboat from spinning or swaying about wildly in the turbulence.

The last detail: drawing in towards the walkway so the ramp could be lowered.

Hadamard bade farewell to Captain Nydar as the ship was moored, then gifted him the armillary sphere. The Grey accepted with a thankful grin, made true and firm by his heavy handshake. The luminary descended the ramp wondering if his model would ever be of any use to the good captain, or if it would just clutter up his already cramped quarters.

Buffeted by high winds, Hadamard stepped onto the pier, legs stiff and feeling very much like they'd been strapped to stilts the whole way. The feeling wasn't so much derived from the strength of the gription or the disorientation imparted by the dim flicker of the ambient light around him—it was more like the solid construction beneath his feet didn't move quite right. It was the same every time, owing to some phantom of the ship's motion that clung to his sense of balance.

The luminary scanned the wharf. The open space bore no barriers, duty posts, or formal guards *per se*, as would be expected at the ports of entry to Gan, Fort Abandon, or Harrow. Instead, a handful of locals garbed in long robes and woven sandals wandered about casually, engaging the wharf's occupants in conversation and mentally recording arrivals and departures. Another craft had docked, built strictly for traversing the nether, while a glideboat was being loaded up with crated goods. *To Gan, no doubt,* thought Hadamard.

The luminary headed for the nearest greeter, a hooded Djinxarai female whose age he couldn't even guess, with gaunt features and a thin-lipped smile. Every fiber of her lean musculature showed through her greyish skin. While he presented his diplomatic colors, one-by-one the unconfirmed prospects wobbled over to gather round, more than a few with pallid faces. Vil'nyan had trouble keeping her dress down, despite the heavy material it was made of.

With voices nervous and unsure, the prospects engaged in broken chatter about the voyage—the sights, the fast turns, the sounds of winds and blades. The sanity of the bold crew was questioned openly. As they shared their experiences, the volume of their combined voices rose to a racket. The tempo of their stories hastened.

Hadamard read his list of travelers aloud to the greeter, pointing to each one as he called them by name. After explaining the reason for their presence to her with care, he received a strong and friendly welcome. She wished the group sure footing and went on her way.

With Nekenezitter at his side, Hadamard scanned his prospects. The conversations between the promising youths had since escalated to enthusiasm and speaking over one another. With a firm clap and a forceful "ahem," he cut their chatter. A few words were in order and they needed to pay attention.

"There'll be time to socialize later," Hadamard began as he studied their faces. They looked enlivened again, energized. "Listen up—there are a few things about Seventh Kaeda that you absolutely NEED to know."

The luminary went on to describe the Djinxarai's gentle ways, their discipline, and their pantheon of life. He provided a brief backgrounder on their culture and explained the openness of Djinxarai society, and how as guests the prospects were free to roam where they pleased—as long as they didn't do so on *his* time. Hadamard told them how to find the Netherdome, and the main settlement of Djinxar, and their way back to Tetherport. Last, he provided an abundance of tips for getting around the Rock and interacting with the locals.

"Get to know them," he finished with. Hadamard paused. There was more. Much more he wanted to tell them. But time, as always, had run short. *The rest can be filled in as we go*, he thought. But with one exception: a description of Seventh Kaeda wouldn't be complete without some mention of the unfamiliar forces at work. He started up again, abruptly.

"Everyone, lift your right foot," he said. The prospects made passing glances to one another; doubt plain on their faces. Hadamard waited patiently for them to comply, keeping his expression even. Seeing that he was serious, feet began to rise.

"The force that keeps you stuck to the ground should feel on the weak side right now," he said. "Go ahead, try it. Do a little hop… Nek, you can take a giant leap."

A handful of prospects snickered. As a group, they did as he bade them. Even Nekenezitter couldn't resist.

"That's right," Hadamard said, making rising gestures with his hands. "Now, that sticky force could easily change to something stronger, or nothing at all for short periods. Or you could casually stroll into an area exposed to high winds that blast you into the nether." He firmed up his tone. "Don't leave yourself vulnerable to an open sky if you feel the Rock is about to get into a serious wobble. Go inside or grab onto something—anything secured to the ground. Look for natural handholds, they're everywhere."

Heads nodded; gazes shifted to the rock wall to scan its craggy surface. Nekenezitter swiveled his head with them and emitted a series of sharp pulses, bouncing sounds off the wall.

His demo complete and his salient points made, Hadamard ushered his group off the pier and to the lift loading area. When they reached the water-filled lift tube, the luminary glanced up. The lift was near the top—the gardens. Slow-moving as it was, he had some time to kill.

While they waited, Nekenezitter started into an impromptu lecture to the prospects on the subtleties of remote psionica and the connectedness of all matter. The luminary groaned under his breath. He couldn't be sure if he suddenly felt heavier because he was trying to follow the crown advisor's convoluted logic, or because the spin of Seventh Kaeda had begun to shift slightly. And as his mind began to wander to things that actually mattered, the Gloom's voice faded into the background. It faded with the bustle of the quay and the hollow-sounding winds.

Hadamard pondered his current predicament. What little solid data he'd acquired through scenario runs only served to confirm the hypothesis he'd known to be true all along: arm the Kith Rangers and to hell with the Queen's Guard—maybe use them as a reserve force, at most, but not the main striker wielders. Otherwise, the weaponry's unique advantages would be wasted.

But Lord Ralador was too pompous to see the reality for what it was. Too pompous, too arrogant, and too glory-seeking on behalf of his precious queensmen.

The battles to come simply won't be their kind of fight.

And they *were* coming. The signs were everywhere.
Ralador...

CHAPTER XVI

RALADOR

(Hadamard)

W HAT HAPPENED TO *the damn night guard?* wondered Hadamard. A muffled voice—male—called from outside the Crimson Tower, followed by more rapping on solid oak. Even with Hadamard's own office door shut tight, the distraction was impossible to ignore. Lightning flashed high above his windows; thunder set them to vibrate. He'd been in the midst of an intricate thought.

Well, the night guard did grumble earlier about a leak in the lower levels… might keep him busy for a while. Heavy rains had dumped on Gan intermittently for three days, spring's way of cleansing the gorge of its last remnants of snow. That day was the worst yet. Its steady patter had started mid-morning and continued throughout the afternoon, with heavy downfalls into the evening.

"Olmi… sin," called the muffled voice, louder than most through the thick barrier.

Hadamard would've been content to remain at his desk and ignore the after-hours summons.

Rap-Rap-Rap.

He tilted his gaze to the ceiling, scrubbed a hand over his face. *Where was I?*

Rap-Rap-Rap.

"Shroud's Well! Enough!" Hadamard slapped his palms to his desk. The rickety thing half-collapsed; notes slid off in a jumbled mess. Heat flushed through the luminary's veins. "Just what I needed," he huffed, glaring at the miserable heap. "Add that to the drawer that won't open." Never mind the fact he'd overstuffed it. "Anything else?"

Hadamard shot to his feet, marched to the office door and burst out of his academic cage. He stormed down the hall to the foyer. Amidst muffled curses, the luminary approached the double doors, fumbled with the lock until it released, then gripped the left door handle.

"Olmi—"

He whipped the door open.

The uniformed man on the other side jerked back at the sudden movement. Spray jetted past him into the foyer. The fan of documents the man had been holding flew out of his hand to scatter over wet tiles, while his other hand angled an umbrella sideways in a vain attempt to fend off the driving rain.

Hadamard stood, glaring. "What? It's after hours."

"Olmi—"

"Get in," he snapped, "before you get me soaked."

The intruder—a well-rounded royal caller—closed his umbrella, shook the water off, and tossed it inside. He scuttled into the foyer, bent over and began scooping up his papers one by one. The man's cap blew off before Hadamard got the door shut.

"Apologies," said the caller. The luminary stood by, watched as the man's frilly shirt and blue jacket rode up his back while his fine, water-soaked trousers rode down. "Please be patient, just a few moments, if you will," the man added.

A handful of Hadamard's colleagues trickled out of the stonework and gathered round, plus a straggler from the Grey Tower, Qyp Reed, who'd happened by on an errand from the Grey Clerk's office.

"An awful mess," Qyp remarked, in the midst of hunkering down to help. He raised a smudged page to his eyes and began examining it. The caller snatched the sloppy paper out of his fingers.

"Thank you, Sir," he said, a hint of sharpness in his voice. Qyp didn't let the response deter him from gathering more pages.

Hadamard's temper slowly cooled as he watched, and by the time the royal caller had gotten himself organized, the luminary's level-headedness all but returned. Just then, the door blew open. Gusty air sent the papers flying again.

Qyp sprang up, shut the door, pressed hard until a click sounded. "The mechanism sticks sometimes," he said.

The second time around, the caller was quick to sort through his clutter. After gathering the papers and his hat, he rose to his feet, unbuttoned his coat and pulled a dainty eyepiece from his breast pocket. Deftly, with the same hand, he produced a handkerchief to wipe the lens dry. He inserted the monocle over his left eye.

Flipping through the documents, he found the page he was looking for. The caller mouthed the words, cleared his throat.

"Ah-hem… Olminsin," he started, surveying the small crowd through the squeezed-in monocle.

Hadamard grimaced. What kind of name was "Olminsin" anyway? "Olly" for short—a great name for a clown. He hated it. He lifted his finger an inch to identify himself.

"Hadamard, if you please," he corrected.

"Yes, of course, Your Lumenship…" The caller's inflated, bespectacled eye scanned the page again. He felt his way to an inner pocket and returned the handkerchief to it.

The caller flipped the page, then cleared his voice again. "Ahem… yes… I see here. Hadamard it is. Again, I apologize…" Then, he took a moment to straighten his posture. His chest expanded. With choreographed poise, he made his formal announcement.

"Lumen Olminsin Hadamard, you are hereby summoned by His Lordship Loraith Ralador to the chambers of Her Majesty's High Elderkin Council. Please make your way to the front gate promptly. An escort awaits."

Hadamard gritted his teeth in silent irritation. *What does he want now? Why me and not Forsetti?* The luminary hated short-notice briefs. "And the topic of the day is…"

The caller rolled his gaze up from the document, gave Hadamard something of an evil eye through that monocle. He spoke in a firm, precise tone. "I am not privy to that information, Your Lumenship."

Hadamard let out a heavy sigh. "Tell His Lordship I'll be right there. I just need to grab my coat and a few things."

"I recommend the utmost expedience." The royal caller removed the eyepiece, tucked it back into his breast pocket. "The Lord of the March does not enjoy being... put off, if you will."

After stowing away the wet papers, the man buttoned his coat. Qyp handed him his umbrella, opened the door and held it.

The caller stepped through, paused, then turned to regard Hadamard. "I will not see you there, as I am off on another errand of the utmost importance. Good evening to you, Sir." He tipped his cap, popped opened his umbrella and descended the glistening stairs to the city street below. Qyp snapped shut the door behind him.

Hadamard swung his gaze to one of his understudies, lounging with the gathered crowd and shuffling his feet. "You're just the person I need, Smat. Grab your things and be back here in three minutes. I need an update on your latest findings, en route."

Smat shrugged, nodded. "Sure. I think you'll be impressed. Kith all the way." He ambled off in the general direction of the stairwell to the lower levels, to his office in the very bowels of the tower.

"Excellent," Hadamard told him, then hastened to his own office. Not knowing exactly what to prepare for, he gathered the latest results of his experiments off the floor. *My recommendations,* he thought, *that must be the reason for the call.* He flipped through his files for one report in particular. *There it is: 'On optimizing the use of strikers.' A vastly important topic.* The luminary folded the report, set it on his bookshelf momentarily. He donned his good coat, then tucked the manuscript into his largest inner pocket. Just as he approached the door to leave, Qyp strolled in. He eyed the collapsed desk and scattered notes.

"A couple of bricks will level that off," Qyp said. Then he turned his gaze to Hadamard, a hint of sympathy in his clear, brown eyes. "Would you mind some company?"

The Grey Clerk's man knew everything about the management side of the project Hadamard was working on. Plus, Hadamard trusted him.

"Do you have a big umbrella?"

"I do," Qyp replied.

"Then of course I don't mind. I should have offered in the first place."

⤳

That was the moment, thought Hadamard, still waiting for the tube lift to arrive. Even with the air bladder deflated, the lift was never speedy on descent, unless loaded to capacity.

That was the moment that set me on this path. During that visit to the palace, he'd faced off with Lord Ralador, overspoken the queen, and worst of all, earned himself a tag-along snitch.

Not a good visit. Not a good visit at all...

⤳

Unsurprisingly, Goremann Smat was not in the foyer when Hadamard and Qyp got there. They descended two levels and met him in his basement office instead, where they found the understudy rummaging through a pile of loose-leaf folders, searching.

The place was a mess—papers everywhere, walls covered in pages of equations and hand-scrawled notes. Water pooled on the floor where more papers lay, half-soaked. Smat was highly valuable to the luminary mainly for one thing—grungy computations that would drive anyone else insane.

"Never mind the nitty-gritty details," Hadamard told his understudy. "Just give me the short version while we walk. Then you're off the hook for tonight." Hadamard gestured to the calculations wallpapering his office. "You can come back and finish this later... is the work you're doing really that complicated?"

Smat's eyes surveyed the material. "Some of the terms might simplify," he admitted.

"I suspect they will," Hadamard said. "When you're done, write up what you think you've found in plain words. Then double-check everything from the beginning. I'll be stepping through line by line with you first thing, so be ready. If I find so much as one wrong factor of two... let's just say I have another task in the bog lands that requires attention."

Smat let out an uncomfortable chuckle. "Still beats Akeda."

He grabbed his coat and, under a single umbrella, the trio departed the Crimson Tower. Luckily, the rain had let up some. On the way to the Hidden City gatehouse, Smat had barely enough time to wretch up the contents of his calculating mind and spew them all over Hadamard and Qyp. It was a remarkable mess, for the most part. When he was done, Hadamard sent him on his way. "Not one factor of two," he called after.

Two palace guards received Hadamard and Qyp at the gate. They promptly escorted the pair to the solar and explained along the way that plans had changed. Hadamard would not be meeting the entire council after all.

"Highly unusual," Qyp commented after the guards departed, keeping his voice low, "to meet with Queen Xara under such private circumstances."

"You would know," Hadamard responded. Being the Grey Clerk's right-hand man, Qyp was required to attend all high-level meetings that his superior could not attend herself. And, according to him, the Grey Clerk had met with the Royal Quarter weekly, if not daily, in times of crisis.

The solar spanned an area the size of a town park—a covered garden with cobbled paths lined with fragrant flowers and vibrant shrubbery. When the pair approached, Queen Xara appeared to be alone, whispering softly as she ran her fingers affectionately along the slender branch of a smooth-barked willow, leaves freshly budding. Soft clicking sounds filled the air, which Hadamard attributed to some exotic insect.

The queen wore a simple evening dress, form fitting green and gold, and she adorned her long, elegant neck with a ruby of such value it could have fed half the monarchy for a month. Her unusual physique only added to the queen's elegance. Xara's Djinxarai heritage on her father's side had imparted an unworldly length and slightness to her frame, but she lacked the wiry toughness that normally balanced it out for full Djinxarai. Xara appeared nothing less than fragile under the sure and steady pull of Theia's gravity.

What is elegance but frailty teetering on disaster? thought Hadamard, as they neared. Qyp led the greeting.

The Grey Clerk's man stood straight as a board, then bowed his tall, narrow frame to her. "Your Majesty," he said. "I bring you Lumen

Hadamard." He gestured to his companion. Hadamard greeted her with a courtly nod and all of the politeness he could muster.

Xara accepted their salutations with grace. "Thank you for coming on such short notice."

"Ahem," came a voice from behind her. A strange little man, obscured by a dwarf spruce, stepped into plain view next to the queen. Hadamard had never seen one of his kind before—from the shores of the Dim Sea. *A Gloom? I thought they were sightless, lacking even the organs to see.* But not this one. This one wore thick spectacles that put his magnified eyes on display. He was also the source of the clicking.

Xara introduced him. "Crown Advisor Nekenezitter has become a valuable counselor, of late. He has some very… interesting ideas."

"Nice to finally meet you, Nekenezitter." Hadamard extended his hand. "I've heard so much about you."

The Gloom took the hand in his small one, shook back gently. "<click> And I of you <chirr>, or more, your work."

"All good, I hope," Hadamard replied.

The Gloom's neck twitched. Qyp interjected.

"We have not been formerly introduced either. Qyp Reed, from the Grey Clerk's office." The two shook hands.

Nekenezitter chirred excitedly. "Indeed." Qyp puzzled over the highly enthusiastic response.

"What sort of advice do you provide?" Hadamard asked the Gloom.

Xara looked down affectionately at Nekenezitter. She placed a loving hand on his shoulder and answered for him. "He is a master of mysteries, this clever one." She paused for a long moment to regard her visitors. "I won't keep you gentlemen long with all of the details."

It was getting late, and behind Xara's refined veneer was a woman exhausted. No doubt, she was exhausted with policy, exhausted with people who didn't know what they were doing, and exhausted with the games people played to advance their agendas and personal aspirations. Hadamard could identify with all of that. He was tired too, and peevish. Qyp was … well, Qyp—annoyingly energetic, standing as perfectly erect as one can stand.

Queen Xara cut straight to the matter at hand. "Lumen Hadamard,

I have discussed your recommendations at great length with Nekenezitter and Loraith Ralador, and I have considered your advice fully."

That moment, the queen's eyes met Hadamard's in a cat's stare, bright amber like those of the ruling class Djinxarai in the Otherworldly Realm—the Jhin Masters. And in her gaze the luminary realized that he would not like what she had to say. He drew in a deep breath.

"My Guard is most noble and brave," she went on. "And they face the gravest dangers. They *absolutely must* have your dancing swords to meet our enemies and defeat them in combat."

Smat just told me basically the opposite. "But the Kith—"

With a gentle wave of her hand and a slight turn of her head, she stopped Hadamard short. "The rangers you suggest should bear the dancing swords are mere scouts. I do not question their loyalty or their dedication to the crown. And they do provide a great service to the Hidden City. But they lack the training, the discipline and… the *lineage* of my Guard."

Hadamard heard the words differently. *Wilders are not true immortals and so they do not deserve the best weapons. They are destined to die anyway, soon enough.*

The luminary didn't care either way what she thought of Wilders, really. And the queen was right about the noble and brave part. *Ralador's words though,* he thought. But bravery wasn't going to win the kind of battle Gan was apt to face. The most likely adversaries were Harrowians—conducting secretive research in banned areas—and the Jhinyari, who already possess the capabilities sought in the Striker Program. The Queen's Guard insists on engaging enemies in close combat on a proper battlefield. Hadamard shook his head. "Close combat is all they ever train for. That attitude will get them slaughtered."

"Your Grace knows best," Qyp countered, in an evaluating way. Lingering a step back, he bowed his head slightly to the queen, then secretly passed Hadamard *a look*: "Leave it be," was his unspoken message.

"No," was Hadamard's unspoken reply.

Qyp's eyes went wide.

Hadamard continued, addressing Xara. "Gan needs fighters who will show persistence and ingenuity when everything goes to hell, fighters who will overcome challenges. Fighters who will improvise."

Xara replied, "And that is not my Guard?"

"The path ahead is clear <tic>," said the Gloom.

What do you know? Hadamard barely contained himself from saying it.

Qyp lowered his gaze to the ugly gargoyle. "Is it?"

Hadamard scoffed, despite himself. "Your Grace," he retorted, "we have new evidence that suggests our Kith rangers are far better suited to the task—stealth, surprise, long range communication and coordination, they all factor in. Their use of animals gives them critical sensing abilities far beyond those of your Guard. Observations made during the initial wave of striker testing confirm this. My best people are running the numbers…"

"Stealth?" said a voice. It was Loraith Ralador, come to the queen's rescue.

The Lord of the March, High Commander of the Queen's Guard, stepped out of nowhere and into the conversation. He was garbed in formal attire, indistinguishable, at first glance, from full military dress. The man walked straight up to Hadamard until the two stood nose-to-nose, where he planted himself. Hands folded behind his back, posture nearly as stiff as Qyp's, Loraith Ralador stared Hadamard down with that hawkish stare of his. The man's wine-soaked words came out stern, carried on a condescending tone.

"What evidence could possibly deny the simple fact that the Queen's Guards are far superior swordsmen—trained from the day they could first lift a sword, some with a hundred years or more to master their skill at arms."

Hadamard did not know how to respond. He hadn't prepared for a debate.

"Well?" Ralador pressed, glaring into the luminary's eyes. "Tell us what you think you've found."

I will, thought Hadamard, *using the smallest words I can think of, so you can spell it out to your gargoyle later.* "The evidence suggests—"

"Suggests?" Ralador's beady little eyes were stabbing. They had a murkiness to them, like dark clouds. His nostrils flared as he inched his nose even closer to Hadamard's.

The luminary held his ground. And he held Ralador's gaze, eye to eye. The two were of a height, on the tall side. Not as tall as Qyp though, or as narrowly built.

"Does something *feel* a little bit wrong?" Ralador egged on. "Perhaps you had a bad dream you would like to share with us, or a premonition, or a little bird told you something."

"Well, basically… it indicates…" Hadamard started.

"Oh jolly, now we have *indicators*. Go on, spit them out," Ralador urged.

Flustered, Hadamard hesitated, searching for the right phrase. It was always harder to explain things on the spot to laymen.

Ralador maintained the stern look of an angry bird. His nose reminded Hadamard of a large, crooked beak. *You're so ugly, up close*, was all he could think about. It was distracting.

Lord Ralador took a step back. "You don't sound very sure of yourself, *Olly*."

Hadamard fumed internally, felt his skin go flush with anger. But before he could blurt out another retort, Xara cut in like a bossy, older sister. Clearly, the queen had no patience for such sparring in her presence.

"Enough!" she said. "Hadamard, begin the preparations necessary to train my guardsmen."

She turned to Lord Ralador. "Together, you and a representative appointed by the Grand Kith Overseer are to evaluate Hadamard's evidence by the end of summer. My preference is that the two of you come up with a unanimous recommendation, for consideration by myself and the Earl of the Gorge." She then addressed Nekenezitter. "You will observe Hadamard's work first hand and aid him by any means at your disposal. Confer with Lord Ralador regularly and update him on the progress made."

Lastly, the queen addressed the luminary and the Grey Clerk's man. "If the two of you can convince Lord Ralador and the Overseer that this new evidence is valid, I shall reconsider. Otherwise, the decision stands."

Xara stepped back. She folded her hands in front of her then looked to each of her subjects in turn. "Thank you all again for coming on such short notice," she said, with firm politeness. "You may leave me now." With those words, the queen gracefully turned away. Casually, she resumed admiring her flora and fauna.

Lord Ralador wagged a finger at Hadamard, then stormed off in a huff.

Nekenezitter stayed in place, awkwardly shifting his weight from one leg to the next, rocking his stout body back and forth.

Qyp sighed. "That went well," he quipped. The luminary didn't think the Grey Clerk man's narrow shoulders had the breadth to slump. But somehow, they did.

❦

"How will I ever convince Ralador?" Hadamard muttered to himself.

Beacon flashing, the tube lift finally arrived at the landing. And as it slowed to a stop, Hadamard jolted out of his lapsing state. Several prospects around him still hummed with conversation about terms in Nekenezitter's asinine equation, while others—presumably those who'd heard enough and were eager to move on—shuffled about and fidgeted as they turned their attentions to the platform.

By all appearances, the lift was little more than a capped-off section of watertight glace tube, with an adjustable air bladder on top. A hooded lantern hung from the ceiling, which doubled as a signal station. Through the double wall of glace and the water in between, Hadamard could make out the middle-aged form of the Elderkin Grey inside. A mechanical sigh sounded as the man pulled back on the air lock lever to seal the doorway. Then he pushed open the porthole door. Squatting to peer through it, he called out.

"All aboard," he announced. The operator recognized Hadamard immediately. "Going down, I take it?"

Hadamard nodded. "My new home." Nothing else was down. Only the Netherdome complex. Without pause, the luminary ushered his prospects into the opening. Then he helped Nekenezitter through before ducking in himself. They all stood tight and straight in the cramped space.

"Fully loaded," the operator told three newcomers as he foot-pumped the air bladder, drawing from the central guide-pipe. He followed with a few words in the Djinxarai tongue. The three Greys nodded, one glanced upwards. *They'd be heading up anyway, to Djinxar,* Hadamard thought, *as most would.*

The operator continued to pump the bladder until Hadamard felt a slight shift underfoot—equilibrium. The man released a blast of air back into the pipe. Satisfied with the buoyancy, he shut the hatch, sealed it, and allowed the platform to begin its descent. All passengers fell silent as the ambient flicker of the Starshine faded out of sight above them. Out of sight and out of memory. And as they drifted downwards, the lantern cast a dim and yellowy glow on the passing rock walls of the deep shaft. The Grey operator winked at Hadamard as he turned the lantern low.

There's something truly morbid about this place, thought Hadamard, as he glanced about. Between Nydar's storytelling about Windswept rituals and Nekenezitter's talk of dead gods, the luminary couldn't help but feel as though he was disturbing a resting corpse. He lowered his gaze to the Gloom, thinking back to their conversation on the *Hyperion*. "I suppose our destination would be the heart of that dead Abindohn god you were talking about then, wouldn't it?"

Nekenezitter's eyes lit up, wide as an owl's in the yellow light. Eager to please, as usual, he nodded back with fervor, chirring as he did so. "A hollow chamber, though, since the heart was stolen." He hesitated. "<tic> A heart of darkness."

"Hollow indeed."

Hadamard fully expected the rest of the day to be humbling to his prospects as they struggled to get a handle on this new environment and experience Jhin thaumaturgy. Humbling and wondrous. But that didn't mean he'd be easy on them. No, Hadamard knew his role. He planned to be fully merciless in all his demeaning ways.

The luminary drew in a heavy sigh. *That's the job.*

Chapter XVII
New moon
(Akrylla, Vey)

~Thieves

Akrylla sized up the three Outlanders she'd bargained with under the new moon. They were despicable. They were scammers. And they were unproductive. Without her plan falling onto their laps, the beast-men had only one scrawny thing hauled out of the dark to show for all their slave raiding. Despicable. As despicable as she. Worse.

I should have never made a bargain under a new moon, she scolded herself. Akrylla felt her stomach harden. *Bad sign. Unlucky.*

Still, the shaman had fared well with the slavers. She'd bargained with all she had when they approached her in the dead of night on the lonely road, rape and robbery in their eyes. After all, she'd been alone and outnumbered three to one. Six strong arms to two tired, aging ones. *If they weren't so pathetic, the bargaining would have been a lot harder.*

Now, as she stood in the middle of the road, watching and waiting for the travelers to arrive, a bad feeling began to stir in that hard pit of her stomach, a bad feeling that was only there because of the moon. Akrylla twisted and squirmed at the discomfort. She knew what was coming. *They will never take my Vey, my Ak'la.* Her thoughts were jolted.

~Liars

They better not lie. The deal is simple: I put the captives under a charm. We all escape. I take the girl, and the slavers take whatever else they want.

S-i-m-p-l-e. How do I keep it that way?

~Favors

Akrylla had read the signs. The one called "Riddik" held the power. The one called "Riddik" could be manipulated. The one called "Cutter"—the other name they called Riddik—stood with a wide stance. Short, bald and brawny; full of hate for everything; not very smart and ugly as a troll. He couldn't hide the Taint in him—Baruush-blooded. *I will give him what he wants,* she decided. She'd given him some already, just enough to make him interested. *I might be seasoned, but I know how to give. I will give him what he wants so he won't take it from her. So he won't take it from my Vey… my new apprentice.* Akrylla felt very strongly about this point. She wasn't sure exactly why.

Riddik the Cutter approached her from his hiding place on the side of the road with the others. Akrylla hunched a little more so she wouldn't be so tall. Riddik didn't like it when she stood straight; when she stood taller than him. He walked right up to her. Close. Too close. His breath was sickening, like puke and rot. The smell of it interrupted her stream of thoughts. Her schemes.

"The handler might fetch a good price if he can fight," Riddik told her. The Taint knew fighting. He had scars all over his face and body.

~Idiot

He didn't know much else besides fighting. Fighting and cutting and catching slaves. They'd been through this before. Akrylla insisted, "Someone has to die to let the world know we're serious." Riddik made a fist and pulled it back.

She received a beating for her insolence, right there in the middle of the road. And Riddik—the Taint bastard—cut her, just like he said he would if she didn't listen. He cut her, but Akrylla didn't scream. She didn't scream because that would foil her plans. The shaman bit her lip and took the pain. *My Vey might hear and turn the coach around.*

Riddik admired Akrylla for that, it seemed, and even made a concession. "The handler we will kill," he told her.

"Unless he can put up a fight, of course," Akrylla replied. The agreeable remark made him grin.

~Clever

And Akrylla convinced Riddik of one more act, an important act: to kill the scrawny dark thing they called "Markine" and leave the body at the side of the trail in a shallow grave—to throw off the Abandon investigators that inevitably would be sent. "Clever, they are, those investigators," she told him. "Too clever not to be careful. Bludgeon him with a rock though—they can trace a blade back to its owner."

The one called "Ang" chimed in on the matter, from her hiding place on the trailside where she squatted behind some brush. She agreed Markine wouldn't fetch much. *I don't think she likes that scrawny thing they hauled out of the dark.*

A flush of adrenaline tingled through Vey's body when she answered the door.

Vice-regent Hersh Tehan personally rang Vey's room when his coach came calling, showcasing a bottle of the Bay's finest red and a slim bouquet of fall flowers. They were blue, white, and violet. The half-giant's voice rolled with great depth when he spoke, and in it still resonated a hint of diplomacy: "Something to express my appreciation for your flexibility," he said, "… changing plans on such short notice." Vey accepted gracefully, if not bashfully. The coach handler, who'd hung back and nearly been occluded from view by Hersh's massive frame, stepped into the forefront. He stooped slightly, reached for her luggage.

"Shall I?" he asked, tone seething of politeness.

Vey nodded. "Thank you. Yes, please."

The handler, sharply dressed and wearing a stiff, blue cap, whisked away Vey's travel case and the new wardrobe bag she'd picked up at the market. And before she could settle into her seat, the vice-regent's carriage was through the fort gates and the three travelers well on their way. Halfway up the hill, before reaching Fairwind's Arch, the handler called back.

"Your Grace, are you certain you do not wish me to raise a security contingent?"

Hersh rumbled back. "Nonsense. Rangers have been scouring the trail from here to Gan all day, searching for rogue Outlanders. The road is as safe as it will ever be."

The handler let out a heavy sigh.

Peering at him through the cabin's narrow front window, Vey might have caught a slight grimace forming on his face. But the handler knew his place and held his tongue on the matter. Hersh slid the panel shut.

After a few hours on the trail, all formalities between the two wayward diplomats vanished. Vey could barely recall what'd sparked the latest fit of laughter…

"I never imagined!" Hersh said, smiling back broadly at her. Red eyes held back the tears.

Vey touched him lightly on the knee, feigned sympathy in her voice. "No need to cry, Hersh." She giggled, herself barely holding back the tears of laughter. "It's all right now. Everything will be better."

That only made him roar. The special assistant burst out laughing with him. After long and vocal sighs, the two calmed down. The moment converged to a decision of what to talk about next. Vey sat contemplating, suddenly conscious of the motion of the coach, the horse's hooves clopping and splashing through puddles, and the tall wheels steadily grinding the sandy earth below—every sound magnified by the wetness of the trail from the passing rain. Her eyes wandered from the cabin to the dim horizon. First, she looked to the glowing wake of a sunset just passed, then felt a slight emptiness at having somehow missed it. The sky loomed orange and red over distant hills, void of its brilliant crown jewel. Second, she looked to the sparkling waters of the Lower Malevuin in its rush to the sea. The river ran deep and fast through the Flats. And third, she looked to Hersh. The half-giant's soaked eyes met hers, reflecting the crimson radiance like pools of oddly translucent fire.

"Dinner was perfect," she offered. "I had my doubts about eating coach…"

Hersh smirked. "The wine might have helped."

Vey whispered. "Your handler must think we're mad."

The vice-regent whispered back, too loud not to be overheard. "He already knows I'm mad, and by now suspects I've passed it on to you, surely."

"Hmm…" pondered Vey aloud. "I have just the dessert."

Hersh feigned offence. "I brought dessert."

Vey insisted, "We can have that too… later." *At my place, perhaps.* Excited to contribute to the fine fair, she fetched her cakes from the Fargoer goods. "These come from the apothecary."

"The apothecary! What, are they drugged?"

"Only a little," she teased. "Clea—who runs the shop now—made them special for me. She really is a dear friend."

Hersh lifted a cut portion, gave it an examining look. Crispy on the outside and moist on the inside, the baked marvel was dark brown, chocolaty and streaked with green bands. He gave it a sniff, quirked an eyebrow, then smiled. "Well, if she is a dear friend, I suppose they're safe."

"If not, I'll be sure to leave you passed out on the side of the road… in front of the palace gates." Vey giggled like a foolish girl.

"With a note pinned to my jacket." Hersh chuckled foolishly. "Please deliver to the queen's bedchamber, at once!"

A reserved smile crossed Vey's face. "Uh huh," was all she said, her tone flat. The young Elderkin did her best to convey her complete lack of appreciation for the jest, hoping to send a message. Hersh was stupid to have said what he said, but she let it pass so as not to lose the moment. *Men say stupid things all the time without knowing it*, she conceded. *It's the sort of thing he'd say to one of his drinking chums.*

The cakes were gooey and decadent, infused with an herbal tang. Vey offered a piece to the handler as well, which he accepted graciously. All indulged and the two passengers washed down their desserts with a second bottle of wine.

With chocolate on his lips, Hersh boasted that he was so gargantuan it would take three bottles all to himself just to get tipsy. Vey believed him.

Time passed, unnoticed. Nearing Turnsby, the special assistant gazed at the vice-regent with tired eyes. The patter of rain on the cabin roof lulled her in slumber's direction. She readied herself to sprawl out across her seat, perhaps even take a nap. Hersh himself was nodding off. Vey glanced out a side window, saw tire ruts leading off the trail, down a slope. She jolted. *The ambush.*

"Tell the handler to slow down," Vey blurted out. She fumbled her words, "There might be… there still might be… there were 'horse thingies' on the road."

Hersh laughed as he slid the front window panel open. A refreshing breeze replenished the air in the cabin. He leaned forward on his seat, called out to the handler. "Did you hear that, good man? The lady would like you to slow down so she can nap without sliding out of her seat. And mind the 'horse thingies.'"

"The horse 'thingies' are dropping as we ride," said the clever handler. "But don't worry, we're leaving them all behind." Despite the fact he clearly didn't know what Vey was talking about, he honored her request.

The special assistant smiled as the handler reared back gently. She closed her eyes and felt the gentle pull of inertia as the horses slowed to a comfortable walk. After slipping away for a long moment, Vey sat up abruptly, straight as an arrow. She was determined to keep the conversation moving forward.

"Where was I?" Vey asked.

"Something about the queen," Hersh replied. "You were talking about the queen."

"That was hours ago, wasn't it?" Vey tried to piece together the time that had passed. "Oh yes," she said at last, glancing ahead to the road—it seemed blurry to her eyes. She turned back to Hersh and gazed into those sunken eyes, set beneath a furrowed brow. *He looks deathly tired,* she thought. Vey felt tired too. *Time to spice up the conversation.*

"Well, then Srylla," Vey began, "one of her ladies in waiting that I got to know very well—"

"I know a Srylla," Hersh said.

"Yes, she mentioned you in passing."

"Why is she in Gan?"

She'd already slept with every eligible man in Harrow, that's why. Gan was next on her list. Vey smirked at the thought. "I bet you know just about all the noble families in Harrow," she said.

"A good many," he admitted.

Vey asked playfully, "How exactly *do* you know Srylla?"

Hersh fumbled for words. "Ahh… umm… I met her father once."

"It's okay," Vey said. "You don't have to tell me *all* your secrets." As she was speaking, Vey glanced to the road ahead. Something shadowy on the path didn't look quite right. Unconcerned, she continued with her story. "Anyway," she said, still staring ahead, "Srylla leaned over and whispered into my ear the last we spoke, and—"

Vey stopped talking, gripped Hersh's wrist. Terror lurched through her. Her words wouldn't come out. She squeezed tight, fingers barely wrapping halfway round.

The vice-regent shot a glance to his arm, then to her. "What is it?"

"Ahead," she sputtered, pointing. A frightful chill passed through her body, as though she'd seen a ghost. She couldn't get another word out.

A lone figure stood in the middle of the trail; a hunched woman clothed in a wet robe. Knotted hair coiled out like a nest of snakes. It was the woman from the apothecary. Milla. She stood confident, defiant, leaning her weight on a thick, warped branch that she gripped with both hands. Behind her, crossways and blocking the road, was a horseless cart with a broken-off wheel.

"I don't like that woman." Vey yawned, then disbelieved it was possible to yawn under such circumstances. "Don't stop," she pleaded, feeling heavy. "Go around her."

"You know that woman?" Hersh nodded off for a moment.

"She gave me the… she gave me the… she gave me the…"

Hersh jolted awake. "Cakes," he said, then shut his eyes again. "Of course. Cl-Cl-Cl"

"Clea," Vey said. "No."

The handler slowed the coach to a crawl. The woman wasn't budging.

"No, don't stop," Vey rasped, as she slid sideways across her seat. Her voice became a murmur. "Run her down."

Hersh's man called out to the soaked woman, strong-lunged yet polite. "Clear the way. Coming through, urgent business."

But the woman forced him to stop the coach, else run her over. She forced him to stop by his own good nature. The steeds whinnied nervously. A lead horse lifted its front leg, then scratched at the earth to protest the vile woman's presence.

Vey closed her eyes, just for a second. *The coachman is too polite.* She heard a loud thunk as Hersh fell sideways into the cabin door. *Wyatt would have... Wyatt would have...*

"Wyatt—" she breathed feebly, urgently.

But the old bogger wasn't there to protect her this time.

Knowledge being Sustenance, it was the One outside all things who created the many universes for her own consumption. To keep watch on the gardens of Knowledge in the many worlds she nurtured, she infused a strand into every single thing and she wove them all together, like a great web.

Then she waited, as any orbweaver would. She waited for a telling sign, a vibration, a wave. And when the signal finally arrived from a distant world, tucked away in a far corner of her grandest garden, the Orbweaver set out to reap what she had sown.

One man on that world learned the secret of the Orbweaver. One man defied her. And when she came for his people and the Knowledge they had earned, he gambled for all humankind… and won.

But the cost was unparalleled. Monumental. Nearly all was lost. All but a precious few survivors, scattered across space and time.

—The Pristine Channeler,
on the Deception of Enormity

CHAPTER XVIII

AN UNEXPECTED TRIAL
(Hadamard)

THE LUMINARY FELT small and grey stepping into the wide-open cavern. Grey because of the grey light that penetrated him, shining from the domed ceiling above, and small because of the emptiness that pulled at him from every direction. *Hollow, like the Gloom said,* he thought, as the warm air of the cavern sighed past him. *But this place is not like a hollow heart… No, more like a giant lung by the way it draws and exhales.*

The grey light was the same grey light as an overcast day when the sky simply would not give up the rain. The same grey as the nether. Hadamard had spent weeks and months laboring in that strange glow. And some days, when he worked in perfect quiet, he could've sworn it swirled above him, ever so slowly.

He turned to watch his seven prospects spill into the dome. Hadamard could judge nearly instantly who had it in them to be a luminary, and who didn't. All he had to do was challenge them, then sit back and gauge their responses. Watch them be brilliant, watch them fumble, or, worst of all, watch them not even try. *This trial will be swift and decisive,* he predicted. *They won't know what hit them.* But becoming a luminary wasn't only up to Hadamard. There were certain conditions outside of his control: the fungus is basically random; the Hurlorns choose their own; the Prime Lumen says yay or nay; and in the end, people do whatever the hell they want to do.

Other than the factors out of his control, the evaluation method was simple enough and consisted of three trials: a written exam to qualify; a personal suitability evaluation; and an oral exam. The prospects had already completed the written portion at Crimson Hall. The marks weren't terrible, overall; neither were they impressive, apart from Seddner Pawl who'd managed a perfect score. Yuri Haulik's breakdown was absent. This coming trial was more important to the luminary though. It came down to finding people he could get along with, who could successfully navigate the work environment, who could carry a heavy load when needed, and who would have the backbone to stand harsh criticisms.

The low, whipping howl of the nether winds outside was silenced when Nekenezitter closed off the chamber. Even then, air huffed out of the breeder caves for a long minute before being drawn back in again to equalize the pressure. Shuffling footsteps broke the dome's hush as Hadamard's prospects gathered round. He waited for his group to settle, then introduced them to the place where everything happened. And by everything, he meant everything vastly important to him right now—everything to do with Jhin thaumaturgy. His authoritative, no-nonsense delivery reverberated throughout the chamber.

"Welcome to the Netherdome," he began, his voice echoing off the walls. "This is where we build and run life-sized combat scenarios, and where we experiment with the Djinxarai's special gift. A gift we are ever grateful to them for sharing with us." The luminary waited for the echoes of his voice to subside, paused for a long moment. "Quiet right now, isn't it?"

Hadamard swept his gaze about the chamber. His prospects' eyes followed. "We're the only ones out here. Not much going on." He gestured to the plain and nondescript building opposite the door they'd entered. "Times like this, between scenarios, are the only times that the source of all the action can be seen for what it is. In the midst of a run, that building behind me—the *COM Center* or *Common Operating Model Center*—might appear as a hill, or a cave, or a thick mist... or some other natural feature of the environment." He waited until all wandering eyes fell upon it, the only structure in the Netherdome. The squat building was tucked into the rounded corner of the elongated chamber. The red glow of its interior lighting shone through the open doorway on the right side, facing.

"There are no windows in the building and only one entry point," Hadamard went on. "Besides housing the most important room—my study…" The luminary hesitated to accommodate a scattering of polite snickers, "… the complex holds the *Red Room* for scenario control; an armory for outfitting mimics; and various small utility rooms stuffed so full of equipment and provisions no one can find anything."

Hadamard raised a scolding finger, wagged it at the group. "But no food. Food is strictly prohibited in the dome to avoid accidental poisoning of the resident shiro beetles. Millions upon millions of beetles support the work being done here." He gestured to the walls. "You'll find numerous small, natural-looking cave openings here and there. Leave them be. Those are breeder tunnels."

Goremann Smat raised his hand. "But where do *we* eat?"

Hadamard answered bluntly, "We don't… at least, not very much."

Smat scrunched his heavy brow.

"Outsiders tend to lose their appetites on Seventh Kaeda," Hadamard explained. "Feel free to dig in though. You can choose between grey fungus and grey-green fungus—next tunnel over, along the lower ledge. I drink water—lots of it. In the same tunnel, you'll find a fountain that draws from the reserve water supply of the lift tube. Don't leave the tap running, or we'll be rock-climbing back to Tetherport in questionable gravity. Now, Smat, what did we discuss on the glideboat?"

"Oh." Smat offered a sheepish grin. "Sorry."

Hadamard got back on track. With his fist, he thumped his chest hard, three times. "The Red Room is the beating heart of the Netherdome. It holds the *assembler*—the main tool of the projectionist. In order to be played out, detailed scenarios like my wargames require a full team of Djinxarai projecting the various elements in tandem. You'll have a chance to experience the assembler later." *I'll leave that to Vil'nyan and Smat.* It didn't faze the luminary at all that the pair would be conducting a tour of a place they'd never been to themselves. The concepts were all familiar. *Should keep them sharp.*

Stepping backwards and gesturing for his prospects to follow, Hadamard drew them deeper into the dome. "Come along," he urged, until they were fully immersed in the vastness of the chamber. When Hadamard halted, his trailing entourage of misfits crowded around him, expectant expressions dancing on their faces. Clicking softly, Nekenezitter set himself apart from the rest and hobbled to Hadamard's side.

The luminary had already decided his address would be unceremonious and abrupt. After all, he had a schedule to keep, experiments to get to, and an exercise to organize. He opened with the only Djinxarai saying he could pronounce… sort of.

"*Kii-dibik-kii-nen moozsin ma'dibik-maasey-agid.*" Hadamard let the words hang in the air for a long moment.

"Or, in other words, 'Fear not darkness, for it is only light upon itself, upended.'" Again, the luminary paused, this time to let the meaning soak into their young minds.

"Did you know the Djinxarai are pacifists because of this saying?" he asked.

Several shook their heads. Not one nodded. Hadamard knew full well there was little chance they could've known that fact. He'd only just learned it himself in casual conversation with Captain Nydar on a previous voyage in. But here was an opportunity to put his prospects off-balance. Nearly everything they knew would have to be turned on its side if they wanted to become successful luminaries.

"You should know that!" he snapped. Then he scoffed, addressed Yuri. "Why are you even here then?" He glared at Seddner. "Don't you read up on a place before visiting? You seem to read up on everything else." Then he turned his gaze to Nana. "Why not ask around? Your shipmates might have known something." And to her scrawny little brother. "Just let your sister do everything for you, right Ogmund?" Last, he locked eyes with Sorral. "If you don't do any of these things, how do you expect to know where you're going?"

Sorral mouthed a response, but no words came out.

Hadamard shook his head in feigned disappointment, then raised his voice, eyes darting from one to the next. "Don't you think that luminaries, protectors of Theia from forces that would tear her apart, should at least know where they're going?"

An uncomfortable uncertainty spread throughout the group. The Rese siblings nodded in blank agreement. *Confrontation avoiders,* Hadamard surmised. The Horse Lord brat must have half-concluded the luminary was toying with them—he wore a cautious smirk that he seemed ready to withdraw at an instant. *On the right track,* Hadamard thought. It was Seddner Pawl who braved a comment.

"I did ask around, but nobody mentioned anything like what you just told us."

"Hmph." Hadamard infused his voice with a demeaning tone. "Let me spoon feed it to you then. The colossus Jhin uttered those words— his last words—to the original people that dwelt here, just after he'd given them the gift of light—the Starshine. And now, the Djinxarai, who hold Jhin's words as the highest attainable truths, refuse to end a life. And I mean *any* life. Not even a bug. That's how shiro beetles infested this place without resistance. Can any of you get that meaning out of what Jhin said?"

Hadamard allowed them another long moment to respond. No one answered. By his shuffling about, Smat certainly had ideas he wanted to blurt out on the matter, but he kept to his bargain and kept his mouth shut. Only the ever-moving dome air dared to disturb the quiet.

Hadamard clenched his hands behind his back. With slow steps, he began to pace back and forth, first in front of them and then amongst them. He gave his prospects ample time to respond. Ample. He scrutinized their faces on every pass, just long enough to make each one uncomfortable before moving to the next. Still, no response.

He halted. "Of course not! Either you don't have the vaguest idea or you don't have the guts to be wrong. And that is why none of you are luminary material." He closed his eyes, rubbed his face in his hands.

"Well, maybe one," he uttered in admittance, then mumbled to himself. "I can only work with what I have." His words were not fully part of the act. The Order Lumen's stiff requirement was beginning to seem out of reach with this lot. One who is deemed Enlightened must be willing to seek out new knowledge at every opportunity, even if it is difficult, even if it feels humiliating to do so. A luminary must feel a certain weight of responsibility when presented with a problem. They must feel compelled to come up with the best answer for anything asked. Anything. And that wasn't happening. *Not even close. Fail, fail, fail on that one; the whole lot of you. No one even tried…*

Well… maybe Seddner, the luminary conceded.

"Obviously," Hadamard continued, a hint of genuine impatience now showing through, "our Djinxarai hosts interpret things differently than we do. Get used to that. Remember it." An empty nod, like artificial obedience, propagated through the group. It looked so phony Hadamard felt like screaming at them all to stop. About to tell them as much, he bit his tongue silent upon seeing the face of one of his prospects.

Vil'nyan alone held her own against the wave. She wore a pensive expression, indicative of deep thought. Hadamard could almost see the sparks igniting in her mind. *She understands*, he thought. *I wish it would catch and spread to the others. Why is it so rare a thing?*

Satisfied he'd explored the prospects' responses to his ruse sufficiently, Hadamard turned his gaze from Vil'nyan to address the group. He spoke as though the episode that had just played out never happened.

"Now, I'm going to tell you how to conduct a proper combat scenario, here in the dome. Listen closely. Besides having a well thought out game plan, you need to first determine the right terrain, the right mimics to use—the actors in your scenario, and you need the right action sequences. These are all aspects of your scenario that will fall completely under the control of the projectionists. You must rely on them for *all* of these things. And you must be thorough with your specifications, or you will discover holes in your scenarios or unexpected additions. Describe everything you can in as many words. They'll fill in the blanks to the best of their ability, but they can't read minds."

"How do they do it?" Smat asked, while scratching under his armpit. "How do the Djinxarai projectionists render a scenario full of mimics and actions, and then run it before your very eyes?" Smat's brown hair was mussed up to the point only one stubby horn was visible.

"You are aware of the legend, aren't you?" Hadamard asked him. Smat shrugged. The luminary surveyed the others. None of them would admit to knowing anything.

Turning back to Smat, Hadamard continued, "Jhin the Colossal granted the Djinxarai complete control of his entire being, just before he died. You are now standing on that entire being. In it, for that matter."

"That's not right," Vil'nyan argued, her voice resonating with antagonism. She placed one hand on her hip, shifted her weight. "Jhin went into a deep sleep," she corrected. "He was to leave this world behind and enter a dream for a thousand years, to discover the *Pristine Truth* and then return. Sleep, not death—big difference."

"That's one version of the legend," Hadamard retorted. "The Abindohn one. There are others, I'm sure you're aware, differing accounts ranging from Ironeagle to the Fountains of Saryid."

She huffed. "They're all wrong."

Unexpectedly, Sorral cut in, orange head bobbing and voice cracking as he spoke. "In the Bloodspill, it was Ekkon the Wanderer of Many Arms and Many Eyes who stole the breath of Jhin the Root and passed it to Asph the Tempting of Ironeagle Peak. Thus, the account is the same at the two extremes, but dips into absurdity everywhere in between."

This one speaks in riddles, Hadamard thought. And by the confused expressions he saw forming on the group's faces, none of the others, including Nekenezitter, had the slightest clue what Sorral was talking about. Hadamard knew the Fountains of Saryid were believed to lie somewhere in the Bloodspill Plain, east of Kel Fariz. And in between there and Ironeagle was the ancestral home of the Abindohns. *In a round-about way, he's saying the Abindohn god is dead.*

Vil'nyan turned to Sorral, looking cross and a tad quizzical. "Are you calling my people absurd?"

The links Sorral had made were fully consistent with known, ancient rivalries and alliances between the colossi he'd implicated. Although a distant link, fraught with uncertainties and not well articulated on Sorral's part, it was an important link—exactly the kind of connection that a luminary must make on a daily basis.

"Precisely my point, Sorral. Well done," the luminary said.

Vil'nyan gasped. "What?" She backed away, threw her arms up.

"Argue your point, if you have one," Hadamard told her. "Luminaries must debate to fully explore the complex dilemmas they are dealt. Only through arguing and bitter confrontation of opposing views does the path forward eventually reveal itself."

The luminary waited for her response, but it was Smat who answered. "Actually," he said casually, "I don't care about some stupid Abindohn legend."

Vil'nyan was beside herself at his remark. She grunted as she stood fuming, shaking even.

Smat just continued. "And the colossi are all full of themselves—you can't trust a single word out of their riddle-laden mouths. I want to know *how* the Djinxarai just make things up and then sit back and watch it happen. That's all I want to know. What law of Nature makes this even possible?"

Hadamard shifted his gaze to his understudy. He decided the time was right to move on to the next phase of the trial.

"I'm glad you asked, Smat. It's easier for me to show you though, than to tell you." Hadamard addressed the group. "Enough discussion for now, as interesting as it has been. Stay where you are, everyone."

The luminary turned his back to his prospects, strode to the very center of the dome. He stopped, tilted his gaze upwards to the high-point of the rounded ceiling, and called out.

"Rise from Jhin."

The luminary's words echoed throughout the cavern. Slowly, he raised his palms. Nothing happened. *Strange. Anya and Crusher should've been expecting me.* He glanced at the COM Center to verify its double doors were still wide open. They were. *At least one of the projectionists must have heard us come in.* Hadamard cleared his throat and called again, louder.

"Rise, I say. Rise!"

They'd better be in there, or I'm going to look like a fool.

Slowly, around him, the flat floor of the dome began to swell. A mound bulged out of the ground, and then another. Farther afield, a long hill began to form, and then a tree line in the distance. Or at least they looked like trees, sort of. More like deadwood. But that didn't matter. Hadamard spun around to face his prospects. Some gasped in awe, others stepped back and away, fearful and uncertain. Hadamard bellowed out again.

"Mimics. Rise forth from the swarms of Jhin the Root."

Another long pause followed his words. Then subtle scurrying sounds began to prick at his ears. Prospects' eyes darted nervously about the dome. The noises began to build. Hadamard smiled. Calmness infused his voice.

"It has begun," he told them. More gasped as the lighting in the dome dimmed. The ceiling became covered with tiny dots, like starlight.

"Fear not the dark," Hadamard added. His words were little comfort to Sorral, whose gaze flitted this way and that way, never landing anywhere for long. The Rese siblings clung to one another.

Scurrying and snapping noises grew to fill the chamber as thousands upon thousands of shiro beetles emerged, their tiny insect parts scraping and grating. They scratched their way out of the earthen floor and they bled out of the walls. They crept out of fissures and they streamed across the floor to congregate in patches; patches that soon ran thick with the large, meaty insects. They even dropped from the ceiling.

Sorral let out a yelp, squishing beetles from his hair. He bolted for the Netherdome door. The luminary called out after him: "They won't harm you, Sorral." But those big boots wouldn't stop running.

Nana Rese and her brother Ogmund eyed the orange-headed prospect as he ran. One after the other, the siblings swung their bespectacled gazes to the nearest mound of beetles, rising rapidly, and then to one another.

Nekenezitter calmly observed the proceedings, while Smat extended his arm and coaxed several of the beetles to crawl on him.

A natural, thought Hadamard, observing how Smat handled them.

The other prospects grinned and bore the experience, holding their own against the onslaught of insects.

Not bad.

"Where do the shiro beetles come from?" Hadamard asked of his remaining prospects.

Smat examined one closely, crawling over the back of his hand. "They look a lot like scarab beetles."

"They're not," Hadamard said.

"The shiro beetle population was originally cultivated by Jhin," Vil'nyan offered. "The insects responded to his every whim." Her gaze shot downward, eyes wide with tempered dread as she watched beetles stream up her ankles. She shook her legs one at a time, and brushed some off her dress.

"Let them explore," Hadamard told her, in a calm voice.

Vil'nyan shook her head. "No way. They've explored far enough."

"Not a big deal." Smat showcased a giant shiro beetle crawling up his arm. "Is this one pregnant?" He flicked it off at his shoulder, shot a glance to Vil'nyan. "They don't bite."

Vil'nyan flashed the Outlander a cross look. Not to be outdone, she closed her eyes and clamped her jaw shut. She winced and moaned slightly as beetles crept up her smooth legs. But she didn't budge. Halfway up, the beetles dropped off, then continued on their way. Soon, they streamed past, ignoring her completely. Vil'nyan gasped. "Why did they stop climbing on me?"

Seddner shrugged. "Maybe because you lead nowhere."

"Huh." The Abindohn let out a shaky laugh, then continued on with her talk of the insects. "The beetles became Jhin's servants—ahh!" She batted one out of her hair. "That's my limit, right there! I'm getting out of here."

Hadamard tried to reassure her. "It just fell from the ceiling."

"Ya, it's not like it was aiming for you," Smat said.

"He's right," the luminary responded. "The beetles won't harm you. They're not interested in us. We're just in the way."

She puffed and tried one more time to get her story out. "And," her voice wavered as another glanced off of her, "and... they became the servants of Jhin's followers."

"Argh!" Frantic, Vil'nyan brushed her hands through her hair as masses of beetles dropped from above. They glanced off her head, her shoulders, her back. Her companions nestled their heads in their arms for protection.

"Correct," Hadamard said, ignoring the new development completely. He casually swatted away those that clung to him. "Well done. Anything else to add?"

The scrawny Ogmund Rese let go of his sister and bolted for the door, mashing beetles out of his shaggy hair and howling as he went.

That's one Abandoner down. Hadamard regarded the remaining prospects. "Is anyone else going to help make my decision easier?"

"No, but I have something to add." Seddner Pawl took a moment to shake an insect off his head and to flick another away that had taken up residence on his arm. "Shiro beetles provide important materials for building, and they can be organized to perform a variety of useful tasks, not to mention their beneficial impacts on the Seventh Kaeda ecosystem."

"Very good," Hadamard said, nodding in appreciation of Seddner's studiousness. "Most importantly," the luminary added, "is the shiro beetles' newest assigned role, and arguably their most sophisticated one—mimicry."

The drone of the insects' noises suddenly shifted to a lower pitch. Hadamard scanned the assembly area. The beetles were largely in place. He addressed his prospects.

"Watch and be amazed."

The shiro beetles had assembled in mounds about the dome floor. And as Hadamard, the Gloom, and the prospects looked on, pairs of thick columns began to rise out of those mounds. Steady flows of shiro beetles clambered on top of one another. On the two closest columns, they stacked higher and higher until two larger-than-life legs took shape. About four feet up, the columns met. A waist began to form, then shoulders, and then the rest of the body.

Faces ripe with astonishment, the prospects viewed the shiro beetles locking in, one after another. The sight always amazed Hadamard. When completed, the nearest mimic stood a solid eight feet tall, shimmering brown and black with the occasional blue flash. Its eyes formed red. This was, by far, shaping up to be Hadamard's favorite scenario yet.

"A giant," he told his prospects. "On the smaller side, this one, the kind you might find serving House Marlin." *Nice addition, Crusher,* he thought of the reddish eyes. *Or is that Anya's touch?* Vivid coloration was a rare trait.

"Once the beetles lock together," Hadamard added, "there's no way to pry them apart short of ripping out their tiny mandibles or terminating the run altogether."

In the next-nearest patch of shiro beetles, another giant began to take shape, larger and needing more time to come together. After prompting the prospects and receiving another null response, Hadamard identified it to be a rarer sort, found only where the Western Tor meets the Upper Malevuin River. Only one such beast, in fact, was ever known to have entered battle. This mimic turned out extraordinarily tall and lean, with a green shimmer and wild braids. It loomed high above them, twice the size of the first.

Meanwhile, on the hill, a solitary, thick-limbed tree mimic soon emerged with a tremendous trunk, oak-like in appearance. The specialized limbs gave it away as a "warlorn"—a fierce subspecies of Hurlorn bred exclusively for battle, with bark six inches thick, club-like appendages for bashing, and long, spidery, spear-like limbs for piercing.

Hadamard stood in awe of the creation. *Amazing addition*, he thought. *Just what was needed. One of Crusher's, no doubt.* Crusher was one of the few people—the only one, actually—who always managed to impress him.

A row of queensmen formed on the hill alongside the massive warlorn—the striker wielders in this latest scenario. Beefing up the giant and Hurlorn content proportionally on the two sides of the conflict had been Ralador's idea. The Lord of the March maintained that the new mix better reflected the changing battlefield. But really, Ralador was desperate to demonstrate a queensmen victory with strikers in hand. *Pitiful*, Hadamard thought. *The Queen's Guard might prevail in this scenario, but the weapons themselves will have less of an impact in a battle between larger entities. You could arm the queensmen with broomsticks and get nearly the same results.* Hadamard chuckled, imagining the look on Ralador's face when presented with such an analysis. Hadamard's theory was yet to be proven though. And it wouldn't be broomsticks— just regular arming swords.

As the last of the shiro beetles snapped into place, the luminary prompted his prospects to explore.

"Go ahead, scout about," he told them. "You can't hurt anything."

Smat made his way to the tall giant, gazed straight up at it. "Can they move?"

"They won't be going anywhere right now," Hadamard replied. "It's simply too mentally taxing for one projectionist to control so many mimics all at once, and maintain the terrain on top. I don't want to burn out my Djinxarai. I need them all fresh for Diamond Saber."

The Horse Lord brat finally opened his mouth to speak: "This is all the work of only one projectionist?"

Nekenezitter, standing next to the brat, answered his question.

"<click> Yes," he said. "<tic> We usually <clack> have one for the terrain <chirr> and <tic> three or four to control the action <trill>."

As the prospects casually strolled through the scene set before them, inspecting every mimic, Hadamard coached them on important aspects of running a projectionist scenario. He included instructions for dealing with the unusual time keeping; the parallel runs; adding weaponry—the projectionists couldn't conjure true metal or wood out of thin air; and the importance of keeping to simple movements and simple rules for casualty counting. The casualty options for a battle were easy to explain: one to three hits per kill, depending on the entity, with no degradation of abilities for those wounded. "Otherwise," he told them, "it would be too hard to quantify and track."

As an exhaustive lull descended upon the conversation, Hadamard pondered his shortlist of prospects for advancement, now set in his mind: *Vil'nyan, Smat, Seddner Pawl… and, of course, Crusher. Maybe Sorral too, if he can overcome his fear of bugs. The Abandon siblings and the Horse Lord brat are not suited for this line of work… not at all.* Then he wondered, *What are the odds at least three of my choices will pan out?*

Nekenezitter chirred, effectively announcing his intention to waste time.

As luck would have it, the Gloom had trouble getting started. And in that chirring moment, the terrain began to change, slowly reverting to its plain, flat-field beginnings. Shiro beetles disassembled from their large, complex structures and scurried off to their hidden hives. The projectionist demonstration had run its course.

Hadamard clapped his hands together, effectively nipping in the bud Nekenezitter's blooming remarks. His hopefuls gathered close around him as he spoke. "All right, prospects. There's a lot of setting up to do before Diamond Saber begins. And I have an experiment to conduct before the dome gets too busy."

"Oh, that reminds me," Vil'nyan said, cringing apologetically. "I have to catch up with Feleg. I spoke to Captain Nydar and he said a ship's heading back through the Veil in about a cycle. And I have to meet someone at orientation…"

"Unfortunate," Hadamard said. "You'd stand to learn a lot if you stayed."

She grimaced slightly, fidgeting with her hands and biting her lower lip.

Hadamard let out a heavy sigh. "Very well," he told her. "But I can't take part in the remainder of the tour—I have urgent business to attend to. So, I'm putting you and Smat in charge. Make sure to walk my prospects from end-to-end, bring them through the breeder caves and the COM Center… show them where the food is. Make them taste it."

Her eyes lit up. "I will," she promised. Anxious to get moving, Vil'nyan promptly started on her way. "C'mon," she told the others, waving them forward. They didn't move.

"You're free to go in a moment," he told his prospects, then called after Vil'nyan. "And when you see Feleg, tell the old grig I'm saving him a plateful of purple fungus. He'll like that."

"I think I hear him belching in respect," Vil'nyan said. She halted, twisted half around. "Oh. When are the *actual* luminary trials, by the way?"

Hadamard hesitated. "The second trial just finished."

Seddner and Yuri stirred; their mouths fell open. But not Smat. He donned a wide-faced grin. Nana Rese's shoulders slumped as she looked towards the exit where her brother had disappeared. Vil'nyan simply frowned.

"That was it?" She pushed a lock of hair away from her face. "How was that a trial?"

Hadamard shrugged. "I have my ways. Be sure to get back in time for the third and final trial."

"I'll be back with the first boatload of Kith," she informed him.

"I'm sure you will. And I expect you to make up for lost time during the exercise." Hadamard addressed the other prospects. "I trust the rest of you are planning to stick around to explore a little and learn more about scenario building?"

To the luminary's surprise and disappointment, Seddner and Yuri fabricated excuses to depart with Vil'nyan, as did Nana. But not Smat. He obviously knew better.

Hadamard studied their expressions, trying to gauge their attitudes. *Did I scare them off?* He'd become accustomed to the environment. Hardened by it. *Or was it too much at once?* They'd experienced a mindful since passing through the Veil, with more to come. *Their brains are rattled, their bodies adjusting.*

And so, the reason for their decision to depart so quickly, despite the wonder of it all, finally came to Hadamard. It was just like Feleg had said. *Tetherport is as beautiful as it is a dive.*

The luminary let them all go as they pleased. They'd glimpsed the sorts of considerations a luminary must tackle in achieving the Order's objectives. That was enough for now. The tour would prove to be an eye-opener on top of that. *Anyone not fully motivated to contribute would just get in the way, at this point. I can get by with just Smat for now—he's eager and he'll make himself useful.*

Before their tour began, Hadamard approached each one to shake hands, express gratitude for taking part in the trials, and to say a personal farewell. While doing so, he discreetly unsheathed his kinship stone and mentally blocked his own affinity signature, so that the stone would respond only to the presence of others. Seddner and Vil'nyan set the fire amber aglow. *That's two confirmed.* Yuri's result turned up null. *Not surprising.* To Hadamard's knowledge, the Royal Quarter had yet to confirm a single case of Hurlorn affinity. Smat's reading was… strange. Inconclusive. *I'll try again later.* Hadamard didn't bother with Nana Rese. She hadn't said two words during the entire trial and he needed luminaries who could bring attention to themselves and get involved in whatever was happening around them. *Perhaps another day.*

Goremann Smat hung back as Vil'nyan took the lead with the prospects. Nekenezitter trailed behind her.

Smat shrugged his shoulders. "Well boss, looks like it's just you and me to put this exercise together…" With a sideways thumb, he motioned to Nekenezitter. "And that big beetle who couldn't find his cave." As the hopefuls headed for the door out, the Gloom got busy offering them a final dose of his sage advice.

The luminary smirked. "You and I will get done what needs to get done. I'll start by touching base with Crusher, my lead projectionist. He's probably in the lab. There's a separate matter we need to attend to. His sister 'Anya' will be around as well—she's always here with her brother. When you get back from the tour, what I need from you is to work with Anya on the terrain for the first striker scenario."

"Is she good looking?" Smat said.

"*Lady* Anya," Hadamard responded, emphasizing the "Lady." The Outlander stared blankly at the luminary. Hadamard rolled his eyes. "She's married to a Grey, Smat, and is one of the few Djins with a royal title. Understood?"

He nodded. "Gotcha."

"Something simple for the terrain," Hadamard went on, "a small hill for the rangers to capture from the queensmen defenders, with some cover nearby—woods, ruins, doesn't really matter—but a good gap in there, at least a hundred feet of open terrain between the cover and the hill. Anya will need consistent details, so don't just make it up. There's a desk drawer full of topographic maps in the control room—mostly old land surveys conducted around some of the smaller communities like Webfoot, Turnsby… Doncaster even. You can use those as a starting point. Just carve out a small section that looks about right; that fits the requirement as I've described it."

"Too easy," Smat said.

"Consider this a well-deserved break. And there'll be more of that later with the other scenarios. Halfway through the tour make an excuse and come find Anya—with luck she'll already be on one of the assembler stations. Introduce yourself, addressing her as 'Lady Anya.' She'll shoot you a bashful smile and say you can just call her 'Anya'— the Djinxarai care nothing for such titles. Then tell her I sent you and tell her why. She'll probably give you a quick demo of how she works the landscape—it's quite amazing."

"Jhin thaumaturgy?"

"Straight from the corpse, or so they say. Get used to it. You'll be seeing a lot of Djinxarai mysticism over the next few days. At times, you might feel like you're inside one of the old Star Sand stories, from the desert."

"The Bloodspill Tales?"

Hadamard confirmed with a nod.

Smat's gaze shifted to the tour group. "Smart bunch—they finally discovered a way to get out of a conversation with Nek."

"I didn't think it was possible." Hadamard chuckled as Smat took off in a jog to catch up with Vil'nyan and the others.

"*Lady* Anya," Hadamard called after him, emphasizing the "Lady."

Smat dismissed the remark with a hand flap response, without even looking back.

"And don't forget to pick up Sorral and Ogmund for the tour."

Hadamard sighed as he watched Smat carry on his way. A sudden lightness overcame him now that the suitability trial was over and done with. A dark cloud lifted from his mind. He looked forward to the next and final trial; a private session with each prospect, prompted by one simple question: Why do you want to become a luminary? From there, Hadamard planned to delve down into the bitter depths of each candidate's core, and unearth everything he needed to know about what they were made of.

Save it for after Diamond Saber, he told himself. *Important work lies in waiting.*

Chapter XIX
The apprentice
(Akrylla)

Whew Akrylla heard the clop clop of hooves approaching and wheels grinding over hard-packed earth, she knew she would have her Vey. And when the coach rounded a bend in the trail—a perfect blind bend for intercepting anyone coming from Fort Abandon—Akrylla stood in the middle of the road just as she'd planned, facing the travelers, her "broken" cart behind her blocking passage. She grabbed her claw-knife and waved her hands. *They will stop to help an old woman.*

~Wyatt

It better not be him. Akrylla spotted an old enemy of hers in town the day she met Vey. An old enemy from the Scarsands. He'd turned to coach-running and was soliciting in the streets for patrons. He would sniff her out. He would run the horses a mile before Riddik got off his ass, and the Taint's legs were too short to catch up. And Wyatt *would* fight—he doesn't eat sweets, he likes everything sour, like he is. *Wyatt could ruin everything.*

~Ekkon's Wheel

Akrylla sighed in relief. The coach rounding the bend was not Wyatt's. It was an official state coach. She thanked "Ekkon the Wanderer of Many Arms and Many Eyes, Who Has Never Been Seen and Who Has Never Been Felt."

The driver called out, "Clear the way. Coming through, urgent business."

In the coach cabin, Akrylla spied one huge bulk of a man teetering to one side.

~Fools

Akrylla waved frantically. *They ate the cakes. This will be easy.* She glimpsed russet-red hair in the cabin as well, beside the huge man. *That oaf better not crush my Vey, or I'll have Riddik chop him into bits so I can put him in a brew.*

The coach halted, just as she'd planned. The driver barely got a word out before the Outlander slavers sprung from the bushes. Amidst sharp growls and shouts, they yanked the coach driver from his seat, straightaway, and dragged him to the side of the road. The driver shouted in protest, and he did fight, but he wasn't very good at it.

The big one and Vey slept through the commotion like milk-stuffed babies. A delicate man, the horse handler was, and probably very polite under normal circumstances. The dark and shadowy beast among the Outlanders killed him, just like she'd asked, growling as it tore the man to shreds, grunting as it gutted him with its huge fangs. *Killing the handler was good advice and they know it. I wish it had been Wyatt after all.* Akrylla had misjudged the power of the growling beast. *A sickly thing*, she'd mistakenly thought. But it was not so sick as it was twisted, and they are two separate things, twisted and sick. Two separate things indeed.

This is going well, for a new moon deal.

~Cover up

Akrylla removed her wares from the cabin when it was over, so as not to be implicated. She had enough troubles already. *And those investigators…*

~Diversion

Akrylla wrote a ransom note using parchment she found in the cabin, addressing it to "The Fort Abandon Bastards" and signing it

"Riddik the Cutter," all in the script of a typical eight-year-old—she felt it appropriate for Riddik. In the note, she informed them to send whatever they felt their steward was worth to Bitterhelm at Ironeagle Peak. *They will bring more ransom that way*, she told herself, *if they come at all.* The syndicates of the council will debate the matter, she knew. Those who oppose the vice-regent or stand to gain from his departure will argue that Fort Abandon should not negotiate with kidnappers, while the guild masters and oligarchs who banked on his support will argue for a payout or a covert rescue mission. *All the while, I will have my Vey. All the while, we will follow the signs together, the way sisters should.*

The shaman also wrote that "I" (meaning Riddik) will send someone to contact the couriers when they arrive, and finished by explaining that the "girl" will be dead by then, just like the coach driver, so don't bother looking for her. "The body is going in a brew, so don't look for that either," she wrote.

~Investigators

Akrylla knew the investigators would be hot on their trail if they were given the note right away. So, with the sharp claw-knife she carried, the shaman slit open a cushion, stuffed the note inside, and then dropped the cushion on the floor of the carriage. *I can count on a day's lead before the note is discovered,* she surmised. *Until then, the body of that strange looking dead thing that came up from the dark will throw them off. As long as we keep to a good pace, the riders dispatched from Fort Abandon will never catch up.* She grinned to herself in satisfaction, and then carried on.

Akrylla's scheme could not have gone any better, except for one rogue detail, a detail that could be for the better as easily as for the worse. She could see that. But it was still upsetting—the connection to the Fargoer, and to Clea who was likely still alive. *The investigators are sure to uncover something,* she decided.

Riddik approached Akrylla with the ferocious one he called "Gutless Kori." The other he referred to as "Ang the Bitch." Akrylla had just met them at the side of the road, but she already knew that Kori survived being gutted by a giant vulture after an unsuccessful raid, and was a damn picky eater. That's why most of the handler still remained. The wolfish brute was the most like an animal, malformed and malnourished, forelegs elongated, and garbed in patchy scraps of armor bound over dark fur. Ang was a lean, venomous creature with crimson skin and jet-black hair covering two stubby horns—a demoness if ever there was one, part Nali. She wore a light and flexible scaled armor that Akrylla did not recognize, black as night. The two were definitely the *wild* sort of Outlanders rarely encountered in civilization, and they followed their master like dogs. Gutless Kori held a slumped Vey in his clutches, unresponsive and unaware. He held her for Riddik. The rabid-looking Wulver bared its fangs at Akrylla when she stared too long.

"Wait," Riddik said to his slaver companions. He pulled Akrylla off the trail.

~Liar

Riddik took more than they agreed upon, more and then some, and gave her nothing in return, save the beginnings of a new scar. And while he was in the mood for taking, he said he might want more than just the big traveler too, who looked important enough to ransom. He might want to keep Vey and maybe even Akrylla as well. Keep her instead of kill her, if she could prove her worth.

Akrylla fumed on the inside as she was being ravaged. *That was not the plan. The plan was they would all escape together to Ironeagle and then part ways. I keep Vey and they keep the half-giant. Simple. Don't change the plan.*

"We had a deal," Akrylla screeched. Riddik didn't care enough to respond. And when he finished his business, he dragged her back to the road. The wolfish beast was waiting for him, the slender redhead still held in his oversized arms. Ang took a step back.

~Vulnerable

Riddik the Cutter went to Vey. He went to Vey and taunted Akrylla with a grin like playful revenge all over his face. He was spent sexually, and so rather than threaten rape, he dangled Vey's life in front of her very eyes. Akrylla feared saying anything. *I thought we'd come to terms.*

I thought I'd gained your respect when I took the pain silently. Plus, I gave you more…

The Taint drew his sturdy but rusted dagger and slid it along Vey's throat, and then he slid it down along her sternum.

No blood, yet. He's teasing, isn't he? The shaman feigned a smile. A nervous smile. *He must like to tease.* Akrylla wished it were true. She wished all he said was just a tease. She wished it true on Ekkon the Wanderer who had already helped so much this time.

~New moon

Riddik shifted the unclean blade to just beside Vey's heart, then pulled her dress down on the same shoulder, baring her breast.

"NO!" Akrylla cried. She raised her palms. Her voice was desperate. "Stop."

But Riddik wouldn't stop. Sneering, he cut into Vey's flesh. Akrylla jolted towards him, but Ang lashed at the shaman's legs with her spear and knocked them out from under her. Akrylla fell, face to the dirt. She raised her head slowly, eyes fixed on the point of Ang's spear in front of her face. The cold steel nicked the skin between her eyes, then Ang withdrew it slightly.

"One wrong move," threatened Ang the Bitch. Gutless Kori's fiendish gaze locked on Akrylla as he held her Vey still.

Akrylla froze, while Riddik continued to do what he does best. He cut into the pristine and tender flesh of her Vey. Akrylla shifted her gaze to read Vey's expression. She saw her apprentice flinch slightly. But Vey did not wake. Akrylla began to sob.

"I benumbed her too much," she cried.

Ang inched her spear closer. "Shut your hole, Hag."

Akrylla squeezed her eyes shut. *I can't look.*

The shaman moaned and turned away.

~LOOK

Akrylla hearkened to the voice inside her. She hearkened and she watched and she choked on the misery that welled up within. *My perfect apprentice.*

~Remember

Akrylla burned into memory the trickles of blood that ran down Vey's chest, soaking into the red dress that she wore. *Pretty red dress.* Then she pleaded with Riddik again.

"Put down the knife. Put down the knife. I have more to give."

The Cutter turned his head, stared coldly into Akrylla's eyes. He steadied his dagger, tip balanced on the middle of the carving he'd made in his victim's flesh. He balanced the tip just above her heart.

Holding Vey's limp form in his dark, furry arms, Gutless Kori shifted his stance. The motion pressed the point of the dagger into the redhead's delicate skin. A drop of blood beaded, trickled down. The Cutter raised the palm of his free hand and made as though to punch the dagger through her rib cage.

"NO!" Akrylla wailed, loud enough to wake the dead, or at least startle Ang the Bitch.

Ang stumbled back. Akrylla took the opportunity to scramble to her knees, in defiance of Ang's spear.

~Favor

She crawled towards Riddik.

"Put it down. I will do anything," she said. Ang flicked her spear at the shaman, slicing into her dirt-streaked cheek. *She likes to cut too.* Akrylla hissed back. Blood streaming down her face, she pleaded again to Riddik. But with a stronger voice this time, one with authority. *He likes to see some backbone.*

"I will give you what is rightfully yours, Riddik the Cutter." She shot Ang a spite-filled glance. "Together, we will teach this bitch what a woman's body is for, in the presence of such a majestic beast."

Riddik sneered.

I have his attention. "I know how she spurns you."

Ang moved to cut Akrylla again, but the shaman scuttled behind Riddik.

"No," Riddik said, raising a firm hand to the demoness.

Akrylla raised the stakes. "I have ways to make her listen and obey," she said slyly. The shaman shifted to a low stance, ready to react.

"Witch!" Ang lunged at her. Akrylla shoved the neck of the spear down, drove it into the dirt. Then she grabbed the shaft.

"NO!" Riddik shouted, his voice as sharp and jagged as the rusty dagger he held. Ang froze. She swung her gaze to the Cutter, narrowed eyes searching for the cue to finish the job.

"Save this witch for me," he commanded.

Ang gasped in disbelief. She shook her head in disgust at Riddik, but nonetheless withdrew her spear and stepped away. Gutless Kori let out a growl. The Cutter regarded the beast, signaling with a nod. The Wulver began to drag Vey away like she was a sack of meat, one long forelimb locked around her neck.

Riddik snapped at him. "GENTLY."

Gutless Kori's ears flattened to his head. He hesitated, grunted, then adjusted his grip to under her arms. Vey's heels dragged in the dirt as he pulled her towards the surrounding woods. She lost a shoe in the process.

~Dominate

Akrylla rose to her full stature. She eyed the wolfish Outlander's every move. *Yessums, I can manipulate that one if he knows I have pull with Riddik.* To test her theory, she called out to the brute. She used a loud, firm tone, the kind she would use on a misbehaving dog. "DON'T spoil her," she warned. "Or you will pay dearly… Gutless." The Wulver continued on without acknowledging her plea.

"Do as she says," Riddik said.

Akrylla grinned.

But Gutless Kori was not as obedient as she'd thought. The beast dropped Vey to the ground where he stood, not far from where he'd dragged the half-giant earlier. He dropped her hard, as though to make a point of it.

"No use to me then," he grumbled. The Wulver fell to all fours, then lumbered into the woods.

~Favor

Akrylla offered Riddik what he wanted again, right there in plain view, in the middle of the trail. She wasn't sure if he would accept this time, but the burly scrapper was pumped up by all the fighting and the strong-arming. He accepted. Out of the corner of her eye, she spotted Gutless Kori creeping back to watch. Ang stared gaping in disgust at the two as they carried on.

The witch gave Riddik more than he wanted, more than even he could take, and on the sly she smiled at the two who were curious. Gutless Kori slunk over to Ang at one point. She rejected his advance with a firm backhand to the snout.

~Jealousy

When Akrylla finished with Riddik, she left him lying on the trail, paralyzed with elation. Without hesitation, she approached the two who had watched on; the two who had gotten nothing. Ang surprised her. Although the demoness would have none of Riddik and none of Kori, her cocked head and inquisitive expression betrayed her interest. Without a word, the demoness thrusted her spear into the ground and came near.

Akrylla obliged. Rummaging through her satchel, she pulled out an erotic salve she'd been saving. With shy uncertainty, Ang removed some of her armor. She loosened, unbuttoned, and untucked her clothing. She allowed Akrylla to rub the salve into her skin, just to get her started. And as Akrylla did so, with slow and rhythmic motions, the shaman whispered into Ang's ears. She whispered the many secret ways of applying an erotic salve to oneself. Ang's eyes widened. She moaned, then collapsed gently to the ground. Akrylla placed the salve container in the palm of Ang's hand and left her to writhe in ecstasy.

Gutless Kori came at Akrylla last, growling and overexcited. Although barely human, his human desires were intact. He diverted and went for Ang first, humping like a dog. She spurned him again, redirected his advance to Akrylla. But the Wulver must've finished before he started.

A hard line to cross anyway, Akrylla thought, as relieved as she ever could be, *even for a shaman.*

When Kori's advance was over with, the witch slipped the beast a brew she kept in a small vial, to soothe his stomach. A salve would be wasted on him. *He'd make a valuable ally though,* she thought, if she could win him over. She pooled the vial's contents in her palm. He sniffed it first, then lopped it up.

Riddik scowled loudly and sneered malevolently when he realized what the others had received. Ang challenged him, asked why he cared. Riddik called her a "demon bitch" and stormed past her. He knocked Akrylla to the ground, vehemently grabbed a fistful of her hair, and forced her prone. Then he drew the second blade that he carried, of the same pitted yet sturdy steel, but longer than the dagger and with a wicked curve to it. Ang and Kori backed away.

He's just adding depth, Akrylla was sure, when she felt him press the knifepoint into the skin of her back. He'd carved her there before. He ran the edge over the very same tracings, and then branched out.

Ang mocked him. "Do you think you're some kind of artist?"

Riddik grunted in response as he pressed down with firmity. Akrylla bit down hard on her lip, until she tasted blood. But the shaman didn't beg for mercy. She wouldn't. In fact, she barely resisted. Instead, she reached deep inside herself to find a way to take this pain just like the last pain, and the pain before that. Just like all the pain. The immense pain she always carried, ever since… *It isn't the first time and it won't be the last. Ekkon's curse.*

~Accept

I do accept, Akrylla told herself. And somehow, that made everything different. Akrylla discovered a power lurking in her endurance, a power for the taking, a power to be harnessed by a witch like her. So, she took the pain and turned it into something different. She took the pain and twisted it around her. The scarred, bloodied shaman drank in the fire of her pain like summer wine. She even rolled it into words. Words of revenge, in waiting. Words of witchery. Words of curse.

~Retribution

In her mind, Akrylla heard a chant:

Cut the Cutter the way he cuts me.

Cut the Cutter, I will, I will.

Cut the Cutter where the sun never shines.

Put it in a brew. Put it in a brew.
Get rid of Riddik. Rid of Riddik. Rid of Riddik.
Cut the Cutter where the sun never shines.

CHAPTER XX
THE 5TH
(Hadamard, Crusher)

H ADAMARD STEPPED INTO the wash of red light beyond the COM Center's double doors, Nekenezitter two clicks behind. A long moment passed before the luminary's eyes adjusted to the dimness. Diagonal and to his left, the main assembler's sands were bright, lively and active. Wisps of forested lands and rolling hills dominated the scene taking shape, confined as though by invisible walls. *Another creation of Anya's*, thought Hadamard. He marveled at the detail achieved by one whose visits to Theia could be counted in the tens. Anya was the only one present in the main chamber, in deep concentration and busy projecting away from one of the stations behind the assembler. *I doubt she even noticed us enter.*

Hadamard gestured to Nekenezitter, pointed him to the right instead. The Gloom nodded. They made their way past the glowing wall sconces and then a training station, arriving at the door to Hadamard's study. It stood ajar and bursts of colored light filtered out around the edges. The luminary creaked it open.

Slivers of structural glace crunched underfoot as they entered the study—a converted back-room storage area of the building. An unexpected sweetness hung in the stuffy air. It numbed the brain, like fresh glue. The Gloom beside him let out an exploratory chirr.

Hadamard sighed at the jumbled mess around him: broken furnishings, books strewn about, rows of unorganized shelves overflowing with odds and ends. Shiro beetles wandered at will. He sighed again. *A work in progress,* he reminded himself.

The luminary quickly spotted his disassembled staff atop a low, three-legged cabinet, near the door. His shoulders dropped at once—a stack of extremely valuable, hand-scribed tomes subbed for the cabinet's fourth leg. He'd brought them from Gan on his first trip in, gifts for the Seventh Kaedan archives. Hadamard scrubbed his face, shook his head. *I should've known better,* he scolded himself. *No archives on this rock.*

The staff itself lay in two pieces, with the deepwood shaft front and center on a custom stand, sporting a new metal gleam which Hadamard recognized to be Jhinyari metal. Behind it, his dual elemental stone sat cradled in a new and elaborate setting. As he watched, the charm flared up again in its unique way. Two confined points of light flashed and danced: one pale red and the other yellow.

"I think he's gone and done it," Hadamard whispered to Nekenezitter.

The Gloom sniffed at the air, trilled softly. "There is alchemical odor about <click>."

Hadamard nodded. "A bonding agent," he remarked, "for the staff."

With a gentle touch, Nekenezitter shut the door behind them. The pair made their way through the clutter towards the workbench against the back wall of the study. Crusher sat hunched, laboring away with his back to them, silvery-white hair spilling over his shoulders. The tabletop held an assortment of colored jars and powders, glace implements, rags, and a small scale. Crusher held a tube of red liquid between two fingers, steadily administering one drop at a time to the hinged bowl in front of him. It was filled with a thick, gooey substance.

"Crusher"—short for Crushermaserann Taerix—had a wiry, minimalist look to him. Although young for a projectionist, his talents had already elevated him to the status of savant, even by his people's high standards. Hadamard had every intention of making the projectionist an offer to work at the Crimson Tower, when the time seemed right.

Prime Lumen Forsetti had already pre-authorized the move. The luminary smirked to himself when he thought of the inevitable by-product that would follow. *Finally,* he thought, *the missing 5th Institute will come into being. Almost like a prophesy.* The Tower had initially labeled its existing eight institutes one through four, skipped the fifth due to a ridiculous clerical error, and then six through nine. That error had persisted for a hundred years.

The 5th, Hadamard repeated mentally. *And none too soon.* The Crimson Tower needed to harness Djinxarai knowledge to give the enforcers of the 1st Institute the edge they'd need to stave off Harrow's technological pursuits, while at the same time equalizing the playing field with the Jhinyari. The luminary intended to explore the possibilities further with Crusher over his stay, fitting in the necessary experiments whenever he could. Hadamard waited until he felt the Djinxarai was done his task before addressing him.

"Crusher?" The projectionist ignored the prompting for a long minute, his steady hand stirring the bowl's contents. Hadamard waited patiently. Finally, Crusher breathed a sigh of relief, regarded his visitors.

"The consistency has to be just right," he informed Hadamard. "When Jhin gifted us with such wondrous ingredients, he could not have foreseen the delicacy of preparing them or combining them for such a purpose. It is too minor a thing. One substance in particular—in the red jars—is a deadly injury poison. One scratch and…" He turned back to his apparatus, snapped the lid of the bowl shut, then snapped shut the lids of the open jars.

Crusher leaned back in his chair, casually locked his hands together behind his head. "But it is done now." He glanced to the Gloom beside him, who'd scurried over to peer over his shoulder. "Hello, Nek. Wasn't expecting you."

"<click> By the order of Lord Ralador, <trill> I am to attend all manner of activities relating to remote psionica kinetics <tic>." The Gloom's response was predictable. Hadamard had heard it a dozen times over.

"Is that what this is?" Crusher shifted his gaze to the luminary. "Lumen Hadamard, so glad you could make it."

"Honored to be here," Hadamard replied. "No easy task, I'll tell you." He gestured to the study door. "Near the entrance... I see you've made progress."

"The staff. Yes. Much progress." The Djinxarai pivoted sideways in his chair, began his usual process for rising to a standing position. Hadamard resisted the urge to help.

"I've since added the white metal of Ironeagle, as we discussed." Crusher pushed himself to his feet, reached for his crutches, then grunted as he tucked them under his armpits. "As you suspected, Lumen Hadamard, it's the same metal the Jhinyari work for their silver swords—this according to the word of a master smith from the Caves of Andulus, who analyzed a sample of both metals."

Nek trilled. His eyes went wide. "The white metal interaction with the slider charm <tic> is what the strikers use to cut through space <click>."

Crusher nodded to the Gloom. "Not just strikers; Jhinyari blades as well—minus the charms." He lowered his eyes. "Jhin's bane, white metal is, for it led to his downfall. But he will rise again, stronger for it." Crusher regarded Hadamard. "I placed the staff out in the open to cure, where the air circulation is greatest. It should be ready soon."

"Lead the way," Hadamard said, ushering him forward with a wave.

Crusher abhorred the thought of being in the way. Seventh Kaeda was nothing if not riddled with winding, narrow passages and steep stairways. Too many times he'd heard the huffs and puffs of those unfortunate enough to be caught behind him. And this spin cycle was shaping up to be a heavy one; his left hip was hurting something awful. *Every time I put weight on it...*

Crusher grunted as he shifted his stance. "I should restore the workbench to the way I found it," he told the Theians. "Please, go ahead without me. I won't be long." He forced a grin. It came out like a grimace.

Lumen Hadamard looked him over, then responded. "Gription weighing you down, Crusher?"

"I'm much more graceful in low Gs," he responded.

"Well, I wasn't exactly dancing either when the shift came—suddenly felt like I had lead boots on. I was waiting for the lift to arrive when things went heavy." Hadamard chuckled. "This damn armor's heavy enough too, and hot as hell. We'll meet you up front, Crusher. Nek and I have a few things to discuss anyway, and it'll give me a chance to shed this bulk for a while." He slapped his shoulder pauldrons, then made the same ushering gesture to the Gloom. "Nek, after you."

With two clicks, the Gloom accepted the prompting and the pair were well on their way back to the entrance. The projectionist shut his eyes tight, grit his teeth. He'd been putting aside the pain shooting up his spine, bearing it as best he could. *Stay on task, Taerix,* he urged himself. He'd sat too still for too long. *It'll only get worse if you stop moving.*

As Crusher's hands worked to tidy up the workbench, he could hear the Theians voices going on about the staff, the white metal, and the oddities of elemental stones. Lumen Hadamard's tone had changed with his diminutive companion in comparison to earlier visits—more conversational and academic; less biting and degrading. In the past, he'd called the Gloom a spy, a snitch, in the way… and several colorful phrases from beyond the Rim that Crusher didn't recognize, but that he knew carried negative connotations.

He wiped the last of the glace implements, hung them on the pegs above the table. His eyes scanned the work space for anything out of place. *Much better,* he thought. Then, one crutch at a time, Crusher shifted his body to a "go" position—favoring his right leg—and turned towards the main aisle. He swung himself forward, landing on his thin but rigid legs, then advanced the crutches. He rounded a corner then swung forward again. The Djinxarai repeated the process, past the many rows of items needing repair and the strange goods from outside the realm, until he reached the front of the study. The luminary and the crown advisor stood to either side of the staff, talking over it while the embedded charm sparked on and off. Hadamard stood slightly hunched in his dark red robe with gold trim. Nekenezitter—dwarfed by the man—was garbed in a comparably drab, brown robe of sturdy material. Hadamard's discarded armor now hung by the door. He finished his sentence to the Gloom… something about the mechanics of timepieces. Then they both swung their gazes to Crusher.

Crusher regarded Hadamard. "Is this what you imagined?" he asked.

Lumen Hadamard rubbed his dark beard, shifted his gaze to the shaft and the setting. He eyed the new creations up and down. Crusher couldn't help but feel a pang of nervousness, a slight rolling in the pit of his stomach. It was as though he, personally, bore the scrutiny of Hadamard's measuring stare.

The Djinxarai re-angled his crutches, shifted his weight to look over his handiwork as well—the object of countless hours of toil. He'd never invested so much time in a *thing to be owned* before. Theians seemed to value gems and metal and the mysterious deepwood greatly. Crusher was still getting used to this concept of ownership. His people shared everything. Items of all kinds were created simply to be used when needed, by whoever needed them the most. *How else would we have survived, with so little to go around? Jhin foresaw this great need to depend on one another, and it is by His will that we live thus.*

Crusher addressed the two of them. "The white metal setting and the coiled strip that wraps around the shaft arrived by glideboat only yesterday. Stout metallurgists at Ironeagle did the forging, based on my designs. Only a Jhinyari weaponsmith could have done better. Unfortunately, my people know little of Jhin metallurgy—that gift the betrayers took with them and never shared, nor would they."

Hadamard asked, "And the bonding agent?"

"My own formula," Crusher replied, "a substance I derived from… what you would call *exotic fungi.*"

The luminary completed the thought. "Fungus that grows only in the Dark Zone."

Crusher nodded. "As far as I know, yes. A blossoming of Jhin's very flesh." Leaning heavily to his right on a single crutch, Crusher freed his left hand and reached for the elemental stone's metallic setting. He'd chosen a flame-like design with elegantly curved prongs to protect the shrouded elemental stone. "The current setting is still an interim solution. I plan to replace the metal with something more protective and at the same time translucent for when the dual charm is evoked to shine bright. Something glace… the Greys are working on it." He offered the set stone to the luminary. Hadamard grasped the piece, rotated it slowly in his hands.

"Impressive. When will the staff be ready?"

"I have a sealant to apply," Crusher said, "after the bonding agent has fully cured. Two, maybe three spins, depending on interruptions."

Gently, Hadamard put the setting back in its place. With a furrowed brow, he eyed the deepwood shaft again, wrapped in its white metal helix. He began to nod slowly. "Not bad," he stated, then turned to address the projectionist directly. His expression softened. A grin began to form. "Masterful, I should say."

Filling his chest and flooding his thoughts, a feeling of immense pride welled up in Crusher. Relief poured over him. *Master Nab will be so pleased to hear the Theian is satisfied.* The project was a top priority to the Jhin Masters.

"Well done, Crusher. Really," Hadamard went on. "You've outdone yourself. Our 2nd Institute alchemists will be impressed." He hesitated. "On a related topic, I'd like to see the mimic you came up with for the staff trials before I get back to Diamond Saber preparations. We should be able to sneak in an experiment some time after everyone departs. I'll make an excuse to stay late. That is… if you think your projection is ready."

"The scene is very simple," Crusher said.

"All the better," Hadamard responded.

"Very well." The projectionist swung his body forward, towards the door. "Come," he beckoned. "I will show you what I have so far, using the Mini. It won't take long." The Theians followed him out of the study to the training station—a private area sectioned off from the main control room. Crusher heard his twin's voice in the next room discussing terrain references for Diamond Saber with a male Theian. *One of the understudies,* he surmised. Crusher glanced to the COM Center's double doors. *Good, wide open, just as I had left them.* That would make visualization easy—he could build the mimic right outside the doorway. *With the staff not yet ready though, the Theians will have to use their imaginations.* He hoped that wouldn't impede them the way it had in the past.

The small operating station held the scaled down version of the main assembler. The "Mini" was basically for practice, demonstrations, or just messing around or trying out new ideas. Like any other station, it could be tied into the main assembler's common operating model with a simple, willful thought. *Another wonder of Jhin.*

Crusher positioned himself in front of the setup. In appearance, it was little more than a basin of sand enclosed in a translucent glace box, rounded at the corners. But to a Djinxarai such as himself, the simplistic device illustrated how his people connected with and manipulated matter in the Otherworldly Realm. *The essence of Jhin's legacy,* thought Crusher, as he reached down into his psyche and honed in on the Divide. The instant he found it, it swallowed itself. And from the void left in the wake of its departure, a churning gateway blossomed into existence. It filled the back of his mind. *Opening.* He basked in the rush of energy that poured through. Thus enshrouded, Crusher brought up the sands. The Theians in the room watched in awe as the first grains swirled into the air, suspended. Crusher kept an ear tuned to their hushed voices as he shaped his ideas into proto-realities. Lumen Hadamard was explaining something to the crown advisor about transmuter charms, which piqued Crusher's interest. And as the projectionist focused his mind on the test scenario to play out, Hadamard's voice took on a hollow quality, as though in a tunnel.

"Based on the sum of luminary experiences," Hadamard explained to Nek, "once a bond has been formed between stone and master, the effects are triggered by raw emotions or sensations."

Yes, Theians, thought Crusher. *This is how Jhin meant for us to connect with the world around us—you are just discovering that? We must feel the ebbs and flows of the Common Will, we must sense every vibration.* Crusher began to mold the sands into fixed structures. One by one the grains deposited.

The voices of the Theians faded. The sands took on their wispy shapes. Crusher had become immersed.

As the sands of the Mini began forming into recognizable shapes, Hadamard swung his gaze to the doorway. Once again, the shiro beetles of Jhin bled into the dome from all directions. They bled in and coalesced just outside the building. Clambering on top of one another, a mimic began to build in front of his eyes, layer by layer. Hadamard glanced back to the swirling sands, glimpsed the diffuse image of the target state. *A soldier,* thought Hadamard. *He's chosen a queensman.*

Crusher had conjured up an early, primitive model. A sensible choice, since a queensman mimic is outfitted to carry a sword and hence could just as easily carry a staff.

When the beetles settled into place, the mimic stood only five feet tall. It was absurdly thin—more like a Djinxarai—with a complexion the shining black of a typical beetle. Its lifeless eyes were the dull white of a rarer subgroup of the species that lacked in pigmentation. *Minimal,* thought Hadamard. Once the beetles locked in, Crusher put the mimic through a few simple motions: marching, stepping, thrusting—all of the basic movements needed in Hadamard's newly approved experimental plan with the staff.

"This will do," Hadamard called to Crusher, wondering if he'd processed the words. "Yes, this will do very nicely."

The sands collapsed at once. The mimic dismantled.

Crusher seemed to recover quickly from his tranced state. There were other times, after long and grueling runs, when he'd nearly fallen over.

The Gloom beside Hadamard let out an uncertain chirr. This demonstration marked the first time he'd actually been inside the COM Center during a projection. Normally, he'd be outside observing the action.

"Nek," Hadamard said, "we need to sort out that time discrepancy you discovered. Tell Crusher what you told me, your observation that since the striker trials began, timelines don't match up with the outside world." He regarded Crusher. "It's been driving Nek here mad. I think it might connect with our staff experiments."

Nekenezitter filled in the details. "Yes <click>. This difference is real and measurable <clack>. I calibrated two timepieces in good working order, <tic> left one in my quarters <clack> and brought the other here during the trials. When I returned to Theia, <click> the clock in my quarters was behind by over six hours <tic>. Somehow, I am six hours older because I visited the Netherdome that one day. I suspect Hadamard is as many hours older as well."

Crusher said, "What exactly did you do in the Netherdome, before you discovered the discrepancy?"

Hadamard answered for the Gloom. "Just striker replications. But during that visit, you brought Nek and me *into* the projection for the first time. We observed the replications play out one after another in succession. Nek tallied the results. That was instead of us simply spectating—staying outside the runs the way we usually do and letting you quickly play them all out and tell us what happened. Remember? At first, I thought you were just executing the runs slower for us, but Nek's measurements tell us that, somehow, that isn't quite right…"

Crusher shrugged. "Of course," he said, as though it were obvious. "Did you expect something different?" He appeared nonchalant, unimpressed. "Yes, the runs are happening all at once when you look at them from the outside. That cannot be helped. When I bring you in, your perceptions realign so that you observe the runs one at a time, and in no particular order. I don't know how to explain, exactly. More time is… happening… but you're not seeing it the way I do: two-way. You only see it one way, one direction. That's just the way your brain works, I suppose… the way you're built, or taught. Maybe with some effort, you could learn to see things the way I do."

"Two-way time?" All of a sudden, Hadamard felt like the grasping prospect. "Forwards and backwards?"

Crusher responded with a so-so nod. "Two directions, yes, but *both* moving forward."

Hadamard rubbed his face with his hands, struggling to understand.

Nekenezitter buzzed in. "<click> This is just… <tic> natural to you, somehow?"

Crusher nodded. "For a projectionist, yes, and some others. You see, Jhin tore a strip out of space and stretched it into light. He joined it to all things confined to the Great Barrier that surrounds us. He even wrapped his children, the Djinxarai, in its glowing tendrils, and infused long life. That same light is familiar to you. It pulses in the Starshine and it flickers within the Hurlorn charms you have brought from the forest to Seventh Kaeda. They are bound, as one, in this respect. I'm surprised you don't know that."

Hadamard, at a loss for words, contemplated Crusher's explanation carefully.

CHAPTER XXI
THE COMING OF THE FIRST MEN

P RECIOUS FEW EVEN *among the colossi can tell of the arrival of the First Men. Under the veil of a new moon, starlight pin-pricking the heavens, the survivors washed up on the fateful shores of Fortune Bay—a few thousand souls of the old world's finest. Across the bay's dark waters, they spotted fires on the rocky peninsula. Seeking all that those without a home tend to seek, the First Men skirted the shoreline and came upon the people who dwelt there. They recognized the small group, numbering hundreds, as the Abindohns, whom they'd set out with on a shared journey, not long ago.*

But the First Men were mistaken, for the tribe had belonged to Theia for eons beyond count. The two groups could barely communicate. Over time, they came to know one another's story. Over time, the First Men learned that, in a sense, they were not wholly wrong in their initial assumption, for those they'd set out with could only be the tribe's lost ancestors.

The newly-arrived survivors settled on the north shore of the bay. They chose an interim leader and made hasteful preparations for the coming winter. "Steward" Taradin, the natural choice to lead, the one they'd all followed on the path from certain doom, sent divers into the chill waters to recover useful items from their displaced city, now submerged at the bottom of the bay. Salvaging what they could and respecting their neighbor's wishes to not disturb the forests, the First Men worked the recovered scrap metal and the resident limestone to build Akeda. Winter came and went. Every man, woman and child had survived, but the new city that rose from the vestiges of the old one lacked a future just the same, for every potential new life in Akeda ended in a stillborn babe.

Fine minds labored night and day over the problem. Old-world tomes, salt-stained, water-stained, and rotting away, were copied by scribes, ever in demand, and deposited in a massive archive. Labs were raised and mechanized equipment manufactured to support them. The power of sun, sea, and wind was harnessed. But the settlers' ingenuity did not suffice: their designs, their labs, and their machines were to no avail. Another winter passed.

Childless, Akeda remained. Worse, over seventy perished in a blizzard that lasted a week.

Yet, across the bay and along the river Malevuin, the mystical Abindohn tribe lived as they had for years uncounted. They told the settlers stories of fulsome lives and small numbers of children, just enough to sustain their population. A spiritual people first and hunters second, they also spoke of unbreakable bonds to all living things, bonds to the living rock and to the sea, bonds to the winds that blustered across the bay, and even bonds to another world where everything floats. The Abindohns grew crops in the flats and fished the bay in narrow boats, content to dwell in simple huts throughout the entire year, exposed to the harsh climate. All this without a grumble or protest, and without loss.

Later that year, before the next winter, everything changed. Torn by discord, the bay descended into chaos.

—Stonebones Clergy,
History of the Bay

CHAPTER XXII
DIAMOND SABER
(Amot)

APART FROM THE "old school" Wilder paint on his face—half-hidden by a grizzled black and grey speckled beard—the man briefing the room was barely recognizable to Amot. The scout was a young teen when last he'd seen his father's good friend, and the years had not been kind to Feleg. He dressed the same, like anyone you might find wandering the streets of Fort Abandon or Harrow. But with the bags beneath his eyes clearly visible and his body trapped somewhere between middle-aged and worked-to-death, he came off more worn out than most. He seemed shorter too, now that Amot was no longer a child, and he'd lost most of his hair. Despite it all, Feleg was still as gritty and down-to-earth as ever, and his manner of speaking was still fast changing and clever. And if Amot let his mind stray for even a moment, the chuckling of his Kith brothers would draw him back in again, about some off remark he'd missed.

The ex-Kith puffed out his barrel of a chest while he shared his views on the be-all and end-all of the coming exercise, waving his hands around as though they were the punctuation marks for his words. His arms looked small in comparison to the rest of his body. Feleg's voice was hoarse and he sounded as though he was always on the verge of clearing his throat. Yet some quality of tone or reverberance made you trust every word he said.

Amot sat in the midst of a dozen or so rows of chairs, near center aisle. Vil'nyan sat beside him, her leg casually brushing up against his. Every so often when Feleg's eyes shifted elsewhere, she leaned over to whisper some comment into Amot's ear. Weeks had gone by since he'd last seen her and she rubbed it in by looking great. She'd tanned well over the last days of summer, giving her a healthy and vibrant presence impossible to resist. Her midnight-black hair flowed over her shoulders. Amot felt more than a pang of guilt for not having written to her while they were apart. If she minded, she didn't let on about it and seemed genuinely excited to be together again.

The drill hall was packed full of Kith and Queen's Guards mainly, together with a mix of luminaries and understudies, regular forces, a few spearmaidens and others involved in Diamond Saber. Dignitaries occupied the two front rows. The queensmen, spearmaidens and regulars were in uniform, together outnumbering the rangers about four to one. The Kith wore their usual leathers and ranger attire, while the luminary types and others dressed in everyday clothes.

Feleg was well-known to everyone present save the newest recruits, by name if not by face. His reputation preceded him. He'd run the guts of nearly every experiment and training exercise going until this latest round. And as a young ranger, the greybeards contend that he'd had a hand in nearly every skirmish or battle from the Scarsands to Ironeagle Peak. That was until, after a serious injury in his middle years, he'd gotten mixed up in Wild thaumaturgy. After that, he never looked back. And now, as the rumors go, he puts his efforts towards work in areas that few can even make mention of.

The ex-Kith went on about how ridiculous an experiment named *Obsidian Rapier* had seemed to him when he was first approached to partake in it, years ago. And how he'd scoffed when a presumptuous luminary tried to explain to him a wild assumption about extraordinary Jhinyari abilities that appeared to go against the laws of physics and common sense.

"I told him that the records could not be taken at face value,"

Feleg said to the assembly, "and that there was too much confusion and contradiction among the accounts to make any sense out of them whatsoever... but that luminary proved me wrong."

Feleg paused to retrieve a pair of spectacles out of his shirt pocket, then proceeded to put them on.

"He can only mean Hadamard," Vil'nyan whispered.

Amot nodded in response. He knew the name well enough.

Feleg adjusted his glasses just right, strode over to a small table at the front of the room. "Listen to these accounts," he said, picking up a short, thick book from the table. "They concern the initial onslaught when the Jhinyari attacked Fortune Bay, of historical record." He flipped through the book's contents, eventually settling on a page near the back cover. He cleared his throat and read aloud.

"'They came out of nowhere and seemed to be everywhere,' was how one person put it," he started, then scanned the page for another fragment. "'Their bright swords flashed out of nowhere,' another said." Feleg flipped through a few more pages. "Ahh... here's one: 'They would strike fast and then disappear.'" He looked up to his audience, eyes peering over the rims of his glasses. They were mounted on a halfway slide down the bridge of his nose. "You all remember the stories. The Jhinyari had taken the Akedans completely by surprise."

"These accounts seem rather consistent with what you might expect for a surprise attack," he continued, "all things considered. Don't they?" Many in the room nodded. "But did you notice anything odd about them?"

Feleg casually strolled down the aisles of the drill hall while his question hung in the air. He moved at just the right pace to hide the stiffness in his gait. The grig studied the faces of those he passed, then singled out a queensman.

"Is that how you would plan a surprise attack?" Feleg said to him. The man was the typical sort among his unit: clean-cut, athletic, and with an air of sophistication about him. He wore a chain shirt bearing the gemmed crown sigil of his order.

"That would be dishonorable," the man replied. "We, the Queen's Guard, would proudly display our banners, announce our intentions, and provide our adversary with an immediate opportunity to surrender or parley. Barring resolution, we would then charge forth and neutralize the enemy elements, in a manner dictated by a well thought out battle plan, leaving non-combatants out of the fray."

"Well said," a comrade uttered. A subdued cheer erupted among the queensmen, heads nodding in approval. His back was soon well patted.

"Indeed," Feleg said. "Well, we know it wasn't the Queen's Guard that attacked Fortune Bay then, don't we?" There was some scattered laughter, during which time Feleg made brief eye contact with a prominent luminary. A knowing look passed between them. Then he moved on.

"One account never quite seemed to fit with the rest," Feleg said next, addressing the room. He flipped through the pages again. "It was written years later by a survivor of that attack. She was a child at the time, hidden in underbrush alongside the main road running north of Akeda. She'd stayed hidden and watched others flee across the road, wondering if she should do the same but too afraid to venture out into the open. Then the slaughter started, right there in front of her." Feleg found his mark and began to read another passage.

"'The desperate runners began to fall,' is what she wrote. 'No Jhinyari were in sight... only bright swords hanging in mid-air that would appear and then disappear like flashes of light, cutting people down as they fled. I had to look away.'"

Feleg tilted his gaze up, scanned the room. He let the silence of the moment creep into the thoughts of those listening.

"Hanging in mid-air," he repeated. "In fact, the attackers themselves are not specifically described at all until some time after the first wave of the attack, when the battle was already won for all intents and purposes."

"Nope," Feleg shook his head as he continued, "that one account never sat well with me. That one account is out of sorts with all the others, yet potentially explains something about them all—the insightful anomaly."

Vil'nyan spoke up. "I've read them all and I noticed that too," she said. "But children are prone to make-believe and exaggerations. They say a lot of things that don't make sense. She was young, confused, and people around her were dying. But, if you were to take her description as valid, then it can only mean one thing: camouflage—I still say it had to be camouflage."

Feleg met her gaze. "I'm sure you *have* read all of the accounts," he said, "and I know your opinion." Then he looked to his audience. "This is Vil'nyan," he said to the room, "my current apprentice and a luminary hopeful."

"Just a prospect for now," she said, "but I hope to be confirmed before Diamond Saber is finished."

Feleg approached Vil'nyan, his faltering step showing itself—a firm but ever-present limp. And as he did so, he encouraged her to explain herself. He rolled his hands in the air, as if to coax the words out of her.

"It's like the cloaks of the Wild Elderkin," she added.

"Ah yes, perhaps," Feleg said in return, meeting her wide eyes. "And drawing on great speed, great numbers, or both, I suppose. Have you ever tried to keep track of a ranger wearing one of those cloaks?"

"Only one," Vil'nyan said, with a crooked smirk. Her knee knocked against Amot's knee. She shot the ranger a sideways glance.

"Well, is it difficult?" Feleg said.

"At first," she replied, "especially in the woods with dense cover… it can be very difficult."

"How about while this fellow of yours is standing in the middle of a road," Feleg said, gesturing to Amot, "with an unobstructed view, in plain daylight, and close by?"

"Not hard at all," she conceded.

Feleg stole a glance at Amot. A greeting passed between the two. The old Wilder had known Amot's father well, his grandfather, and Amot himself as a child and young teen. He flicked his eyes to Vil'nyan for a moment, then back again. Amot responded with a childish smirk. Feleg winked at him before turning away. Casually, the grig strolled front and center, turned and faced the hall. He started a new topic.

"Obsidian Rapier was an *experiment*, to test a new concept," he said, "a new type of weapon that defies all logic—queensman logic especially. Crazy, yes, but the test was a complete success. And now we have new questions to answer… many new questions." Feleg snapped shut the book he was carrying, held it up for all to see. It was bound in red leather. "Questions far beyond what the contents of this book can answer." He strolled over to the small table near the front and left the book to rest on it. Then he removed his glasses, folded them, and stuffed them into his shirt pocket.

"Many questions," he reiterated. Feleg let the quiet linger again as he limped down the central aisle with his slow step, studying the faces of the audience, gauging each one as he passed. A queensman coughed. Amot craned his neck and watched as the grig made his way to the eighth row of the dozen, before turning back. He halted near the front, then turned to face the crowd. Feleg stood motionless for long moment, arms hanging casually to either side. Then he raised a fist to his mouth and cleared his throat. It didn't seem to do much good. When he started speaking again, his voice was as gruff as ever.

"The scenarios in Obsidian Rapier were too simple to provide conclusive answers about how to use these new dancing swords," he explained, "and who should wield them. So now, it's time for us to accomplish just that: to replicate the reality of the combat environment that Akeda faced in the past—that Gan may someday face—and to discover those answers."

A queensman coughed again, barely disguising the words "Queen's Guard" in his voice. Others around him chuckled.

Amot huffed, glanced over to Vil'nyan. She took one look at him, bumped him with her elbow and whispered in his ear, "Clearly, they feel entitled."

"They're all that way," he whispered back, loud enough so his Kith brothers could hear.

Feleg grimaced, then mumbled: "Some have yet to accept the true meaning of that reality." He shook off the queensman's veiled remark and raised his voice, intonating as he spoke. "Diamond Saber, unlike Rapier, is an *exercise*. I cannot stress enough the importance of this event. What happens here will inform the decisions that dictate how we will defend our forest realm and how we will meet our enemies in battle."

A hush came over the crowd.

"The objective here is to validate the effectiveness of *strikers* in different roles, plain and simple." Feleg paused. When he started again, he emphasized every word: "*These weapons are like no others, I guarantee you that. A full description will have to wait… this hall is not cleared.*" He turned his gaze Amot's way, addressed the scout's girl.

"Even Vil'nyan, who is involved in the striker program, does not know the full extent of their capabilities. I suspect she may change her mind about what is behind the accounts I've just read to you, once she finds out." Whispers rose up among the ranks, and Feleg let his words sink in for a long moment.

Vil'nyan leaned over to Amot, whispered a quiet question to him. "Where do they get these names? They don't make any sense to me. 'Obsidian Rapier'—no one makes a rapier out of obsidian. And 'Diamond Saber'—that's just impossible."

Amot grinned to himself for knowing the answer, despite this being his first field exercise.

"They pick a precious stone and then a weapon of some kind," he replied. Amot skipped over the fact that he'd just asked Berendt the very same question on the journey in. "The value of the gemstone speaks to the game size or importance. The weapon part is alphabetical."

"What weapon starts with 'Z'?"

Amot shrugged.

"What about 'X'? 'I'?"

Amot didn't have time to come up with an answer before Feleg resumed.

"Rest assured," said the grig, "we will pit rangers against queensmen in two of the three scenarios." A wide smirk crept across Feleg's face as he observed the building reaction. The crowd murmured and there was some subdued laughter, scoffing really.

Amot eyed the Queen's Guards around him, overconfident and completely full of themselves, it seemed. They knew they lacked nothing and had no reservations flaunting their privileges—the best education, elite swordsmanship training, family money for the highest quality armor and personal gear… Amot could hardly blame them. And on top of all that, connections to clergy endowed some with exceptional battlefield healing skills.

The ex-Kith ranger continued on. He explained that the first day would be dedicated to training, the second day to enacting two mock battles against one another, and the third day to a coordinated offensive against an enemy force, played by a mix of regulars and mimics.

"Mimics?" a familiar voice asked. It was Rix, the redheaded spotter from Fort Abandon that Berendt had brought into the ranger fold. The two had gotten to know one another better in the months since the Akedan raid. "What the hell are mimics?"

"Oh, didn't anyone tell you?" Feleg said. "We'll be heading out to Tetherport in the morning." He slapped his forehead. "Of course no one told you… it was kept secret, up until now."

Cheers erupted from rangers and queensmen alike. Admission to the Otherworldly Realm was by special invite only and deemed highly prestigious, normally reserved only for the highest ranks and social orders in Elderkin society, or those involved in special trade or projects.

Feleg waited for the ruckus to subside. "In the final scenario on the third day," he continued, "rangers and queensmen will be expected to work together. But only the most *worthy* group will wield the strikers. That will set the stage for their incorporation into the combat force structure." Murmurs filled the room again.

One of the lords seated in the front row answered to Feleg's words as though they were a challenge. The man wore a decorated uniform from the Royal Quarter, well-adorned with medals and badges of honor.

"Queen's Guard, most obviously," he said, and then swiveled his head around to face the Royal Quarter attendees. The queensmen cheered him on and pumped their fists in the air. He, in turn, nodded his approval. Kith rangers scoffed and grumbled under their breaths.

Again, Feleg waited patiently for the commotion to die down. "That remains to be seen," was all he said.

The outspoken lord's jaw dropped. "The Kith don't have a chance," he stated bluntly.

Feleg overspoke him, addressing the room. "Before I let you all go, I just want to remind you to get a good night's rest and be ready to depart at sunrise from the royal wharf. During the trip, STAY ALERT. That means no allowing yourself to be rocked to sleep along the way. And hook in. *Stay hooked in.* I don't want to lose anyone in Kaeda's Temper before we even get started. We only have three glide ships lined up, so we'll have to make several trips. Organize yourselves into groups of a dozen or so."

With that last remark, the same woman who'd opened the meeting—a distinguished officer sitting in the front row with raven-dark hair—stood up and dismissed the hall. She wore the winged sigil of Order Valkyrie.

Afterwards, Amot joined his comrades for food and drink in the mess hall, checked on his stabled horse, then signed out a raven so it could have a good fly and maybe catch a mouse or two.

Later, nearing sunset, he met up with Vil'nyan in a secluded glade. The two made camp and slept under the stars.

The "Scarsands" is a desolate, volatile territory bordered by lush, stable nations and a nearly impassable mountain range. Once a thriving city-state, the region fell into ruin after the onslaught of a mysterious plague. Neighboring rulers and regents were quick to close their borders to the stricken people; the inhabitants and their descendants became sealed within for time unmeasured. Few now remain who recall the stone faces of the Guardians of the Wanderer, the white domes of the Garden Temples, or the tall golden towers that kept watch over the fair city of Kel Fariz. Once per year, bards still sing of the hypnotic winds and rolling dunes that envelop the ruined city, immortalized in song as the "Star Sands."

—*The Pristine Channeler,*
on the coming of the Scar

Chapter XXIII
The shaman's satchel
(Akrylla)

THE LONG HAUL through Turnsby Corners in the middle of the night had been grueling, but it was the rough patches in the mire that had done Akrylla in. Her, the three slavers, and their quarry headed east to the city of Outlanders. East to Bitterhelm.
~Witnessed

Akrylla hated having crossed paths with ore haulers—Stouts from Ironeagle, their faces shrouded in the hoods they wore. By lantern light, they led their mules and hummed in low tones to the steady beat of heavy hooves and heavy boots. *Keep your narrow minds on your own businesses,* Akrylla had thought of them, *or I'll cut out your tongues and use them in a brew.* At least they kept their heads forward-facing, dozens of eyes blind to the slave trade. Perhaps they profited from it. Akrylla still didn't consider *herself* to be a slave. Not yet. She was glad when the Stouts' lanterns winked out of sight.
~Enough

Akrylla'd had enough of the rough bush trail—treacherous in the dark, more so alongside a horse with faltering steps. Her own legs felt ready to collapse under her weight, knees and elbows scraped and bruised, feet blistered and chafed. Yet the shaman trudged on, eyes straining to resolve the ground ahead of her toes, one hand pressed upon Vey's middle back in case she slid off her horse again or the steed stumbled. The cart she'd purchased at the stables bumped along ahead of them. It wasn't big enough for both the redhead and the bulky steward, neither of whom had woken since the ambush. And every time it got stuck, Akrylla had to help push it out.

~Fool

The Cutter had killed Akrylla's horse—a stupid move in her mind—and had taken two horses from the steward for hauling. He'd sent the empty coach into the Flats with the remaining pair still hitched. *Not bad,* she had to admit of that last move, begrudgingly.

The shaman raised her weary head. Riddik the Cutter led the horse pulling her cart, Ang the Bitch led the horse bearing Vey, while Gutless Kori—the only Wulver she'd ever known to have ventured so far from Whisperwood—prowled somewhere behind. At times, the beast would catch a scent and slink off the trail to creep through the woods. She gazed past the Outlanders, through the trees to the horizon. A bright patch splotched the sky ahead.

First light approaches. Shroud's Well, I've been walking through this slop all night.

The slavers rounded a bend, came upon Blackmuk Creek. Riddik halted, gave orders to dump their human quarry on a bed of moss and then to mind the horses. Gutless Kori and Ang obeyed the Taint without hesitation, while he disappeared off the trail and into the woods.

~Assess

With heavy eyelids and heavy steps, Akrylla approached the crossing and surveyed the starlit waters. *Slow-moving and silent.* Its trampled bottom was muddy and the ground on both sides of the creek eroded by foot traffic. Even with the water level low as it was, there was no way the slavers could lead a limp half-giant through the waste-deep middle—not until he came to. Nor would the cart bear their prize slave without getting bogged down. Riddik had commented that the steward must have weighed three hundred pounds.

~Signs

Akrylla glance up. *The ore haulers.* She smiled when she saw the system of pulleys the Stouts had used to ferry their precious cargo across. *They must've spent the day here and left their ropes behind.* She couldn't decide whether she'd mention it or not. She had no use for the half-giant.

~Rest

Yessums, rest, thought Akrylla. *I could use a rest anyway. But will Riddik allow it?* It was like he ran on pure hate. *Why aren't his stubby little legs tired?* Akrylla could hear the mean little Taint up to something new already, in the bush, hacking away at some tree. It worried her.

His mind is always bent on torture, that one. Who knows what he's cooked up in his mean little head over the night? Evil thoughts. Yessums, evil, no doubt. A short while later, Akrylla heard him whittling the wood down.

~Apprentice

Akrylla backtracked along the trail to where the cart had been discarded, then stepped off and navigated a path between the mossy boulders to where Vey lay motionless. Ang the Bitch hadn't been careful setting her down. First, there was the blood the shaman spotted on a nearly hidden rock that bulged up through the moss. Vey's hair was blood-soaked on one side. Second, her body lay contorted. The shaman straightened out her Vey, her *Ak'la,* and laid her body out flat. She checked Vey's breathing with the palm of her hand.

Satisfied when she felt shallow breaths, and after verifying that the headwound was superficial, Akrylla rummaged through her satchel for her needle and thread, plus something to sterilize the wounds. Fighting drowsiness, she got to work stitching up the nasty wound on the redhead's chest. The shaman shook her head in disgust. *Horrible, what Riddik has done to you, my dear,* she thought as she worked, steady and diligent. *Horrible.* She stitched until she began to nod off, fortitude only for a rush job.

After tying the last knot, Akrylla bit through the thread and stowed away her healer's kit. Her gaze wandered, scanning the area for a comfortable resting place: a place to watch over her Vey. *There,* she thought, eyeing the base of a thick cedar, *both vantage point and cover.* Body exhausted, mind tired but fixated, the shaman curled up in the tree's sprawling roots. She closed her eyes and let her thoughts drift.

~Liars

Akrylla wanted the original deal back: the slavers take the half-giant for ransom or auction in Bitterhelm—she didn't care which—and she goes her own way with her new apprentice. *My Ak'la.* It burned her insides the way the slavers handled the bargain, the way they manipulated her, the way they didn't respect boundaries, the way *he* threatened to renege. *Mind the signs,* she scolded herself. And then Akrylla reminded herself of something else, something her weary brain was almost too tired to remember. It drained her to drudge up the memory, small as it was. But it was a memory she clung to, small and precious, before the desert winds brought the Scar to Kel Fariz. *Not the worst deal, I suppose, for a new moon. But still…*

~Consequences

Yessums, there must be consequences. Thoughts heavy but still churning, Akrylla started making her plans for the slavers. She started making plans and she started thinking dosages. She'd kept her satchel with her the whole time and her purchases at the Fargoer had helped to keep her going through the night. It contained everything she needed from the apothecary. Everything. *What shall I do? —make ill, paralyze, send tripping, or kill outright?* The shaman couldn't decide. Not yet. *If, in the morning, the slavers let me leave with my apprentice, maybe I'll go easy on them. Maybe. Lucky for you, Riddik, saved only by the new moon.*

Her mental machinations were interrupted by a sucking sound, the sucking sound of a boot retracted from the muck along the creekside. *He's coming?* Heavy footsteps trudged through the wet earth. Next came the snapping sound of crushing sticks.

Riddik was not nimble. He made more noise than two blind bears in the bush. Akrylla craned her neck to peer around the root base of the large cedar she'd nestled into, eyes fixing on the creek. The Cutter had returned to Ang and Kori. He gathered his followers close, and the three exchanged low-volume words, low enough not to be overheard. *Fool,* thought Akrylla. *He's scheming against me. Against my Vey. Something evil.* They all glanced her way. She ducked down. *Shroud's Well, not just him. They're coming. All of them. They're coming for me and they're coming for my Vey... Did they spot me?... No. They were looking to where they'd dumped the bodies.*

~Protect

Akrylla had read the signs correctly. *This won't be easy.* Dealing with slavers was never easy. *I need to get my edge back.*

She reached into her satchel, retrieved a small bag and undid the drawstring. Between two fingers, the shaman pinched a portion of the fine crystals within. *No time to dab it,* she thought, her preferred method of ingestion. So, instead, Akrylla lifted the powder to her nose and snuffed it up. It would only be a minute or two before she felt something. Before she felt the way she needed to feel, to confront, to survive.

Peering back between the cedar's curling roots, Akrylla watched as the slavers made their way towards her. The stocky half-breed was in the lead. He carried a freshly cut walking stick, burled and twisted. The demon bitch in scaly black strode a step behind, spear in hand and whip coiled at her side, while the displaced Wulver hung back, half-dragging himself along—a misshapen hell hound in the dim light, dark and shadowy with gleaming red eyes.

Akrylla turned her gaze away, pressed her back against the trunk of the cedar. Her body tensed. She cursed 'the Nine' for her predicament, she cursed every one by name, even Ekkon the Wanderer. She cursed them all and then she regretted it. So she said she was sorry, and then she cursed them all again.

Kick in, damn it. Akrylla needed the boost. Muscles stiff and aching, eyes barely open, by sheer determination she slid up along the trunk from her seated position. She forced herself up to face the coming slavers. Akrylla winced, drawing shallow breaths as she waited. *I must show strength.* The Outlanders closed in.

Akrylla staggered out in front of them. She steadied herself, straightened her hunched back and made herself tall. It felt good to be tall again. And just as the rush hit her, Akrylla's eyes locked with the approaching Taint's. She called out to her captor, voice envenomed with accusation. "What are you doing with that stick, Riddik?"

The Cutter grunted back. "Not your concern, Hag. Out of my way." Riddik pushed her aside, tried to sidestep past. But the shaman's hand flashed out. She grabbed his new walking stick, gripped it tight and held it firm.

"Not so fast," the shaman told him. Her heart raced at the sound of her own words. Riddik turned, glared at her, his gaze laced with hatred and disgust. He tugged and grunted, but her grip was like iron. And when he snarled at her, every scar on his face stood out. He took a step towards Vey and yanked hard on the walking stick. The force sent Akrylla off balance. She stumbled along with him. But she held firm, dug her heels in.

Ang's voice lit up behind the shaman. "Let go, old hag."

Akrylla ignored the Bitch. Riddik kept his hold, but flicked his gaze just past her, and low. Then his eyes shifted back to stare into Akrylla's. A grin crept over his trollish face.

~Dodge

Ang grunted from behind. Akrylla twisted her body sideways. A sharp, stinging pain erupted on her torso—a quick jab, followed by the slick withdrawal of the spearhead's metal tip. Blood soaked into Akrylla's robe, warm against her skin. She pressed a hand to the wound.

Akrylla screeched at Ang. "Put that thing away, Demon Bitch, or I'll shove it up your hole."

With a swift motion, Riddik wrenched the staff away. He raised it above his head, ready to strike. Gritting his teeth, he swung at the shaman's head. Akrylla flinched, eyes shut, body tensed for the impact.

Nothing hit her. And when she opened her eyes, Akrylla saw that he'd stopped the ball-end of the staff an inch from her nose. Riddik held it there just as the second rush shot through her. A higher rush. Intense. She could hardy take it, pulsing through her brain. Then something about the walking stick made an impression on her. *A sign.*

~Snakes

The walking stick seemed an odd choice to Akrylla: its wood warped and twisted. Along its length one branch strangled another, and a heavy burl sat on top with a definite likeness to it—serpentine and staring, as the shaman stared back at it. *A snake coiled on a branch.* Frozen with the realization, Akrylla's mind scrambled to interpret the meaning of this great omen. *Splendor? Rebirth? Knowledge? Enigma?* Her head spun with the choices. *There are so many.*

Riddik mistook her reaction for submission. "Hmph," was all he said, satisfied. The Cutter spared her the hit she had coming to her. He withdrew the gnarled staff, turned his back to her and continued on to where the captives lay. Ang followed cautiously, raising her spear to threaten Akrylla as she passed. Gutless Kori rolled out a low growl.

As Riddik poked at Vey with the stick, Akrylla's mind continued to search for meaning. *Rebirth,* she decided, lining up all the signs together. *It has to be rebirth. But who? When?* She looked to her helpless apprentice. *Vey? Or me?*

Vey hadn't reacted to Riddik's prodding, so he nudged her with his boot to the same null response. And with Ang covering his back and eyeing Akrylla suspiciously, the burly Outlander strutted over to the half-giant and poked him as well. The steward was just as dead to the world. The Taint grunted. His gaze focused back on the shaman.

"How much longer?" he asked.

The shaman hesitated. *Careful what you tell him,* she reminded herself. Light-headed, she slumped down on a root. *I'm losing blood.* Akrylla pressed harder on her wound.

"Well?" Riddik wanted an answer.

"Well, it depends on how much they ate."

Riddik shifted his stance. The snarl he wore showed his lack of satisfaction with her answer.

Akrylla squeezed her eyes shut for a long moment to compose herself. She buried the dizzy feeling, gathered her wits about her, then met his gaze. "If the two of them consumed the same amount of cake," she explained, "the big one should be up any time now. But if he stuffed his face and the girl held back, she will be up by sunrise. Worse case, the redhead stuffed herself and the lug didn't take a liking to it. The redhead could be out another eight hours and the big one would be listening to everything we are saying right now."

Riddik pointed with his stick at the half-giant's left cheek. "His face still has cake on it."

Gutless Kori let out an unusual growl—an expression that bridged the gap between pain and laughter of some kind. Akrylla didn't tell them that she'd drugged the big one extra to be sure he'd stay under. She'd never drugged anyone so big before.

Riddik wound up his leg, delivered a swift kick to the ribs with a resounding thud. The half-giant only grunted.

Riddik sneered. "I say he pigged out." He started to snicker.

Gutless Kori's growl morphed into a subdued, barking laugh. Then he started to moan, one long paw-hand holding his half-eaten gut. "Sto-rr-p," he gruffed.

"Stop screwing around, you two," Ang chimed. "We have to put more distance between us and the road to Abandon, as soon as we can."

Gutless Kori swung his head to the demoness, rumbled off a warning. Then the wolfish brute shuffled over to Vey, stooped, and sniffed her crotch. Akrylla sprung to her feet. She raised her hand the same way she saw Ang raise hers before smacking the Wulver's snout.

"Get your nose out of there," she scolded. Gutless Kori's fiendish eyes swiveled her way, then narrowed. The beast barred its teeth, let loose a throaty growl.

A chill ran up Akrylla's spine. She suppressed the urge to bolt. *Show no fear*, she told herself. But she became dizzy again. Her stance wavered. She backed away, put a hand to her forehead—her bloodied hand. Then she put it back to the wound.

Sensing weakness, smelling blood, the Wulver shifted its dark mass to face her straight on: shoulders high, head low, eyes glaring.

~Danger

Legs shaking, Akrylla steadied herself against the tree. Sickly as the beast was, she knew those massive jaws could tear her to shreds in a minute. But the shaman held her ground. She pushed herself back upright, stood fast.

"Be gone," the shaman spat, eyes locked with the predatory gaze of the half-starved beast. She'd thought Kori was different, at first—once left for dead and gutted by vultures. That made him vulnerable to her. She'd eased his pain with her medicines. She'd eased his pain and this was her reward. *Biggest liar of them all,* she decided. Akrylla would've given him something to help with his digestion, out of pity. But now she saw in those wolfish eyes that this was truly a predator staring back at her, and that pity only put her in the beast's sights. And so, she did what desert shamans do. Akrylla raised her hands and made the many-tentacled sign of Ekkon the Wanderer. She made the sign and invoked his power.

"I curse you, Gutless Kori," she uttered, judgement and hate in her voice. "I curse you to pain unimaginable:

Forever pain, forevermore;

forever a pain in your half-eaten gut.

Feel the vultures tearing at your innards,

feel their beaks pecking at your flesh,

string by string pulling out your insides.

Forever pain, Gutless Kori.

Forevermore. Forever pain for you."

After a long minute of low growls and a steady stare, Gutless Kori's gaze wandered to his master, who stared back without word or a sign.

The Wulver sniffed at the air, then shifted its stance again. With a slow and uneven gait, Gutless Kori lumbered towards Akrylla. Every muscle gripped her insides as the beast dragged itself past her. She expected a quick turn, a lunge to her throat. It didn't happen. She breathed a heavy sigh of relief when the Wulver continued to the creek.

Riddik addressed the shaman with a sharp voice. "Get the half-giant to wake up, then get him across the river."

"The half-giant's your problem," Akrylla retorted. "I don't trust

Giant blood. And there's something of the desert in him." The shaman had caught a hint of the distinct odor in the night. She made her way to the slumbering half-giant, kneeled, and sniffed the side of his face and neck. *Yes, I knew it.* She tilted her head to Riddik. "Some Djin blood in this one."

Riddik grunted. "No one cares, Hag. Strength and title are the profit for this sac of meat. He needs to look more like a regular giant though. Why isn't he bald? Giants are always bald and that's what buyers want to see in him. Being bald adds grit."

Akrylla thought the comment self-serving, but refrained from answering him. No one answered him.

Riddik scoffed, then let his gaze wander to Vey, up and down her body in the revealing dress she wore. He narrowed his eyes slightly. "I'm shackling them both up." The Taint grasped the pair of shackles he carried on his belt and dangled them over Vey's body. A true slaver. ~Protect

Hands off, fiend. In her mind, any purpose of Riddik's was guaranteed to have an unpleasant twist to it. "You're not putting those iron things on my Vey," Akrylla said. "They'll tear her tender wrists apart."

Ang spoke out. "And those shackles won't fit the half-giant."

"I'll use rope then," he replied. "I'll make a soft shackle."

"You don't have enough rope for both," Akrylla snapped back. "And if the big one awakens…"

The demoness promptly agreed. "The hag's right. All he has to do is get you in his grips and your done for. Not that I'd care."

Riddik frowned heavily at the Bitch.

Ang continued, "Tie up the half-giant with everything we have. We can't afford him going berserk on us. We can pawn off the draft horses at the trading post and get more rope in the exchange."

"Steal the rope," Riddik countered. "We'll get more for the horses at Irongate."

"Gutless will keep an eye on the girl." Ang shifted her gaze to the Wulver, called out to him. "Won't you, Gutless?"

The beast growled in response. Ang glanced at Vey, then her dark eyes swiveled back to Riddik. "The girl is as soft as they come—not much fight in that pampered little thing."

~Ignorance

Soft? Akrylla grinned to herself. *How little you know of my Vey... my Ak'la.*

Riddik took a long look at the incapacitated redhead lying at his feet. He stood rubbing his chin. The Taint's brow furrowed, contemplating Ang's words.

~Scheming

What's wrong, Riddik? thought Akrylla. *Didn't get your way? You want her completely helpless, don't you? Wasn't I enough? Hmm...* The shaman discreetly patted a small pouch of "herbs" that bulged out of her satchel; a pouch she'd taken from the Fargoer labelled "for getting rid of pests." The motion went unnoticed to the Taint. *Even the Cutter has to eat or drink, eventually. And when he does...*

She patted the pouch again, then let the memory of the night's events soak into her soul and fuel her loathing. Like a slow burn they took hold, one by one...

Chapter XXIV
Strikers
(Hadamard)

FELEG SHOULD BE here any minute, thought Hadamard. He considered tidying up the lab, but a quick glance around had him wondering where he'd start. *A minute's peace then,* he decided. The luminary picked up one of the discarded books, found a comfortable crate against the wall, leaned back and began flipping through the pages. The topic was metallurgy.

Only three days and change had passed in the outside world since Hadamard set out to Tetherport, but the scenario runs had stretched the clock out for him personally—he'd operationalized scenario time. Over that duration, the luminary's prospects had trickled in to work with the projectionists—beginning with Smat who'd never left the dome, then Vil'nyan on the first glideboat in, as promised. Surprisingly, she'd convinced the remaining prospects to accompany her, with the exception of Sorral. The luminary's modest team of hopefuls gelled quickly in the Djinxarai facility, worked hard, innovated, and accomplished feats it would've taken others weeks if not months to even begin to explore. To be fair, more than a week had passed in the Netherdome as the scenario trials piled on, run after run, until every piece of terrain was in place and the range of mimic actions carefully scripted.

The door to Hadamard's study creaked open. He put the book down and made his way to greet his friend.

Feleg limped through the doorway. "Nice digs," he said, then swept his eyes across the disarray laid out before him, "… for a pack rat."

"The rent's cheap," Hadamard quipped. "And the place has potential."

Feleg grimaced. Of late, he'd spent most of his days at House Aokwan on an island in the Dim Sea, midway between the westmost edge of the Isles of Lore and the underground maelstrom. He'd never see the cramped study the way Hadamard saw it, the way it could be with a modest investment of time, money and energy.

"There's a workbench at the back," the luminary added.

"All I need is a place to sit." Feleg's wandering gaze settled on a low table amidst the clutter. With a loud scrape, he pulled it from the heap, planted himself on top. The grig extended his left leg, rubbed it up and down, then leaned back against the shelf behind him. "I'm getting too old for this sort of thing."

Hadamard dragged his crate next to his friend and sat down.

"How's the training coming, since I left?" Hadamard said.

Feleg frowned. "Terrible. I need a drink."

Hadamard grunted. "You won't find any hooch in these parts."

The grig's eyebrows lifted. "Don't be so sure. You know, I got talking to one of them glideboat captains on the ride in, and I told him I'd seen some of his Greys at the Wolf'N Stein. I asked him 'what have you got to drink out there on that rock of yours?' 'Well,' he says, with a grin forming on his lips like he knows I'm going to cringe at the answer, 'other than water, all food and drink is derived from fungi.'"

"Did you cringe?"

Feleg nodded. "I did. 'That sounds terrible,' I told him. Then the captain said not to tell, but some Greys are experimenting with a mushroom wine and some 'fungussy' beer. Can you imagine that? Fungus beer?" He placed a hand on his belly and made a sour face. "With my stomach already queasy on account of the dips and turns, the thought of that beer nearly pushed me over the edge."

"It can't be any worse than the Wolf'N Stein."

Feleg puffed out a laugh. "That's exactly what he said." The two thaumaturgists shared a good chuckle.

"Nydar, must've been," Hadamard said.

"Yep," Feleg nodded, "that was his name."

"You got the 'fun' Nydar. I got the 'sentimental' Nydar this last trip in." Hadamard organized his thoughts to tell him about the Windswept, but Feleg flicked his gaze to meet Hadamard's eyes, beat him to the punch on another topic.

"How did the tour and the scouting go?"

Hadamard huffed in discontent. "I need a drink."

Feleg smirked. "I can help both of us with that." The grig pulled a squat bottle out of the sidepouch he wore, then two shot glasses. The bag deflated without them. He held the bottle up in clear view. "Salt Blood Whiskey," he proclaimed, a proud grin on his face. "Contraband, from Dim Lake. The best contraband."

Hadamard protested, his tone firm. "You can't have that in here." He hesitated for a long moment, relishing in the sudden change in Feleg's expression: the low-hanging jaw, the uncertain gaze. Hadamard sighed, then put the grig out of his misery. "Pour swiftly, friend, but keep it out of sight."

Feleg got to pouring straightaway. "Not a problem." He passed Hadamard a glass, which the luminary sipped. Then the grig poured one for himself, downed it, and quickly poured a second.

"That bad?" Hadamard said. "Tell me, how did the first phase of the training go?"

Feleg swallowed his second shot, then cleared his throat, his eyes suddenly watery. He pounded his fist on his chest. "Damn it." His face went beat red. "I have to stop doing that. Don't ask me a question while I'm drinking."

Hadamard snorted. "That would mean a lot less questions."

Feleg ignored the remark, filled his glass a third time. He flicked his eyes to Hadamard's glass, saw that it wasn't empty, then answered. His voice was hoarse. "Those simulated strikers are just plain creepy. Made of bugs? Really?"

Hadamard shrugged. "Mimicry was the only way the projectionists could track the motion and count hits, the same way they do in the runs. The wielder swings the bug sword, and with a successful hit the target mimic—a hundred feet away or whatever—bursts open with a gaping wound."

"I'll give you full credit for creativity. But I have to say the participants are too distracted by the mechanics and the biology of it all. They're not used to all this weird shit like you and your team are. And rangers are all saying they'd rather use a bow."

"It's just to give them a sense of what it'd be like to use a striker, before they log time with one of the few prototypes."

Feleg lifted his eyebrows, nodded. "The sword vibration—on a successful strike—now that's a nice touch."

"The feedback mechanism: That was Vil'nyan's idea—by the way she's one of my top prospects now. Her and Anya—the sister of my Djinxarai prospect—invented that feature from scratch in a day."

"You're going to steal her away from me, aren't you?"

"You bet."

The grig scowled slightly. "That leaves me with Nahm."

Hadamard grinned. "Your problem. Not mine."

Feleg sighed. "The price I pay for helping a friend."

Hadamard gripped Feleg's shoulder. "Look, I'll send a couple of prospects your way. They won't make luminary, but they might have potential in your line of work."

"What about that other new assistant you had, the one seconded from the Grey Tower?"

"Vey Lancer." Hadamard let go with a quick pat, downed his shot. "The Grey Clerk clawed her back for a mission to Abandon. Word from Qyp is that the Grey Tower is looking to revive the alliance, and at the same time slow down Harrow's investment in the area."

"Shit Hadamard. Have another drink. I thought she was off sick or something. You raved about her."

Hadamard responded with a dismissive wave. "I think it's a good idea, actually—maybe she'll buy us the time we need to field these strikers. I heard the Grey Clerk's even willing to offer up access to the archives." He paused, held his glass to Feleg. "Who am I kidding? Hit me."

"Hmph, that's weird," Feleg said, as he poured the luminary another. "The last time I tried to access *my* compartment at the archives, it was no longer there. And now you're telling me the Grey Clerk wants to open them up to foreigners?"

"Allies. The access would be *limited*. What do you mean your compartment wasn't there?"

"Relocated. Haven't you heard? All the really sensitive stuff is being moved to deeper tunnels."

Hadamard shook his head. "I haven't gone down there much lately, only for the odd enforcement case. There really isn't anything in the archives to help with my current projects."

Feleg changed the topic back to the exercise. "So, we have a dozen simulated dancing swords—which don't dance at all, by the way—and you said... half a dozen prototypes, right?"

"Less two. One's a civilian-style rapier—too dangerous and has no place in battle—and one's a dagger that doesn't really fit into any of the scenarios."

"An assassin's weapon."

Hadamard nodded. "Between you and me, yes. Are the participants ready for the real thing?"

Feleg grunted out a chuckle. "Not even close. I made a short list of three rangers and three queensmen that might have some talent, and who seem to have enough imagination to be open to the concept."

"Only three each?"

"Like I said, most rangers don't see the advantage over a bow. Plus, Morty Short and a few old-timers complained that they only fight with an axe." Feleg chuckled again. "Rockhound doesn't fight at all, and says if he ever had to, it'd be with his pick. As for the queensmen, most turned their noses up—they'd rather face their enemies eye-to-eye."

"I bet Ralador didn't count on that response."

"Don't be so sure. Either way, it won't matter to him—it isn't enough to convince him to back down. He'll ram the strikers down their throats if he has to. Lord Ralador's stubborn and determined."

Hadamard downed his shot, acknowledged the bite with a nod, and handed Feleg back his glass. He stood up and felt a mild but unexpected rush from the alcohol. He shook it off.

"Come with me," he said. And while Hadamard brushed the dust from his robe, Feleg finished his own shot, then carefully returned the emergency drinking set to his sidepouch. Hadamard helped the grig to his feet and, after a few stiff steps, led him on to a certain cabinet in the room. When they got there, the luminary squatted to his haunches, pulled the bottom drawer completely out. The drawer itself was nothing special—it held an assortment of old robes and other clothes for messy jobs. But underneath was a secured false-floor compartment. Hadamard released the catch under a nearby tile. The lid popped up, he shoved it aside. Within the compartment lay the striker prototypes—Hadamard's dancing swords. Their keen edges were each protected by a thin, blunt sheath, clipped in with white metal bands, both to safeguard the prototype from damage during training and to prevent accidental injury.

Feleg's eyes widened. "I thought you said there were only six? What's that curved one, without the protector?"

"That's an authentic Jhinyari blade," Hadamard said, "unearthed from the Akedan ruins. The Djinxarai even have instructions on how to use it, straight from a Jhinyari source. They're split into factions, you know—the Jhinyari: constant infighting. The Djinxarai are providing aid to a group they feel is moderate. If they can get a foothold…"

Feleg squatted down beside Hadamard, pulled his spectacles out of a shirt pocket. "Damn lighting in here," he said, as he put them on. He reached for the grip of the silvery Jhinyari blade, then stayed his palm. "May I?"

"Sure. Just don't accidentally invoke it—I don't know if you can. Apparently, the Jhinyari can detect when one of their swords is used."

Feleg snorted, gave his old friend *a look*.

"Djinxarai lore," Hadamard added, disowning the information as much as he could. "They never said how and I don't know if it's true, but we don't understand exactly how it works either…"

The grig's silence and bitter smile said it all—he didn't believe a word of it. He carefully lifted the bright sword out of the compartment and into the light where he could examine the workmanship. "You made your strikers based on this?" Feleg asked, as he checked the sharpness with his thumb and slowly rotated the weapon in his hands, observing the gleam.

"That's right," Hadamard replied.

"This one's sure kept its shine." His eyes fixed on the grip. He made a passing glance over the others, then met Hadamard's gaze. "Your strikers all have slider charms embedded just forward of the hilt; this one doesn't."

"I've improved the design," Hadamard said. "The Jhinyari dancing swords are line-of-sight only. My strikers tap into Hurlorn thaumaturgy to provide an image of *hidden* targets, the one you can't otherwise see. It's fractured, mind you, and there's no color, but it's a big advantage."

"How's the image formed?"

"Acoustics."

Feleg wrinkled his brow. "You're shitting me. Acoustics?"

"The Hurlorns use sound we can't hear, not only to communicate, but to form images as well."

"Out here? I didn't see any Hurlorns."

"That's the part I don't understand."

Feleg huffed. "Shit."

"Shit is right." Hadamard didn't mention the fact that a few Hurlorns actually do grow on Seventh Kaeda, but not a lot and not enough. He began bundling up the swords. When he had the four that he needed, he called out.

"SMAT," he shouted to the open doorway. In a softer voice, he told Feleg, "Put that one back for now." The grig obliged.

When his prospect arrived, Hadamard rose to his feet, plunked the four strikers into Smat's outstretched arms, then patted him on the shoulder. "Bring these out with Feleg here. We're starting Phase Two of the training."

Feleg's gaze wandered to the largest striker. He ran his fingers over the half-grip, intended for one- or two-handed use, then eyed the compound hilt which was for improved handling. Hadamard could see his friend was impressed by it.

"I wish I'd had one of these bastards thirty years ago," he said, a way back look in his eyes. The grig turned to Smat: "I'll carry this one, you take the rest."

Smat handled the remainder: two standard arming swords and an officer's rapier. The latter was needed to explore the concept of a light striker weapon in combat, and was of a different design than the civilian rapier kept stowed away.

The pair ferried the weapons out the door and towards the dome, bustling with activity.

Hadamard hung back to close up the secret compartment. He placed his elemental stones inside for safekeeping. Before setting the lid, he paused. Then he removed the dagger, pondered slipping it into his belt. *In case I need to demo a striker projection,* he thought. He'd tried out all of the prototypes personally. Hadamard was no swordsman though, nor would he ever be a swordsman. He wasn't an assassin either. Yet, the weight of the dagger felt right in his hands, and he'd practiced using it considerably. With a little concentration, the luminary could strike an unseen target at fifty paces—if Nekenezitter provided the range and bearing. And without the Gloom's assistance, Hadamard could do the same after a few tries, as long as his initial guess at where the target lay hidden was decent.

The luminary questioned himself, *is that really why I'd be taking this striker—to demo it?*

Hadamard shook his head, lowered the dagger back into its place next to the Jhinyari weapon.

Live by the sword, die by the sword.

Swords and daggers, and whatever else, were just not for him.

꩜

Before getting out to the exercise, the projectionists in the Red Room sidetracked Hadamard for a good hour sorting out last-minute exercise details. When the luminary finally exited the COM Center, he scanned the grounds. A few select rangers and queensmen were trying out the prototypes. Others appeared to be searching for something.

Over the years, Hadamard'd learned how to blend into the background of an exercise, even one that he was running. It was the only way to observe what was really happening. *A fly on the wall*, he reminded himself, notebook and pencil in hand as he hid in plain sight. *Should be easy.* He hadn't yet introduced himself to most of the participants.

The mid-afternoon scenario sun hung high in the dome by the time the luminary caught up with Feleg. It was a false brightness from above, lacking in warmth, and he could stare straight at it without hurting his eyes. Feleg's rasping voice was easy to single out over the hustle and bustle of the training.

"That worked well," he barked scornfully at some young Wilder after the lad took a swing with a striker. Nekenezitter, who'd been facing the intended target and sending out a flurry of clicks, turned to the grig and shook his head. Hadamard moved in closer as Feleg egged the ranger on with a mix of criticism, impatience, and encouragement. "Just get'er done, the way your old man would've. Think it. Do it. Simple. They're one in the same."

The Wilder—a ranger familiar to Hadamard—shook off the remark. He focused on his task, slowly raising his striker with a strong, two-handed grip. He wielded the largest weapon of the lot, the gleaming hand-and-a-half sword. With a far-off look in his eyes and in full concentration, the ranger adjusted his stance until he stood square to the distant target—a giant of Tor Lord lineage. The Wilder's eyes narrowed. He took careful aim at the mimic in the distance, swung again. Nekenezitter sent out another flurry of clicks.

No impact.

No projection.

Nekenezitter swung his bug-eyed gaze to Feleg, shook his head a second time.

"This isn't like the simulation," Feleg explained to the ranger, irritation showing through, "where some projectionist does everything for you. No. This is the real thing. You must project the sword yourself: with your own mind and your own thoughts. Focus on the objective."

"I will," the young ranger replied. He raised his sword again, adjusted his stance, and refocused his thoughts.

"Amot," continued Feleg, a hint of disdain entering his voice, "I hate to tell you this, but you're the only one not getting it. Your father would've had this licked by now. Hell, so would your grandfather." The ex-Kith ranger shook his head in disappointment. Out of the corner of his eye, he caught Hadamard watching, shot him a wink. The defeated ranger breathed a heavy sigh. For a long moment, he just stared into nothingness, pale frustration showing through. Nekenezitter offered a sympathetic chirr.

"Never mind," Feleg said to the Gloom.

Feleg was outright lying and Hadamard knew it. Glancing about, the luminary could see the looks of frustration on ranger and queensmen faces alike. It wasn't as rosy for the others as Feleg made it out to be. In fact, it was dismal, and his old friend was playing the naïve Wilder for a fool. *Damn it Feleg, don't be so hard on him. I need at least one ranger to figure this out.*

Hadamard discreetly wandered off, with plans to return. From his observations throughout the larger dome area and the fragments of conversation he overheard, only three subjects were able to get *something* to happen. Two of that elite group had lost their grip and the priceless weapons had slipped into some kind of void, with an air-sucking pop. One striker had been recovered in a hollow thirty feet behind the wielder, and the other was still missing. However, a distinctive clang had been heard at the same instant the weapon disappeared, so it probably wasn't far.

I better not have to shut down the scenario to find that one. He'd selected a simple terrain recommended by Smat and Anya, based on the map of a grassy field north of Turnsby—open space with a small hill situated a few hundred feet from a tree line, dense with pine.

In another section of the training area, a swordsman distinguished himself by being able to hold on to his hilt and gain respectable accuracy at several tens of feet. He was a queensman by the name of Eriff Haulik with blonde, short-cropped hair and a disposition as pompous as they come. *Another Horse Lord brat,* thought Hadamard. *Probably driven by his desire to prove himself better than everyone else, at every-thing—typical of his sort.*

Hadamard looped back to Feleg's project. Snuck up on them, really. His friend had started over with Amot, grinding over the striker operating procedures word for word, Wilder to Wilder. The luminary maintained a careful distance, at an angle that kept him out of their peripherals so as not to distract.

"It just doesn't add up," he heard Amot say. Hadamard had been optimistic for this one, especially compared to the century old martial types of the Royal Quarter. He'd met the Wilder at various ceremonies and other events where the Order Kith and Order Lumen mixed. It was obvious to Hadamard that the scout possessed a high degree of knowledge about Hurlorns. *It probably comes naturally to him, from his upbringing—third generation Kith ranger and all.* Beyond that, Amot came off as the sort of bright mind who would catch on quickly. And no doubt, he was physically strong enough to overcome the forces at play. *Persistent as well, which helps immensely.* According to Hadamard's notes, over three quarters of those who'd tried so far and failed blamed their lack of success on the device itself.

Hadamard jotted down his impression of the scout:

Amot's hard on himself.

He thinks something's wrong with <u>him</u> and not the weapon.

Those traits were positive as far as Hadamard was concerned, traits that might push the scout to eventually overcome the obstacles he was facing. But Amot was still unsure, his own worst enemy. *Disbelief is stifling his progress.* Hadamard contemplated returning to the lab, retrieving the dagger, and providing a demonstration after all.

Feleg urged Amot on. "Just relax your mind," he told the young ranger. "You can't focus to a point. I know that's what you want to do. Spread out your thoughts instead. Let the scene on the other side pour in from all directions."

Not bad, mused Hadamard. *Clever.* The luminary had never thought of it that way and it wasn't exactly correct, physically speaking, but there was some truth to it. The far image, when it appeared, was warped by the way it projected around the body. Worse still, it came fractured in tens of tiny, disjoint bits, and never appeared as more than a faint, colorless trace. The accesses drifted and faded in and out, so one never really knew when and where the next opportunity for a strike might emerge. *You must anticipate. There's no helping that.* But once a connection was made and the white metal blade thrust through it, the steel *projected*. The access channel bonded to the blade, stuck to it, then slid with the hand movements of the swordsman until fully withdrawn. All motions were restricted to the arc of the projection. The Djinxarai called it the "fighting circle."

Feleg's coaching of Amot attracted unwanted attention. Hadamard watched as Lord Ralador approached the pair, walking stiff with his hands behind his back and his chest puffed out. He was accompanied by Eriff, his most promising queensman, sauntering over. Ralador addressed Feleg, square on.

"No rangers yet?" No doubt, in Ralador's mind, his long-held notions had been confirmed yet again: Kith were impulsive, undisciplined and ultimately unreliable. For his lackey Eriff, Hadamard imagined the rangers' failure would be the talk of the day at the mess hall. Plus, the matter gave the queensman the perfect opportunity to brag about his own success, however limited. The luminary added as much to his notes, still keeping to a low profile.

"Getting there," Feleg replied to the March Lord, in his "accommodating" voice. Hadamard knew better. He knew it was forced.

"In fact," Feleg went on, "Amot will be the second ranger to clue in. He has a lot of talent. That's why I gave him the most difficult sword." The grig swung his gaze to the young Kith. "Isn't that right?"

Amot returned a prompt nod. "That's right, Uncle Feleg."

Eriff gave them both a stern look. "Uncle? Well, did I miss something? Has this 'boy' struck the target?"

"Close," Feleg said, before Amot could open his mouth. "Very close. He's just about to demonstrate his superior abilities."

You're a good bullshitter, Feleg. But you might be taking it too far this time.

"Then I shall observe," Ralador said.

"By all means." Feleg shifted his attention to Amot. "Whenever you're ready. Show them what you've got."

Just then, a mass of weary exercise participants happened by, making their way out of the dome for lunch. Sensing conflict and competition in the air, the way crowds do, they all stopped to watch the action.

To Hadamard, it seemed Feleg had inadvertently set up Amot for an epic fail, one likely to reverberate in the halls of the Queen's Guard for as long as they had walls and a roof. *I need to put a stop to this,* he thought, then made a quick gesture to interrupt. But he was too late.

The ranger's ink flared as he took aim. Light distorted around him. Amot swung his striker. The onlookers gasped.

Tired but motivated, the young ranger suddenly was brilliant. At twenty-five feet, he sliced through the sword of the closest stationary mimic. That was on his first try. Then came three hits to the body before losing the trace. The crowd around him steadily gathered, whispers rose. A hush fell over them as they watched on in awe.

At fifty and then one hundred feet, Amot struck animated mimics programmed to defend themselves. Even better, the targets appeared vaguely queensman-like. Hadamard chuckled to himself. He knew Anya wouldn't have done that on purpose.

Eriff and Ralador observed with the sourest of expressions as Amot, at five hundred feet—nearly the length of the dome—sunk his blade into the belly of a mimic concealed to him, as confirmed by Nekenezitter. The shiro-made automaton never even had a chance to react before being cut down.

Hadamard turned to the crowd, bellowed out, "We adjourn for three hours. Be back for Scenario One, the Hill Assault." He waved them off. "Until then, enjoy the sights of Seventh Kaeda."

He swung his gaze back to Amot. With a heavy sigh, the scout handed the bastard sword to Feleg. "Thanks, Uncle."

A satisfied grin crept across the luminary's face.

He's arrived.

CHAPTER XXV
CRYSTALLINITY
(Vil'nyan)

Vil'nyan stood wrapped in Amot's strong arms, buffeted by mighty winds on a plateau overlooking the cradle of Djinxar. The winds whipped over the valley below, and they whistled through the crystalline spires of Seventh Kaeda's Gardens of Light. As though in a lightning storm at night, the splendor of the unworldly terrain unveiled itself one flash at a time, with every electric flicker of the Starshine. *Wondrous,* she thought, as the two lovers gazed in awe at their surroundings.

The Abindohn leaned back against the Wilder's chest, away from the edge of the high precipice, shielding herself slightly from the warm, moist winds of the nether and the brilliant flashes of light that left black spots floating in her vision. Anya and Crusher lingered back from the cliff, patiently waiting for the two Theians to take in the scene. Anya sat on a large, glassy stone riddled with sheer surfaces, while Crusher leaned against a crystal pillar, pale red and jutting. Vil'nyan never dreamed such a place could've existed. And the view of the valley was only the half of what she beheld: The glowing Tendril Forest rose above the city's core. Its ropey vines shot up and away through a vast expanse of misty nether, and then plunged into the Starshine. The forest's hulking mass was rooted firmly at both ends. And like a storm never-ending, the turbulent Kaeda's Temper swirled in the backdrop. Amidst the thick of the forest, Vil'nyan glimpsed a section of high wall that peaked through the foliage, overgrown and nearly hidden. She pointed.

"Look," she said to Amot, "in the forest."

Anya answered instead, calling to her above the wind's howl. "The outer wall of the monastery."

Vil'nyan glanced her way. Dark robe flapping, the gaunt but stoically beautiful Djinxarai wore a satisfied grin on her face. A proud grin. Crusher stood by her, restless it seemed and shifting on his crutches. *Still has work on the brain, that one,* thought Vil'nyan. It was Anya that had dragged her twin brother away from his assembler station, protesting. But Crusher needed a break from Lumen Hadamard's slave driving. They all needed one. *He'll work you to death if you let him.*

Amot pulled Vil'nyan in tighter, but her mind was suddenly alert, probing. She broke away, recalling that the monastery was the homestead of the ruling class. Amot let her go, gently. She turned to face Anya, one hand still finger-locked with Amot. "Do you live in the monastery?"

Crusher answered, "We both do."

Amot's gaze followed the vines from their base upward. He raised his free hand to shield his eyes from the light. "I don't know if I could stand it here, all day every day. Do you people even sleep?" He swooshed his hand through his tousled hair.

"Most are sleeping now," Anya said, pushing herself from her seat. She meandered towards the couple, making her way through the heavy chunks of crystal strewn about. She stopped nearby. "But only for one or two spins."

"Spins?'" Amot said.

"A complete rotation," Vil'nyan replied, "like a wheel."

"How long is that?" Amot said.

Vil'nyan shrugged.

Anya's eyes scanned the turbulence around her. "You can judge the time better when the Temper is still," she said, then turned her gaze to the Wilder. "The way the visibility is now, you'd have to rely on one of your time pieces, like the one Nekenezitter has. He told me two spins translates to about four… what do you call them?" Her eyes swiveled up, searching for the word, "hours."

Vil'nyan turned her attention to the gardens. She gasped in awe when a long flash of light lit up the tips of the spires before her. She grasped Amot's hand fully and led him to where the light was shaded, away from the precipice and away from the Taerix twins. She led him between two tall, crystalline structures, red and blue and bifurcating, bearing crystalline nodes that gleamed like prismatic fruit. At the base of the spires, mushrooms grew. She led her man down a translucent path, feet crushing the soft bed of colored pebbles underfoot, to where no one else could see. The flickering light of the Starshine danced through all that surrounded them, vivid and eye-catching, with a saturation of color that non-netherfaring artists could only dream of.

High gusts suddenly arose. The couple tilted their heads up as zones of lensing began to push through the higher reaches of the gardens.

Crusher called to them. "We shouldn't stay much longer. The Temper is brewing."

"A storm?" Vil'nyan called back. This time she pulled Amot in tight. She whispered to him. "I love storms." She pressed her body against his.

Amot kissed her forehead, then pivoted his gaze upwards again, peering through the crystals at the Temper beyond. "Maybe not these storms," he said.

"I hate to say it," Anya called, "but Brother is right." She sighed. "Brother is always right."

Vil'nyan felt a pang in her chest. She squeezed her man even tighter. Hadamard had insisted that, once the exercise was over, she stay behind at the dome with Crusher, Lady Anya, and Smat, to help with his experiment. That meant she wouldn't be leaving with her man. Vil'nyan buried her face in his chest. She closed her eyes and inhaled deeply, savoring the moment. Then she looked up and gazed into his dark eyes, and planted a long, soft kiss on his lips.

"Are you coming?" Crusher called. His voice echoed through the crystal spires.

The couple didn't answer.

⋖

It took several long minutes for the lift to sink down to the last shaft, during which time the inseparable pair remained joined at the hip. As Vil'nyan leaned into Amot, she took in the otherworldly scenery through the water-filled glace tube. Her mind freed itself from the moment and bent to the far away future. She would reach old-age one day. It was inevitable. And when that happened, Amot would outlive her youthfulness by decades. She imagined herself old and tired and grey, with wrinkled skin faded by time and a hunched posture, bent and twisted by life's burdens. And then she imagined Amot in his veritable forties. He would be handsome, still, and strong, with a look of wisdom well beyond his outward years. He'd have that unmistakable ruggedness all Kith rangers seem to acquire over time.

I need access, she decided. *Making luminary is my only ticket to rejuvenation.*

She pushed the thought aside, let her mind drift back to the moment. The moment was good. Once returned, Vil'nyan couldn't figure out exactly why her stomach felt full of butterflies. Maybe it was the breathtaking view of Tetherport gliding by that made her feel so, or the descent into a dark and wondrous place, or the lingering after-effects of experiencing the Gardens of Light. *Or maybe it's just being with Amot?* She giggled at the ridiculous thought, despite herself.

CHAPTER XXVI
BLOOD HEART
(Vey, Akrylla)

A LONE CROW'S RASPING call. Buzzing insects. A squirrel's angry chatter.

Morning sounds.

Cool air, laden with liquid scents of earthy decay. Beneath, the uneven ground jabbed at the special assistant's ribs: stones, sticks, moss. But there was something else: a sound. Dull scraping on metal, it came and went…

Where am I? Vey rubbed her eyelids, all gummy and glued shut. Light lingered on the other side. With her fingertips, she split them open and beheld the sky above, then turned her gaze to the terrain.

A line of pregnant hills basked in dawn's early light. *Where?* They looked familiar but she couldn't quite place them. Her chest felt tight, numb; her neck muscles stiff, sore. She massaged the kink in her neck. Vey's whole body felt out of whack. And something else. A rush of heat flushed through her head…

Tension. She fought, denied. *A dream. Just a dream. Did I dream? But why am I here… who…*

Vey's mind scrambled to piece together the events of the night. She concentrated hard on the beginnings: *The treaty… Fort Abandon, the coach, and…* she shook her head. *Such a blur.* Jumbled thoughts. She felt a pounding in her head, throbbing. *That scraping again, grinding.* Vey clamped her hands over her ears, squeezed her eyes shut. *Why can't I remember?* She shook her head again. "Stop it," she pleaded, her voice weak and wavering. A disturbing metal ring pierced the back of her skull. Then silence. Finally, a clear thought. She deciphered the sound to be a sharpening stone, honing a blade.

Her heart added an extra beat.

This is wrong... very wrong. Vey placed her hands on her chest. She felt the material of her dress. *Doesn't feel right.* She pulled the slidden-down strap back over her left shoulder. *Ouch!* The sting—her chest—the garment stuck to her skin. When she slipped a hand beneath the fabric, her nail caught. Her skin wasn't smooth. *What?* She glanced down at her chest, gasped. *Blood.* Cringing, she peeled the fabric from her skin and peeked underneath.

Vey moaned at the sight. The dried blood. The cut. The stitches. With her fingertips, she traced the tender flesh. Red. Numb. Raw. Her pulse raced, thoughts in a whirl. *How did this happen?* A precision wound, centered around her heart. In the shape of a heart. Vey whimpered.

And that sound... scraping... honing... the damn knife is sharp enough. "Stop it," she said again. The pulsing wave grew in her head. Louder. Reflective. Resonating. *I have to get out of here.* She glanced this way and that way. *Trees silhouetted. Rocks. Darkened sky.*

"Hersh?"

Heartbeat pounding, Vey withdrew her hand from her wound. She rolled over onto her side. Lichens crunched underneath. She lay in thick moss, amidst fern-covered boulders. Vey tugged her dress straight. It had twisted in the night.

"Hersh," she called out again, her voice thin and crackly. *He must be near.* A surging memory jolted her. *Gan! We have to get to Gan before it's too late. Are we far?*

The special assistant propped herself up on one elbow. Dots of color flashed. Her vision blurred. Burning pain shot through her chest. She gritted her teeth. Gasping, she called out, "Hersh. You are going to miss—"

An image flashed in Vey's mind. She gasped: The Scarsands woman, in the middle of the road.

Shroud's Well... it's her. Smiling, but in a false way. The woman in the image looked at Vey haggardly, unruly hair standing on end. *Her eyes. Something cold.* The image only lasted a second, and then went dark. *What was she holding?*

The memory flashed again. This time closer, with the object raised to eye level. *Black, shiny, curved... a hook... a claw.* Vey grasped the bloody wound on her chest until it hurt. *That hag carved me up with a dirty old claw?*

Her ears pounded. Everything a haze. Vey remembered the cake. *Of course.*

This is bad. Very bad.

I need to run. Vey wiggled her feet. She felt a shoe on one foot and flung it off.

Then she heard something stir. Close by. The hoarse voice of an old woman called out to her. "Good morrow, my dear."

Vey jerked at the sound, a sound she knew. She tried to turn around, but didn't make it. The twisting motion tore at her stitches. She clamped over in pain. Grasping the wound, she let out a long, muffled groan. She peered between her fingers and gasped at the oozing rawness, then felt along the cut. *I think it's still closed... mostly.*

"You did this to me," she moaned. "Why?" Vey didn't hold back. "Because I wasn't polite and talkative? Because I could tell you were a Scarsander?"

"Keep quiet," said the voice, low and raw-throated, consoling in a matter-of-fact way. "Not me, my dear, no. Don't worry. You should heal up fine. I purified the wound. I sealed the wound. The wound is good, it is. I did everything but lick it better. And gave you something for the pain—NO sudden movements."

Vey wanted to sob. She continued to hold her hand to her chest, tight. Her body rocked back and forth. Blood trickled down between her fingers. "Darn," she huffed. "It did open up. Who did this?"

"Don't ruin my stitching," The woman scolded. "I was rushed.

You're pressing on it too hard. Leave it be and stay still." The woman hesitated.

Vey relaxed her hand. She damped her rocking motion to a gentle sway, kept her moans to herself. She hadn't turned to see the woman yet, but she knew who it was. She knew the voice from the apothecary.

"We—the vice-regent and I—we have to hurry to the Grey Tower. If he doesn't catch the Grey Clerk before she leaves… if she doesn't sign… the vote—Ahh!" Pain ripped through Vey's chest, like the wound had split open. She gritted her teeth and grunted through them.

"Not your concern any longer," said the woman.

Vey waited for the shot of pain to subside. "Who?" she asked again, this time in a cold, firm voice.

The woman sighed heavily, as though giving in. "Plucked by slavers, my dear. I was waving your carriage down to warn you and to beg for help. I'm sorry. I didn't know they were so close, so strong… such is Ekkon's Wheel, and we are but the pins on its outer rim."

"Slavers?" Vey's eyes went wide with the realization. *That Wilder knew… Amot. He was right all along. He wanted to hunt them down.* Vey shot a quick glance at the woman. *It's her all right—from the apothecary.* Then her eyes darted around her. "Hersh?"

"He can't hear you," the woman said. "But I can. Talk to me."

"You don't understand," Vey pleaded. "Fort Abandon will vote to forsake the Treaty of Nature. If that happens…"

The woman nodded knowingly, a slow grin forming on her face. "Ekkon's Wheel, I should have seen the signs." Her eyes brightened with realization. "It has begun."

Vey was taken aback. "What has begun?"

The Scarsander gaped. "And by my own hand, no less."

The scraping sound suddenly stopped. The woman glanced over her shoulder. Keeping low, she scuttled closer to Vey, leaned in and whispered. "The big one's bound and out cold. But don't you worry, my Vey. I'll get us out of this, I will. You and me. But you have to do as I say. You have to trust me, yessums. Now here's what you need to know for starters: Guard yourself against the nasty little one—Riddik the Cutter. He's the one to watch out for. A degenerate scum of the

earth, even for a slaver. Not the worst I've ever seen, but close to it."
She glanced over her shoulder again.

"And don't run," she went on. "A man-wolf creeps among them,
sometimes on two legs, other times on all fours—Gutless Kori. He'll
gnaw your ankles off if you try to escape, and then... you don't want
to know what happens next. The last one, Ang the Bitch, she's a devil's
child. Don't cross her."

Vey felt soft material brush against her hand, a small bag. She eyed
it carefully.

"Take this," the woman said.

"What is it?"

"Something to help with the pain. A pinch every few hours, but
no more. Sniff it if you need a fix right away. The powder will help to
keep you going."

Vey accepted the bag. It fit easily into her palm. Careful not to tug
at her stitching, she straightened up. Wincing at the pain, she slowly
adjusted her position. She turned to face the old woman full-on, but
the hag had already skittered off. Flattened ferns slowly lifted where
she'd been crouching.

... Milla, that's her name.

Despite what the woman had told her about running, Vey's first
thought was to run, to escape. *But where? The nearby road? The hills?
Some random direction in the forest? Should I scream? Who would come,
out here on the Outland Trail?*

While she sat contemplating, her ears homed in on a small sound...
the sound of short breaths. She cocked her head and then oriented her
gaze towards the direction they came from. First, she spotted long locks
of light brown hair scattered over the moss—Hersh's hair. Then she
spotted the steward, lying among boulders as she had been, out cold
as she had been. Bald now, little cuts crisscrossed his scalp. Like Vey,
he appeared to have been dumped there. Unlike Vey, he was bound in
heavy ropes, hand and foot.

Why him and not me? she wondered, but the reason was obvious.
They don't see me as a flight risk or a threat. She looked about discreetly,
staying low among the boulders. The coach handler was nowhere to be

seen among them. *Could he have escaped to tell others? Gotten help?* Her stomach dropped. Something inside told her "No."

A short distance away, a rough, male voice grumbled unintelligibly. Angry tones. Vey ducked down, flat. A second male responded, all harsh edges and just as cryptic. The voices brought vague visions of a wild place to her mind. Uncivilized. But something about the rolling rhythm of the words and guttural tones had a familiar ring to it as well. She reached back to her training in linguistics to piece it together. Another muffled exchange took place.

Ironeagle… Stouts, she surmised. *Stout words roll off the tongue. No. Baruush. But Baruush speech is even more harsh.* A bead of clarity opened in her mind. *A combination of the two.* It was common knowledge that the Stout settlers of Irongate and the native Baruush of Bitterhelm had grown close in recent years after decades of conflict, with many a Taint to seal the union.

Vey straightened up just enough to peer over the boulders. She quickly spotted two horses, a cart but no coach, and the three Outlanders Milla had warned her about, including a short bald one that had to be Riddik. The three stood together near a quiet creek. *The Blackmuk. It has to be.* The redhead felt a tingling all over. Suddenly, she knew where she was. *The road out of Deepweald crosses the same creek, but miles to the north. What did Wyatt call that boggish scent on the breeze? A skunk's arse?*

If I run, maybe I could get there. Following the creek was a better option than the road or the hills—a few miles through the woods along the river bank would bring her into familiar territory. But with a wolfish tracker in their midst and horses at their disposal, the implication was clear. *The horses I can outrun in the woods, but the man-wolf?* She remembered her lack of footwear as she watched the monstrous Wulver stand up on its hind legs, its elongated form misshapen and crooked. Vey gulped. *I don't want to mess with that thing. It'll catch me before I get anywhere.* She'd never seen one of his kind before, only in books. *A terrifying creature.* As it shuffled about, she noticed the old woman had made her way to them.

There she is, Milla. It seems she'd left Vey's side to confer with her captors. Even stooped as she was, Milla towered above the burly

Baruush that stood facing her, taller by a span. Two if you included her hair, shooting out haphazardly every which way. Vey strained her ears. What Milla told the little brute startled her.

"I'm taking the girl and leaving now," the old woman said, straight up.

Vey's heart drummed in her chest. Milla had to be crazy to simply walk up to a slaver and state such a thing, demand it. Especially with him carrying a long, curved blade, holding it the way he was, fingers toying with it. *That's what he was sharpening.* The special assistant gazed intently to gauge his reaction and the reactions of the others.

The Taint glared up at Milla. And as he did so, he slid the blade into the sheath at his side.

Vey sighed. *Good.*

"I don't think so," Riddik replied, his voice low and rasping.

Uh-oh.

The Taint widened his stance and, with a swift blow to the head, smashed the old woman hard to the muddy ground. Vey gasped. He'd landed a solid hit. She wanted to help, to scream, but all she could bring herself to do was keep watch as the old woman struggled to get up. He hoofed her in the ribs next. Vey heard the crunch. Down the woman went again, sprawled out, face to the ground.

Even from a distance, Vey could see the smirk Riddik wore on his face, and his hateful gaze as he watched the old woman writhe in pain from the blow. *He's enjoying this.* The mangy Wulver dragged himself a step closer and sniffed, while the demonic female crept towards Milla, keeping to a low stance with her spear readied. She was an athletic female—young teens maybe—with two stubby horns, shining black hair and beguiling looks.

Milla lay barely moving for a long moment. Slowly, her limbs began to stir. She rose to her hands and knees, head bowed, tresses of hair dragging on the mud. The Taint didn't kick her this time. Shaking and hunched over, Milla wiped her lip with her robe sleeve.

Vey felt terrible for her, despite herself. *She won't last. I have to do something.*

The special assistant shuffled over to Hersh. She shook him vigorously, slapped his face and his newly bald head, and pinched his arm hard. "Wake up," she begged. He didn't respond. She shook him again. *It's no use.* She tugged at the knots that kept him bound, but he was well-tied.

Back at the creek, Milla cried out. "We had a deal, Riddik!" She spat at the Taint.

Deal? Vey swung her gaze back in time to see the old woman steadying herself before attempting to rise to her feet.

The young demoness threatened Milla, prodding with her spear. "Stay down and shut your ugly hole, Hag, unless you want Riddik to carve you another one." Ang's voice pricked the eardrums, high and biting. "Or shall I do it for him?"

"You shut up, Ang. You're the little whore. Ang the Bitch aye? *HANG* the Bitch, I say." Milla narrowed her eyes, grunted, and then spat at the girl's feet. The demoness hopped back, a disgusted look on her face.

Ang lowered the shaft of her spear, set the point to the Scarsander's neck. "Call me a whore again."

Frantic, Vey worked the rope. *If I could just get this off… I know I can wake him up.* Grunting with the effort, she pulled frantically with all her might. The rope *might* have budged… slightly. She broke a fingernail trying, and then another. Vey winced in pain. The knots weren't giving. *Too tight.*

~Disrespect

Akrylla had half a mind to kill Riddik on the spot. She'd jab him with the giant scorpion stinger she was saving and be done with it. Gutless Kori would rip her to shreds and Ang would feel lucky to sink her spear into Akrylla's belly. Nevertheless, the shaman would die a satisfied death, satisfied to watch Riddik turn blue and suffocate when his throat constricted.

~Not yet

Her words laced with scorn, Akrylla cried out to the burly Baruush-Stout. "Ridicule me now, Riddik. Intimidate me, ya, ya." She raised her voice.

"Do it!" she dared. "You can cut me; you can screw me. But break your deal and I'll rip your worm off and toss it in a brew." She narrowed her eyes and stuck her neck out at him, boldly pressing her flesh into Ang's spearpoint until it drew blood. "Rip out your foul tongue too, I will. Rip out your tongue and rip your little worm off, and put them in a brew."

The demoness grimaced, full of disgust, while the skinny dog-face howled at Akrylla's remarks. Riddik smacked him across the snout to shut him up. The Wulver snapped back, growling. Riddik raised a single, firm finger to the beast, rested his other hand on the grip of his long knife. Gutless Kori slunk back, ears flattened to his skull. Then Riddik shot Ang a hard glance. She withdrew her spear slightly.

Riddik turned his dark, beady eyes on Akrylla. "You're starting to sound like a witch," he told her, glaring. He drew a different blade, wide and short, with an orange handle. "Are you a witch?" He ran his thumb along the edge, verifying its sharpness. "Because if you are, I'll carve you up again. If you confess now, I'll make quick work of it."

Akrylla scowled fiercely at Riddik. "I will curse you, Riddik the Cutter, curse you to suffer even worse than Gutless Kori, curse you to hang bleeding until maggots creep out of your rotten balls. How's that for witchery!"

Ang scoffed at Akrylla. "You can't do any of that. You're not a shaman. You're a useless old woman."

"Oh, but I can and I will," Akrylla assured her. "And you will hang too, Ang. You cross me and I will watch you both hang." She raised her voice. "Flies will feast on your rotting flesh."

~Mistake

Akrylla quickly realized she had gotten herself in a tizzy and gone too far. She had revealed something best kept secret.

I was angry, she explained to the voice that interrupts. But she knew the excuse was lame. There was a good reason why, early on, she'd told the Outlanders that her satchel was full of roots and herbs she'd gathered for cooking. And there was a good reason why, when Ang searched it, she'd skillfully explained away the snake tails, horse teeth, and raven's claws that the Bitch found inside.

A very good reason, in fact, she told herself. *A very good reason indeed, now in jeopardy.* The demoness had already frowned at the snake tail. *And now this?*

Ang, at least, had been contentious from the get-go about ascribing any mystical talents to Akrylla, and this played into the shaman's designs. Akrylla nodded slowly to herself as she considered what to do about Ang. *She's the brains of the operation. But the Bitch has a weakness. She downplays others' skills and won't admit anyone is better than her. At anything.* The shaman pondered the thought for a long moment, decided the personality trait suited her purposes. *Keep her that way.*

Rather than look alarmed by Akrylla's threats, the devilish Ang smirked fiendishly at her, then remarked, "You can have your little red-haired slut if the brothels don't want another soft, scrawny thing from the West that the cat dragged in. They don't fare well. Not for long."

Again, she misjudges, thought Akrylla, *my Vey is stronger than she looks.*

Riddik added, "She won't last a week if they do take her. I've seen how it goes."

~Take heed

Ang she couldn't trust—the girl misjudges and she could be trying to get under Akrylla's skin, nothing more. But Riddik, no, Riddik was not one to mess with. By the Taint's even tone and his unwavering expression, Akrylla judged he spoke the truth as he knew it. On top of that, rumors about the treatment of slaves in Bitterhelm were fully consistent with what the Outlanders were saying: torture, experimentation, fighting pits, and sex slaves. The same could be said about Jakka and the Scarsands. Akrylla made a vow to herself and to the voice that interrupts. To herselves: *Under no circumstances will I allow my Vey to be sent to the brothels of Bitterhelm. None whatsoever.*

Vey felt a hardening in her stomach. Jaw clenched, she banged on Hersh's bonds with her fists, trying her best not to whimper. She wanted to scream. *These damn ropes are impossible… and he won't wake up. Stupid oaf.* She simply couldn't make progress with the half-giant.

Down by the creek, the situation between Milla and the Outlanders had gotten out of hand. The old woman was about to get herself killed, or severely beaten at the least. And Vey needed her. Vey needed Milla and Vey needed Hersh too if she was going to get through this. *And all for a… for a stupid treaty.* She pounded her fists on Hersh's chest, let out a frustrated grunt. Most of all though, Vey needed to find something within herself. Something to help get them out of this mess. *Unless… maybe that Wilder will pick up the trail, or the Aerie will send out a gryphon.*

But the only way she'd ever heard of captured slaves escaping Bitterhelm was through buybacks. Vey sighed a defeatist's sigh. She wouldn't hold her breath waiting to be rescued. In the meantime, she'd torn her wound again and it hurt like hell. As the back and forth arguing continued at the creekside, she opened the small bag that Milla had given her. She glimpsed purple within. *What else can I do?* She wasn't sure if she trusted the old woman. *What else do I have?* Vey pinched the powder between her finger and thumb, sprinkled it onto her tongue, then licked the rest off her dainty digits. She wrinkled her nose at the bitter-sweet taste. *Not so bad,* she thought.

Vey waited for a long moment. *I don't hardly feel anything,* she told herself. The special assistant thought twice about the amount she'd taken. *How much exactly is a pinch anyway? My fingers are small compared to Milla's. I'll just take one of 'her' pinches.* Vey ingested a second helping of the powder the same way. Next, she drew the tiny drawstring tight, then tied the bag into her hair where it wouldn't be seen.

When she was finished, Vey sat still and let the substance do its magic. The reaction began almost immediately. She closed her eyes as numbness began to set in. She let the feeling permeate her consciousness. Then came a gentle drifting sensation. After that, her pain seemed much less of a concern—like something put aside, for later. *Compartmentalized.* Vey smiled, proud of herself for yet again having come up with the perfect word. She spoke it softly. "Compartmentalized." Vey giggled. After a long minute, she sighed restlessly. *I'm ready.*

Vey Lancer took a deep breath. She took a deep breath and stood up among the boulders, barefooted and proud. The head-rush from her quick rise made her dizzy. She didn't care that her legs were wobbly and she didn't care that she felt light-headed. Vey cleared her throat. No one but her seemed to hear. Tender-footed, she stumbled on a rock, then found her footing. Vey cleared her throat louder—much louder. The arguing by the creek ceased. Heads turned.

Fully conscious of the sudden attention, the special assistant took a long moment to straighten her red dress again, soiled and stained as it was. Vey hummed as she did so, then faced the Outlanders. All three of their beastly faces stared back at her this time, along with Milla's, which wasn't much better. "Really nasty, really ugly," Vey said aloud. Then she told them everything she thought they should hear. "I'm not sure I like the bald head you gave Hersh," she started, eyeing the Cutter, then she lost her train of thought. Vey paused, then started again.

"Ang, Riddik, I heard what you said about me. You're both right. Why would a self-respecting slave trader pay top dollar for me?" She stretched her arms out and examined her lankiness, rotating each limb about the long bones. "I'm scrawny and I won't last. Waste of time and effort." She narrowed her eyes and pointed to Milla. "And what are they going to do with an ugly old lady like her?" She tapped the top of her head. On the third tap, she missed and tapped her nose instead, which made her giggle. "Not smart," she went on. She tapped the top of her head one more time, slowly. "You can get much better… much more… by turning around and bringing us back. I'll pay you double what you would get for me at the auction, no questions asked and no hassle. Triple even. Milla too. My family's good for it." She gestured to Hersh. "And you have the mighty Steward of Fort Abandon here. Think about it. That's lots of free money." She nodded an exaggerated nod, eyes wide. "Lots of it."

"Mighty Steward," Riddik repeated, "I'll remember to carve that into his forehead."

"Ooh. I think he prefers 'Vice-regent,'" Vey said. "What were you thinking while you were shaving his head?"

Riddik answered, "I was thinking how much I wanted to cut his throat. Now I'm thinking about yours."

Undeterred, Vey continued. "The vice-regent's estate keepers will easily pay out... ten times what the slave traders would offer. For all of us, in fact. Just name your price."

"What do I tell my customers?" Riddik asked.

"Tell them..." She couldn't think of something to tell Riddik's customers. "Tell them..."

Ang scoffed. "If Abandon wants the vice-regent back so bad, they can come and get him in Bitterhelm."

The Taint took a long look at Vey, eyes feasting on her body as he ogled her up and down. The Special Assistant to the Grey Clerk lowered her head, swept her hair in front of her face, then stuck her fist in her mouth to gag. "Ugh," she said, under her breath. Hair got in her mouth. She spit it out. The hair tickled her nose. That made her giggle, then she stuck out her tongue to get the rest of the hair out. "Plah," she said, then peeked at the Outlanders between long strands of red. Her eyes fell to Ang's bitter face.

The demoness offered the Taint advice. "Our negotiating position is strongest from Bitterhelm," she insisted.

Still staring, Riddik nodded. He swung his gaze to Ang.

"Gather the horses. We're getting out of here now, before someone comes looking for the steward." Then he addressed Gutless Kori, "Kill anyone who tries to leave." Last, he regarded Milla.

"Wake up that slumbering half-giant or I'm going to carve him into a dozen pieces and toss them in the creek. I don't care what he's worth. You and the redhead will make up the difference in profit. As for the deal, the deal was that you give me what I want and I give you the girl. Well, maybe what I want *is* the girl, and then you can have her. Until I decide, you come with us to Bitterhelm."

No, no, no, thought Vey. She blurted out, "You must reconsider."

Riddik only scoffed.

A wave of hopelessness overcame Vey, but it drained away fast. It drained away fast to a place she didn't know. *I think that bad feeling is keeping the pain company*, she told herself. She shrugged. "Oh well."

The old woman slowly rose to her feet, holding her side. She took a long look at Vey, but not the same kind of look Riddik did. *She has crazy hair.* Vey giggled.

Milla met Riddik's gaze. "No more carving her."

Vey nodded with exaggeration. "Oh, good one… Haggy," Vey said to Milla. "I don't like it when he does that. Do we have any more of that cake?"

Riddik slid his second knife back into the smaller of two sheaths on his belt. "One wrong move and your Vey goes to the brothels," he told Milla. "I'll break her in for them myself. Even you might be worth something, to someone. Miners maybe."

Ang chimed in, already on her way to the creek. She called back over her shoulder, "Not the hag. She's too old and ugly for the brothels."

"Well," Riddik said, "someone can always use her in the kitchens."

~Opportunity

Akrylla knew she had to play this gift from Riddik just right.

"Go to hell, Riddik. I'm not cooking, not for you, not for anyone."

Riddik furrowed his brow. His mouth contorted into a grimace. "If cooking's what I want, you'll do it, Hag. That's the deal."

~Lure

Akrylla threw her arms in the air. She cursed and spat and scowled malevolently.

"I did everything for you already," she ranted on. "The deal is done. I'm taking her."

"For what?"

"For my own purposes. Mind your business, if you know what's good for you."

The Taint shook his head. "We feast at dusk. Gutless Kori will provide the game. Only afterwards will I consider closing the deal."

Vey started singing. Something about a game. *She took too much. I told her a pinch, no more.* While she sang, Gutless Kori's wolfish eyes watched the shaman, gauging. Akrylla couldn't decide if it had something to do with her preparing a meal, or potentially being one. Either way, his vulture-pecked belly would be full.

Akrylla ignored the distractions and scoffed at Riddik's offer.

Riddik called out to Vey, "Redhead, I'm coming for you."

Vey squealed in delight. "First you have to catch me." She spun around in circles, then fell on her ass.

Akrylla breathed a heavy sigh. "Fine," she told Riddik. "But only this once." *Once is all I need.*

"Hmph," he responded, with a sly grin.

He thinks he's won.

"And you better do it good, Old Woman. Gourmet. Else someone's gonna get a new carving on their face." The Taint turned his back on Akrylla, then caught up with Ang to gather the horses.

So glad they're not too worried about the witch thing, thought the shaman. *Riddik especially. Typical degenerate male—exactly what I'd expect coming from Bitterhelm. Just like them, to underestimate women.* In her mind, to be underestimated was the greatest advantage she could hope for right now. Akrylla was also glad she'd purchased the smelling salts at the Fargoer... for the half-giant. Otherwise, he'd soon be in pieces.

Chapter XXVII

Rules, rules, rules
(Hadamard)

T HE BURLY GRIG stuffed three pinches of flake into his pipe, tamped it gently and struck sulphur. When the flame settled, he put it to the bowl. With long, even draws, he got the weed to flare up. Mission accomplished, Feleg shifted his gaze to Hadamard. "The Kith don't have a chance in hell, do they."

Hadamard sighed. "You're not supposed to smoke in here either."

Feleg responded through clenched teeth. "Can't you see we're outside?" His voice rolled into a laugh, despite himself. The Djinxarai had dimmed the lighting in the dome to the usual grey of an overcast day. The expected animal and bird sounds of a real woodland scene were absent though, such devices beyond the projectionist's power to mimic. But not the drone of insects. And several rangers added to that humming noise, as they practiced imitating the resident shiro beetles' sounds for the purpose of disguising future communications.

"Besides, it's only simulated smoke…made of bugs, like everything else in here. Except tiny, little bugs that float around in the air."

"And cling to your lungs," Hadamard remarked.

Feleg's laugh morphed into a hoarse cough, which he muffled with a loosely clenched fist held over his mouth.

Hadamard shook his head. "Let's at least get behind the building." Before anyone took notice, the pair ducked behind the control center.

"So, how's that simulated buzz?"

"Not bad," the grig replied, "not bad at all." Feleg sucked back with small, occasional draws. He seemed at ease, for a few seconds at least, until he became acutely aware of the presence of his new shadow. The little bugger stared up at the grig with those owlish eyes. Feleg took one look into them and winced, as though in great pain. His voice was pleading.

"Ahh … don't look at me like that, Nek," he said. "The Djinxarai won't mind." The imp opened his little round "o" of a mouth to speak. Words crackled into the air.

"<clack tic> This isn't really outside <click>," he scolded.

"Really, Nek?" Feleg closed his eyes, drew another short breath through his pipe, then let out a relaxed puff in Nekenezitter's general direction. The Gloom took a step back. Feleg's "fix" had arrived, his mood had normalized, and he wasn't about to let the little imp ruin it.

Feleg turned his attention to the exercise grounds. Peering out from behind the building, he swept his gaze over the activities in the field. Hadamard did his own quick assessment.

The coveted "Take that Hill" scenario was rapidly coming together and both teams had committed to mapping out their strategies for the forthcoming exercise. Only Kith rangers would be armed with strikers, numbering three. They were to attack a long, low hill defended by queensmen. There would be no mimics in this scenario, the first of the trio of circumstances the dancing swords would be wielded in.

"The situation isn't as hopeless for the Kith rangers as you might think," Hadamard said. "The queensmen are exposed while the rangers have some cover to work with." The mocked-up terrain offered little protection for the defenders from an advancing enemy—just a simple hill in the middle of a "grassy" field—the grass being long strings of shiro beetles. And the tree line could prove to be a considerable threat, edging to well within confident sighting range for a decent marksman.

Feleg removed the pipe mouthpiece. "The Queen's Guard is a highly organized unit, and they'll be determined to hold their ground at all costs, with a strong shield wall and a capacity for decisive counter attacks." He hesitated. "Experienced too—some have decades more than our old-timers even, without loss of youth's vigor." He returned his pipe for another draw and puff.

"Hmph." Hadamard shrugged. "We'll see."

On top of that, Hadamard knew honor and pride were at stake, not to mention possession of what promised to be the most elegant weapon ever forged. Even if some queensmen snubbed the idea of dancing swords initially, the Lord of the March was sure to rally them behind his cause, to instill in their hearts and minds that strikers belonged in the skilled hands of the elite, not some disheveled band of wandering miscreants. Tradition and destiny demanded that the Queen's Guard prevail. Tradition and destiny demanded that they maintain their status as something to aspire to, the envy of all.

For the rangers, it was different. Much different. Strikers would just be another tool in their arsenal to get impossible jobs done; a practical necessity to achieve certain missions.

Garbed in his usual ranging leathers, Kith Commander Berendt Garondi approached the three "delinquents" hiding behind the building. His eye patch and the mutilated skin around it roughed up his look considerably from the last time Hadamard had seen the ranger, months back in the Akedan ruins. Berendt had his pipe going too, but unlike Feleg he didn't bother concealing his habit from the Djinxarai, not in the least.

"Gentlemen," Berendt said to the group when he arrived. He extended his hand to Hadamard's good friend.

"Feleg, good to see you again." He shook the grig's hand vigorously. "It must be five years now… outside Turnsby, wasn't it?"

"That sounds about right," Feleg said.

The ranger eyed the Gloom next, introduced himself. "I've heard about your kind, but never actually seen anyone from Dromeron Odoon before." He shook hands with Nekenezitter. "I've never been underground, you see. You're not what I expected. Your eyes…"

"He's just here to keep Hadamard honest," Feleg remarked with a grin.

"Nekenezitter," the Gloom replied. "True. I am different. <click> I am not blind. Vision is a rare gift among my people. <clack> They call it 'The Fifth.' There is much I would like to discuss with you. <tic> And when I am done, you will long to visit the rocky shores of the Dim Sea."

"Sure, anytime but now." Berendt turned to address Hadamard. The two shook hands, then the ranger got down to business. "The *hit callers* are asking about the rules of combat," he told the luminary. "They never received confirmation on the specific instructions for calling hits and kills in the scenario, and we're about ready to begin."

"That's because Lord Ralador never gave me an answer about the scoring system." Hit callers were Hadamard's way of officiating the combat. "We need to find him and get this sorted out."

"Better run," Feleg said. "Otherwise…"

"Shroud's Well, I know. He'll make the calls himself."

How to count wounded and kills in the scenario was the only parameter remaining that could be tuned to ensure a fair fight. Hadamard had already fought and lost on the issue of the attackers to defenders ratio. Three to one was standard, all else even, but despite the well-known rule of thumb, Lord Ralador had insisted on making the battle more "balanced." In reasoning out the advantages and disadvantages of the two sides, he'd argued that the terrain counted for at least one factor in favor of the rangers in the three to one ratio, and the lack of ranged weapons for his queensmen another half. Never mind that the scenario forced direct and close combat for Kith that were trained for stealth, surprise and, yes, ranged attacks. Never mind that, under standard operational procedures, the rangers would have carefully selected their time and place for an ambush after careful reconnaissance. But there would be no surprising the queensmen and stealth was limited to buzzing out comms and the use of a precious few wilder cloaks, in broad daylight conditions no less.

As the self-appointed officer in charge, Ralador's rules won out. Hadamard had no choice but to let him have his way. The Lord of the March even rejected Nekenezitter's offer to build in a provision for chance encounters and circumstances that could imitate a real surprise situation. The modified scenario featured the ambushing of a Queen's

Guard foot patrol, forcing them to retreat to the central hill where they would mount a hasty defense. The disagreeable lord shot Nekenezitter's idea down on grounds that it was too last minute to implement and that it would spoil the exercise by complicating it unnecessarily.

In the end, the ratio settled at three men to two, in favor of the rangers. To bolster the Kith numbers, over a dozen queensmen were put under ranger command, but only to fulfill roles that kept them out of the main fray—namely fire support and surveillance.

Berendt drew one last long, even breath from his pipe. Then he tamped out the burn with an already blackened thumb. "I'll round up the hit callers," he stated, then left the way he came.

Hadamard dropped his gaze to the Gloom. "Nek, are you coming with me?"

The Gloom trilled as he shook his batty head. "No. The Lord of the March <click> might get the impression I'm siding with you."

"Of course." The luminary felt a pang of disappointment, despite himself. *Too bad, I could've used the help.* His gaze shifted back to his old friend. "Feleg, Nek's all yours. Keep an eye out, in case I need you."

Hadamard turned to face the open area of the dome. He spotted Lord Ralador straightaway, garbed in full military dress and in the midst of a dozen distinguished guests. Hadamard hastened towards him. A diviner from the Chamber of Aelish stood at the March Lord's side, scepter in hand, white hair tied in a high bun in opposition to his white beard, which narrowed to a point. He was shorter than most. The pair's low-toned conversation was straight-faced and even-browed, with the occasional slow nod shared between them. The diviner wore the typical red and gold robe of his order, wide-cuffed and blended with elements of decorated plate armor. High ranking officials from the Grey Tower, the Hidden City, the River Guard, and the Gryphon Aerie surrounded the pair, socializing with one another.

When Hadamard arrived, he interrupted loud enough and forceful enough to put a stop to all conversation in his midst. "Lord Ralador, it's time to begin the first mock battle. We must finalize the scoring."

Ralador's reaction was a pinched expression. "Talk to the battle commander, Champion Eriff Haulik."

Champion was just a squad leader rank in the Queen's Guard hierarchy. Hadamard had expected a gallant.

The March Lord waved his hand in the general direction of his queensmen participants, together in a close huddle. "I am in the midst of discussing an important matter."

Hadamard countered, "Isn't he busy right now, preparing his men?"

"Nonsense." Ralador swept his gaze over the queensmen, locked eyes on one of them.

"ERIFF!" he shouted. The queensman stood casually in full plate armor, holding a tall helm in one hand as he addressed his men, surrounding him. When the queensman turned around to look, Ralador pointed at Hadamard's head. He mouthed something. Something that the luminary didn't quite catch.

Hadamard felt his face flush. Pointing at someone's head and mouthing a secret message to pass that person off was nothing short of rude and derogatory. The luminary widened his stance, folded his arms across his chest and with a firm tone addressed the March Lord squarely. "You need to be part of this discussion," he told Ralador. "I need to run everyone through the particulars of the mock battle one last time, and I need everyone to be on the same page when it comes to the rules."

Eriff arrived, having left his men and jogged over.

Hadamard continued, raising his voice to the next level. "What I *don't* need are interruptions and bickering, like during the last exercise."

"Rules, rules, rules." Ralador breathed an impatient sigh, muttered something under his breath, then turned to his guests. "Forgive me," he told the group. "It seems I must supervise every minute detail that remains, right up until the first sword is drawn." He turned his gaze back on Hadamard, his eyes like daggers. "Or shall I comment on that as well?"

Hadamard scrubbed a hand over his face, shutting his eyes tight for a moment. "No, Lord Ralador, that will not be necessary." *I simply don't want you to argue the calls, or have any excuses when you lose.*

"We understand," a young woman cut in, wearing a skirt and jacket that seemed almost military. In contrast, her hair was freefalling and full of loose curls, deep brown and rich-bodied as it draped over her shoulders.

Hadamard pegged her as Hidden City lineage—the palace.

"Your work is never done," she continued. "When do you ever sleep?"

Lord Ralador absorbed the compliment as though it were sunshine. A mature woman in the group, garbed in dark leathers and practical furs, turned away and scoffed discreetly. She wore the markings of Order Valkyrie.

"It's impossible to get good help these days," added a tall, lean dignitary with Outlander facial features, complemented by a dark moustache and goatee. He wore dark, loose clothing of fine material. "Every good worker I know quit after thirty or forty years to become an artist."

Definitely Grey Tower.

"That's Gan," grumbled the diviner in response. He turned to regard Ralador. "We shall leave you to your last-minute preparations. We can finish our discussion afterwards."

"Apologies, Ascendant." Ralador grasped the diviner's hand firmly in both of his.

"May Aelish's glow be upon thee." The diviner exchanged a knowing glance with the March Lord before they released their hold on one another.

Hadamard took note. *Obviously, something's going on between those two that I don't know about.*

As the dignitaries sauntered over to the viewing area, gabbing as they went, Berendt approached. He brought the hit callers with him, as promised, and a few extras.

Hadamard took control of the conversation. He began by explaining how the Kith rangers were charged with the unfamiliar task of storming a hill, defended by fully armored soldiers. For the most part, he addressed the callers, but was sure to make eye contact with Berendt, Eriff, and Ralador as he spoke. If for no other reason, to gauge their reactions to his words.

"The ranger objective is to retrieve the queensman flag, planted somewhere on the hill," he told the group. "They have to acquire it by sheer force as opposed to stealth, deception or speed. When scoring hits, any solid tap constitutes a hit from the weapon doing so—be it sword, blunted arrow, axe… whatever. Glancing blows and shield impacts will not to be counted. To register as a hit, the keen edge of the blade, the tip of the sword, or the tip of an arrow have to make firm contact with the body, whether armored or not."

"Yes, yes, they know all of that." Ralador addressed the Queen's Guard battle commander. "Eriff, describe your forces to these…," at a loss for words, he looked the motley crew up and down, "… these good citizens."

Eriff promptly responded, "Gladly, my lord." He turned to regard the hit callers.

"The Queen's Guard number thirty. Chain-armored fighters outfitted with training longswords constitute the primary line of defense—a kite shield wall to hold the high ground by blocking access at the base of the hill. They will prove to be an impenetrable wall, for sure. A separate chain-armored force, bearing round shields and training longswords, will act as reserves and lookouts, and they will handle any excursions that might arise. The main flag protectors are plate-armored officers, bearing round shields and true longswords—they represent our most skilled swordsmen, so there is no real danger of injury."

"Berendt," Hadamard said, prompting the Kith commander.

The one-eyed ranger regarded Eriff. "Kite shields? You mean the tall, curved ones? Tower shields."

"Yes," Eriff replied. "Eighteen."

Berendt grimaced, then turned his gaze back to Hadamard. "Rangers number thirty as well," he said, "outfitted with light armor and personalized weapons of various types, blunted or guarded. We'll have no choice but to rush the hill. Three strikers will be wielded from hidden positions. I inspected the blade guards and they're all secure."

Eriff furrowed his brow. "What about the fifteen queensmen under your command?"

Berendt turned his head back to Eriff, shrugged. "What about them?"

"Where will they be? What will they do?"

"As little as possible." Berendt's tone hinted at derisiveness.

Eriff's head jutted back, his eyes narrowed. "Whatever do you mean? Surely—"

Berendt folded his arms and stated his reasons. "After the reactions I got from your queensmen when I gave them their tasks, I don't trust them. And even if I did, if we can't use them to rush the defenders and break their ranks, they're no good to us. As it stands, they'll loose blunted arrows onto the hilltop from the tree line before the main ranger charge." He huffed, shook his head again. "They'll have to coordinate their fire on a high arc trajectory to have any chance of neutralizing their targets. They should be able to deter excursion forces, at least, if they can aim at all."

Hadamard cut in before the queensman could contest the ineffectiveness of his comrades. "Eriff, be on the lookout for arrows and make sure your men keep their visors down. Berendt, be wary of those longswords. Your rangers shouldn't need head gear, right?"

"I hope not, because we don't have any—you know Wilders." Berendt hesitated. "The archers were instructed not to fire if doing so would put a ranger in the line of fire."

Eriff sighed, then shrugged. "Your call."

With the queensman seemingly satisfied, Hadamard went on to explain the casualty model. He started by addressing Ralador and the two commanders.

"Our seven hit callers here will call out strikes and make judgements on damage. Every fighter of each team will carry a colored flag with a number on it—red for the Queen's Guard and blue for the Kith."

Hadamard handed Eriff and Berendt each a stack of colored, numbered flags. "Distribute these randomly within your teams—don't number people by rank or else the other side will be able to separate out your high value targets. Tell everyone to memorize the number they are given; I don't want corpses running around and screwing up the dynamics because they forgot their number, which was called out. A lethal hit call means you are out, non-lethal means you are still in, simple as that. The hit callers' rulings will be both immediate and final." He glanced to Lord Ralador. "NO ONE shall halt the action to argue a call." His eyes swept over the commanders. "Live with the judgements and move on. Understood? We can sort out any discrepancies afterwards."

Through eye contact alone, Hadamard coaxed a nod out of the two commanders and then Lord Ralador. He turned his attention to the hit callers. "Do you get it?"

The hit callers accepted with a group nod. They were an odd mix, composed of luminary prospects, regulars, and a Djinxarai.

"As a safety measure," Hadamard added, "a striker appearing within two steps of a queensman counts as a hit."

Lord Ralador interjected, "I have reconsidered the hit scoring method."

"Say again," Hadamard said. It was the last thing he needed to hear right before commencement of the first scenario.

"It is not fair that a single hit equally should bring down a ranger in leathers, a queensman in chain, or a queensman in plate," he said.

"We discussed this," Hadamard said. "One solid hit, one man down. It keeps the accounting simple."

"It is not realistic, and leaving the hit and kill system that way will discredit the outcome. It should be one hit to neutralize a ranger, two hits for chain armor, and three hits for plate armor."

Hadamard grunted his dissatisfaction. "That won't do; that won't do at all. You've tipped the scales in considerable favor of your Queen's Guard. The ratio is supposed to be three to one in favor of the attackers. We've already whittled that down. And you heard Berendt—your extras are practically useless to him."

Eriff butted in on the argument. "My men are well-prepared, my lord. I propose one hit for leather or chain armor, and two hits for plate armor."

Berendt shrugged, "No bother. My men are used to shit odds."

Hadamard scowled slightly, despite himself. With reluctance, he gave in. "That seems reasonable enough."

"Agreed," Ralador said. "Begin the match, immediately."

The two commanders proceeded to their teams. The hit callers took their places and a few luminary prospects manned observation posts. Lord Ralador went off to rejoin the group of dignitaries that had come to observe.

Hadamard sighed. His hopes rested squarely on the young ranger who'd shown the most promise in the trials leading up to the mock battle. The other two budding striker wielders, one Jull Dinser and one Tirma Burq, had also shown potential.

Now that potential will be put to the test, Hadamard thought. Every nerve in his body tingled with apprehension. *Everything rides on this outcome.*

Feleg and Nekenezitter joined the luminary in the viewing area to watch the mock battle.

CHAPTER XXVIII

THE SIGN

(Hersh, Vey, Akrylla)

HERSH ABRUPTLY BECAME aware: mid-stride, soaking wet, wrists tied. The skin of his neck burned raw. The steward felt as though he'd teleported into a body that'd been functioning all on its own, up until now. His swishing step tipped him off that his ankles were tied, loosely. The time preceding was lost to him. Cool, light rain pattered his face and the top of his head. *What the…?* Even that didn't feel right.

His entry into the conscious world had the character of a dream. The half-giant slowed to make sense of his new predicament. But before he could come to a complete stop, a strong tug on his neck sent him stumbling forward. A harsh, raw-sounding voice scolded him.

"Don't slack off," the woman ahead of him snapped. She glanced back over her shoulder, scowling from the confines of her hood. "And don't open your mouth, if you know what's good for you." Wiry tendrils of hair spilled out, grey-streaked and dripping wet. Her posture was hunched and she wore a crossed expression on her face, etched there like it would never go away. She, too, had a rope around her neck, attached to his by a cord that ran between them. Her lashing complete, the woman turned her head forward again, keeping step as she did so. She traipsed along the muddy trail in her brown robe, threadbare and ragged, and her worn, leather sandals. One of the sandal straps flapped with every step.

This woman was the middle person in a chain of three captives tied by the neck, although only Hersh's hands were bound. Ahead of her, a much younger woman with red hair and a red dress plodded on with heavy steps. *Vey.* The half-giant's heart sank into the pit of his massive gut when he saw the special assistant, the way she was: downtrodden, her dress soiled and wet, trudging shoeless through the mud. She didn't look right at all. Her head hung low and she stumbled several times in the few moments he watched. *What have they done to her?* The older woman nudged her forward at times when she slowed, or tugged on her rope left or right to set her on the proper path like she was some kind of mule. The three of them were being led by a male and female riding bareback on draft horses—his draft horses. Neither had yet glanced back.

Hersh didn't give a damn about the ragged woman's warning. "Vey," he called out, his voice weak and scratchy, as though he hadn't used it in a week. While he cleared his throat to try again, the ragged woman whirled about, soaked robe swinging with her. She made the evilest face he'd ever seen: glaring eyes that burned with malice, pursed lips, and her face shook with anger. Were Vey not on the same line, by that face alone he would have jerked the rope back and swung the old woman around him, strangling away the ugliness.

"Shut your giant trap," she snapped. "Blubbering ogre. You'll just make things worse. Your brain is mush, the girl is deadened, and your words are flying ants to her right now. So keep your nonsense to yourself."

Flying ants? Hersh shook his head at the strange comment. In an odd way he felt like apologizing. The woman huffed, whirled back around. She muttered something under her breath. True to her words, tiny floating dots suddenly appeared, swirling about his head. They faded into the rain.

What the…?

No one else took notice. Hersh blinked and did a double take. The dots were gone.

And although a haze yet lingered in Hersh's thoughts, and although he couldn't be certain that he was thinking straight, the half-giant still maintained a trace of his usual level-headedness. *Keep quiet and keep walking,* he urged himself, *for now... until you know what's going on. These are rough, desperate people. Dangerous people. And Vey is... delicate. Precious. Lives hang in the balance.*

The vice-regent surveyed the lands ahead. A mountain loomed in the distance. A bright patch hung high in the sky and to his right. *My bearing is east,* he surmised. *I must be on the Outland Trail, heading to Ironeagle Peak. Bitterhelm.*

Hersh remembered his manners. He quietly thanked Stonebones that Vey was still alive. With the image of that cold stone golem in his mind, the half-giant slipped into *recall.* He retreated mentally into the sanctuary of his still mind. It was an ancient trick he'd picked up in Glace Valley. A gift from the giants who dwelt there, part of the training he'd never finished. Hersh hummed to himself softly, low enough that the haggard woman wouldn't complain. He hummed in a tone that settled his mind.

Suddenly, Hersh arrived.

Although many years had passed, he felt as though he'd never left. The air was fresh, cool, and pine-scented. *Mountain air.* There was no rain. Great winds howled through the snow-tipped peaks surrounding him. He breathed deep through his nostrils and held the air low in his gut.

From his place next to a gurgling mountain stream on a high precipice, protected from the winds by a small stand of tall pines, the half-giant contemplated his fate. It didn't take long to discover the decanter was empty.

Empty.

For now.

That was a good thing, for it meant nothing stood in the way of him filling the decanter with free will.

For now.

The only other sounds in the mountainous setting were disconnected ones: footfalls slapping wet ground and horses' hooves thudding, the occasional murmur of low conversation, and a strange animal growl—canine in origin. They came to him in the form of echoes, reflected off the facing bluff from the nearest peak. Hersh turned his gaze from the stream to the bluff, wide and wind-smoothed. He rose to his feet and walked to the edge of the precipice. Beneath him, a dizzying drop. And as the echoes from the far-off land vibrated his eardrums, the same gentle rain that he'd felt on the trail pattered his skin.

I'm Here and I'm There—the two "wheres" he wanted to be. Had to be. The steward rubbed his head. *So that's the problem: I'm bald.* He shrugged it off. *Seems fitting enough, to be bald again among the giants.*

Hersh focused his mind on the rhythmic trudge of his own step, not *Here* but *There*, and then he focused on the voices that filtered in from the bluff, calling up from the drop. They were louder now, the voices of the Outlander slavers. To go to them was to take a giant step, in the *Here*.

And the voices were talking about him. Arguing. The conversation may have been prompted by his brief awakening, but he couldn't be sure if it was now or had just been—that is the way of *There*.

A chiming girl's voice insisted that if the ransom didn't come through, a guild master in need of a thug would top the offers. *She must mean Bitterhelm.* The haggard woman's hoarse voice came next. She believed a warlord looking to build a formidable fighter would win out. And, if that didn't work out because of his bad attitude, dismembering the vice-regent would send a clear message to Fort Abandon about the consequences to those who choose to meddle in Bitterhelm affairs. *A bit unnerving,* thought Hersh. One named Riddik gruffed that the Stout mining camp would outbid them all, hands down, arguing the mine managers stood to make a fortune off giant-blooded laborers, with a modest investment in some custom machinery. *Custom machinery?* His claim went undisputed. Hersh had never heard of Stouts using slaves before, and he privately wondered what the Outlander meant by "machinery." And he wondered where such equipment might come from. He sighed. *Realistically, it would have to come from under my very nose.*

Hersh closed his eyes and retreated deeper into his thoughts, far beyond *recall*, to a place where the voices could not reach. He retreated to the Pool of Invrin.

⌇

Vey collapsed to the ground after the long day's march, soaked from the hard bouts of patchy rain that had fallen throughout the evening. She felt she had her wits about her again, but her body was tired, her chest throbbing in pain, and her skin badly chafed from where the rope burned.

They'd only stopped because Gutless Kori killed a fawn. He'd already eaten the guts out before dragging the carcass to where Riddik said they could make camp, alongside the next river in their path.

This was after Riddik had already skinned three hares the Wulver had brought back en route. He used a small orange knife with a serrated blade that cut through hide and flesh effortlessly.

Riddik had used the same knife to cut Vey free, stating he wanted the red marks from the ropes to disappear before tomorrow's auction. He freed Milla as well, ordering her to tend to Vey. Hersh's bonds remained. As "confused" as Vey had been throughout the journey, she knew that Milla had never strayed far from her side. And she knew the old woman had given her water, forced berries into her mouth, and, just recently, rubbed a soothing salve over Vey's burning skin. Milla had a tendency to mumble to herself when she focused on a task, in low tones and strange tongues that the special assistant struggled to decipher.

The half-giant stood still as stone, glazed eyes staring straight ahead, unresponsive as though in a trance. *Milla must have given him an extra pinch,* thought Vey.

When Riddik caught her staring, he warned Vey to keep her distance from the half-giant, or he'd tie her to a tree—around the waist so it wouldn't leave a mark. That was the last thing she wanted to deal with.

The Taint went back to his task and made short work of the deer, quartering it and stripping off the back meat in under ten minutes. Vey watched, wary of Riddik's skill with that orange knife, wondering if he'd cut her the same way. Every slice with the small blade was precise and confident. He never grunted once about something not going right. When he finished, he hung the carcass and rinsed the blood off his hands in river water. Then he moved on to finding suitable branches to suspend the meat for roasting.

Meanwhile, Ang built the fire. Milla collected deadwood for her while intermittently preparing the hares. Gutless Kori licked his chops. Every so often the beast glanced at the captives, one by one. And while Milla and the Outlanders were thus occupied, Vey ran her fingers through her hair. She reacquired the tiny bag Milla had given her, discreetly retrieved two pinches of powder from it, sprinkled them on her tongue and waited for her pain to float away.

Riddik bellowed out, "This will be a feast." The declaration came while busy cutting a heavy spit and sharpening it to a point. With the fire going strong, he sent Ang off with Milla to gather herbs for the roast. "Keep an eye on her," he warned the demoness.

As Vey lay on the ground, she gazed up and watched the sky. The inky darkness of late evening had begun to set in. The night would be pitch-black: moonless, cool and wet. She felt a pang of hunger in her stomach when the meat began to cook, and she wanted to dry off by the fire. But moving would mean effort, and there was something in her stillness that she simply did not wish to disturb. With the comforting smoke of the coming dinner filling her nostrils, Vey slipped into a deep, dreamless slumber.

⚜

Akrylla awoke beside the firepit, her stomach hollow despite the night's feasting by the Outlanders. Riddik had begun to stir, while the others slept soundly. Gutless Kori lay curled up by a half-charred log, like a hound. Stiff from the rain and the chill air, the shaman forced herself to her feet, then ambled softly to a tree that'd been uprooted by strong winds. There, she made herself comfortable. From her position among its curled roots, she had a clear view north between the treetops, north to Blacktip Mountain in the distance—the "other" mountain in the region. She gazed at the twilit sky overtop it, eyes fixing on the clouds that churned there.

~Unease

The storm wasn't even near, yet the birds were silent and every living thing in the woods lay hidden.

~Unsettled

Lightning flashed behind the clouds as Akrylla watched on. Then again, and again. Each new flash lit a pale orange eye in the sky. *A pale orange eye.* The heavens were electric orange that morning.

Thunder rolled in after. Akrylla felt divine purpose in the works, but she could not put a finger on exactly what it meant. *Tell me more, Norwin of the Dawn,* she urged the northern sky. *Tell me more, Song of Light, that rumbles in the distance. Tell me more, Song of the Wind, that rattles leaves and makes trees groan.*

Lightning flashed again. This time, two powerful channels, massive and bright, split over the mountaintop like a forked tongue. *A forked tongue... a forked tongue...*

~A sign

Akrylla knew of the ruined and snake-ridden city of Jakka, scattered throughout the mountain's roots. And she knew of the great behemoth that lay nestled in its grand snake-pit. A desert creature originally, known from the days of old. The only one to have ever defeated Shroud.

Gorganna. She calls.

CHAPTER XXIX
THE FALL OF SHROUD

*O*N A STARRY *night in mid-summer when the Star Sands was still lush, Shroud journeyed from the North to claim a new land for his followers. He was so confident there would not be trouble that he left his Shield Maidens behind. But Shroud met the Great Mother of Snakes, Gorganna, in a mountain pass near the Great Bend of the river Dekka Kur. The Serpent lured Shroud into her den with twisted promises of power and riches and wisdom and women. Then, in the dark, the Serpent felled him with a single poisonous bite. Gorganna dragged Shroud's body to the surface, bit off his right hand and tossed it away. Thus was formed a great hill in the shape of a hand. She then proceeded to drag the body back to the North. Thus was formed Gorganna's Trench. But Shroud was not dead, and as he came to, he heard a dreadful hiss. With his left hand he drew his sword and fixed his eyes upon what he saw to be a red serpent. He swung mightily, but his vision was not right from the poison and he hit a mountain instead. He sliced the mountain in two, and the top shattered into pieces so small they became the desert sands. It was a fiery streak across the sky Shroud had seen—not the Mother, and so what is left of the mountain is now called Slice of Fire.*

Shroud succumbed to the poison again and Gorganna dragged him farther, until he awoke once more. This time, he saw a serpent in the shape of a crescent and swung his mighty sword. But again, Shroud's vision was not right and he had swung at the moon, only to hit another mountain, split it in two, and send the shards flying to become small rocks. That mountain is now called Slice of the Moon. Driven by anger, in a moment of clarity, Shroud swung at the Serpent's face and split her tongue. Gorganna was quick to respond though, and bit him one last time, filling his blood with her deadly venom. Before falling under, Shroud threw his sword. It flew through the air and sliced though all of the other mountains in the land, smashing their tops to sand and rocks. Whirlwinds formed as the sword spun and the rainclouds in the sky were sent far and wide. Then Shroud fell hard. He fell so hard his blood splattered for miles upstream, and the land bent beneath his broken body. That land upstream is now called the Bloodspill, and the earth there is red. The muddy waters of the Dekka Kur then rushed over Shroud's body and hid him in their murky depths. Gorganna would have pursued him further, were it not for the Shield Maidens of Shroud. They rose from the sands riding great black scorpions. They drove the Mother off of Shroud's body, back through the trench and to the safety of her den, which, they discovered, was nothing more than a giant worm hole. The Shield Maidens drove Gorganna from there as well, and chased her a hundred leagues east to the swamps of Jakka.

—The Pristine Channeler, on Shroud's demise and the coming of Gorganna to Jakka

CHAPTER XXX

THE WALL

(Akrylla)

"Ikkubar had many years to construct his place of rest—many years and many wives and many cats with many lives. Yet, when he died, the monument to his glorious rule was still incomplete." Osha brushed her fingertips against the huge cat carved into the heavy stone door that blocked passage into the ancient tomb.

Her memory is intact, Akrylla thought, *a good sign.* Yet, she prodded. Every day she tested her little sister, a child of eleven, just to be on the safe side. "One should never venture inside," Akrylla told her. "Remember?"

Osha recited the next phrase of the legend, from memory. "And although betrayed by his own brethren and by eight of his nine wives, Ikkubar was well respected by those he ruled. Especially the catfolk. Artisans of all trades took to the secret task of finishing his tomb and devising ingenious traps to guard the treasures he would need in his afterlife."

"Exactly," Akrylla said. "We should go now. To the Wall."

"Are the catfolk real?"

"I have never seen them." Akrylla forced firmness into her tone. "The Wall, Osha."

"But we have weeks before the borders are sealed." The girl's big, brown eyes brightened beyond compare. "Today, we can explore, all to ourselves. But once we leave…"

"Osha, we're going NOW."

"You go. I'm staying." The eleven-year-old made her best pouty face.

Akrylla, being seven years her senior, responded by doing what older sisters do. She knelt down beside Osha and softened her voice, gently rubbing the girl's back as she did so. "One day, we will return. That tomb will still be here when we get back."

Osha huffed, averting her eyes.

"Please, Osha," Akrylla pleaded, "the wall guards won't let me pass without my ak'la, my apprentice."

"That's not true."

"It is true. Everyone who leaves to study healing at the Chamber of Aelish needs an apprentice. Just like a knight needs a squire."

"Is that *really* true?"

"Yes, it is. Don't you want to be a healer someday too?"

"I like archaeology more."

"But don't you want to come back someday and help make everybody better?"

Osha shrugged, eyes tracking up along the length of the intricate stonework.

"Well, you can do archaeology *and healing*. That way, if you set off a trap while exploring one of these old tombs—a poison gas trap for instance, or rocks that come tumbling down on you, or whatever—you'll know how to make yourself better."

Simple arguments that spoke to immediate desires worked best with Osha. She breathed a heavy sigh and swung her gaze to Akrylla. "Promise?"

"Promise."

"All right then. I'll go."

The sisters collected their belongings, drew their cloaks tight about them and ventured away from the protected gash where they'd sheltered for the night, into the open wash plain. High winds gusted about; sand whipped through the air. Akrylla wondered if she should burden her sister with a bedroll to carry, lest her frail frame be carried away. *No, she decided, the poor thing's too weak.*

Osha called out over the roar. "The Angry Wind God is out today," she said.

"At least he's at our backs," Akrylla replied.

Now desolate and dried up, the Wash of Shroud had become a land of parched, hard-packed sand and old tree snags, and for those who believed the coal miners that lived nearby, the place was terribly cursed by the "unrejuvenated"—angry, vermin-infested bodies set adrift from Kel Fariz at the Scar's onset. The miners claim the corpses settled to the bottom of the wash, before the waters were dammed, and now lay buried beneath the cracked mosaic of the wash-bed. Not fully dead, the miners say the corpses still wait, unforgiving and full of hate for all who dare to live, even more so for those who dare to stride casually upon their shallow graves.

Fire box stories, Akrylla told herself. And as nervous as she was about the bodies, she didn't let it show. Not to Osha. Not in front of her little sister. There was only one direct way to the Wall and they were damn well going to take it.

Osha and Akrylla passed the flat-topped Slice of Fire mesa in good time, and then the palm trees, small round huts, and rubbled halls of the Mystic Dunes oasis. Instead of laying over like they usually would and delving into the archives of the Sons of the Deceived, the siblings pressed on through Gorganna's Trench all the way to Ekkon's Pass, where they spent the night, before cutting north towards Kel Samu. Ahead, in the general direction they were traveling, a column of smoke rose high above the hills and mesas. Akrylla wondered if the smoke originated from the city or its outskirts. Kel Samu—the only major center of the Star Sands not to have fallen to the plague—had become the gateway to the East, by way through the Stout outpost of Kalkakham and onward to the Outland Trail.

Akrylla patted her cloak where, on the inside, she kept her entry documents closely guarded. She felt the rectangular shape of the folded parchment pressed between her palm and her left torso. *Still there.* The invitation to study at Gan's Royal Citadel had been signed by the Fifth

Ascendant of the Chamber of Aelish. She could even read the name, but that didn't matter. All that mattered was the seal the document bore and the authority that it represented: the seal of the Pristine Channeler. Officially, Akrylla had been chosen as a Healer Prospect.

It had been a queensman, though, not a diviner, who had discovered Akrylla's talents as she toiled away in one of the healing camps; a queensman with some healing skill of his own, who happened to be part of the expeditionary force providing security for humanitarian aid to the region. Most importantly, he was a queensman she'd fallen in love with. And when the valiant Duelist Marec was called away on duty to escort an eastern dignitary to the Wall, he'd begged her to accompany him.

Akrylla glanced back to Osha, trailing slightly behind. *I did the right thing,* she told herself, *to take heed of that little voice inside.* Osha had helped Akrylla in the camp, and it was there she'd fallen ill. She'd helped ever since the two of them had to rely on one another for everything, ever since their parents were killed during looting in Kel Fariz. *Had I left her to relatives, I would not have been able to live with myself.* And her little sister was stronger now, much stronger, nursed by Akrylla's expert knowledge of medicinal herbs found only in the Star Sands. *More than strong enough to make the journey,* she was sure.

᠃

Ekkon's Pass cut a northeast line through the highland terrain. The steep hills and cliffs on either side gave shelter from the dry, desert winds. The mid-morning sun came welcome that day, after such a chilling night and a long, shady morning.

Rounding the final bend, the Wall came into view, about half a league distant. The tall, stone-block structure stretched hundreds of feet end-to-end across the pass, barring passage into Kel Samu. A crowded tent city had sprung up at the base of it, since last Akrylla had visited. She finally got her answer about the smoke. She swung her gaze to the northwest where it billowed up into the blue sky, thick and grey. She knew of a canyon there. *Probably burning garbage from all those people in the camp,* she decided.

"Look!" Osha called.

Akrylla more than half expected her little sister to be pointing at the Wall. Far from it—when she turned to see, instead she beheld the girl kneeling on the sand before a pile of loose rocks on the side of the hard-packed path.

Akrylla halted. "What have you found?"

Osha shut one eye, held something small up in front of the other eye. The object glinted in the sunshine. "A bead," she replied. The girl rose to her feet and rushed the find over to her big sister.

Akrylla pinched the piece between her forefinger and thumb. She, too, examined it closely. *Yellowy-orange, translucent, tiny specs inside...* "Amber," she said at last.

"Ekkon the Wanderer," Osha added. "And I found it in *Ekkon's* Pass."

Akrylla reoriented the bead in her fingers and noted the many tentacle-like appendages. "Indeed, it is. A good omen to those who would venture forth into the unknown or the uncharted—you've heard the phrase 'Ekkon's Wheel' haven't you? Many in this city are followers of the behemoth who slips between the dunes. Today is your lucky day."

"Can you hold it for me?" Osha asked, eyes squinting in the sunlight. "I don't have a good pocket and I'd hate to lose it."

"True. You are always losing things," Akrylla responded. She squirreled the amber away in her satchel then pulled out her waterskin. They both drank deep.

"We are close now," Akrylla told her, then stepped off the trail and strolled behind a sand dune. After spotting for snakes and scorpions, she beckoned her sister to follow. "Come along," she said. Osha obliged. Behind the dune and among the fallen rocks, Akrylla unpacked two garments and laid them out flat in a private space: a blue dress with flowers for her to wear and a similar-patterned green dress for her sister.

"Today, we are going to make ourselves very pretty," Akrylla told Osha. She started by taking a cloth, wetting it, and wiping the girl's face. Then her arms and then her legs. Next, she dumped a measured amount of water over Osha's head and ran her fingers through her hair. She squeezed her sister's cheek, smiled into her face. "Pretty," she said, then gestured to the green dress. "Now put this on."

Osha crinkled her nose. "Marec makes you wear clothes like these."

Akrylla gasped dramatically. "He does not." She raised a hand to her chest. "I wear them because I want to. I happen to like them."

Osha giggled.

Akrylla went on. "Everyone on the *other* side of the Wall likes them." She picked up the green dress and held it for her sister to take. Osha's hand flashed out and grasped it. With a high, sweet voice, Akrylla intonated a warning to her. "Careful, you are going to crinkle it." Ignoring her completely, Osha tossed the dress on the ground and began to change clothes.

Akrylla sighed. *At least Osha's acting normal.* She prepared herself next. And after changing into her blue dress, she pulled a small mirror out of her satchel and gazed into it. Several days had passed since she'd seen her reflection. Akrylla grimaced at what she saw: tired eyes staring back at her; the dullness in her hair; her skin not nearly as radiant as it had once been. And when she held the mirror at arm's length, she couldn't help but notice her bent-over stance.

Despite her aching bones, Akrylla straightened her posture. She could still stand elegantly. *Just tired,* she told herself. Then she brushed a wet hand through her hair to style it. Between her fingers, strands of hair came out in clumps. *Diet,* she surmised. *I have not been eating proper meals.* She smiled into the mirror. Decay was beginning to show on her teeth as well. *I need to take better care of myself.* A terrible thought entered her mind. Straightway, she denied the idea. On the strength of her skin still being unmarred, she dismissed the notion that she could be showing early signs of the Scar.

Akrylla huffed a disappointed huff at her declining physical state, and then unpacked two fresh pairs of sandals. "Throw your old ones away," Akrylla told her sister, a slight sharpness to her tone. She couldn't help it.

The girl laughed nonetheless as she whipped her sandals at the cliffs. "Goodbye, stinky sandals," she called after them, as they spun through the air. That made Akrylla smirk. Refreshed and bright-looking despite all, the siblings returned to the trail and continued on their way.

On the outskirts of the tent city, vultures fought over a small, furry carcass. They took flight when a pair of laborers got too close, having just exited the uneven line of structures that marked the camp's boundary. They led a donkey cart with two squeaky wheels, its covered contents on such a tilt Akrylla imagined them sliding off at the first bump in the road. Some ways behind, a sellsword in leather armor casually followed, before stopping to chat with someone. *A guard,* she surmised.

Smells of smoke, cooking, urine and incense assailed the two sisters' senses as they approached the tents. Akrylla could smell the sickness in the air as well, circulating on wayward currents. Just like at the healing camp, she tried her best to ignore it. Voices swelled as they neared, the sounds of people going about their daily business. Pots clanked. Children ran. Tent fabrics flapped in the breeze.

Akrylla and Osha crossed into the encampment and zig-zagged through the maze of animal-skin shelters and makeshift lean-tos, stepping through the filth and over the occasional passed-out occupant. Cats roamed about freely, eyeing them as they passed.

A few minutes in, Osha went pale. Akrylla stopped and took the girl's hand, clammy in her grip despite the heat. "Are you feeling a little queasy?" she asked.

Osha nodded, wide-eyed.

Akrylla quickly looked her over, the way she would a new patient. She saw no ridges or red coloration on her arms. She noted some dark around the eyes and color drain in her face, but no open sores or wounds to speak of. Just like yesterday, and the day before that, and the day before that. *Still no telltale signs of the Scar,* she thought, and thanked Ekkon the Wanderer. *Just a little overpowered by the horrid stench is all.*

"We haven't much farther to go now," she assured her little sister. "Soon, we will be on the other side of that big wall."

Osha lowered her gaze to the ground. At the sight of a soiled blue blanket, she put her hand to her stomach, pressed hard, and moaned. Her pain infused her voice. "Can we go back to the pass, to the open air?" she asked.

"No Osha, we cannot," Akrylla replied. "That would send us in the wrong direction." She offered her palm. "Now come along, my ak'la, to freedom from this land until the Scar passes." Osha accepted.

Eventually, they reached the wide, cobbled road that led to the gates. The line-up to the wall was at a standstill—hundreds of people long if not a thousand, some standing and others sitting. Some carried their children or belongings, while others had carts or loaded pack animals. At least a dozen queensmen in chainmail patrolled the line. They did so with relaxed strides, swords hanging from their belts.

Akrylla lifted her sister up into her arms, held her close. The girl weighed almost nothing. As each queensman walked by, Akrylla scanned his face, hoping. She even asked a guard who wandered near if he knew of a duelist by the name of Marec Haulik. The man shook his head apologetically, noting in kind and polite words that he knew the family name, but that there weren't any Hauliks in his unit.

She was shocked to hear the hateful conversations that rose up in the crowd around her, behind the man's back after he'd left. Akrylla covered Osha's ears at the foul names they called him and his comrades. They went on to complain that Gan was not really there to help, and lamented about how the mystical Djin had turned a blind eye to the desert people's suffering. Some accused both societies of taking part in Harrow's cruel experiments with rejuvenation, the experiments that caused this mess to begin with.

"No one is really getting through the gates," one woman claimed, "we're all diseased as far as they're concerned." A man in his twenties insisted some had been let through, only to be beheaded on the other side, their bodies tossed into mass graves. That much, at least, was contested by several in earshot: "Get out of line then," those behind the man urged, "if you're so sure you'll die on the other side." They had a point.

⟡

Afternoon had turned to evening. And following many hours standing in the stinking crowd under the hot sun, a woman in red regal armor finally ushered Akrylla and Osha to one of the nine administrative desks—simple stone-slab tables set up in front of the gates.

Each had a metal box underneath stuffed full of papers, and each had a wooden chair on either side. Tarps protected the busy clerks from the sun as they worked their ink and their paper.

Akrylla took the seat offered her, lifted Osha onto one knee. The balding, bespectacled man facing her from the other side of the desk wore a tan robe with gold trimmings. He introduced himself with a forgettable name, in a voice so low she could barely hear it. Then he eyed the two sisters with a measuring look. She knew that look.

"You both probably have the Scar," he told them straight out. "But don't worry, you won't be contagious for weeks."

"What?" *Did I hear him right?*

The clerk sighed, upped the volume of his voice slightly. "The Scar. Chances are, you have it."

Akrylla jerked her head back. *That doesn't make sense.* She shook her head at the man. "What do you mean?" She stretched her arm out to him, then rolled her forearm in front of his eyes. "No red, wavy lines showing through… see? I volunteered in one of the aid camps. I know the signs."

"Then you'll know when it's full-blown. I can't let you pass."

"But I've been accepted to study in the Chamber of Aelish, Gan's most prestigious healing institution…" The letter was still in Akrylla's cloak, which she'd rolled up and stuffed into her carrying bag when she'd changed into her dress. One handed, she fumbled through the bag's contents. "One moment… I have documentation from the Citadel." Akrylla found the pocket and slid her hand in. With a few short tugs, she pulled out her acceptance letter and handed it to the clerk. "Look at the signature and the seal. You *have* to let us in."

The clerk sighed, then slowly unfolded the parchment. A chunk of the wax seal plunked onto the table. Skepticism on his face, he adjusted his round-rimmed spectacles and scanned the document, then raised his eyes to hers. "How do I know this isn't a forgery?"

Akrylla didn't answer, put-off by the insinuation.

The clerk flattened the letter on the table, then gestured to the cracked seal. Pieces of it were barely attached. One finger tapped the signature block beside the seal. "On top of that, the signature date is *before* the absolute quarantine. Therefore, this offer is invalid."

"Invalid?" The word burned her insides. "What do you mean invalid?" Heat flushed to her temples. Lips pursed, trying to be gentle, Akrylla lowered Osha to the cobbled ground. "And the seal," she explained, "that letter has been through a lot. *We* have been through a lot."

His voice was soft but firm. "The offer is invalid. Even if it were not, you are still showing signs…"

Akrylla stood up, blood boiling in her veins. "I know the damn signs." Towering over the small desk and the man seated behind it, she glared down at the clerk and enunciated every word. She spoke with forced kindness. "I have come all this way to study at the Citadel." She rested a hand on Osha's head. "I have come all this way to bring my sister to safety—look how young she is. She needs a healer. And I have come all this way to find the man I love, Marec Haulik. He is waiting for me on the other side of this stupid wall."

"I'm terribly sorry, Miss. There is a hospital tent you can visit for the girl. Our healers will do what they can—"

"Do what they can?" The words rang in her ears. Akrylla raised her arm and pointed past his head to the gates. "What you can do is let us through those gates before I… before I…"

A queensman at the gate stepped towards them—a different sort than the ones patrolling, outfitted in heavy armor and bearing a polearm. The clerk raised his hand to stay him. Akrylla heard murmurs in the crowd. She glanced about, many eyes upon her.

The clerk rose from his seat. He stood shorter than her by several inches. He leaned forward and spoke softly, making subtle, calming gestures with his hands. "Come back in four weeks," he implored. "If the guards don't tackle you, put you into a sac and throw you onto a cart because you look like walking death, then perhaps I was wrong and we can make an exception."

"I demand to speak to Marec Haulik." Akrylla's voice began to falter. "He is expecting my arrival. He is…" She had to force the words out. "He is to meet me here."

"I'm sorry, I don't know who that is. I know the family name, but—"

Akrylla folded her arms, firmed up her tone. "I want to speak to Marec."

The clerk gave her a measuring look, turned to face the guard at the gate, then waved and called out: "Gallant, do you know of a Marec Haulik?" Without hesitation, the queensman made his way over.

"Yes, I do," he replied when he arrived. His tall helm and regal armor gleamed bright in the sun. He loomed over both of them. "I am sorry to say that Marec was assigned to escort the Pristine Channeler himself back to the Citadel, and later posted to the Hidden City."

The clerk asked, "Did Marec leave any instructions or make any special arrangements?"

The queensman shook his head. "He had expected a hasty return, but plans changed. Everything changed."

The clerk turned to Akrylla, eyes pleading. "I really am deeply sorry, Miss. Why don't you leave your entry papers with me and come back in four weeks? I will send a caller into the encampment to find you and your daughter."

"My *sister*. And her name is *Osha*."

"Osha, then." The clerk continued where he'd left off. "If you both seem healthy, you may pass the gates and stay in our holding facility for another four weeks. Then, if all goes well and your claim checks out, you may proceed to Gan."

Akrylla stood staring at the man for a long moment, pretending not to notice the guard motioning for her to leave, signaling that her time with the clerk had come to an end. To either side of her, interviewees were being turned away, sent back to the crowd. No one was getting through, just like the woman in line said. But behind her, something was stirring. Behind her, as she stood glaring at the balding man, the murmurs of the crowd seemed to grow louder. She sensed their collective frustration. Uncertainty. Anger. Whether directed at her, or the establishment, she did not know.

Osha began to weep. Akrylla broke eye contact with the man and picked her sister up. Feeling Osha's body against hers, Akrylla's anger melted away. It melted into sympathy. Sympathy for Osha. Sympathy for herself. She wiped away Osha's tears while holding back her own. And as the wash of emotion overcame her, the clerk outright asked them to leave. He asked them to be mindful of others still waiting in line. Akrylla buried her face in the girl's hair.

"Next," the man called towards the front of the line.

Four weeks, Akrylla thought. *Shroud's Well.* Four weeks seemed like forever away. The clerk could just as easily have said a hundred years for all the good it did her. She turned her back to him. Not knowing exactly what else to do or where else to go, she left the Wall, back in the direction she'd come.

⋙

Akrylla made her way back through the crowd, holding her Osha close. She didn't know what to think, what to feel—disappointment, fury, embarrassment, hopelessness, hate… they all took turns coursing through her veins. In the end, only numbness. For hours after, neither sister spoke to one another as Akrylla wandered the encampment searching for an unoccupied tent. Every patch of ground seemed taken.

As night began to fall, the twenty-something man who'd stood next to Akrylla in line, the one with the conspiracy theories, greeted her. He started talking. He started talking and he never stopped talking. He gave her his name. She forgot it instantly. It had a 'd' in it somewhere. The twenty-something man told her how Harrow started the plague and he told her how Gan studied it. And then he told her the only thing she cared about. He told Akrylla he could find her and Osha a place of their own among the tents. She smiled at that and thanked him profusely. But he wasn't finished. The man kept talking. He also told her to try the lineup another day because different administrators make different decisions. That was useful too. He told her a great many things about daily life in the tent city. Finally, as he led the sisters to an empty tent, Akrylla looked at him—*really* looked at him. The twenty-something man was seedy in appearance, with dark hair slicked back and a lean build, but he wasn't ugly and he wasn't stupid. And he seemed to know everyone.

⚘

Two weeks later, a morning came when Osha never woke. And when Akrylla heard the creak of the daily cart rolling up, she let it pass without a word. And when the trailing sellsword quietly announced himself, lifted the tent flap and ducked his head in for a quick look, he simply curled his nose before proceeding to the next tent. Osha had become so thin he hadn't noticed her under her blanket.

Lifting a bundled-up Osha into her arms, Akrylla shadowed the cart on its meandering path. In her two weeks in the camp, she'd learned that the cart was loaded with loosely-wrapped bodies—two or three this time, she guessed, by the size of the towed heap. And she'd learned many other things about the tent city in her time there. She'd learned greed and pettiness and that people are foul. She'd learned there are predators and there are victims. She wasn't sure which were worse. She'd learned men were unreliable and only ever wanted more for the little they gave her. And last, she'd learned how easy it can be to turn a blind eye.

Akrylla followed the grim procession out of the tent city. She watched from a distance as the cart rolled into the canyon she knew of, to the fire that never stopped burning, to the fire she'd thought consumed garbage. But it wasn't garbage consumed, it was souls freed, souls of The Scarred, ascending above the canyons and the mesas, into the clouds. Even the Angry Wind God let them be, it seemed, for the smokey column never wavered on its course to the gusty heavens.

Akrylla kept going. She slipped between the sand dunes of Ekkon's Pass, until she came to the place where they'd changed clothes, where Osha had found her bead. There, Akrylla put to rest her little ak'la, garbed in her special green dress. She put her sister to rest in a shallow grave of sand, and then piled stones over her body.

Grief-stricken, Akrylla made her blurry way back to the stench of the tent-city, back through the refuse and back to her own tent. She gathered her belongings together for a quick departure.

Exhausted and numb, Akrylla unrolled Osha's bedroll. She collapsed onto it, relishing in the scent that lingered in the material. Osha's scent. But the pain she could not bear, so she reached into her satchel, portioned out a triple dose of the most potent medication therein, and soon passed out.

Later that night, a group of intoxicated men and one stumbling woman visited her tent. Akrylla's muffled screams went unanswered. In the midst of her horror, horror in the company of despair, a pulse jolted Akrylla's thoughts. Intense. Abrupt. In her mind, an inner voice opened. Not just any voice—the inner voice that had always guided her. But wider now. One simple word.

~Persevere

And when the night was over and Akrylla was left alone, she knew exactly how to respond: She waited. She waited in her tent for three days until, in the dead of night, a small, grim figure darkened the opening. She'd been gnawed on here and there, but seemed otherwise intact. When Akrylla stepped out to greet her sister in half a moon's light, she finally beheld the Scar along Osha's arms, dormant for so long, streaking crimson and bulging from under greyed skin. Akrylla took Osha's tiny hand in hers, gazed tearfully into her sister's dull eyes. She stooped slightly.

"They will pay," Akrylla whispered into her ear, spotted with grains of sand. "Harrow, Gan, the Djin; they all will pay."

Another pulse jolted Akrylla's thoughts.

~Retribution

"Others must pay first," Akrylla added as she lifted her sister up into her arms, limp head resting gently against her chest. With tender strokes, she ran her fingers through Osha's matted hair. Akrylla whispered again, "I must leave you for a short time, my Ak'la, but I will come back for you. Listen for my call." She carried her deathly frail sister to the only well in the tent city, dropped her down into it, and then headed for the open desert.

CHAPTER XXXI
THE MOTHER AWAITS
(Vey, Akrylla)

VEY FIXED HER eyes on the haggard woman's hunched form, perched among the roots of a fallen tree, lost in thought. The woman seemed oblivious to the gusts of wind beating at her body and whipping her hair into even more of a frenzy. Milla's blank eyes stared east. East to the morning sky and to the looming mountain that blocked out the rising sun—Ironeagle Peak. Occasionally, she'd pivot her gaze north to a second mountain, farther off and black-tipped, that rose beyond Deepweald Forest's vast reaches. The sky was dark that way. The scraping sounds of Riddik with his knives sounded in the background.

Another dawn had come. By nightfall they'd reach Bitterhelm, the group's final destination in the shadow of Ironeagle. Vey's chest tightened with apprehension. *Are these really our fates—a life of whoring for me and slave labor for Hersh?*

Vey shuddered at the thought and quickly decided she'd rather take her own life than become a plaything in some Baruush establishment. *I'd do it now, if only I could.*

The special assistant lay still, curled in a ball and pressed against the hard ground. Someone had tied her wrists in the night, behind her back. Not overly tight though, and a strip of wrapped cloth kept the rope from chafing her skin. The wind whipped overhead. Riddik added coughing and cursing to his blade sharpening sounds. Vey's ankles, having been free during the previous day's march, were also bound. The rope was black, thick, frayed and wet. She struggled against the bonds, let out a frustrated grunt. They burned and wouldn't loosen in the slightest. In fact, they felt tighter for the effort.

Riddik's coughing escalated to an all-out fit. After an intense bout of hacking, he let out a huge and forceful wretch, cleared his throat, then spat. The projectile had such a hard core Vey could've sworn she heard it plunk into the river water. Riddik sighed heavily when he was done, let out a few retrospective curses, then went on the move again. His footfalls crushed the groundcover of the trail.

Vey gasped. *He's coming.*

Tied the way she was, Vey could only imagine what the slaver might do to her. *And how much can I rely on a haggard old woman like Milla to stop him?* Vey didn't have an answer for that. Her body tensed. She closed her eyes tight and lay still, dreading his arrival. But before he got to her, the Cutter moaned and veered off the trail. Tree litter snapped and split underfoot.

A long pause ensued. A slight shuffling, a grunt, and finally the unmistakable sound of liquid spouting over fallen leaves—Riddik relieving himself. When he was done, he coughed some more, then made his way over to Vey after all. She lay still as he poked her twice with that gnarled walking stick of his, before opening his hateful trap.

"Get up, Red Whore," he gruffed. "Bitterhelm's waiting. There's a line forming at the gates. They're lined up to have a go at you."

Vey remained as limp and dead to the world as she possibly could, hoping he'd move on. But her stomach felt tight as a drum as she anticipated the worst. After a long moment, she hazarded a thin glance at the Cutter, through one eye barely open. The stocky Taint loomed over her, two hands gripping the branch he'd cut for himself the day prior. He leaned heavily on it. Behind Riddik, the old woman's bent frame rose slowly from the root she'd been sitting on.

Thank goodness for Milla. She can handle Riddik better than I can.

Milla wasn't much to behold, but she was all Vey had between her and the Outlanders.

"No," Akrylla told the Taint, a tired and sorry air of defiance in her voice.

Riddik swung around to face Akrylla. A flash of anger contorted his scarred face.

The shaman continued. "We're going to Blacktip instead."

He scowled and frowned at her absurd suggestion, then widened his stance.

"What are you going to do, Riddik," Akrylla said, antagonizing, "clobber an old lady again? To prove that you're a man? You're so predictable… and pathetic. You and that sick puppy who wants you dead, not to mention that demon whore who'll take anyone but you."

Riddik put his fist to his mouth instead of her face this time, coughed profusely.

Akrylla egged him on. "What's the matter, Riddik? Catch something?"

"To Shroud's Well with that." Riddik coughed again. Holding his gut, he spat at the ground. "It's Bitterhelm, old witch. Get that through your ugly head." He raised his staff to the woman, shook it at her.

Akrylla didn't flinch. Riddik readied a strike but convulsed into another coughing fit. As the Cutter hunched over, the shaman looked him up and down, settling her eyes on his spotted groin area.

Riddik noticed her stare, glared back. "What? <cough> Want some more? <cough cough>"

"You pissed yourself," she replied flatly.

He scowled. "Bitch of a wind."

The shaman feigned a look of concern, spoke in a consoling tone. "You poor thing. Does it hurt to piss?"

Riddik winced at her statement. "Why would it?" Suddenly, he seemed uncertain. "What's it to you?"

Akrylla grinned fiendishly. "Did you enjoy the hares we roasted? How was that hind leg of venison you gnawed on for half the night?"

With a forceful grunt, Riddik lunged at her and swung the staff. But Akrylla was ready this time. She dodged the blow with ease.

"The serpent strikes," she said, "and misses its mark. No serpent will harm me now, Riddik."

"What are you talking about, crazy witch?" His voice filled with rage. "And what did you mean when you asked 'Did I enjoy the hares… or the venison?' What does that have to do with anything?"

Riddik followed his questions with another coughing fit. He spat blood.

Rather than answer right away, Akrylla let the implications of her silence soak in. And then she let them build. And as she waited, with the Cutter bent over trying to control his fit, the shaman raised her chin slightly. She raised it and looked down upon the slaver, her captor.

Riddik grumbled to himself, "The hare tasted a bit funny. Bitter-grass, I thought." Finally, the wave of realization washed over his face.

Akrylla smiled to herself, knowingly. "You had the lion's share of the meat last night, didn't you, Riddik? Not so much left for Ang, but she eats like a bird anyway. And Gutless Kori? Well, he ate the guts early on but not much else. I had to settle for a leg of hare myself, some herbs and some roots. And your poor slaves got next to nothing."

The Cutter's eyes narrowed. His words were coarse. "What have you done, Witch?"

The shaman studied his expression. Inside, she relished in his pain. Yet, she wore the face of one concerned. "How do you feel, Riddik, this fine morn? You look a little flush to me. I'm guessing Ang is a bit crampy too."

He fell to one knee, wretched. Vey sat up, pushed herself away from the disgusting Taint as best she could, bound as she was. Riddik wiped the side of his mouth, fixed his hateful gaze on Akrylla. "You're dead, Witch. I'll cut your face off."

You're mine, Fool.

"Maybe Ang picked the wrong herb when I let her help last night, the li'l devil." She paused. "Let me lay it out for you, Riddik the Cutter of Flesh—my flesh, my Vey's flesh, the half-giant's flesh… Surely, continuing to Bitterhelm will be the death of you—there's no medicine there. None; none that works anyway. Only corruption, filth, blood money… whores…" She glanced at Vey. "But not the whore you were hoping for. Lucky for you, Riddik, I know of a remedy that grows in the swamps of Jakka. I can give you a little something along the way to help get you there. But you must give me something in return."

Riddik winced in pain, holding his gut. He shifted to a sitting position. "Give it to me now."

"When we get there," Akrylla continued, "you will bring me to the 'Mother of All Snakes.'"

Riddik blasted her, "GIVE IT TO ME NOW, WITCH!"

That stirred the others, near the river. *They'll be here soon.*

"Do we have a deal?" Akrylla pressed. She kept her voice even-toned and steady. While the Taint coughed away, the shaman grinned a satisfied grin. And when the coughing ceased, Riddik fixed his dark eyes on who he knew to be a witch. Akrylla could see it in his disturbed gaze. He hesitated before he said anything, now drawing heavy, forced breaths. Airy spittle dribbled down from his mouth and blobbed onto his shirt. He didn't expend the effort to wipe it off. He rubbed his bald head.

"Gutless Kori will gnaw your guts out for this," he told her.

Akrylla responded matter-of-factly. "If he does, you'll die. And so will that bitchy little Ang."

A long moment of stillness came over Riddik. His jaw hung open as he considered his options. Another bout of the foamy liquid drained out. "How do you plan on getting to Jakka?"

"Through Deepweald, of course," Akrylla replied.

Riddik cleared his throat. "The terrain… the horses…" His voice was weak. He looked pale.

The shaman responded, "You won't be riding a horse, Riddik, nor will Ang. I'm setting them free. The way is rough and you're both too sick to handle them—they would only be a burden. Mules maybe, but not horses."

Struggling with the effort, Riddik rose to his feet. He took a threatening step towards Akrylla, staggered, then collapsed to the ground. Breathing heavily and completely drained of energy, Riddik writhed and moaned. Wincing in pain, he curled into a ball and kept his thoughts to himself.

Did I dose him too much? He's smaller than most. If he hadn't made such a pig of himself...

Ang made her way over, slightly hunched and holding her own stomach.

"Bad case of the monthlies?" Akrylla said.

The demoness glanced at Riddik. Her eyes widened with the spark of realization. She swung her gaze to Akrylla. That moment the shaman knew the demoness understood what Akrylla had done. The realization in her eyes soon turned to fear.

After a long minute, Riddik regained his composure, sat up again and wiped the spittle off his mouth with his shirt sleeve. He drew a deep breath. "The Line of Control is a dangerous place, Witch. Wilders set traps and they feather us with arrows. Hundreds of Baruush have died there."

Akrylla crossed her arms, raised an eyebrow. "Then we go around and you die on the way to Jakka. Is that what you're suggesting, Cutter?"

Riddik has no choice, thought Vey. She'd backed away a safe distance from him, just in case his energy returned. *But why Jakka?* She tried to make sense of it. *That can't be completely good.* Stomach fluttering, Vey blurted out a question. Her voice wavered as she spoke. "What about the Jakka Outpost on the outskirts of Gan? Surely, whatever you need can be obtained from the Lord of Scales, and it's closer."

Her query was greeted with a pinched expression from Milla.

Vey added, "I hear the stronghold is stocked with all sorts of antidotes to all sorts of poisons—Jakka being what it is…"

"Not for flesh-peddlers like him," the shaman responded, a slight sharpness to her tone. Milla turned her gaze to the Cutter. "But if he insists that I take him there…"

Riddik scoffed at the suggestion. "What about my half-giant slave?"

"You can still sell him in Jakka," Akrylla said, flatly.

"He'd fetch a better price in Bitterhelm." Riddik drew in short, heavy breaths as he spoke. "The mines—" Ang spared him the words.

"Stop arguing. You're going to die."

"Go to hell." Riddik coughed, pressed his gut tight, then swallowed deep. "Why are you on her side, Bitch?" He paused to cough again. "The Bitch and the Witch, together at last."

Ang shifted her gaze to Milla, then back to the Taint. "I'm *not* on her side." Eyeing Riddik's hand on his stomach, she suddenly stooped over, held her own gut, then let out a frustrated moan. She straightened slightly. "I just want to live, Riddik," she told him. "Jakka's a different market: Bitterhelm slaves are for work, mostly." Ang winced, squirming with the pain. "Jakka slaves are for entertainment," she forced. "And I know the people who run the fighting pits. I can build the half-giant up. The Blackdagger auction will fetch top dollar."

The Cutter shifted his narrowed eyes to Milla. "I'm already down one slave because of you, Witch. Two if you count yourself."

"Shut up," Ang snapped.

"Three," Milla responded. "You already know I'm taking the girl with me."

Riddik chuckled slightly, grimaced. Vey couldn't tell if the pained look on his face was because of his condition or because of the arguing. Finally, the expression washed away. Riddik nodded.

"Jakka it is," he capitulated, "through Deepweald. Now give me what you've got."

And while Milla busied herself preparing "medicinal" tea for him, Vey kept her eye on Riddik as he studied the old woman's every move. And when Milla wasn't looking, Vey saw how he narrowed his eyes and curled his lip at her.

He's going to cut her again. Vey knew it was true. *He's going to cut her up and kill her the second he gets the chance… but then what happens to me?*

But Riddik didn't get to Milla that day. He was too slow and too sick. So, they slogged on through the wild and spent the night just off the trail, en route north to Blacktip Mountain.

CHAPTER XXXII
GALEWIND
(Galewind)

GALEWIND HADN'T SEEN Berendt since the disastrous temple attack. Disastrous for him personally, but even more so for some of those who served under him. And she knew he'd be extremely busy with his unexpected role as commander of the entire Kith contingent in the exercise. *He's had a rough few months. We've both had a rough few months.*

The knightmaiden tried not to think about the terrible injury her friend and confidant had been struggling with; she tried to push it aside in her mind. It pained her. Too much. And she feared the worst. *He had such a handsome face…*

She tried to console herself, convince herself that maybe the injury wasn't so bad. After all, the rugged look worked well for the Kith commander—an extra show of strength.

But I loved those eyes. A pang of longing washed over her, despite herself. She squeezed her own eyes shut, briefly, to remember the way he looked at her, the way his gaze dove deep into her core. *I loved how he looked at me.* Berendt's greatest strength might have been measuring a person's worth, recognizing who someone really was. She craved that look. Worse, she NEEDED that look now more than ever. *Maybe the luminary got to him fast enough and he'll make a full recovery. It might not be so bad.* She breathed a heavy sigh and faced the practical truth. *If I can make it better... easier somehow, I will. I must.*

Despite Galewind's clear duties as Order Valkyrie liaison, she'd waited until the last glideboat was about to depart Gan before deciding whether or not to attend Diamond Saber; whether or not she would show her face among her juniors and peers. *This is a good thing,* she tried to convince herself. *I needed to get away. And here I am, as though nothing has changed.* She'd simply taken her place among the March officers in the viewing area, passing time not unlike the rest of them before the exercise commenced, absorbing the wonders of this unusual venue.

Her stomach sank at the mere shadow of a thought about the *other* disaster. Her disaster. Not Berendt's. Although his, in all likelihood, contributed to the root cause of hers. Most of all, the knightmaiden didn't want to think about what had happened to her celestials, her trainees. *Naïve, precious...*

The knightmaiden's chest tightened. As discreetly as she could, she pressed a hand there and quietly gasped. Tension grew on the inside and she fought to keep it down. She fought to keep the emotion from welling up. She glanced about nervously, mentally assailed by her own destructive thoughts. *What is the Judiciary discussing right now, back in Gan?* she wondered. *What are they thinking?* Her insides quivered. *They can't believe it was my fault, can they? I told them what happened, straight and truthful.* Galewind rewrapped her body in the furs draped over her shoulders, for comfort's sake. She needed to feel warm. The gustiness of the dome had come as a surprise, rising and falling like the gentle sighs of a sleeping titan. *I told them everything. What more could they want?*

But Galewind would never forget the committee's cold stares when they finally gave her the chance to tell her side of the story. She would never forget the cold stares, the cold questions, and the cold silence that followed when she was done. Blank looks from faces too young and too placid to bear wisdom. *Now I know why law breakers call it the Ice Tower,* she thought. The monolithic structure was the center of law and order in Gan, but it also held the Aerie of the Gryphons on its craggy top. Galewind tried not to think of the worst-case scenario. She tried not to think about what the Judiciary Committee might decide. *They can be so cruel.* Ironic the very same tower she devoted decades of her life to now deliberated her fate on its lower levels.

But that wasn't even the worst of it. *Will this be my last official duty as Aerie Liaison Officer to the Palace, as knightmaiden?*

She cut off her train of thought, turned her attention to the incoming rangers. She had to. It was a welcome distraction—ranger watching. Galewind felt her hair coming undone… again. *Damn gusty place.* As the Kith began to stream in through the Netherdome entrance one after the other, rogue locks of her hair slipped out of place to dangle over one eye. She pushed them aside and adjusted her wing clips once more, this time just tight enough to keep the hair out of her face.

The rangers must have just finished at the mess, she surmised. She could easily pick out the few that had just glideboated in, by their agoraphobic looks as they ducked through the doorway and took in the sights.

Galewind snickered, shook her head. *Quite the characters,* she thought. Most appeared at first glance to be woodsman or hunters, prospectors, or adventure seekers of one kind or another. They dressed to blend in on the trails. And none displayed their clan badges. That would give them away. Those entering wore fur-lined bush leathers and old woolen shirts, weather-stained cloaks and worn leather boots. Compared to the clean-cut queensmen, they were rugged and unpolished. And although still largely drawing from men of the Wilder clans, she could see the mix was changing. Abandoners, Stouts and Taints numbered more than a few, and several women walked among them. The age demographics had diversified as well. *Some too old to hold a sword, others so young they should be brandishing a wooden one.*

The knightmaiden remembered her duties, retrieved her fountain pen and flipped open her notepad. Lady Apsarla would want to know all the latest details—the up-and-coming talent, the future leaders, anyone that might be of use to the Aerie. She'd also want Galewind's opinion on the new dancing swords.

Exactly how Prime Lumen Forsetti's lead man at the exercise could bring himself to argue that such a ragtag force of Kith brethren should wield the strikers was a mystery to nearly all, especially among the

Queen's Guard—undeniably Gan's finest swordfighters. But it wasn't a mystery to Galewind. *Olmi… Olmi… Olminsin, I believe his name is*, she reminded herself. *Yes, Olminsin Hadamard.* She wondered how he'd try to showcase the potential of this motley band of outcasts, the same group the Royal Quarter tagged as miscreants. She didn't wonder openly, of course. Not yet. First, the Kith rangers would have to prove themselves worthy. Then, she would offer her support. *It won't be easy. I'm sure Loraith has the outcome stacked in his favor. But there is another option…*

Galewind knew something of the Kith command structure going into this exercise, thanks to Loraith Ralador's unbridled criticism of it during the voyage in. Her beloved Berendt, apparently, who was free to choose his second-in-command, had chosen an inexperienced scout for the job. *Why not choose Tallman if he really wants to win?* she wondered. Tallman—shorthand for "Tall" Hallman—was an officer in need of command experience and a full kithblade, a rank above scout. Galewind had worked with him on an operation when he first started. He'd simply amazed her. But Berendt was never one to let rank get in the way. It was always about who was best for the job at hand. *Or maybe he was too busy kissing the ass of the March Lord to think the matter through.*

Galewind snickered aloud at the totally unfair thought, again despite herself. She would tease the Kith commander later, in private, about his "secret" desire to someday join the ranks of the Queen's Guard. She glanced about. No one in her immediate vicinity took notice of her private outburst. Lords, ladies, palace officials and clergy—they all kept to their cliques. *Berendt can always swap out the scout for another if he needs to, for the next scenario.*

Just then a young, broad-shouldered Wilder with long, dark hair in tied locks strode into the dome, garbed in ranging leathers. *That must be him,* she figured, thinking back to a description she'd heard of the scout. *What's his name again?* Loraith had mentioned it to her in passing after his soon-to-be son-in-law—a Horse Lord brat by the name of Eriff Haulik—had jibed about the ranger scout's prospects, his choice of armor, and even his hair. "Get cleaned up and for Ekkon's sake, get a serious haircut," Eriff had said, in a mock confrontation to keep the banter going with his chums, "and drop that leather for a solid breastplate. Then maybe you will have a chance. This is battle, not bird-hunting."

Although somewhat snobbish to others, Eriff had evidently accepted Galewind into his circle without hesitation. He could be charming in a staged way. *He's to marry into House Ralador—that can't be easy. No wonder he acts as he does. How much of a choice does he really have?* She didn't fully trust the queensman's intentions though. *But he's worth being civil to,* she conceded. Eriff was, after all, a good duelist. He could be useful.

She penned her first entry:

Eriff Haulik: talented swordsman, ego driven (can use that), natural commander, well-connected, high upward mobility.

"Hmph," Galewind said aloud, as she fixed her gaze on the ranger scout. Her impression of him completely contrasted Eriff's derisive words. She quickly realized he stood out in nearly every way a young man should. At least, Galewind's kind of man—give him another ten years. She could picture the wind riders at the Aerie fawning over him now, though. Catwings certainly would be all over him, and she'd flat out reject Eriff's first point, about the hair. Rainsong, well, Rainsong would be Rainsong and likely tease the young man to death. Storm-bringer, a level-headed spearmaiden, would consider him handsome, but nonetheless would lean on the noble's side on both counts, more so regarding proper protection. *She's quite sensible. But throwaway breast-plate for a queensman would cost a year's wages for a typical ranger,* she thought. Added to that, many of the Wilders served only for status in their tribes. Galewind doubted Loraith or his son-in-law had any idea about such complications.

The scout casually wandered near Galewind and the other spectators that had gathered. *He's gaining perspective on the battlefield,* she noted, as he gazed out over it. She observed his choice of weaponry—he bore what must be the heaviest of the striker swords. One look at his arms told her that he possessed the means to wield it. *Hallman has nothing on him there,* she conceded. *He must be somewhat clever and adaptable as well, being one of the few in the training portion to have taken to far fencing. These are beginnings though, not ends.*

The knightmaiden sighed, then reconsidered. Despite the put-downs and the obvious lack of experience, something about Berendt's prospect undeniably came off a bit like surprise and a bit like promise. Berendt, a seasoned veteran, always had good reasons for doing what he did. She gave him a lot of credit for his rangers—they reflected well on him, usually.

A small group of March officers around her also took note of the scout's presence. But rather than marvel at his obvious potential as she did, in low tones and behind his back they called him a hick, uneducated, and went on in unkind ways about his broken family and jaded past. She interrupted, speaking loud enough to be revealing to all within earshot.

"Perhaps this Kith-boy will surprise us all," she told them. "Rangers have a different philosophy. It's the bow that teaches the archer, they say."

"Yes, Knightmaiden," replied one of the officers. "Well said," remarked another, among nods of feigned agreement. *Kiss asses,* she thought, *real ones.* That was the last she heard of their snickering.

And as the young ranger shot the crowd a sideways glance, his name popped into Galewind's head. *'Amot'—that's it!*

She added two more entries:

Tall Hallman: forceful, heavy load for a gryphon - good for ground surveillance.

Amot: strong fighter, considered unpredictable - wildcard, use caution.

The scout turned his attention back to the field. As Galewind discreetly looked on from her place among the March officers, she took careful note of Amot's measured expression. It reminded her of a much-younger Berendt, back when she'd first met him. Back when her body was mature and the Kith commander's was youthful. She'd since been through rejuvenation. *We should be on par now,* she thought, *physically.* A slight smile formed on her lips—a personal one, indulgent, meant for her pleasure only.

As the scout continued to survey the Djinxarai-generated terrain, Galewind had her own thoughts to ponder. And when Amot left to be with his team, she let those thoughts wander freely. She let them wander to places she'd never let them wander before.

⤳

A hush came over the Netherdome. All eyes fell to the combatants as they took their positions. A scattering of whispered commentary in the vicinity of the knightmaiden centered on the competencies of the favored queensmen and the shortcomings of rangers. In their bright mail, regal dress and fine weaponry, the well-trained and highly disciplined Queen's Guards were victors by all outward appearances. *Hard to deny,* she had to admit.

Galewind took notice of a young Abindohn woman standing near, in traditional dress. Just a girl, really. She occupied the natural rift that had formed in the crowd between the March officers and the regulars or Grey Quarter types. The girl seemed awkwardly detached from both groups. The Abindohn gazed at Amot, wearing her fondness for him on her sleeve. Galewind watched as the two locked eyes for a moment, the same way the knightmaiden had locked eyes with Berendt earlier—one eye, in his case. She'd seen him only for an instant. She felt again the rush that went through her. But Berendt's gaze had been quickly diverted—some imminent crisis to handle, it seemed, messaged by some junior ranger. *I'll catch up with him later,* she promised herself.

The knightmaiden leaned over to the Abindohn girl, raised a hand to her lips and whispered. "That Amot will give them a run for their money, just wait and see."

The girl smiled as she watched the scout disappear into the terrain cover. She folded her arms, turned her gaze to Galewind. "I heard what you said earlier," she responded. "You're absolutely correct." Her voice teemed with conviction.

"I saw you watching him. You must be so proud that he's leading the charge."

She looked confused. "Oh, he won't be, Knightmaiden. Haven't you heard?"

"Well, I…"

"At the March Lord's urging, the Kith are to maintain their original battle order. That mean's Commander Garondi, then Hallman. My Amot's third."

Galewind glanced at the battlefield, hoping to spot Berendt. She was too late—he'd already passed into the scenario woods where the rangers lay hidden. "Who will stand up for the Kith during the exercise?" she asked the girl. "Berendt's place is here, to ensure a fair fight." *What's that Loraith up to?*

"Lumen Hadamard has accepted that role."

"I see," Galewind said. *He's not even military. I don't like it.*

The Abindohn extended her hand to Galewind. "Vil'nyan," she said, introducing herself. "I'm with Lumen Hadamard's crew."

The knightmaiden accepted and responded using her alias. "Please, call me Galewind." They exchanged polite smiles. "Shouldn't you be on the field observing or refereeing?"

"Oh. Next scenario. This is my break."

That moment, Loraith Ralador stepped onto the battlefield. He scanned the final set-up like a hawk. Hands clasped behind his back, the man stood proud and stern in his full military dress. The emblem of the March blazed red and gold on his puffed-out chest. He spoke no words, but the confidence he projected announced to all, loud and clear, that today would be his day. Everything rode on the outcome of the coming mock battle and the two scenarios to follow. She guessed that as far as he was concerned, there was little actually hanging in the balance of it. *He will be vindicated so long as the moon is round.*

An assortment of other spectators resided in the observation area: a support group of regulars, extra queensmen slated for later scenarios, and one of her own—a spearmaiden hopeful named Tess, from Fort

Abandon. Feleg, a Wilder and former Kith whom she knew from way back, was also nearby, conversing with Lumen Hadamard. All but a few of Olminsin's team had taken up positions around the grounds, ready to observe and take notes. An eager bunch they seemed and highly sociable to one another, at least on intellectual fronts.

Galewind leaned in to the Abindohn girl again, whispered. "They're about to begin. I'm sure your rangers will bring honor to their order."

The girl laughed. "Oh, don't worry," she replied, a bit louder than Galewind would have preferred. "The Kith are gonna kick their lily-white asses right out of the dome and into the nether."

The knightmaiden discreetly added one more entry before the battle began:

Vil'nyan: pretty, able-bodied and athletic – good candidate for training. Optimistic, perhaps naïve. Abindohn.

Chapter XXXIII

SEPTEMBER ROSE

(Akrylla, Vey, Hersh)

*A*NY SIMPLE, EDIBLE *plant from the swamp will do for a 'remedy,'* Akrylla told herself, thinking ahead to the wet lowlands among the Jakka Hills. *They won't know the difference.* The shaman paused to hike up her robe, then stepped carefully over yet another half-charred log. Patchy sleet had made every surface slippery, and the passing storm in the distance made for a dark day in the stark landscape they traversed. Lightning flashed in wide forks and thunder rolled in, dispersed and jagged sounding. The smell of smoldering bush lay thick in the air.

The biggest event of the morning had been the unusual statue they'd come across in the middle of nowhere—a huge Baruush warrior in the midst of a deathblow, wielding a monstrous, spiked club. The meaning of the lifelike piece haunted Akrylla, obviously fashioned by a master sculpturer. *A warning from Bitterhelm?* she wondered, *to any who would dare enter these contested grounds?* Their new path skirted the Line of Control between Gan and the Baruush stronghold, the easternmost line in Deepweald Forest. She couldn't even determine what the statue was fashioned of. The shaman shook her head. *Never beheld such a thing—a sculpture so large and yellowy, all crystalline.* It had appeared worn and weathered. Ang's keen eyes had spotted what might've been another figure much the same, glinting in the distance to the north-east. She'd told Riddik it resembled a mean bear.

The shaman peered back over her shoulder. The three Outlanders had fallen behind, now bringing up the rear. Riddik's forced steps were the slowest, leaning heavily on his serpentine staff as he struggled to keep pace along the old logging road. Akrylla grinned. *Payment for your gluttony.* More disturbing was Ang. Her reddish skin had taken on a more pallid tint, and her athleticism seemed slightly diminished by the way she carried herself. But the biggest indicator something was amiss with the demoness was that she now permitted Gutless Kori to travel by her side—a sight Akrylla hadn't witnessed before. She'd routinely spurned him, until recently. *A new alliance?* the shaman wondered. *What hold could she have on him?* Ang's newfound affinity for the beast made practical sense—the Wulver was the least affected by the shaman's brew and would be the most capable defender… or attacker. *Damn picky eater.*

~Hurry

Akrylla conjured up a kind voice with which to address them. "Make haste, darlings," she called over her shoulder. Then she sharpened her tone. "Your time is running out."

Riddik the Cutter shot back venom in return. "I'll slice you open if it's the last thing I do, Witch." He immediately stumbled, cursed, coughed twice, then found his footing and kept on.

Persistent little skinhead, thought Akrylla as she swung her gaze ahead. She almost admired him for it. Riddik had inadvertently received enough dose to kill a horse.

The demon bitch, on the other hand, held her tongue. She didn't even lift her eyes Akrylla's way. Ang's expression was obvious: the tightness in her face, her silent look. *Lying low, contemplating her options, is she? That demoness's mind is busy.* Her stooped posture could've meant many things, but one stood out in the shaman's mind. *I sense worry in her. Why else would she cozy up to Kori, whom she despises? And the way she's ignoring me… worry and spite: the battle rages. Perhaps she wants out… something better.*

~Bitch knows

It was obvious to Akrylla that Ang was a good judge of intentions. Too good. *I have to be careful around her. She's skeptical. She might see through my plans. It takes a bitch to thwart a witch.* Akrylla wondered if she might have room for two apprentices. After all, she would've taken Clea from the Fargoer. *I'll wait for a sign,* she told herself, and left the notion to simmer in the back of her mind. She'd never had an apprentice before, never mind two.

Akrylla heard the voice of the steward directly behind her, low and sonorous. He'd been babbling to Vey, beside him, for the better part of the morning and into the afternoon. The two of them slugged along, occupying the space between the shaman and the slavers. *Probably mumbling nonsense,* Akrylla thought, without so much as a pinch of concern. *And even if it isn't nonsense, my Vey will think it is, with the dose she's had.* Akrylla sighed. The going looked rough ahead along the road, and not much rougher off of it, having fallen out of use decades ago. *Another hour and we'll be among live trees again,* she reminded herself, *the shrinking edge of Deepweald.* Being out in the open along the Line of Control unnerved her.

~Fake cure

Akrylla mulled over her options again for the bogus, herbal cure she planned to administer to the slavers when they reached Jakka. Getting a brew out of her head wasn't easy, once the idea had been planted. *I have to stage the search—it can't be too easy—the gathering, and the preparations.* She considered the landscape. *Something pleasant,* she thought, picturing the rolling terrain in her mind and all that grows there. *Sweet Gale, or perhaps Sweetfern if I can find a dry patch.* She thought there must be others to choose from, but it had been years since she was in Jakka. *Fall is difficult.* In the meantime, Akrylla would serve her blend of "medicinal" tea to the slavers regularly. The effects of the first batch were just beginning to taper off. Each round, she planned to reduce the dose of the poison that kept them subdued, while upping the dose of the mild hallucinogen she laced it with, to keep them wanting more. *String them along, I will. And when I make them tea in Jakka, they'll feel so much better—cured of all woes and ailments. I'll even put a little extra something in for elation.* The shaman smiled to herself at the idea. It was a good one.

Then they must guide me through the hordes, to the Mother. Without a guide, Akrylla would never get past the Nali and the Baruush guards. They'd kill her to look at her. They'd kill her for being too human.

~Double-crossers

Live up to their end? Akrylla almost laughed. "No," she muttered, so low no one else could hear. "That Taint is a liar. That Ang is a demon bitch. Gutless Kori… perhaps. But he's a sick Wulver, rejected by his own pack in bedeviled Whisperwood." The Outlanders would skin her alive the moment they knew they were cured. Akrylla had another good idea. She nodded to herself slowly. *I'll make a 'cure' that requires several doses. Days, if need be. They'll get the last dose when we part ways.*

Suddenly, Vey's worried face flashed into Akrylla's mind, followed by her inner voice.

~Ease

In the morning, Akrylla had seen that her Ak'la was under great stress. She'd seen that Vey needed help. *An extra special tea for her, I made.* She smiled at what she'd concocted—the elixir she slipped her, and only her, while the rest drank poison. *It will propel her through the day, and more.* Vey had accepted the offer readily. *A good sign. She trusts. It's almost time for more.*

~Farseer

Akrylla knew the devil was in the dose. *The hit will open her mind. It will help her to see the signs, to be a good apprentice.* Vey's extra special tea was the very same active substance that had debilitated the Outlanders, but in a slightly different form and a different dose. *That changes everything.*

The shaman crested a low ridge, then halted to survey the bleak landscape.

~Scorched

Everywhere she looked the land was charred. This part of the forest had never been the same after the torching of the Hurlorns. Years later,

Ironeagle woodcutters had made a mess of what was left of it. The Baruush never let the land heal, setting it ablaze, section by section. Here and there, life sprung up. But it was meager, struggling. On the hillsides, the rains and winds had eroded away the bared soil. Half a dozen parcels of land smoldered around them.

~Pretty

A splash of red caught Akrylla's eye. A lone rose. *It's just like Kel Fariz. Just like Kel Fariz. Just like Kel Fariz.* The shaman fixed her gaze on the small, red miracle of life; a vibrant life among all that is barren.

The Star Sands. Images came to her in a flood. Beautiful gardens. Utter destruction. A single red flower peeking through the ruins. Her hand reached out to touch it. *You promised…*

Riddik interrupted, crude as ever. "I can make your neck blossom just the same, Witch. Or maybe your ugly face, if I cut off your nose."

He's close. Akrylla snapped back to reality. She whirled around, fixed her gaze sternly on Riddik's face. He'd picked up his pace and passed the others when she wasn't paying attention.

"Kill me now and you die too," the shaman snapped back.

The Taint's eyes were glazed over like a madman's, and he wore a murderous sneer. He trudged towards her; staff raised in his right hand. Riddik held his curved blade in his left hand, almost casually, as if he didn't care whether he swung it or dropped it. The Cutter hadn't cut into flesh or sharpened his instrument in hours.

I should've taken that thing, Akrylla scolded herself. Riddik had never quite gone under though, and she knew he'd kill her for trying with his last ounce of strength.

Before the Taint came into reach, Akrylla turned her back nonchalantly to him. She turned her back but tuned her ears to any sound that might indicate a bold action on his part. Pushing ahead at a brisk pace, she patted her sidebag. *Shroud's Well, it's mostly air.*

Riddik kept to his normal pace. Akrylla's efforts put her well ahead. She breathed a sigh of relief that he didn't pursue. But the shaman had more on her mind than just Riddik. She'd been watching the half-giant as well, looking him up and down over the day's trek. He seemed to grow taller as the day progressed, looming over them all.

~Control

When Akrylla reached a calculated distance ahead of Riddik, she stopped to peek inside her satchel. *I can't keep them all down much longer,* she thought, fumbling through the contents. *That damn lug's a huge drain.* Soon, dose would be a problem. A big problem. *Riddik and Ang will surely turn on me…*

In her mind, the voice that interrupts did so again.

~Kill

This time, Akrylla shook her head in defiance of the voice. *No, I need the slavers for safe passage through the gates of Jakka, and slavers need a slave to put up for auction.*

~Overpower

Akrylla pondered the notion, in reverse. The steward was a man of honor. If he became lucid, he wouldn't stoop to overpowering an old woman, but he'd be quick to overpower the Outlanders. *By all rights,* she thought, *he should kill them all and have mercy on me. That lug longs for Vey and I protected her from the slavers. I sacrificed. And I tricked the Outlanders into being drugged. Me. All me. In fact, he should give me a reward for all I've done.*

~Gold

Akrylla considered an offer of gold and shook her head again. *No,* she told the voice inside, annoyed at the suggestion. *Not gold. I would demand service.*

❦

Dark and limbless, the skeletal remains of the forest jutted up from the scorched earth all around. Vey let her eyes relax. She imagined the blurred apparitions were spirit soldiers rising from the ashes in defense of their wraith kingdom.

"You can't see us, dark spirit warriors, because we're invisible," Vey informed them, then giggled. Smiling, she swung sideways to share her good humor with Hersh. The half-giant plodded along slowly, a dazed look on his face. She frowned. *Giants are stupid. No fun.* She took a longer look. *He's still cute though, even bald.* Vey avoided making eye contact with the Outlanders behind Hersh and she avoided looking Milla's way, who was ahead of her, in case the woman turned around. *She has an eye in the back of her head. And she'll give me a mean face if she catches me spying on her.* That didn't leave many places to look.

When the old woman did turn around, Vey pretended to be looking straight up. Almost immediately, she tripped and fell. "Oopsie," she said, sprawled out on her hands and knees. Vey scrambled to her feet this time, unlike the last time and the time before that. She quickly brushed the damp, soily ash off her dress, shook a black glob off her hand, and continued on her way as though nothing untoward had happened. She walked with a limp though, because her knee hurt, and she couldn't bend one arm much when she swung it—the elbow stung too much.

Vey let her gaze wander over the ground ahead as she closely followed Milla's pressed impressions in the ash. She picked a careful path between the rocks, the blackened stumps, the pits, and the fallen logs. Her moccasins, the ones Milla said she'd found in her satchel, were coated in the grey substance. Ang tried to tell Vey that Milla stole them from the trading post. *She doesn't steal,* Vey thought, remembering the apothecary. *She doesn't even haggle. She just orders, pays and then some.* Vey didn't believe Ang after that.

As the path became rockier, the special assistant used every ounce of focus she could muster to not fall. She'd been that way since they left the old road.

She fell anyway. It seemed Vey tripped and fell every few minutes, in fact. Sometimes she didn't remember falling but knew that she must've since she was lying in something gooey. Sometimes she laughed, because falling can be funny. Vey covered her mouth to giggle. *Nobody noticed I went pee that time.* Most times she just lay on the ground, staring up at the grey sky. She'd lay there until someone hauled her up. Usually it was Milla, grabbing her under her arms and lifting her to her feet, grumbling as she did so about having to backtrack or about who-knows-what in some unworldly tongue. Other times it was Hersh, silent and strong. He made her feel like she could fly. Never Riddik though, or Ang, or Gutless Kori. Milla wouldn't allow that.

She was in charge now. She was in charge and everything was better. Not much better, but better. And Vey still hurt. *Better hurts, sometimes,* she concluded.

Vey's tumbles had left her bloodied and bruised. Ash and charcoal streaked her skin and her dress. The sockets of her shoulders throbbed from being pulled to her feet so often. She felt relieved when they finally reached the edge of the living part of Deepweald, the part that hadn't been hacked or burned. She halted, glanced to her left. The forest was vast in that direction, on a rising slope, spotted with trees that'd discovered their fall colors early. She glanced to her right. In that direction, the forest's edge ran down the slope until the ground leveled off, where it met a rocky plain that nothing grew on.

Riddik, still moving slow but having gained some color in his cheeks, sluggishly scouted to the left. Vey frowned. *I feel better when he looks worse,* she thought, and then shrugged. Gutless Kori lumbered along with the Taint, skirting the tree line and sniffing out the territory. Ang rested on a fallen log untouched by the wildfire. Hersh had stopped to stand beside Vey. He didn't respond to her playful smile and wave. She reached up and snapped her fingers right in front of his eyes. He didn't even notice, and his eyes were still glazed over.

Milla approached, looking windblown. It wasn't a good hair day for her. "He's in another place," Milla explained. Then she gave the half-giant an examining look. "I can't say it's all my doing. I don't like half-giants. They were never meant to be. Sterile, you know, except the odd one. There's a good reason for that." The old woman grimaced as she searched through her satchel of herbs, powders, vials, and animal parts. *Is she looking for more powder?*

"I have some," Vey blurted out. She gestured to the pouch tied in her hair.

"No, dear, but kind of you to offer," Milla replied.

Sometimes she can be nice.

Vey asked, "Where's Riddik going?"

Milla gruffed, "To find the trail we're supposed to already be on."

Oopsies. She pinched a finger and a thumb together. *That tiny little thing about the trail made her mad again.*

Milla shook her head, grumbled under her breath and pulled out a small pouch of powder. It looked the same as Vey's.

The special assistant looked up and down the slope again, then craned her neck to peer around Hersh at where they'd been.

"There's no trail, silly," she told Milla. The old woman was in the midst of portioning out her special powder to the half-giant. "That wasn't a trail we were on." Vey pointed as she spoke. "No trail up there, no trail down there…" Then she shrugged. "There was never any trail." Milla ignored her. Vey nudged the old woman with her elbow and laughed. "Why do we need a trail?"

"Ahh!" Milla screeched. She whirled around, glared at Vey. The woman's eyes stung like wasps. *She gets ugly really fast.*

Vey noticed the purple powder on Milla's robe. "Oopsie, you spilled some."

"Don't—touch—me—when—I'm—working!" the old woman spat.

Vey turned away, wiped the spit off her face with the wide strap of her red dress. *Now she tells me.* Avoiding eye contact with Milla, the special assistant wandered away and found herself a grassy hollow to sit in. *I'm not pouting,* she told herself. There, she retrieved her own pouch. She shook the special powder to the bottom, then peeked in. It was almost empty. *I'll only take one and a half pinches.* After sniffing it in, Vey stretched out, laid herself down and closed her eyes. She felt her mind begin to twist and drift. A rush of good feelings flooded her body.

Suddenly, in the midst of a dream about crying, she felt herself being hauled up again. It was Hersh. But this time, the half-giant carried Vey in his big arms. He carried her in a way that made it seem like he wasn't going to put her down this time. Vey kept her eyes closed and let her body go limp, even though she was fully awake. And after a long way, when she heard the wind rustling in the treetops and smelled decaying leaf litter, she opened her eyes.

As difficult as the going had been over the logged-out terrain, she preferred the grey openness of the fields to the dark of the forest, and the grasses to the tall trees that now loomed above her. Vey squirmed in Hersh's arms. Slowly and carefully, he lowered her to the ground.

Gutless Kori led the way with Riddik and Ang behind him. In that marching order, Akrylla could keep an eye on the Outlanders. They seemed more alert and energetic in the woods than they had been on the open slopes, despite Akrylla's recent doses. Even the half-giant showed signs of lucidity. *Too soon,* thought Akrylla. *The Jakka swamp is still a day's hike, or longer. Then what?* She might have to choose. *Riddik and the half-giant are the priorities,* she decided. She pressed her lips together firm, in the knowledge that if either got out of control, she was done for. *Ang the Bitch, I can handle. Bring her to my way of thinking. Gutless Kori—the Wulver's cruel, but a follower. I can bend him to Ang over Riddik.*

As Akrylla's thoughts churned, she took note of the backs of the Outlanders' heads, swiveling one way and then the other as they made sideways glances about them. They'd entered a sheltered grove. She slowed her pace. A second later, the shaman stumbled upon a third crystalline figure, fallen over. It was life-sized like the others, covered in broad-leafed, creeping vines. *Baruush again.* An uneasy feeling took hold of her gut as her own eyes now darted about. The seldom-used path had become fully overgrown, and she saw what had to be several other sculptures, positioned here and there in various poses. Hunching and angling her head just so, she peered into the dark woods before them.

Akrylla called ahead to the Taint, her tone accusatory. "This trail doesn't look right, Riddik," she scolded.

Riddik scoffed, "What does it matter, Witch, as long as we're going in the right direction?"

"It matters because the path you've taken us on runs higher on the slope than I remember," Akrylla retorted. "It matters because your path is more winding. And it matters because I see old growth ahead, which makes this Wilder territory."

"The Line of Control is miles to the north," Ang said, in Riddik's defense. "You just don't like the statues. I saw the way you looked at them. Get over it."

~Schemer

Yessums, she plays both sides. She's scheming something. I know it.

"No one knows exactly where the Line is out here," Akrylla replied.

"It's just a line on some map. One thing I do know is that the Wilder tribes couldn't care less about the younger woods to the south. But this old growth…" She eyed a suspicious looking tree as she walked past, then stopped. They all stopped. "No," Akrylla said, her voice firm. "We're turning back to search for the proper trail, downhill. This route will draw us to the edge of the Hidden City, I'm certain of it."

Riddik countered, "We're only a few miles from where Bitterhelm beat back the Wilder tribes and the Queen's Guard, and then roasted the Hurlorns."

"Mind your tongue in these parts!" Akrylla snapped. A branch creaked a loud, long creak. *Now you've done it.* She crouched low, eyeing the treetops suspiciously. "Like I told you, old growth. Deep roots. Why do you think the Baruush stopped where they did?"

A soft "thwunk" sounded in the wilderness. Gutless Kori yelped and twisted, struck by an arrow in his side. His head jerked back. Then he was still. A thrumming sound arose as the Wulver's hulking form blurred and split into a thousand shifting planes. The ringing grew, amber light flashed. The many divisions crackled as they pinched out of sight.

Then silence.

Akrylla gasped at what was left behind—a perfect statue, like the others, yellowy and translucent. Static. Gutless Kori's snarl remained frozen on his face, eyes wide and crazed.

Riddik stood gaping as he stared at the Wulver. He double-blinked. "Kori?" Then he drew his small orange knife.

Akrylla's pulse quickened. She lunged at Vey, knocked her to the ground. "Down!" she urged the others.

Riddik and Ang ducked low, glancing into the woods this way and that way. Only Hersh remained standing, unresponsive.

They waited. An uneasy silence filled the woods.
~Verify

"Wait here. Don't move," Akrylla whispered to Vey. She crept to where Gutless Kori stood. *He's not right at all.* In the dim light of the grove they'd entered, she reached out to stroke his fur. The striated surface was hard and smooth to the touch. Her eyes weren't lying. Gutless Kori had gained a new translucency.

~Bonecasters

"What is this?" she said aloud to the voice that interrupts. It did not respond. "Who are the Bonecasters?" The voice remained silent. Around her, the woods began to knock and snap. A blur rushed past, a flash out of the corner of her eye. *An animal?* By the time she whirled around to see what it was, it was gone. She drew her claw dagger, stepped back. Leaf litter rustled on the forest floor. "This is Hurlorn country," Akrylla told the voice. "No Bonecasters dwell here."

Suddenly, a viny root snatched the shaman's leg, hoisted her into the air. Inverted and under a wide swing, she spotted Riddik slashing away at encroaching roots with his weapon, grunting with the effort. He was quickly overwhelmed. Up he went. His knife dropped and clanged on the rocky ground. The Taint cursed the Hurlorns as he struggled against their sinuous bonds. Next was Ang. In a matter of moments, the three hung together, entangled.

A loud thud sounded—the half-giant toppled to the ground, barely missing the ice-like figure of Gutless Kori. Roots and branches wrapped around his limbs, neck, and waist, holding him firm. Hersh, it seemed, didn't have it in him to struggle. *I benumbed him too much,* Akrylla feared, *I misinterpreted the signs.* Anger rose up in her—anger at herself. *THINK.* She could've scratched out her brains through her eye sockets. *Only the half-giant can stand against a Hurlorn.*

As she wallowed in self-pity, lithe branches tightened their hold. They wrapped around her body and squeezed until she could move no more. Completely immobilized, Akrylla labored just to breathe. She heard the others in the trees beside her, struggling with muffled grunts and gasping for breath as she did. Only one thought comforted the shaman, as she closed her eyes and began to slip out of consciousness. *My Vey… my Ak'la… my apprentice… spared.* The ropey branches had simply let her be.

So, this is how it ends?

Everything went dark.

⇜

Kemgi, you're a hard woman to find. Until Hersh confronted his superior in the third and final trial and survived nine rounds of combat, he could not gain the title of *Distance Walker*, the title he'd failed to obtain so many years ago. He'd passed the first two stations with difficulty—he was out of practice. *Silent Shadow of the Forest* was never his thing. Even the full giants bested him on that one. *Nameless Kindheart of the Streets* tested his will to its limits. It takes enormous strength to be gentle and kind, especially in the face of battle. And his current station, *Wanderer of Mountain Paths*, presented an even greater challenge. Pathfinding where there are no paths and fighting on slippery slopes was not exactly his forté.

The previous two trials had combined some form of sparring with everything he'd ever learned in the stations. Endless sparring, it seemed. Exhausting sparring. *I'm getting closer to her, though, I can feel it.* He'd searched the valley end-to-end, asking everyone he'd met on forest paths or village streets where he might find Master Wayfarer Kemgi. Everyone knew her name, but none gave answer. Not one. No one, that is, until Hersh tapped a hooded man on the shoulder from behind— normal-sized, not even a giant. It was midday. The sunlight filtered through the trees at the mountain stream where Hersh had stopped to drink. The man wore a purple robe of light material with a reflective sheen to it. And when the person swung around, Hersh bellowed out his usual greeting. This time, though, he greeted a man without a face. Or a woman without a face. He could not tell which. Hersh's voice slowed as his question spilled out of his mouth. The words had formed on his lips by reflex. "Please, good traveler, can you tell me where to find Master Wayfarer Kemgi?"

The answer given was a nod, the first nod he'd seen since the beginning of his quest. And then the person bolted up the nearest slope.

Hersh followed. He followed glimpses of the *Faceless* up the mountainside. *Is this person leading me to Kemgi?* Just when Hersh thought he'd lost sight of the Faceless, he'd see a glimmer of purple in the sun.

Always out of the corner of his eye, always higher, always more vertical. Soon he was scaling a bluff.

The half-giant paused, clinging to the rockface as he surveyed his new location—a steep cliff, sheeted with ice. Cold wind howled through the peaks around him. *Distance Walking is not for the faint of heart.* He waited there for the next sign, the next flash of purple. It never came. Flattened against the rock and exposed, chill winds cut through his clothing. The cold burn of the mountain-peak air found his bare skin and seeped through his flesh, down to his bones. His fingers and toes tingled as they slowly froze.

And then the Faceless came. The Faceless dropped from above, out of nowhere it seemed, fists flailing. The artistry of the fighter's balance in quick motion was nothing less than perfect. The Faceless scaled the slope, up and down like a spider before it lunged at Hersh and beat against him, attacking his face. The half-giant absorbed the first three punches. He raised a numb hand to block each attack, but each time the Faceless jabbed past Hersh's defenses. The half-giant swung back, but missed. The next solid hit came to his neck. The sharp blow nearly crushed his larynx.

A surge like fire flushed through Hersh's body. It warmed his cold flesh. He wanted to lash out at his attacker, swing wildly. But he knew that balance and strategy were everything in this place. So, he tempered the raging fire within and maintained his composure. *To lose control is to die here*, he told himself.

And so, when the half-giant saw his opponent preparing to lunge again, he let go of the rock hold. He let go, tilted away slightly, and, as the Faceless came at him, Hersh found peace in a moment of perfect balance. Relying on his superior reach, with a swift, fluid action, the half-giant thrusted his fist into his opponent's chest. He used the counterforce of the blow to reinforce his own stance and regain his hold, one-handed. *Finally, a hit. It can be hit.* Lightning fast, he delivered another smash. He felt the crunch of ribs under his knuckles.

The Faceless dropped into the chasm. And even as the limp body plummeted, two fresh combatants appeared out of nowhere, one to either side of the exhausted half-giant, poised to strike. Hersh was perched too precariously to defend himself in a balanced way—he hadn't counted on another attack. One Faceless delivered a punch to his face. He blocked the next two blows, and as he felt himself begin to topple, the second Faceless delivered a kick to the neck. Hersh gasped. *I can't breathe. How can I fight with one hand if I can't even breathe?*

Jaw clenched, he executed a sharp kick. The Faceless blocked him easily, while the second delivered a precise blow to the supporting leg. Hersh's knee erupted in pain. His stability faltered. He nearly lost his balance on the snowy mountain bluff.

Hopeless. Impossible.

A voice called out to Hersh. A young boy's voice, nearing maturity. *Now I'm hearing things.* He ignored it. *They have no mouths.* A third opponent appeared, or reappeared—Hersh couldn't tell them apart. The three attacked at once. Always the face. Hersh struggled to defend against the flurry of strikes. Sweat and blood stung the half-giant's eyes. His vision blurred. The three seemed to merge and then split effortlessly as they punched, kicked, pushed... eyes, ears, nose, chin... Hersh found another hand grip and buried his face in his arms. He had mass and strength on his side, but combined, the Faceless were winning, beating him down with speed and precision. Risking injury, he craned his neck around, peering downward. *A deadly fall.* If he dropped, he would end up *There.* His foot slipped and, for a long moment, he dangled by his grip on the rock hold. One of the Faceless darted up the slope, dislodged a loose rock and smashed it against Hersh's fingers, clinging to the rock face. The other two came straight at him, attacking his face again. Hersh let out a frustrated grunt. "You just love attacking the face, don't you? Why? Are you jealous?" He drew the injured hand from the cliff just as it was about to be smashed again, and punched one of the Faceless in the blank space where a face should be. He felt a crunch, and punched again. His other hand erupted in pain, smashed by the rock.

I can't hold on.

Hersh let go, slid down to the next ledge—glare ice. To halt his descent, he drove his fingernails into the frozen pillar. Body pressed against the ice sheet, he struggled to grasp a proper hold. *Nothing solid.*

One by one, fingernails snapped. Blood trickled down the ice sheet. He grunted with effort.

The boy's voice called again. It didn't seem to belong on the side of a mountain in Glace Valley. It also lacked the hollow quality of sound carried on the winds, and it lacked the play of an echo bouncing between cliffs. *Too plain and direct, this voice.* Undeniably near.

"Vice-regent, awaken."

Hersh felt himself being shaken by the shoulders. A terrible smell filled his nostrils. He gasped. *My body… lying down. Confined.* Someone slapped his face. *Don't touch the face!* The mountainside, the Faceless… everything… began to fade. Except his grip on the rock hold. His grip kept him *There.* And except the rage. The rage burned within. *To hell with control.*

"Vice-regent," the voice said.

The half-giant let go of the rockface. He felt himself fall. Weightless. Drifting. The cold air of the chasm whirred past his ears.

Hersh opened his eyes. *Ice?* His mind scrambled to understand. *No.*

A glassy Wulver stared back at him. Familiar. *Gutless Kori?* Through the translucent figure, Hersh's eyes caught movement—something swaying in the treetops. He scanned above. *More.* His eyes narrowed on one specific target wrapped in thin branches, hanging helpless from a tree, snake-like staff jutting out.

Riddik. Hersh put his self-control aside.

"Oh good, you're awake," the voice said. A man's face leaned into view. *He has a face.* Angular. Chiseled.

Where's the boy? Hersh's mind struggled to put the three faces together: boy, man, blank. *What's happening?*

Hersh grunted. He tried to move his arm. It was restrained. A snap sounded when he jerked it free. Gritting his teeth, he palmed the man's face, shoved it aside.

"Riddik!" Hersh boomed—one face he didn't need to see. He tried to scramble to his feet. *Stuck… ropes… no, they're tree roots.* With his free hand, he tore the bonds from his neck and then freed his other arm. As he pushed himself to a sitting position, roots and branches snapped and pulled against him.

"I'll kill you, Riddik." Hearing his own voice say the words sent a rush of pure elation through his brain. *This is too easy.*

"No."

That voice again. The tone was firm.

"Vice-regent, don't—"

Hersh ripped the last of the roots binding his legs and rose to his feet. The man with the angular face shot in front of him. Hersh shoved him aside and approached the helpless Riddik.

"So sad to see you like this," Hersh said, sarcasm in his tone. He massaged his fists as he eyed the fiend. "Riddik the Cutter. Riddik the Cutter of an old woman. Riddik the Cutter of Vey Lancer." He scoffed. "Riddik the Haircutter." With his massive fist, Hersh smashed Riddik. The worthless sack of slaver flesh flew like a punching bag. The Taint squealed in pain as he swung high. Hersh wound up for a second strike.

"How many others have you cut, Riddik? Killed? Enslaved?"

"STOP!" shouted the boy with the man's face.

Hersh smashed Riddik again. The blow sent him flying. This time, the Taint broke free of the branches. Riddik crashed to the forest floor. And as he writhed and moaned, Hersh shifted his gaze to the suspended Ang.

"Your next." The demoness hung there, still and unresponsive. *She's better off that way,* Hersh decided.

That voice sounded again, getting in the way of revenge. This time, pleading. "Have mercy. Let me bring them to true justice. The cores of their souls have been stolen."

Hersh wondered, *Is this another test?* He halted, and his gaze wandered over the scene. Clearly, he was in the domain of *Silent Shadow*, and yet, the scenario lent itself to *Nameless Kindheart*. The half-giant breathed in deep. He let the forest air collect in his belly, and then he slowly exhaled. His fists dropped to his sides. He unclenched his fingers. Hersh's heart melted, as it had on the streets of Glace Valley's main settlement.

This is not a battle for fists, he realized.

❧

The half-giant and the Wilder druid sat cross-legged and across from one another on the forest floor, in the grove where the Wulver had been turned to crystal. Both were shoeless, baring their calloused, earth-stained feet to one another. Hersh had no idea what had happened to his fine boots. Beside the half-giant, Vey lay resting. Above them, Milla and Ang hung silent, tightly cradled in Hurlorn branches. Riddik's body lay crumpled, motionless on the ground where he'd fallen.

Hands folded in front of him, eyes lowered and wearing a somber expression, the Wilder spoke. "Quite the storm I see, to the north." Slashes of wilder ink stained his sunken cheeks. "So far, seems to have passed us by. Hoping for a wind shift to bring it our way. That would slow Ironeagle's advances and give me some peace."

Hersh understood that the one sitting across from him could use some rest. *A hearty meal as well,* he thought. Beneath the wilder ink and patchy scruff, the individual's features were sharp and drawn. Hersh couldn't sort out his age—he seemed to be a combination of ages. His pale skin tightly wrapped the jutting bones of his lower jaw and cheekbones. Wide streaks of crimson disguised the bags under his eyes. The druid's frame seemed child-like though, shrunken under the worn leathers and weather-stained cloak that he wore, as though he'd once filled them more wholly. All of his clothes were sprinkled with forest matter. His black hair was mussed up and matted like a careless child's, and had more than a few twigs in it.

Hersh asked, "How do you know who I am?"

The Wilder met his gaze with bright green eyes, discerning and keen. Then he smirked, reached to the ground beside him, picked up something and tossed it over. Hersh caught the leather wrap against his chest, then sighed when he realized what it was. "Of course, my diplomatic colors." Somehow, the half-giant had managed to hold onto them.

A quick grin formed on the Wilder's lips, and his eyes grinned along with them. "What? Did you think you were famous throughout the land?"

Hersh grunted. "Infamous perhaps, if you believe my political opponents."

"They are many, and they are not confined to the Fort Abandon guild masters."

He knows more than he lets on. Hersh studied the man's ink more closely. "You have the markings of a Chieftain." He glanced about. "And yet I see no tribe." Hersh fixed his gaze back on the Wilder. The man's grin had disappeared, replaced with a pensive expression. He sat with his jaw slightly dropped, eyes downward. As thin as he was, he seemed to have deflated slightly. The half-giant pressed on. "Who are you? And what do I owe for this favor?"

The Wilder druid rubbed his scruffy chin. After a long pause, he shifted in place and re-crossed his legs. Then he raised his eyes to meet Hersh's gaze. "I grew tired of my comrades falling around me," he said. "I go it alone now. Bitterhelm believes these woods haunted, and the Queen's Guard in Gan has it in their heads that a Wilder tribe defends this Line of Control. I'd hate to disappoint."

"But it is only you."

The Wilder confirmed with a nod. "And the Hurlorns of course. Many Sleepers in these parts have been awakened, but not many even remember how to move anymore. Most are content to live their lives as normal-seeming trees. Without my prompting, they'd never budge." He hesitated. "And I get updates from wind riders now and again, but their patrols are few of late." The Wilder gave Hersh a measuring look. "I go by the name of Anexxander, and I protect these sacred woods."

"A good name. After the Legend."

"I am the Legend... or what's left of it."

Hersh did a double take on the Wilder, trying to match what he saw with tall tales of great deeds from long ago, in the days before the First Men were scattered throughout the lands. *Wilders are not true Elderkin. They don't rejuvenate.* He'd heard the company of Hurlorns could drive a man insane. *That must be it. He's gone mad. Delusional. They've whispered things to him. Terrible things to make him go mad.*

Anexxander spoke. "You owe me nothing, Vice-regent Tehan." He hesitated. "I may have a favor to ask of you though, one day. A favor you will have to weigh the consequences of with the times. I will not bind you to it."

"I'd rather settle this here and now. I can offer you notes, property… a high position in the Fort Guard—they could use a man like you." *If you aren't mad.*

The Wilder shook his head. "Spare me your burdens."

The half-giant sighed. "Very well, then. When the day comes, consider me bound." He extended his hand. "Many thanks, Anexxander. And you can call me Hersh."

The Wilder druid leaned forward. He took Hersh's hand and shook it with a pointed grip. A grip so gnarly strong it could crush the blood out of a stone golem.

The half-giant still in his clutches, with a rolling motion of his free hand Anexxander ordered wine. Red.

Chapter XXXIV
Crystal arrows
(Akrylla, Hersh)

~Listen

Akrylla jolted awake. It was dark. She gasped. *Can't move.* She tried to spread her arms out, kick her legs. In response, the branches holding her redoubled their grip. She grunted as they squeezed. Her body swayed with the effort, struggling, suspended in its twig cocoon. Stiff, gnarled fingers clenched her throat—at least they felt like fingers.

"Let me go," she pleaded, her voice a rasping whisper. The shaman glimpsed the evening sky through the colored leaves and the twigs, then gasped for air as her throat constricted. *Too tight.* She gargled, "Stop."

~Relax

Akrylla took the hint and let her body go limp. She waited. *No struggling.* Hoping. *Relax,* she repeated to herself, *conserve energy.* The wood's unrelenting grip held her fast. *I can barely breathe.* Her pulse quickened. She tried to contain it. She tried not to panic. *Relax.*

Wait.

A long minute went by. Then another.

Wait.

Akrylla's breathing slowed and shallowed, but she remained fully conscious this time. She remained conscious long enough to feel the tiniest release, the tiniest slack around her neck. The sensation spread to her shoulders and down through to her toes. The grip loosened.

Relief washed over her. The shaman deepened her breaths, grateful for the newfound freedom to expand her ribs, if only slight.

"How about letting me go," she mumbled to the Hurlorn, as best she could with her mouth stuffed full of twigs. The branches didn't budge after that. She heard talking.

~Listen

Akrylla perked her ears to the conversation below, in the grove. She recognized the deep, soothing voice of the half-giant.

"What do we do with them now?" he said, and then crunched on something.

She listened intently for the response. *This is what I need to know, isn't it? With whom the big one speaks?* A child's voice responded to the half-giant—a mere boy.

"Not sure about the hag. I wanted to ask you about her." He paused. "Take the two slavers to justice in Gan, I s'pose. There's a bounty."

Hersh repeated the word, "Bounty?"

"Nine hundred griffs a head," the boy explained, "but I opt for Beads of the Nine instead."

Beads of the Nine? Slowly, carefully, quietly, Akrylla twisted her body around. Part way, she spotted another twig-wrapped body, hanging beside her. A splash of red peeked through the branches. *Ang.* The body wasn't moving. *Unconscious, like I was. She lacks patience.*

The shaman completed her spin and peered down through the branches. Her gaze wandered over the dimly lit scene. She spotted Riddik first, curled in a ball beneath her. One leg twitched as she watched. He'd been ejected and was coming to. Vey lay passed out on the forest floor, her chest heaving slightly as she breathed. *Sneaking pinches, she was,* Akrylla surmised, *incapacitated by her own devices.*

Next, the shaman fixed her eyes on the new Gutless Kori. The half-giant stood leaning casually against the crystallized beast, eyeing Riddik while chewing on something. He held a goblet in one hand and a fist full of nuts and dried berries in the other. Not far away, someone sat cross-legged on the ground... the boy... she couldn't quite see...

Speaking with his mouth full, Hersh stated, "The hag is a victim." He sounded convincing, authoritative.

A second wave of relief washed over Akrylla. She knew those words meant she'd be set free.

Hersh swallowed. "Were it not for you, I would've killed the wretched slavers. How can you think to do otherwise, after all these years fighting Bitterhelm?" He washed down the trail mix with a swig from his goblet.

Akrylla angled her body for a slightly better view of the boy.

"The Chamber of Aelish put up the bounty—for live capture," the boy said, tracing out the shape of the 3rd Institute's domed roof with his fingertips. "It's been in place for years."

The boy seemed to communicate as much with words as with his arms, waving them freely, one hand brandishing his goblet. Red liquid splashed up and out, then sloshed back again as he carried on. His voice quickened. "Some highfalutin do-gooder *ascendant* recognized the situation in Bitterhelm... the users and abusers, y'know... and wanted to make a name for himself, but without actually doing much of anything that involves work. The bounty is his way of giving a few desperate people a chance at a new life, one they could never have without intervention."

"Compliments of his followers."

"Of course," the boy said, throwing his arms wide. "Nothin' like spending others' money."

"And the goal is to..."

"Send them back to Bitterhelm with a new perspective on life: first take them in under Aelish's graces, to 'heal' them—body and soul. They might even get rejuvenated if they qualify. And then, as I said, eventually... You must've heard, being in your position, how Bitterhelm has become hooked on the 'charm dust' of Irongate, if you gather my meaning. It takes many forms." The boy downed the contents of his cup, let out a satisfied sigh. He wiped his lips with his sleeve. "A good vintage. Sometimes it's a bit vinegary."

Hersh nodded, "The dust that makes its way to Bitterhelm is manufactured in the Bay area—illegal alchemical operations. Treaty enforcers busted one a few months back in the Akedan ruins. A lot of bad substances came out of there. They'd even managed to weaponize some of their creations."

The boy raised his pointed eyebrows and nodded, then reached out to grasp a bottle nestled in among the rocks and the ground cover beside him. He bent forward and raised it to Hersh, who stooped to accept the offer with an extended cup hand. The boy topped up Hersh's goblet first, emptied the remaining contents into his own, then flung the bottle into the trees behind him. It whipped through the branches, smacking leaves and twigs along the way, but never landed.

As Akrylla continued to spy, the boy's gaze shifted to Riddik, whose stirring had become pronounced. He frowned, shook his head at the slaver. Hersh's gaze followed, and he stiffened his stance at what he saw. Never taking his eyes off the Taint, the half-giant carefully balanced his goblet on the nape of Gutless Kori's neck. He downed the remaining trail mix and brushed his hands together.

Leveraging his staff, Riddik was in the midst of a silent attempt to rise to his feet. Hersh stepped towards him, but the boy's raised palm stayed the half-giant. With a casual, rolling gesture from the same hand, branches bent down from the treetops. Long, viny roots crept along the ground towards Riddik.

It's true, this child commands Hurlorns, he does.

Before Riddik knew enough to react, the branches entangled him again and jerked him into the air. He cursed malevolently. The staff dropped to the ground as he fought against his bonds.

"Let me be, Druid," the Cutter spat, voice full of malice. He whipped his body around and dropped a few feet. Riddik nearly broke free, but for a vine that drew him back in. He cursed again. "I'll cut off your fingers and stuff them down your throat, Druid. I'll burn every tree in this cursed forest." Struggling and swearing, spite oozing out of every cell of his body, the Taint was hauled up into the high branches and forcibly put in his place, to hang next to Ang. Riddik cursed them all with death by blades, until brightly colored leaves stuffed his mouth and his words turned to muffled grunts.

After a dismissive wave and an exaggerated sigh, the boy uncrossed his legs, pushed himself to his feet. *Not much taller than Riddik,* Akrylla thought of him when he stood, dwarfed by the half-giant he faced, *but so thin. I doubt he's a hundred pounds.* The shaman could see the boy's face clearly now and quickly realized this was no child. *Dark hair, sharp features... a hard, youthful look.* Her gaze narrowed in on his facial markings. *Wilder paint... yes, Riddik is right. A Wilder druid.*

The boy slipped a hand under his collar and pulled out a leather cord, looped around his neck, then held it up. The beads strung along it were tiny carvings, amber in color. He dangled them in front of the half-giant.

"Beads of the Nine, towards rejuvenation," the boy said. He spread his hands along the cord and pulled the necklace taught, hooked by his thumbs.

Hersh leaned towards him for a closer look, squinting. "The nine original leviathans and behemoths," he remarked.

The Wilder wagged eight fingers in response. "I have eight so far. Just one more to complete the set and gain another rejuvenation session—as much as the process disagrees with me. Every ten slavers earns me a single bead."

"Which bead are you missing?"

"Ekkon the Wanderer."

A pulsing shiver passed through Akrylla. *A sign.* A realization flashed in her mind. *Not a trivial sign, either.* Heartbeat racing, the shaman wriggled her hand to her satchel and felt inside, to the very bottom corners. She felt through the contents until she came across something small, roundish and hard. *Is this it?* She pressed her fingers on the shape to discern its features. *Yes, I can feel the tentacles.* Her sister had found the trinket among the ruins of her homeland and given it to her.

The shaman had pleaded to Ekkon for years in the desert... since before she was a shaman. Alone and assailed by the dry, open winds, she'd pleaded and prayed for help. The beast never answered her call. *Perhaps he did answer,* she theorized, *perhaps this was his way.* All she'd ever received from Ekkon up until that point was a useless bead, or so she believed. Akrylla grinned and withdrew her hand, leaving her miniature idol behind.

She turned her attention back to the half-giant and the Wilder. She'd missed the bulk of whatever it was they'd gone on about in the meantime. Politics, it seemed, from the fragments of conversation she'd overheard.

Hersh sipped from his goblet, nodded to Anexxander. "Not a bad idea, in principle. At least someone in the Royal Quarter has a heart."

Anexxander huffed. "They're the ones at fault. It was the Royal Quarter that created this mess in the first place. It's not something they advertise, y'know, but Gan used charm dust to prop up the Ironeagle Stouts." He bore a cross look. "This whole dependency problem was orchestrated to pacify Bitterhelm and thwart the warlords by taking away their soldier's will to fight, thereby decreasing attacks on Irongate. Gan provided Irongate with the original means to manipulate the situation to their advantage, but then cut off the supply when it blossomed into… into degrading and controlling the Bitterhelm population to provide cheap labor for the mines. And now…" The Wilder druid had begun to pace. He waved his hands about frantically, in disbelief. "Bitterhelm's gone right mad with a new variety of charm dust that has much the opposite effect—pure aggression. The warlords are in on the production now, recruitment is on the rise, and *I* have to deal with berserking fighters that fear nothing, not even death."

The Wilder halted to face Hersh square on, eyes wide and piercing. "Mad, I say." Anexxander threw his arms in the air. "And that's not all."

The half-giant jerked back in response. "I had no idea," he said.

Anexxander continued with his rant. "I don't know what's in the latest batch, but I can't hardly tell who's who anymore: half the men dress like women and half the women dress like men." He sipped from his cup. Hersh could hardly believe there was anything left in it, the way he sloshed it around.

"It isn't the charm dust, Anexxander," Hersh explained. "It is one part of many great shifts occurring among the colossi."

"Shifts?"

"Bitterhelm's leviathan, Asph the Tempting, is in the process of changing gender in anticipation of breeding with Sinfon of the Dim Sea."

"You're kidding." Anexxander's jaw dropped. "This, after a decade of war with Jakka over failing to breed with Gorganna?"

"The Mother of All Snakes tried to devour Asph after mating. It's the sort of thing colossi do. I don't pretend to understand it. Sinfon is the dominant male from the brood of the White Whale. If the change takes and the two breed successfully, it will unite the undercurrents of Harrow and Bitterhelm. And if Queen Xara actually goes through with her planned marriage to King Taeglin, one of the colossi offspring could attempt to fill the power void left behind when Aelish finally passes in Gan and begins transcendence."

Anexxander grunted. "The death of the God of Healing."

"Not a god," Hersh corrected.

The Wilder druid grunted again. "I know. You get what I mean."

"This situation is a huge concern in political circles," Hersh continued. "Back to your observation, I suspect that members of Asph's clergy have followed suite, out of respect... to the extent they can."

"By making *the change* with her?"

Hersh nodded.

Anexxander puffed, eyes full with a child's wonder. "Oh. Well, that's different then." He shrugged. "I thought it was the charm dust. I'm glad we had this conversation, Hersh. At first glance, I thought you might be one of them giants south of Ironeagle. I almost... you know..."

Hersh rapped his knuckles on the glassy Wulver. "I get it."

Anexxander pressed his lips together and shook his head. "Nasty creature—not about to take a chance on that one."

Hersh grunted. "One-tenth less of a bead though." He swept his gaze over the other statues in the grove. "Where do they go? Where, exactly, do your arrows send them?"

"Somewhere hellish, I'm sure," Anexxander responded. "A place where terror reigns free." He averted Hersh's eyes and shifted about uncomfortably, yet continued to speak. "I choose my targets with great care. I'd been tracking the six of you since early morning." He shifted his gaze back to meet the half-giant's. "Would you say I judged the Wulver correctly?" Anexxander waited expectantly for Hersh's response.

The half-giant nodded firmly. "A foul creature. As foul as they come."

The Wilder druid puffed out a heavy sigh. "Good, then." He swiveled his gaze upwards to the hanging slavers, then to Milla. He scratched his head. "I'll release the hag to your care. You're free to return with me to the gorge when I collect, or go your own way. Up to you, Vice-regent."

"I'd much rather travel with you and sort everything out in Gan. I was on my way there to begin with, before getting sidetracked by these slavers." He turned his gaze to Vey. "Me and my traveling companion, that is: Vey Lancer, Special Assistant to the Grey Clerk. We were on an important diplomatic mission…" A wave of sudden dread overcame the half-giant as the greater purpose of the mission swelled up in his mind. *The Council. The vote.* The memory pulsed in the veins of his forehead. He swung his gaze, eyes wide, back to the druid. "What day is it today?"

Anexxander shrugged. "Beats me. Nigh on October by the chill in the air and the changing of the leaves on the early turners."

Shroud's Well. "The vote has come and gone." Hersh squeezed his eyes shut. The power generators, the machinery, built off of old-world knowledge and hidden deep within the maze of tunnels beneath Fort Abandon, had already passed the prototyping stages and were being primed for production. Mechanized weaponry was the first priority, to outfit those who would defend the wave of industrialization to follow. Vey's words resonated in his mind: *Who would you rather work with? Gan or Harrow?* The Grey Clerk's willingness to share the archives with Fort Abandon could have been a turning point. *Can it even happen now?* Breaking the treaty would shatter the prospects of a renewed alliance with Gan. The half-giant dropped his giant head low. One hand massaged his forehead.

Anexxander's voice cut in. "What is it?"

The vice-regent didn't respond for a long moment, mulling over the folly. He knew the guild masters were on the take from Harrow and that they'd have voted for the project even if they knew Gan would take action because of it. On top of that, Hersh was convinced that half of the guild masters would be happy to see him dead. *But the oligarchs… the oligarchs I could have turned. And that would have been enough to win the vote.* Hersh was certain they'd have listened to him and was certain they'd have taken heed of the Grey Clerk's veiled warnings about the Jhinyari. *That business about protecting all humankind would have fallen on deaf ears though.* Hersh decided he'd keep that one to himself, at least for now. He sighed, opened his eyes and turned his gaze back to the druid. Then he shook his head.

"Nothing that matters now," Hersh told him, "except to say that even more power shifts are at play than the 'colossal' ones we were discussing earlier. Everything is shifting at once… the very ground beneath our feet moves." The vice-regent knew he'd have to deal with the consequences later. Much later. But the process would still be reversible for some time. Months of production line testing would be required before anything could be manufactured.

Anexxander's eyebrows drew together in a concerned look. "I'm sorry for all you've had to endure. Tell me if I can help. And that special assistant—a nasty cut she has. Is she going to be…?"

"She'll get through it—I'll see to it personally that she does. She's tougher than she looks and very smart. As for you, Anexxander… I'm afraid there isn't much more I can ask of you than to keep holding the line."

The Wilder druid nodded knowingly, then whispered into the branches of the trees above. A breeze seemed to pick up his words and propagate them through the canopy. Gently, the Sleeper that held Milla in its grasp lowered her to the ground. As she lay immobile, the branches that had her bound and gagged slipped away from her body.

◆

~Grateful

Akrylla scrambled to her knees in gratitude to the Wilder and the half-giant. She hugged the steward's shins, then scuttled over to the boy and clamped her arms around his thighs, ignoring his humble protests.

The boy's wine spilled and he seemed genuinely uncomfortable with the attention. He told her "it was nothing."

Akrylla cried tears to him about how terrible it was to have been taken by the slavers, and she cried tears about being manipulated by them. She told her rescuers their names. She told them everything she knew. And she told them she thought Ang was worth saving, that she could be turned around. The boy liked the sound of that. She even whispered to Hersh about the dark, scrawny thing that Riddik had killed. That made the half-giant scowl and massage his fists.

I can get by without Riddik now, she decided.

Vey stirred in the midst of all the commotion, the first signs that she was ready to awaken from her slumber. Akrylla shot her Ak'la a discreet glance. The eyes of her young hopeful opened wide and sleepy, coming out of her daze. They immediately sought the half-giant, begging for his presence. He went to her straightaway. She sat up, and he settled in beside her.

While they're occupied... Akrylla turned her attention back to the Wilder. She'd heard the name "Anexxander" before. The voice inside had been right about him all along.

~Secrets

I know, I know. This man-child is a gift from Ekkon the Wanderer. This man-child has secrets. Secrets from way back. Secrets I can use.

When Akrylla decided she'd groveled enough, she squatted on her hinds and extended a hand to the boy. He hesitated, and then, it seemed, he tried to cover up his hesitation with a quick grasp of her hand. As Anexxander hauled her up, his wiry strength caught Akrylla off guard—she stumbled to her feet.

And as the shaman met the Wilder druid's gaze, her ears homed in on the words of comfort passing between Hersh and Vey. The half-giant was telling her everything that had transpired.

The boy's eyes shifted to Akrylla's satchel. In her scuffle with the roots and branches, her giant scorpion stinger had poked through the seam.

"Oh that," Akrylla said with a dismissive wave. She tucked the stinger back into her satchel and shrugged. "I dabble." The Wilder boy's eyes shifted again, this time to the sandspider claw that she'd hooked back onto her robe sash. The shaman pretended it wasn't there and grinned. "I'm Milla, from Fort Abandon."

The Wilder druid hesitated, then downed the last of his wine. He casually dismissed the shaman's poisonous weaponry and introduced himself formerly as "Anexxander Strife."

"No need to worry, Milla," he assured her, patting his own sidebag. "I have my own supply, which you are welcome to." Then he offered her some roots, a thin wafer, and a drink from his own waterskin.

Akrylla felt comfortable in Anexxander's company. *He has that way about him.* All smiles and without even hiding her teeth, she readily accepted all he had to offer. She held on to the waterskin longer than she needed.

~Distract

Akrylla swung her gaze to the crystallized Wulver. She put a hand to her chest, gasped in awe. "How is this even possible? You must be a Master Thaumaturgist." With her other hand, she slipped a powder pouch from her satchel and hid it in her palm.

"I'd love to claim the credit," Anexxander said, admiring the statue alongside her.

The shaman sipped from the waterskin, swallowed, then wiped her lips with her sleeve. In the same action, she dumped half the pouch's contents into her mouth.

Still eyeing the statue, the Wilder shrugged, his expression humble. "But the credit is not mine."

Keep him talking. Akrylla did her best not to sound like her mouth was full. "Then whose?" she said. "Who gets credit?" In plain view, she took a swig from the container again, swished the water in her mouth to dissolve the powder, then discreetly backwashed it all. She wiped her lips again then handed the boy his waterskin.

Anexxander grasped the container. "I found the arrowheads in a dugout," he replied, "exposed by the passing of wildfire and the erosion of loose soil." The Wilder druid dipped his waterskin for a quick swig, put the cap back on, then pulled an arrow from the quiver at his side.

He held up the tip of the arrow to the grey light of the fading day. Slowly, he rotated it in front of Akrylla, keen eyes fixed to the crystal that formed the arrowhead. "I only found a dozen, so I use them sparingly."

The druid offered the arrow to Akrylla.

~Take

The shaman grasped the shaft, focused her eyes on the tip. It was yellowy-red and translucent with silvery veins inside. "This crystal is infused with metal," she remarked.

~Apprentice

Akrylla glanced to Vey. She could only think of one way out of her predicament. One way to regain control, to regain her Ak'la. One way to respect the signs she'd been given.

The shaman returned her attention to the arrowhead. Holding it up to the diffuse light, she began to wander casually through the forest grove, scrutinizing the crystal closely as she did so. She wandered behind Vey and Hersh, acting as though the illumination was superior there.

"White metal," she added, at last. The half-giant shot her a sideways glance.

He's watching me. Akrylla knew that sooner or later though, the boy would draw Hersh's attention. *Sooner,* she thought, *I know the perfect question.* She regarded the Wilder boy.

"What tribe fashioned these crystal arrows, so long ago?"

Anexxander rubbed the scruff on his chin. "Ahh yes," he replied. "A very good question. There's a single legend that makes mention of the use of a crystal arrow—to slay a greedy giant that had bent over to pick up a gold nugget the size of an apple. He became a hill of crystal."

Akrylla let out an exaggerated gasp, as though she'd never heard the story. "I know that hill. It's in the desert."

Anexxander furrowed his brow. "Where did you say you were from?"

Hersh suddenly appeared uncomfortable. He swung his gaze to Anexxander.

"Who? Who shot the arrow at the giant?"

The boy hesitated, his expression suddenly blank. He moved his hand from his chin to his forehead and rubbed. He winced and shut his eyes for a moment.

Vey interjected, addressing the Wilder druid. "Are you all right?" she said, concern in her voice.

The powder's working, thought Akrylla. The shaman casually stepped into place, closer still to her Vey. *Keep him distracted.* She spoke firmly to the boy. "Yes Anexxander, who shot the arrow?"

The Wilder druid composed himself and answered. "Those who walked these woods before the Wilders came. Abindohns, perhaps."

Bonecasters, Anexxander. You, of all people, should know that. Bonecasters.

Hersh asked, "Then who exactly is greedy?" The tone of his voice had turned confrontational. Akrylla relished in the passion showing through. He went on.

"Is it the giant? Or is it the Abindohn who shot him to keep the gold? Giants are not wealth-oriented, I'll have you know. The giant was probably just curious."

~Act

Arrow in hand, Akrylla lunged towards Vey. The shaman grabbed her by the hair, yanked her from Hersh's side. Vey screeched. The half-giant's arm lashed out but missed its mark.

"Stop!" Vey cried, as Akrylla dragged her to a stand-off distance. "What are you doing?" She struggled against the shaman. "Hersh!"

The half-giant scrambled to his feet, but he was too slow. Akrylla had Vey exactly where she wanted her. The shaman locked her arm around Vey's neck. She held it firm, pressed the arrow's tip to the red-head's throat.

"Not one move," Akrylla said, her gaze switching from half-giant to Wilder. Vey went wide-eyed and still. Hersh froze, but Akrylla could see his muscles were tensed, ready for action. Anexxander backed up a step, stumbling as he did so.

Akrylla narrowed her eyes at the druid. "Not one gesture or she dies," she told him. "And back off." She watched him step back. "Move over to the steward."

With his shoulders high and shrugged, Anexxander held his hands up in front of him where she could see them. "What is this?" he said. He didn't look so much alarmed as confused.

The shaman raised her voice. "BACK OFF." Anexxander did as she bade him, until he stood next to the half-giant.

"Don't do this, Milla," Vey pleaded. "We can help you."

"Silence!" Akrylla snapped back.

Hersh addressed the shaman. "What is it you want?"

"I want you to kill *him*," she said, flicking her gaze to Anexxander, and then back to Hersh. She'd kept the small bag of powder in her hands, which she now dangled the half-giant's way. "And then I want you to take this."

Akrylla spoke quietly into Vey's ear. "And you, my dear, I need you to take another pinch of your own stash. You know where to find it."

When Vey didn't budge, Akrylla pressed the crystal arrow harder into her skin.

"No," Vey begged, glancing to the Wulver. "Don't do this." Tears streaked down her cheek.

"I'm sorry, my Vey," Akrylla replied. Her own eyes felt wet. "It has to be this way."

"Wait," Hersh said. Eyes fixed on the crystal arrow, he addressed the Wilder. "Anexxander, will that arrow work on Vey the way it did on the Wulver?"

"Not a chance," Anexxander replied. "It needs a good draw weight and a firm smack to activate. Stabbing her with it won't do anything out of the ordinary."

"He lies!" Akrylla screeched.

The vice-regent kept his voice calm. "Have you ever stabbed a person with one, or been cut by one accidentally?"

"No, I'm always careful."

"The druid doesn't know," Akrylla insisted. "He doesn't even know where they come from." She glared at Anexxander. "Bonecasters, you fool," she hissed at him. "Not Abindohns. Bonecasters!"

~Shroud

"Shroud himself was one of them."

The Wilder druid made a sudden step sideways, correcting his balance to keep from falling over. He double-blinked. "What have you done to me?"

Akrylla grinned to herself for her deft handiwork, then shifted her focus to the half-giant. Hersh paused in thought for a long moment. She could see the indecision on his face. *Here it comes.* Akrylla dug in her heels to brace herself, in case he lunged at her, and she firmed her grip on the arrow's shaft. *Don't test me. I'd do it just to spite you, before you smash my old bones into pieces.*

Hersh closed his eyes, then breathed a heavy sigh.

~Troubled

By his harried expression, Akrylla could see that the decision weighed heavy on him.

The half-giant grimaced, bit his lip, then spoke to the Wilder beside him. "Thank you for the wine and the nuts, Anexxander."

"You're most welcome," came the boy's uncertain reply.

In a flash, Hersh's hand lashed out at Anexxander, smashing his chest. The boy flew through the air and crumpled to the ground.

Vey screamed.

Akrylla cackled, the thrill of the moment surging through every vein.

Anexxander didn't get up. *Out cold,* Akrylla thought. *And maybe a few broken bones.* "Now finish him!" she commanded Hersh.

The half-giant slumped down to a sitting position, crossed his legs. He shook his head at Akrylla then looked to Vey with sad, tired eyes. "Vey," he said, "take your powder just like Milla told you to. Then bring mine over and dump it into my mouth. Let's get this over with."

Sobbing, Vey shook her head. "No," she said, her voice feeble and shaky. She glanced to Anexxander and whimpered. "No. Not again. I won't do it. I won't go through this again. I won't be a slave, or a whore, or… I don't even know what this woman wants with me. I wish she'd just leave me alone. No one owns me."

"It's for your own good, my dear," Akrylla said. "I will teach you to read the signs, that is all. That is everything. Then you are free to go."

Hersh locked eyes with Vey, his voice warm and comforting. "Milla won't harm you. Just give her what she wants and she will protect you." Hersh shifted his gaze to the shaman. "Isn't that right, Milla?"

Akrylla nodded. "Yessums. I would never harm my Vey, unless forced to. Any more than my own child. My own sister."

~Sister

The well. Akrylla squeezed her eyes shut, then forced the memory back where it belonged, back somewhere in the dark recesses of her mind.

Hersh continued. "Milla, I'm not going to let the Outlanders kill or enslave Anexxander. You need to leave him alone too. In that spirit, I propose, in exchange for my cooperation, that we cut Riddik and Ang down and I carry them far away from here before removing their bonds. You can do what you want with them after that. Deal?"

~Convince him

"I know of this man-child, this wild thaumaturgist," Akrylla said. "If you don't kill him, he'll hunt us down."

Hersh folded his arms. "Do we have a deal? Or do I take Anexxander's word about the arrow and tear your limbs off one-by-one, then hang your shredded corpse in a tree myself?"

Akrylla hesitated. *The Wilder's probably right.* She spat.

"Deal, Vice-regent, but I'm taking his supply of herbs. He offered them to me fair and square, and I'm taking him up on that offer."

"Surely, under the circumstances, he—"

Akrylla groaned. "He should have thought more carefully about circumstances before making the offer. He should have read the signs. He knows better. I know he knows better."

Hersh sighed heavily, paused to think, and then nodded to Vey. Hand trembling, the redhead reached into her hair. She retrieved her pouch and emptied out the last pinch to use on herself. Next, Akrylla passed Vey the small bag meant for Hersh. Following closely behind, arrow pressed to the side of Vey's neck, Akrylla ushered her to the half-giant. The redhead sprinkled two pinches into his mouth.

That's the last of it.

Hersh stood up and collected the slavers in short order before falling under the spell of the powder. While he did so, Akrylla pilfered Anexxander's necklace of beads, then poked at his neck with the crystal arrow's tip. Blood trickled down to his collar. Otherwise, no change.

"Hmph," she muttered under her breath. "The child was right." She tossed the arrow onto his chest and left him be. As she strode through the grove, she accidentally tripped over Riddik's staff. Akrylla squatted to pick it up, then tried it out for balance. *Not bad,* she thought, as she examined its snake-like pattern. *He'll need it when I dope him up again.* ~Haste

Akrylla huffed to herself when she thought of the woodland trail ahead and how close it would bring them to Gan. She had no choice though, not now. *Time is running out, and it is the shorter path.*

Her voice was sharp, addressing the half-giant. "We march through the night," she told him. He gave no response.

On her way out of the grove, the shaman paused at the crystal statue. She took a long look at Gutless Kori, immortalized in translucent glass, gleaming in the end-of-day light. "Better than you deserved, Gutless Kori. Your pain is over too soon." Akrylla horked up a nugget, spat it on his ever-snarling face, and walked away.

Chapter XXXV
Far Fencing
(Berendt, Hadamard)

BERENDT KNEW THAT most took him to be the calm, steady, predictable type. The ranger assault that he devised was anything but that.

What I wouldn't do for a good archer right now though, he thought. He'd brought the redheaded spotter from Fort Abandon in last-minute, as an alternate, but Lord Ralador disqualified Rix because he wasn't listed on the original roster—the same reason Amot couldn't take control of the operation. A part of Berendt felt good to be in command instead of standing on the sidelines watching and complaining, but another part wondered if he was up to the job. He hadn't been in a skirmish since Akeda; since his injury and others' more horrific; since he'd lost men and women under his command.

The skin under his eyepatch burned, and it itched constantly. He had to drain the ooze out of the wound every morning and every night, and rinse it thoroughly. The radiance channeler at the Citadel told him he might never see out of his left eye again. "No problem," Berendt'd replied. "I aim with my right anyway." He smirked to himself.

That enforcer and his staff of light would come in handy right now too. Without Lumen Hadamard at Akeda, surely there would've been more casualties, and I… Berendt didn't need to finish that thought right now.

He had another urge to satisfy, other than self-pity. *Others got it worse.* He glanced left and right to see who was watching. His rangers had all disappeared, just like they were supposed to. He scurried behind the nearest scenario tree. Leaning back against it, the Kith commander reached into his sidepouch and pulled out his flask. He unscrewed the cap, drew a quick swig, and screwed it back on again. The liquid soothed as it burned down his throat, the way it always did. He quickly and discreetly tucked the flask away. The whiskey would help him ignore the throbbing pain and the itch for a time, and that's what he needed right now. He couldn't remember what his excuse was before the injury. The battle horn would soon sound.

Berendt peered around his fake tree, heaved up from the ground by some bizarre Djinxarai projectionist. At least it wasn't made of bugs like some of the other scenario features—the "grass," for instance. *Long chains of damn shiro beetles.* He wasn't looking forward to the scenarios beyond the hill assault, the ones with larger bug entities—the mimics. Berendt was not a fan of the dome set-up in general, and he didn't like the games Lord Ralador was playing either.

"It all stinks," he told himself. "And that's why we're going to win this." In his mind, what Ralador and the queensmen failed to realize is that rangers are used to the smell.

One thing was for certain: the fight had to be quick and decisive for his rangers to prevail. The queensmen's tactical training, superior armor, impenetrable shield walls, and, as much as he hated to admit it, fine swordsmanship, would wear away at his Kith brothers in a standoff. *Early gains, before they know what hit them. That's what I'm aiming for.*

Berendt's two runners and callers showed up at his side just as the horn sounded. He'd need them to pass the commands he didn't want to shout out loud. The Kith commander cocked and loaded his hand crossbow. The battle had begun.

Hadamard scowled as the Queen's Guard readied their defenses. "Damn tower shields," he fumed. He turned to Feleg. "Did you see that shield wall go up? It's a damned fortress." Lord Ralador had simply written "shields" on the equipment list, "some round and some roughly diamond-shaped." Hadamard could tell by Berendt's expression when he heard the news that he wasn't fond of the kite shields either. But the Kith commander didn't protest and so the luminary, in his place, would be hard pressed to make a case of it.

Easily called a knoll, the long, low hill that the queensmen were to defend sat amidst a flat field. It was barren and featureless, apart from windswept scenario grass. The flag had been planted on a patch of the summit, near to the crowd. An inner circle of four plate-armored defenders stood ready to protect it. In position behind the shield wall, the rest of the summit was occupied by eight chain-armored defenders—spotters and the reserve force Eriff had mentioned. Since the queensmen wore helms with visors, it wasn't clear to Hadamard exactly which figure was in command, until he took a closer look at their armaments. One carried a cutting rapier—more rightly a civilian weapon than a military one. *Only the highest officer would do that,* Hadamard guessed.

Feleg acknowledged Hadamard's comment about the shield wall with a sorry shake of his head. Perimeter shieldmen fully protected the long hill from anything that might come charging at them from out of the tree line. And they didn't have much to worry about from the Kith-controlled queensmen archers either, many of whom hadn't been trained on the bow. Nekenezitter, standing slightly in front of the grig and the luminary, kept to himself on the matter.

The horn had long sounded yet nothing was happening on the battlefield. The silence of anticipation filled the dome, broken only by windy sighs rushing through the shiro beetle tunnels. Hadamard focused his gaze back on the scenario. He stood and watched for another long minute, waiting for the flurries of arrows to rain down on the hill before the rangers charged it. The opportunity to take out a few queensmen without opposition would be lost once the real fighting started. The Guard's spotters nervously eyed the tree line.

The arrows didn't come. Hadamard glanced at the crowd. Heads turned; people whispered. They were getting restless.

Finally, a shrill call filled the air—an ear-piercing battle cry. Screaming like maniacs and swinging their weapons wildly, rangers charged out of the tree line at great speed and as a single force. Gasps and cheers of encouragement erupted from the crowd. Tall Hallman led the way with his long stride, great axe swinging, a trail of hardy Stouts in his wake.

The sound and the action together were startling... unnerving. Hadamard felt chills ride up his spine like danger. And the visual of the rush, the power in the sprinting legs, and the Wilder's striking ink inflamed for battle, bleeding through to paint their crazed faces, was enough to turn all but the most hardened enemies.

"Woe," Feleg said. "I'd run like hell if I saw that coming at me." He'd voiced Hadamard's sentiments exactly.

Nekenezitter clicked in, "The rangers <tic> have insufficient numbers to fight the queensmen that way, <click> to surround the hill."

Feleg scoffed. "Based on what? Simulations? Don't be so sure." As the attacking rangers barreled towards the broad side of the hill, they formed a wedge pattern. "They're gonna punch through, Nek," he said with a grin. "Put that in your equation and solve it."

The grig was right. The crowd cringed in anticipation of the two forces colliding. Ranger bodies slammed against the tower shields in a tremendous clash of armor, wood and metal. Fighters on both sides scattered, trampled, and crawled over one another as more poured in. The scenario hit callers shouted "lethal" in a steady stream, identifying "red" queensmen and "blue" rangers in equal numbers. The Kith had plowed through the queensmen shield wall by sheer force. A tough squad of Stouts quickly gained the high ground, while steering clear of the staunch defenders at the flag end. Every other unscathed ranger scrambled up the hill with them.

Disqualified soldiers rolled on the ground and groaned, holding their wounds, taking the pain.

"Imagine the broken bones in that pile up," Feleg remarked.

"More than a few," Hadamard replied.

The displaced queensmen regrouped, then charged up the slope from all angles.

"QUILLS!" Berendt shouted. Hadamard swept his gaze to the Kith commander. He'd just stepped out of the tree line. He cupped his hands around his mouth and shouted again, to a different part of the forest. "THORNS!"

And as the queensmen fought their way up the hill, a flurry of arrows met them from behind. Berendt himself worked his crossbow, firing alongside his two defenders. The projectiles flew low to the ground on fast arcs.

Hadamard's pulse quickened. "The Guards, they're caught."

Flag defenders faced a barrage of arrows as well, while their shield-men were drawn into the fight to retake the summit.

As the two archer groups let loose, rangers on the hill ducked down behind the Guard's own tower shields to protect themselves. Some queensmen mistakenly turned their shields to the archers, leaving themselves open to ranger melee attacks from behind. Hit callers shouted out the strikes and tallied them against armor type.

"Two fronts." Feleg turned his gaze to Hadamard, eyes gleaming. "The queensmen have to fight the rangers stuck in the middle of them, uphill no less, and at the same time protect themselves from arrows flying up their arses." He snickered, then lowered his gaze to the Gloom. "What do you think of that, Nek?"

"Not only that," Hadamard added, pointing. "Look!"

A flash of silver appeared in mid-air behind a queensman, then disappeared. A rush like adrenalin overcame the luminary. "Perfect." Soon hit callers' voices rang out loud and clear, relaying a symphony of damage.

"RED 21 HIT STRIKER LETHAL," called a hit caller.

"RED 12 HIT STRIKER DAMAGE," called another. Number twelve red wore plate armor.

"RED 19 HIT STRIKER LETHAL," called a third.

"RED 12 HIT STRIKER LETHAL," came the fourth striker call of the battle.

Nekenezitter chirred. "Impressive."

Rangers Tirma and Jull wielded their strikers from opposite sides of the hill at the edge of the tree line, partially concealed. Amot faced the hill straight on from the direction of the original charge. There were two guards assigned to protect each far fencer.

"This might be a quick win," Hadamard said. He glanced at Lord Ralador and chuckled. The man's face was as stern as stone. "He doesn't know what hit'em."

Feleg traced Hadamard's gaze to the March Lord. "The tactic is a variant of the old 'thumb-pinch' maneuver," he explained. "You conceal force elements in the midst of an enemy camp, then attack the perimeter at the same time those elements pop up to fight from the inside. It can be quite effective."

Indeed, it was. The Queen's Guard were losing men quickly on the perimeter, and as many to strikers as to arrows. The strikers were fewer in number, but arrows came from predictable directions easily defended by the tower shields. Strikers could come in from virtually anywhere. On the interior front, ranger and queensman loss exchange ratios were stacking up about equal.

"BLUE 18 HIT STRIKER LETHAL," said a hit caller. "FRATRICIDE."

Hadamard shook his head. "That was unfortunate."

"Still worth it though," Feleg said. "You have to expect some of that."

As queensmen pushed their way farther up the slope, arrows began to fly a bit high.

"BLUE 5 HIT ARROW LETHAL," said a hit caller. "FRATRICIDE."

"Oh shit." Hadamard felt his stomach rolling on the inside. "Not good."

Lord Ralador called out. "ARCHERS, CEASE FIRE. You are hitting unarmored rangers on your own team."

The ranger's borrowed archers stopped firing immediately.

"Objection," Hadamard called to Lord Ralador, despite the impact of recent losses. "Rangers are trained to dodge. Fratricide is a risk for Commander Berendt Garondi to sort out."

The March Lord sneered. "Absolutely not. It is too dangerous. Overruled." He faced the field and called out again, "Carry on, only clear shots at queensmen are permitted."

Feleg grunted. "At least he threw you a bone."

"Ya, but look," Hadamard replied, eyes on the queensmen. The break in rhythm was all the Queen's Guard needed to rally. Hadamard huffed as they mounted a "pinch" attack of their own in retaliation. Fully plated fighters from opposite sides of the hill made a coordinated rush up the slope.

Berendt saw what was happening. With his small group, he charged towards the foray. But by the time they neared the hill, the queensmen had already forced their way to the summit. The defending rangers were divided and surrounded along the hilltop, a good many pressed against the intimidating flag defenders.

"BLUE 7 HIT STRIKER LETHAL," said a hit caller. "FRATRICIDE."

Tirma, with her striker, had attempted to help out her comrades in need, but her projection came too close to one of her own teammates. Berendt and his two fighters fired six shots before drawing their swords. Four hit their marks, but two of those went unnoticed and uncounted. Berendt's two.

"Did you see that?" Feleg said to Hadamard, after hearing callers name only two out of the four hits. Ranger and reg force elements of the crowd erupted in protest as he spoke.

The luminary turned his gaze to the dignitary section and contested again, calling out to Lord Ralador. "RED 18 and RED 3 should be out. Commander Garondi hit them both with crossbow bolts."

"I did not see it," the lord replied, "and I am not going to second guess the hit callers. They are the ones officiating. Not you, and not I."

Feleg turned to Nekenezitter. "Nek?"

"<click> Both hit," responded the Gloom. His sensing abilities were unparalleled.

"BLUE 9 HIT LETHAL," called a hit caller. It was Berendt. RED 18 and RED 3 had successfully counterattacked. The Kith commander was out.

"BLUE 14, BLUE 1, HITS LETHAL."

Out went Berendt's defenders.

Uproar and ruction spread through the crowd. A woman cried out, her voice strained, but her tone was firm and demanding, "Take the two queensmen out and leave the Kith commander and his two men in, Loraith." It was the Knightmaiden of the Aerie. "The queensmen were hit first, plain as day."

Lord Ralador scoffed, then called back, "Stick to recce, Valkyrie." He shook his head and lowered his voice to a conversational tone. "And to think I stood up for you when the Judiciary came calling. I thought you had better sense." Officers and dignitaries around the March Lord snickered to one another—some openly, others discreetly covering their mouths as mocking words passed between them.

Hadamard clenched his jaw. Heat flushed through his body. His legs tensed, restless. He took a step towards Ralador but Feleg grabbed him by the shoulder.

"Let it go," he implored. "We were lucky to have Berendt in at all. With the Overseer a no-show, his duty was to observe as the high-ranking Kith officer in attendance."

Hadamard breathed heavy through his nostrils, scoffed. "This isn't the end," he promised. "I will interrogate those two queensmen when this is over, and under oath to Aelish. They wouldn't dare…" Biting down on his lip, he turned his attention back to the fight.

Without harassing fire from the borrowed archers, the Guard had gained full freedom of movement along the protected summit of the hill. They quickly used it to advantage. Besides easily cutting down rangers, queensman spotters scanned the tree line from their new vantage point. Their prying eyes locked onto the two far fencers in the flanking positions: Jull Dinser and Tirma Burq.

In short order, eight queensmen in chainmail charged out towards the two striker bearers, four per side. Early in the fight, such a maneuver would have left the flag vulnerable. But the queensmen were now ahead in the count and the forces left behind still favored the Queen's Guard, accounting for the double hits needed to down plate armor. The archers' bows twanged as they loosed arrows upon the chargers, without a single hit. A striker felled one queensman before reaching his objective. The remaining forces crossed the field unhindered to confront the far fencers and their defenders.

Jaw hanging, Lord Ralador's eyes riveted on the scene. Looks of excitement shone on the faces of the esteemed guests surrounding him. The battle had taken a turn. It was going the March Lord's way now, and he would be nothing if not boastful about a victory, should it become his. The two skirmishes that pitted small teams of his most promising protégés against far fencers and their protectors proved closer, perhaps, than he'd bargained for.

On the side with the full complement of four fighters, the queensmen quickly overwhelmed the rangers, with only one loss. On the other side, two queensmen were downed before the rangers incurred any losses. It appeared as though one striker bearer—the stronger and more capable Tirma—might prevail. In a one-on-one battle, she fought with advantage until her opponent flicked away her sword and sent it spinning from her hand, through the air and into the long "grasses" of the field. Moments later, the burly queensman had her pressed to the ground, "neutralized" as per the rules of combat.

Ralador's grin could hardly be contained as the two teams hustled back to the hill and joined ranks, strikers in hand. Amot managed to cut one man down along the way, but even that could not dampen the clapping and cheers that erupted among the spectating queensmen and their invited supporters. And as they called out words of encouragement, a smug look grew on Lord Ralador's face. He wore it like a badge of honor.

At the hill, a plate-armored queensman traded his cutting rapier for a nearly identical dancing sword. Protected by the flag defenders, he began to wield it.

"BLUE 17 HIT STRIKER LETHAL," said a hit caller.

"BLUE 2 HIT STRIKER LETHAL," said another.

He's good. That can only be Eriff under that helm, thought Hadamard.

Feleg threw his arms to his sides. He turned to Hadamard.

"They can't do that!" he called out in a huff, loud enough to be heard throughout the entire dome. "They can't just take the strikers!" Up in arms, it was his turn to step towards Ralador, no doubt to give him a piece of his mind. Hadamard barred his way with an outstretched arm.

"Wait," he said. "In our rush to get everything done, we hadn't considered the fact that the strikers could be captured and used against our own forces." The luminary paused to remind himself of all that was said and planned concerning the scenario content. He shook his head. "And nothing in the rules covers commandeering equipment—a definite oversight. Don't waste your breath. Ralador will only argue it's fair game. Let them play it out."

"There's more at stake here than satisfying your curiosity," Feleg retorted. "No enemy of Gan even knows that strikers exist. They'd be untrained. Surely, they wouldn't be able to... pick them up off the ground and use them the way the queensmen are about to."

"Spies are always, ALWAYS among us," Hadamard said. "And we're always training outsiders on our kit. Even if an adversary was blind-sided for one battle, they'd be sure to find out what they had to before the next."

Feleg didn't need the latest innovation in wilder ink on his face to show his utter disgust for the situation. Nevertheless, he turned a blind eye to Ralador's underhandedness and calmly refocused his attention on the disaster unfolding in front of them. "Unless we learn to fight the Jhinyari way," he retorted, rather after-the-fact. "One attack and the enemy is decimated—conflict over. No concept of proportionality."

"Now that's a scary thought," Hadamard said. *Live by the sword...*

Over the few moments the two friends had argued, with relative ease the Queen's Guard had fully retaken the hill. By the end of their advance, its base had become littered with prone bodies. Only six scattered Kith remained to challenge a line double their numbers. Worse still, some opponents in plate armor remained untouched.

Amot stood in full view of the situation, at a safe distance, final striker in hand. He stood alone; his two defenders having joined in the melee. With Berendt down and his second down as well—Tall Hallman—the young ranger was now in command.

He buzzed out a call to his fellow Kith. The rangers at the hill began to execute a controlled withdrawal. But even as they backed away, a coordinated rush by the queensmen broke their ranks, scattered them again. The rangers fought back hard, individually, and the queensmen paid a heavy price for their bold maneuver. But in the end, the Guard prevailed.

The result: Amot and his two protectors—the only two rangers with enough energy to escape the queensmen's rush—stood virtually alone against exactly six opponents. Virtually alone because tower shields fully protected the queensmen from the archer groups, who weren't permitted to fight close quarters.

Feleg turned away from the fight, as though he couldn't bear to watch. He fixed his troubled gaze on Hadamard, silently shook his head. Hadamard knew the feeling.

A member of the Queen's Guard raised his sword hand, called for parley. He bore a rounded shield and wore plate with elaborate etchings. He also carried a captured striker—an elegant weapon, the slim cut-and-thrust blade referred to as the "war rapier."

In response, Amot called off his defenders and his archers. All complied to hear what the heavily armored soldier had to say.

The queensman sauntered forward to within thirty feet of Amot, stopped, and then removed his helm: Eriff Haulik, of course, Ralador's future son-in-law. Blond hair soaked in sweat, the squad leader stabbed his striker into the ground and wiped the wetness from his brow. He called out across the field, to Amot.

"Now what, Kith-boy?" he said. "Are you going to make us chase you around the dome?" Queensmen supporters in the crowd hooted and hollered at the suggestion. "You've lost your commander," he went on, "you've lost your second, and you've lost most of your rangers." He paused to make sideways glances at the two archer groups. "Your archers are useless against our shields. You have a single striker; we have two strikers. Surrender, I say. On your knees and beg for mercy. You have three bushmen up against six of the finest swordsmen you will ever find, and fully armored at that. Admit you've lost, Kith-boy. Yield as you would yield in a real battle lost, to spare the lives of those few lucky ones who remain."

The young Kith ranger stiffened his stance. "If this were a real fight, we'd have won three times over." Even from a distance, Hadamard could see the wilder ink bleeding through Amot's skin, putting his resilience on display—the dark red slashes under his eyes, the dark green and chaotic swirls surrounding his eyes and brow. "Your fighters' armor was overrated, our archers were stifled by unnatural rules, and the hit callers missed critical strikes that everyone else didn't have trouble seeing."

Ranger supporters cheered and woo-hooed in support of the ranger's retort, loudest among them Vil'nyan. Berendt, technically downed, pushed himself to his feet where he'd been felled. The Kith commander brushed off his armor, turned to face Amot. He shook his head slowly.

Amot's dark eyes swiveled his way. "You're dead," he told his commander. "This is my call." He had support from his side of the spectators.

Berendt's eyes narrowed, gauging. He sighed, nodded to Amot, then swung his gaze to Lord Ralador.

Lord Ralador rolled his eyes. "Carry on in desperation, if you feel you must."

Nothing like a crushing defeat to end the striker debate, thought Hadamard. The luminary knew he'd never live this one down.

With nonchalant steps, Eriff retrieved the rapier, then made his way back towards the knoll. He raised a gauntleted backhand to his comrades when they tried to follow. Confused, they stood and watched. When Eriff got to the flag, he grasped the flagpole. Someone among the spectators asked, "What is he doing?"

Leaning his weight casually against the pole, Eriff made an offer to Amot. "How about I make it easier for you, bushwhacker," he said. "Come and get our banner, just me against you. If you defeat me, it's yours. So simple, even a Wilder can understand."

Feleg perked up instantly. He whispered, more to himself than Hadamard or Nekenezitter beside him, "Take it." The grig's eyes watched Amot intently. "Take it," he repeated.

"Stand down," Amot commanded his rangers. His two defenders hesitated. The scout removed his wilder cloak, tossed it to one of them, then raised his voice.

"STAND DOWN!" he repeated. He shooed them off and made the same gestures to the archers. "Go on now," he told them. The borrowed queensmen were quick to abandon the battlefield. They exited together, tossing their bows into a single pile at the forest's edge. After a few words exchanged in low tones, Amot's defenders slowly backed away to join their Kith brethren on the sidelines.

"No hit callers," Amot demanded to Eriff.

"Agreed," Eriff replied. He spun around to face Ralador. "Taps?"

A sinister grin crept across the March Lord's face as he signaled his approval. "I also agree—no hit callers." He then wagged a finger. "But you shall fight until one of you yields. As always, head shots are discouraged."

A collective expression of shock developed on the face of the crowd.

Eriff hesitated, then straightened. "Very well," he replied.

"Whoa," someone remarked, in the midst of outcries.

Hadamard swung his gaze to Amot. Without hesitation, the Wilder nodded his approval to the March Lord's conditions. The contest between rangers and queensmen had developed into a dangerous game, and not one the luminary could protest easily. *The participants are willing. To speak against this fight would insult the Kith Order, and withdrawal or softening the rules of combat would dishonor it.*

Feleg cleared his throat, then spoke in a rasping voice. "Someone's going to get themselves killed." He hesitated. "I know Amot. He'll never yield. And that queensman is not just champion in rank, he really is a champion—a champion swordsman on the fencing circuit."

Nekenezitter's eyes darted nervously to Hadamard, to Feleg, and then to the spectators. The Gloom gasped, tried to speak but swallowed his click.

Feleg asked, "What's gotten into you, Nek?"

He chirred in response, "Wait!" Patting his chest, the Gloom scurried over to Lord Ralador. He stopped in front of the March Lord, drawing the eyes of all in the crowd. "<click> I strongly," he puffed, "<clack> advise against this action <tic-tic>. It is not safe. Not safe at all."

Ralador raised an eyebrow to the Gloom. "Is war safe, Crown Advisor Nekenezitter?"

The Gloom shook his head. "<click> This is completely unnecessary. We have all the data <tic> we need."

"Well, I do not. These men are warriors," Lord Ralador continued. "A true test of strikers in real combat is needed before I can make my final evaluation. What better way than to pit the best ranger against the best queensman?"

Nekenezitter didn't seem to have a quick answer for that. *But he'd opened the door...*

"Nek's right," Hadamard said. He chose his next words carefully. "Eriff's original request for 'taps' would provide enough of a demonstration. We can't predict what will happen in uncontrolled combat conditions."

Ralador's tone was firm in response. "Exactly my point. We can't predict, so we must observe. The yield condition remains. You may leave the guards on the strikers." The March Lord turned his gaze to the battlefield and shouted. "CLEAR THE WAY."

Oh shit, thought Hadamard. The uneasy feeling that he had earlier returned to the pit of his stomach. He regarded Feleg. "This won't end well for someone, will it?"

The grig frowned. "You got that right."

Beaten and bloodied, the fallen fighters gathered their belongings and made their way to the sidelines to watch the final duel. Amot and Eriff positioned themselves fifty feet apart, facing one another. Eriff stood at the base of the hill, in front of the flag he was to defend. He tossed his helm aside as though it were trash. Amot stood half-way to the tree line. His watchful gaze never strayed from his opponent.

Chapter XXXVI

One on One

(Hadamard, Eriff, Amot)

A N UNNATURAL SILENCE filled the dome—an air of seriousness different than before the battle had begun; the tension seemed to build with every heaving sigh of the chamber itself, every rush of air through the shiro beetle tunnels. No voice dared disturb it. No soldier so much as shuffled. This was not, after all, friendly sword-play they were about to witness. The duel unfolding before their eyes was real. It was Queen's Guard versus Kith. It was High Elderkin versus Wild Elderkin. It was Establishment versus Exiled. The prize—dancing swords. Swords of power. Anticipation hung suspended, saturating the air like the brewing of a great storm.

Amot's stance carried a wild look to it as he waited for the horn to sound. A slight snarl curled his lips. Ink flaring, his gaze fierce and focused, the Kith ranger stood slightly crouched, powerful legs ready to spring. *A cornered animal,* Hadamard thought. Wolverine came to mind. The Wilder's tousled hair hung past his shoulders like a dark stallion's mane. The way his entire body lined up behind the two-handed grip on his bastard sword had an odd, awkward-seeming balance to it. The luminary had seen Amot adopt this stance before, during the latter stages of his training session. His hold on the striker had more thrust than cut to it, as though he expected to push a great weight that required every muscle in perfect alignment—a single, direct channeling of force.

The queensman champion, on the other hand, took on a more roguish stance for one of his order. With perfect poise and lines like a dancer, by appearances he belonged in the royal theater, not some gritty, drawn-out battle. Hadamard had become accustomed to the typical middle guard approach taken by the Queen's Guards, a flexible stance with the sword held at a medium height as the name suggests, its point threatening the face and throat of adversaries on the other side of the shield. From middle guard, the sword could be quickly lifted to the high guard position—the second most popular stance of the queensmen. But not Eriff. He, like Amot, had resorted to a low stance, deceptive and countering. He held his rounded shield well forward and leaned that same way, while his rapier pointed backwards, long and low, the angle chosen carefully so as to occlude it from his adversary's view.

Back guard, thought Hadamard. Uncommon, but a naturally strong stance for the sword to thrust from an unseen angle, or cut swiftly under and around.

The horn sounded. Spheres of distorted light sprung into existence around the swordsmen as they invoked farseeing. The light wavered and refracted while shards of imagery swirled about.

The first move was Eriff's: a lightning-fast thrust. The deadly rapier punctured the space between the fighters, bursting forward. It fell short of its mark by about fifteen feet.

The Wilder parried the attack with a swift swipe of his own striker, blocking with the flat of his sword. The two projected blades clashed in mid-air to an electrifying snap. White metal flashed and sparked. Onlookers gasped at the charged display.

A chill ran down Hadamard's spine. *If that'd hit, it would've killed him.*

The bastard sword vanished and reappeared to rap on Eriff's shield. The crowd gasped in amazement, and Hadamard along with them at the sheer accuracy of Amot's counterstrike. *A warning.*

Even Eriff nodded in appreciation. He withdrew his blade and made the rapier whole again. The refracted-light shell around him dampened out of sight.

"Not bad," Eriff shouted across the field. The queensman adjusted his stance. "Or was that just dumb luck, Kith-boy?"

Amot didn't respond. Nor did he let down his guard. His shell blurred the space around him.

Eriff called out again, "Let's find out just how lucky you are." His sphere flashed on as he swiped the blade—a horizontal cut.

Again, the attack fell short, and again, Amot's striker made sparking contact with the rapier, slapping the white metal down in mid-air. He then retracted his blade, this time without a counterstrike.

"I'm over here," Amot called back, taunting. His Kith brothers and sisters chuckled on the sidelines.

Eriff shifted his stance, aligning once again for the same back guard position. When perfectly still, he responded to the slight. "Shall we dance, then?"

And then the real fighting began.

Eriff lashed out, striking at the lower legs with an upwards diagonal cut. His rapier found its range. Amot leapt up and back, barely dodging the blow. Eriff followed through with a diagonal cut from high, missed again, and then began a series of controlled thrusts. The queensman's swift sword was gaining in accuracy. Forced back, the Wilder focused on dodging, but the cuts and the thrusts were getting closer. The air around Amot ignited in bursts of light as he parried one blow he couldn't dodge, struggled to block a second, and weakly tapped a third to divert it—a narrow miss.

"Eriff's damned fast," Feleg said. "He's made about eight attacks before Amot made one."

Grunting with the effort, the ranger retaliated with a wild swing of his own. White metal flashed above Eriff's shield, in front of his face. The queensman stumbled back, behind the flag.

Amot jumped on the opportunity. Bringing his sword around to a high guard posture, he made a downward slice at Eriff. The projected blade smashed the queensman's shield. The force of the two-handed blow sent Eriff stumbling backwards again. He lost his footing on the hill slope. A second smash to the shield knocked him to his back. He landed with a clunk.

The queensman took shelter under his shield as a flurry of blows rained down on him, one pounding strike after the next. He held his rapier crossways in front of his shield to repel the blade. White sparks flared. Onlookers gasped when the protective sheaths of both weapons flew off at once, into pieces. Eriff attempted to regain his footing, but was beaten down. His shield split.

"Hadamard," Feleg said. His tone prompted action.

The grig didn't need to say another word.

We can't start this way.

A splinter off the shield had penetrated Eriff's forehead, devoid of a helm. Blood soaked into his light hair and ran down his face. The queensman scrambled backwards, still clinging to the shards of his battered shield in one hand, rapier in the other. He rolled behind the knoll and beyond Amot's visual.

The luminary rushed towards Ralador, whispers from the crowd rising as he did so: "He needs help"; "Where's the medic?"; "Are they going to stop?" The implications resonated in his mind. *This is to protect our own, not to kill one another. No, we can't start this way.*

When he got to the March Lord, Hadamard looked him in the eye. He kept his voice to a forceful whisper. "Lord Ralador, end this. Your future son-in-law's life is at stake. He needs a medic."

Berendt had followed from his place among his rangers. "I agree," he said. "We'll call it a draw and move on to the next scenario."

The March Lord's gaze shifted between Berendt and Hadamard. Stopping the fight would mean admitting defeat or parity. And to that man, parity was as good as defeat—the defeat of clear superiority. The asshole shook his head.

"By the will of Aelish, Champion Eriff Haulik will prevail. Watch and learn exactly why the queen's guardsmen are the rightful wielders of the dancing swords." He turned his gaze from the pair and fixed it on the fight. And while he was at it, just an inch, he turned his nose up to them as well.

Bloody hell. His vision blurred, Eriff tossed the rapier beside him where he sat, his back leaning against the hill. He de-gauntleted, wiped blood and sweat from his face. It still stung his eyes. He rubbed again, but couldn't keep the fluids out. The Wilder called to him.

"Yield, Eriff," he demanded. "You've lost."

The bastard sword ripped through the space between them, flashed above Eriff's head. He froze.

"I know where you are, queensman." The sword danced in a tight circle above him, angling this way and that way. Anticipating a plunging strike, Eriff scrambled out of its way. Heart pounding in his chest, he grasped his rapier and brandished it defensively.

To prove his claim, Amot stabbed the striker's tip into the earth, inches from Eriff's leg. "Did that scare you? It should have."

He's mad.

I need to buy time.

"Just take the flag," Eriff called. "Those are the rules. Capture the flag and you win. You don't have to kill me for it."

The blade jerked from the ground and vanished.

Eriff sighed. He rested his rapier on the hill slope and clamped both hands to his forehead, pressing the gaping wound there. Summoning his talent as a radiance channeler, he began a soft chant to Aelish the Resplendent—the dying leviathan whose good graces he'd been in his entire life. *Please help. I hope you have the strength.*

Amot approached the hill with cautious steps.

"Enough, Amot," Berendt called to him, from the sidelines.

"You're still dead," Amot retorted. Apart from one gnarly old Stout with a beef against everything, there were no snickers from his comrades this time.

Was that an order? Amot wondered, then decided *'No.'* It'd come off more like a suggestion. He glanced the way of his commander. Berendt stood with Lord Ralador and Lumen Hadamard. But it was the March Lord's hawkish gaze that locked with Amot's eyes. The March Lord shook his head.

He's the one calling the shots, Amot thought. Undeterred, the Wilder continued. He quickly scanned the crowd as he strode, gauging. Looks of concern traced to the other side of the knoll—*Dead Gnarl's Knoll near Turnsby*, at least that's what the hill reminded him of. *That queensman must be injured,* he surmised. He'd seen the broken shield in his imagery.

A second interpretation popped into his mind. *Shroud's Well, what if he's on the move, about to strike?* He halted, took on a middle posture with his sword raised forward, and invoked the farseeing shell.

White metal flashed in and out of the thin air as he projected his striker in a search pattern. Fractured imagery of the other side of the hill sprung up around him. He quickly spotted the blurred, colorless outline of Eriff. He'd barely moved. Nonetheless, Amot rotated his wrist slightly—at this range, the resistance to his motions was almost nothing. Manipulating his grip and the hilt's annulets, he danced the blade above Eriff's body once more.

"You can yield any time," Amot called to him. The threat was an empty one—as long as Eriff stayed where he was, the ranger didn't intend to attack. Nor did he believe Eriff would ever yield without a blade to his throat—a feat he doubted he had the control to exercise at this distance, not yet. With minimal concentration, Amot kept the striker hovering above his opponent as he proceeded towards his objective. But something felt wrong, a knot in his stomach that wouldn't go away. Eriff's offer of the flag didn't quite add up in the ranger's mind. It seemed more like a bluff or a lure, to catch Amot with his guard down. Unexpectedly, he heard a familiar voice call to him.

Uncle Feleg?

"Amot," his father's old friend begged. "Stand down."

Does he have a bad feeling too?

"Don't listen to him," Lord Ralador snapped. "Carry on to the bitter end."

Steps away from the flag, the Wilder slowed his pace, struggling to understand. He'd always trusted his uncle. *Why would he say that to me?* The swirling imagery around him dizzied his mind. Amot felt queasy, a heaviness settled in his stomach.

Out of nowhere, a thousand whispers assailed the Kith ranger's ears.

The image of a pine forest flashed in his mind. Then fire. A burning tree filled his vision. It burned around him and it burned in his mind. It burned a fiery red, until darkness washed over him, black as coal.

Did Feleg get through to him? Hadamard wondered.

After a few stumbling steps, Amot staggered to a halt. He lowered his eyes to the ground. Something had changed in the volume of space around him. His sphere darkened into swirling chaos.

When he raised his eyes again, they had a far-off look to them. With a two-handed grip, Amot raised the hilt of the sword above his head. He raised it high with the point aimed downwards, as though to slam it into the earth. The refracting sphere around him wavered. In a flash, the blade tore out the space directly above Eriff.

Coup de grâce?

The next moment, Amot prepared to thrust down hard.

But the queensman had recognized that something was different, that the threat had changed. He'd sprung to his feet, rapier in hand. A sphere of white light activated around him, pulsing.

"The glow of Aelish," someone said.

Eriff had planted his feet firmly, one in front of the other. He'd shifted to a hanging guard position, forearms high with the hilt and the blade angled slightly down. His intense gaze focused on the hovering bastard sword.

The projected blade needled towards him. Eriff flicked his rapier to intercept. The two strikers clashed. Sparks flew and snapped in a dazzling display of pyrotechnics. The air buzzed with electricity. Both fighters flew back, whipped to the ground. Amot's bastard sword flung from his hands, spun twice around, and then blipped out of existence with a loud pop.

Onlookers gasped. Murmurs rose up and surprised looks raced between them.

"What happened?" Nekenezitter asked.

Feleg hurried towards Amot, lying on the ground near the flag, while two Royal Quarter officers jogged behind the hill to Eriff.

Lord Ralador shot Hadamard a scornful look. But the luminary's eyes were busy elsewhere, darting across the field, searching. He scanned the hill, the tree line; the missing striker was nowhere to be seen.

Queensmen grabbed Eriff under the arms and hauled him to his feet. Blood-smear was everywhere. His rapier jutted out of the ground beside him.

Before Amot's Kith brothers could reach him, the Wilder shook off the rattling and scrambled to his feet. He tilted his head upwards, eyes wandering over the grey ceiling of the dome. He spoke something, almost in a daze, his voice barely louder than a whisper.

Was that a name? Hadamard wondered. He strained his ears as the ranger repeated the single word a second time.

"Elise."

Chapter XXXVII
Old acquaintances
(Anexxander)

"WAKE UP," A croaky voice said, vaguely familiar and from long ago. A strong-fingered grip shook the Wilder druid's shoulders as he lay on the forest floor. The air smelled like morning air. His head hurt. Anexxander blinked his eyes twice to get rid of the blur. He rubbed them, then blinked again at who he saw leaning over him.

"Wyatt?" The bogger's hair had thinned and his head had shriveled, but the bright green eyes were the same. Anexxander's gaze wandered over the bogger's attire. *Ranging leathers?* "I thought you were out, decades ago."

"I am out," Wyatt said, annoyed at the asking. "I'm looking for a redhead in the company of a half-giant, and perhaps a haggard woman from the Scarsands. I tracked them to this area. Have you seen them?"

Anexxander ran his fingers over the bump on his forehead. It was a whopper. His chest felt heavy when he breathed. "Redhead?" A long moment passed before he was clear-headed. "Yes, I've seen them. I rescued them from slavers." He sat up and waved in the general direction of the glassy statue in their midst. "Meet Gutless Kori; he was one of them. There were two other slavers: a stoutish Taint and a Nali, or part Nali—the nearly human kind. The half-giant must've knocked me out—the damned Vice-regent of Abandon, no less." The Wilder druid glanced about him. "I guess... I guess they've run off."

The old bogger lowered his gaze to the ground and shook his head, wincing. "I should'a never left. I should'a stayed in Fort Abandon and waited for her. Never, never, never..."

"What are you talking about?"

Wyatt grimaced, drew a deep breath, and raised his watery eyes to face Anexxander. He gripped the druid's forearm, firm. Desperation filled his croaky voice. "I need your help, old friend." The bogger slowly nodded, eyes pleading. "Yep. Help is what I need."

CHAPTER XXXVIII

PROJECTION

(Hadamard, Galewind, Eriff, Amot)

HADAMARD WATCHED AS yet another volunteer recovery team rushed out of the Netherdome. The luminary let out a heavy sigh, his own legs weary from the search. *They won't find anything,* he thought. Little else but solid rock and sheer cliffs lay beyond the dome's walls, and Amot's dancing sword would be long gone if it'd projected farther, into the open space of Kaeda's Temper. *Irrecoverable.*

A second team, composed mainly of Stouts, made preparations to enter the larger shiro beetle tunnels. *Slim odds there too,* he had to admit, despite the fact expert miners stood among them. An insect-like chirr interrupted his thoughts.

"<tic> The meeting," Nekenezitter buzzed, as the pair trudged on towards the control room. "We're late."

Hadamard glanced down at the Gloom hobbling along beside him. "They won't start without me, Nek. Ralador will want someone to point his finger at and Amot's ducked out of sight for now. Feleg snuck him into my study so that the Kith commander could give him some coaching before the March Lord puts the screws to him."

Nekenezitter responded with one of his quizzical, mantis-like tiltings of the head.

Hadamard hesitated, out of instinct. *Do I tell him more?* It had become clear during the exercise that the crown advisor wasn't really a snitch after all. The luminary sighed, giving in despite himself. "At this point, no one really knows what happened. Lord Ralador will use that ambiguity to do everything in his power to pin the blame on Amot and rangers in general, in order to serve his greater purpose to arm the Queen's Guard with the strikers."

"<click> Why is it that the Kith <clack> and the Queen's Guard cannot share <chirr>?"

Naïve little creature. "Nek, you know very well there simply wouldn't be enough strikers to fulfill both rolls—ask Smat and he'll go over the scenario numbers with you on what's needed."

The Gloom let out a low buzz at the remark. Hadamard hadn't heard it before, but it sounded like he'd taken offence. "I know the numbers <tic>," Nekenezitter retorted.

Hadamard decided not to elaborate on all the problems with producing strikers in great numbers: that only a handful of elemental stones with the right properties had been found, the rarity of the white metal and the difficulty working it, not to mention the intricate practices needed to integrate the two. Currently, the Tower had access to one person for each of the necessary steps and no one person could perform all of the steps. The luminary crafted a carefully-worded response.

"As you know, every blade is precious and virtually irreplaceable. Every skilled person in the production chain is precious as well, and also irreplaceable. I floated the idea of having a ranger detachment embedded within the Queen's Guard. That way, the dancing swords would be in the right hands and the capability would be available to the Guard as well, when they needed it. At least until we build up numbers. That's as close to sharing as the negotiations came. Well, Lord Ralador would hear none of it. He wants them all to himself. Period."

Nekenezitter nodded. "Yes <tic>, I can see that." He trilled to punctuate his sentence.

"The arguing will only get worse," Hadamard added. "I'm sure you took note of the Order Valkyrie knightmaiden present during the exercise—no doubt the Aerie has designs on the swords or perhaps a variant, such as a striker spear." Hadamard refrained from mentioning yet another option on his mind—one he wasn't comfortable with in the least. It was the option that had driven the creation of the dagger prototype, which he'd personally opposed, and the option that scared him the most: that neither the queensmen, the valkyries, nor the rangers would be the recipients. Rather, the Blue Tower's 4th Division, known as "The Silencer," would be reactivated to receive them. In essence, the Blue 4th was an assassin's guild, currently dormant until needed to counter any emerging existential threat to Gan, or one of its close allies.

The dome itself seemed to sigh at Hadamard's ruminations, and the nether winds gusted through the dome's opening to the outside as the luminary and the crown advisor passed by. Ahead of them, the COM Center's double doors had been swung wide open. Two strapping queensmen in short-sleeved scale shirts—dull gold and black—stood guard in the doorway. Their protective gear gleamed with martial regalia and the gemmed crown sigil of their proud order.

A few steps from the guards, an untidy assortment of scruffy rangers loitered about, boisterous and coarse, trading exaggerated but entertaining tales of passionate encounters while on the road and in the wild. The Gloom drew curious glances as he and Hadamard navigated their way through the group.

The guards stood facing one another on opposite sides of the doorway, arms crossed as though in defiance. Hadamard peered past them into the Red Room. Light from the wall sconces flooded the space with a devilish glow. Apart from the area dedicated to the projectionists and their assembler stations, the place was crammed and stuffy. It buzzed with the chatter of twenty conversations all happening at once. *Half the officers from all four commands must be standing around in there.*

"Have they started yet?" Hadamard asked the door guards. "The meeting," he added, as if the context wasn't obvious.

The guard on the left responded. "No, Lumen." His eyes darted to the rangers and then back. "If that were the case, I'd have the pleasure of insisting these *vagrants* shut their traps."

"What was that?" retorted a Stout, standing wide and squat among them, stuffed into his hide armor and gnawing on his unlit pipe. He scowled. "Start by shutting yer own trap!"

The guard ignored him, and continued to address Hadamard. "Lord Ralador has exited the dome and will be returning shortly." With a sudden sallow look, the queensman gestured at Hadamard to enter. Accepting with a nod, the luminary allowed himself to be escorted inside.

"Apologies," the guard said, as he walked them in.

"For what?" Hadamard said.

The guard flicked his head back to the rangers outside the door. "Them."

Hadamard responded, "They might seem a little rough around the edges, but those rangers are as good as gold."

The guard didn't look convinced.

"Absolutely," Hadamard emphasized. "We're lucky to have every tick-bitten one of them. You really should try to meet as many as you can while they're all here. This is a great opportunity. They know everything that happens in their territories, like the backs of their weather-beaten hands." Hadamard passed the guard a quick wink. "The eyes and ears of Gan, without a doubt."

Half-way in, the guard halted. "Yes, Lumen, of course," was his polite reply. Then he sucked air into his lungs, ready to bellow out an introduction.

Hadamard raised a staying hand. "No need for that," he told the guard. "I'd rather quietly mingle first."

The queensman puffed the air out. "As you wish, Lumen." He nodded courteously before heading back towards the doors.

A grin had formed on Nekenezitter's face in the meantime. He looked up to Hadamard and chirred. "You never know. Maybe <tic> rangers and queensmen will learn to get along... someday <chirr>." The Gloom shrugged as though the effort might be hopeless, then let out a flurry of clicks to doubly scan the chamber.

Hadamard spotted Crusher straightaway, propped up on his crutches and manning the central station behind the main assembler. He'd tied his white hair back into a low ponytail, and his eyes were scrunched shut. Despite the calamity around him, Seventh Kaeda's premier projectionist appeared focused, in deep concentration.

On the station to his left stood Crusher's twin sister, Anya. The resemblance between the two was undeniable. When the sibling projectionists actually worked together instead of arguing, they could perform nothing short of miracles. Hadamard could see by the beyond-gaunt look on their faces that they'd stretched their talents thin again. *Nearly spent, the both of them,* he noted. *What exactly have they been doing?* He shifted his gaze to the scene forming within the main assembler. It was complex.

The setup was much larger than the Mini, illuminated from above by boxed lanterns. Unlike the Mini, the main assembler lacked the containment of the transparent glace shell. That, apparently, was for amateurs. The contraption consisted of a long and narrow slab table, about waist height, that sectioned off the control room. Fashioned of the same native rock as the building, it had been hollowed out to form a shallow trench. Seven piles of shiny dust were held within, each one a slightly different hue. In the space above them, flecked and sparkling and constantly in motion, streams of the light particles jittered about on currents of air. Formless shapes, wispy and rising as high as the box lanterns, briefly coalesced into larger, grainy masses before coming undone again.

Behind the table were half a dozen individual stations, each with its own smaller table where projectionists could shape reality for their individual pieces of the larger model that brought them all together.

Hadamard surveyed the four empty stations. "The twins could use some help," he said to Nekenezitter, while his gaze wandered over the room in search of the remaining projectionists. "Have you seen any of the others?"

The Gloom didn't answer.

"Nek?" Hadamard looked down but the Gloom wasn't there. His eyes darted about. The crown advisor had disappeared into the crowd.

Just then, from a nearly hidden position near the Mini, the luminary's good friend Feleg clapped loudly. The grig cleared his throat, then raised his raspy voice above the crowd's murmur.

"May I have everyone's attention," he called out. As the room quieted, the ex-Kith sauntered in front of the long slab table. Behind him, the sands continued their wispy dance. A shape resembling the knoll in the scenario formed briefly, then broke apart.

Feleg winked to Hadamard before he started. "As you all know by now," he began, "we've experienced some difficulties since the onset of this exercise. They started small: difficulties training, difficulties due to the small numbers of strikers available, difficulties due to rushed timelines and lack of equipment. All of these problems were resolved. But they didn't end there. New problems arose regarding the combat rules and the scenario mechanics. Those, too, were resolved. Unfortunately, one problem persisted. One problem did not get resolved. Occasionally, one of the dancing swords went missing... temporarily. But shortly after, the weapon was always found not far from where it was lost. Always, that is, until now."

Hadamard edged closer to the front, while officers in the crowd exchanged opinions on the matter. Feleg raised his hands to hush them.

"Just to update you," said the grig, "the missing dancing sword has not been found. The search is ongoing and we remain hopeful. The weapon is a bastard sword—a hand-and-a-half sword about four feet long, designed for thrusting and slashing. It has a sophisticated grip and hilt that allows for precision maneuvering. This weapon is a well-balanced, well-forged piece of kit and the metal is virtually unsurpassed. Make no mistake, this striker is a dangerous weapon in the hands of anyone capable of wielding it."

A hush propagated through the crowd, followed by murmurs. Feleg's gaze surveyed the crowd, then rested on the luminary.

"Lumen Hadamard, do you have anything to add?"

Hadamard cleared his throat. "Yes, I do," he responded. "Two teams are still searching—one outside the dome and a second ready to crawl through any shiro beetle tunnels big enough for a Stout miner to fit into. So far, no luck." He hesitated. "Unfortunately, Feleg, I don't share your optimism. I have no reason to expect that either team will turn up the sword."

A queensman officer spoke up. "How do we know the sword hasn't wedged itself into solid rock?"

Hadamard answered. "In all of our tests, projected blades consistently appeared in the less dense medium available. For instance, when projected near the surface of a body of water a striker will come up above it, unless you put a lot of force behind the push."

"What kind of 'push' did that ranger put behind the sword?" asked another queensman. "He was raving mad. He could've killed our commander." The sentiment was seconded. "Bring that ranger before us. He must answer for what he did." Another spoke out. "Order Kith must answer. Was this the plan all along?"

The Queen's Guard officers lent support with more incriminating outcries. Rangers in the crowd were roused to defend Amot and to defend the Kith. They pointed fingers and shouted queensmen down, citing stacked forces and biased officiating. Flared tongues turned to pushes, pushes turned to shoves.

Hadamard forced his way through the crowd to Feleg. "We're going to have a brawl—" Hadamard was bumped by a ranger. He shoved the Wilder back into the foray and started again. "We're going to have a brawl on our hands."

"Let them brawl," was Feleg's response. "There's no way I'm subjecting Amot to any of this." Then he sighed at Hadamard's stare, turned to face the commotion and slapped his palms together in one loud clap. "Calm down! Hey, hey, hey." Feleg might as well have said "get a good punch in while you can" for all the good it did. The ex-Kith put a hand to his mouth, coughed into it.

Hadamard glanced at the twins, surprised to find they were still carrying on, unhindered. *That can't be easy.* He shifted his gaze back to the crowd, shouted over them. "THAT'S ENOUGH."

A few heads turned just before the room erupted into total mayhem.

The knightmaiden backed away from the ruckus, towards the rock wall of the Red Room. The luminary's request had gone unnoticed, and not for lack of loudness. A burly Stout ranger and athletic queensman came stumbling towards her, grunting and locked in a battle of grips. Galewind stepped aside as the pair toppled to the floor. She rolled her eyes at them, huffed when she got bumped by a flailing limb.

"Schoolyard bullies," she scolded. The whole lot of them were acting that way. Galewind shut her notebook. She'd been going over her entries, but that would have to wait.

The wrestling match continued at her feet, each combatant attempting to gain the upper position. The Stout was winning.

Where the hell is Berendt? Galewind checked the doors. *He'd put a stop to this nonsense in an instant.*

Just then came an announcement from one of the guards at the entrance. His words, though, were lost in the clamor. The knight-maiden turned her gaze to the double doors as four hooded Djinxarai strode in, nether-grey robes flowing behind them. They halted once inside, gleaming eyes surveying the turmoil. Although gaunt and under-nourished by all appearances, their cadaverous forms in no way detracted from the power of their presence. Rather, it seemed more the foundation of their lean strength and iron wills.

The Jhin Masters, thought Galewind. At the palace, Jhin Masters handled all correspondences with Gan's Royal Quarter, and they were the closest thing the Djinxarai had to a warrior cast. Most resided at the monastery-like complex in the thick of the Tangles.

The Jhin Masters pushed forward into the chamber to make room for Lord Ralador, who entered next, accompanied by Champion Haulik. Following the officers, more Djinxarai. The March Lord's stern visage quickly turned to anger. He directed his gaze to Feleg.

"Is this how you conduct a meeting?" he barked.

Feleg responded with a defeatist's shake of his head and wave of his hands.

And as heads turned to the back of the room, queensmen shut their mouths and braced themselves, not daring to lift a finger even while rangers continued to shove, tug, and badger them. A heartbeat later, the rangers, seeing little game in browbeating docile opponents, dampened their aggressions.

As the scuffling died off, a petite waif of a Jhin Master approached Loraith. She addressed him in the Djinxarai tongue. Eriff leaned towards his soon-to-be father-in-law. In a low voice, he appeared to translate the message. When finished, the March Lord prompted him with a short nod. The queensman abruptly stepped forward of the dignitaries. Standing firm, he raised his voice, addressing the room.

"Clear the area," Eriff bellowed. "Children of Jhin, Grey and Kith Quarter representatives, and essential command elements only."

Galewind assumed she fell into the latter category. Voicing muffled complaints, the bulk of the crowd began their exit. The knightmaiden re-opened her notebook to an empty page. *This is important,* she told herself. She would record everything about the coming meeting for Lady Apsarla, and, upon returning to Gan, pay a visit to the Aerie at the earliest opportunity. For starters, Galewind added Eriff's language skills to his profile, then entered what she'd been working on before being so rudely interrupted—her overall impressions of the new weaponry:

> *Dancing sword / striker weapon - potentially powerful asset for Order Valkyrie. Try to secure one. Can be game changer for precision strikes, devastating if in the wrong hands (may have been better left undiscovered). Limited numbers: requires "slider charm" - rare variant of the usual fire amber. Elements of unpredictability require careful consideration.*

❧

Extraordinary, thought Hadamard. *I never would've guessed.* While the Red Room emptied of nonessential personnel, three of the four Jhin Masters exchanged hushed words with Lord Ralador and Eriff. But it was the fourth, when he removed his hood, that drew Hadamard's attention—the luminary knew him.

Following behind the Jhin Masters were two Djinxarai involved in Hadamard's scenarios, together with a third they'd been training. And as the newly arrived projectionists wove through the departing lower ranks and took to their assembler stations, the fourth Jhin Master joined them. His abridged name was "Bender," known to Hadamard simply as a talented and tireless specialist at mimic actions, who never said much. The projectionists readied themselves for Jhin thaumaturgy with the main assembler, but paused before raising sands of their own to mix with Crusher's and Anya's.

Feleg lingered about the slab table, ready and waiting to resume his role as facilitator. Meanwhile, a handful of Kith and Royal Quarter officers had crowded around the main display with him, entranced by the rhythmic flows of the Taerix twins' mental machinations. Waiting, it seemed, for something profound to reveal itself. One poked the dust with his finger, as though to confirm it was real.

At last, Commander Garondi emerged from the study to join the gathering, while officers parted way for the March Lord as he sauntered through the crowd. Ralador planted himself directly in front of the contraption's silvery display, head swiveling to track the bulk motions within.

As they all watched on, the fine particles began to merge. Lord Ralador's eyes narrowed and his lips curled. "What is this mess?" he asked, furrowing his brow as he stared. "It is beginning to look like... like... something."

Feleg answered. "This 'mess' will soon render a depiction of the scenario terrain."

Hadamard observed as the Djinxarai newcomers raised their mental imagery to the main assembler and joined sands with the twins. A pause ensued as the formations began to take on wispy shapes. During that pause, Hadamard heard the guttural, otherworldly tongue spoken behind him by a female Jhin Master. Based on Hadamard's limited understanding of the language, Eriff, in turn, seemed to follow with a Djinxarai translation of Feleg's recent comment.

Focusing back on the display and straining his eyes, even Hadamard had trouble interpreting exactly what he was looking at. He'd observed reconstructions displayed on the assembler many times before—clumpy, unclear, and always in motion. He addressed Ralador.

"Give our Djinxarai friends another minute to bring up the full projection."

Eriff relayed the message to the Jhin Masters again, in Djinxarai.

"Translate everything for them," Ralador told his subordinate. Eriff nodded.

The luminary casually strolled behind the display and approached the twins. By all appearances, Crusher and Anya had become fully immersed in the trance-like state characteristic of the practice of Jhin thaumaturgy. Hands actively shaping, some motions were forceful, swift and cutting, while others manipulated thin air as though molding clay, or fitting together the unseen sections of some three-dimensional puzzle.

Hadamard placed a gentle hand on each of their shoulders to indicate his presence, then whispered softly, "Crusher, Anya… we're ready whenever you are." The twins responded with subtle nods. The luminary didn't concern himself with the other projectionists—he knew they'd follow suit. So, he made his way back to the officers on the other side of the assembler table.

Under the red light of the chamber's box lanterns, the swirling dust before the observers came together in isolated regions, and began to take on solid forms. On the near end to Hadamard, a fuzzy depiction of a grassy hill emerged, suspended in midair. The hill drifted along the length of the viewing space to the opposite side, slowly rotating and stretching in and out, gathering detail as it went. Finally, a dull shine like metal came over the shape before it migrated back to the middle of the assembler. The replica had set.

That moment, the sand boundaries sharpened. A clear representation of the hill that the rangers and queensmen had been fighting over materialized.

"I see it now," Ralador said, clenching his hard, boney jaw as he gazed at the dune-like structure before him. In side profile, the bridge of the March Lord's nose shot nearly straight out before it plunged sharply downwards, prominent like the beak of some bird of prey.

As the silvery replica slowly rotated, bursts of colored sand suddenly appeared in the space above it.

Ralador's jaw dropped slightly. "Flashes—red and blue," he muttered, almost to himself. He swung his gaze to Hadamard. "What do they mean?"

Hadamard didn't have an answer. He looked to the grig, who only shrugged.

The bursts repeated themselves. After each one, the colored sands dispersed and became lost in the circulating volume, only to recombine into dense packets in the same positions later on, to burst out again, one timed slightly after the other. Feleg spoke up.

"Maybe that's a question for the projectionists."

"Then ask them," Ralador demanded.

"Not yet," Hadamard interjected. "They need their space to stay focused. Let them do what they need to do." Whatever the twins were up to, the luminary could see by the intense looks of concentration on their faces that they had not yet finished. And he knew from experience how fragile their shared state of consciousness could be.

When the flashing pattern showed itself again, Galewind raised her left hand to the base of her throat. "That's what I saw," she said. Straining to raise her voice above the din of the enclosed space, she called out to Hadamard and Feleg: "The swords."

Her words went unnoticed. Feleg's and Hadamard's furrowed brows and scrutinizing gazes remained fixed on the sands, as though to make certain they wouldn't miss anything.

Galewind didn't know if it was her flight experience that allowed her to process the image of the spinning hill better than the others, or whether she'd just had a better view of the last few seconds of the fight between Amot and Eriff than everyone else. Either way, it seemed obvious to her that the colored flashes in the Djinxarai projection corresponded to the flashes of light she saw when the two strikers clashed, and then again when Amot's spinning sword had disappeared.

"The swords," she repeated.

Berendt homed in on Galewind's faint cries. He spoke for her, voice cutting through the room. "Listen up," he gruffed. "The knightmaiden has something to say."

All eyes turned from the sands to Galewind.

Feleg said, "Sorry?"

The grig's tired eyes met Galewind's. She'd known Feleg when he was younger and still a ranger; a sharp contrast to the slouched figure standing before her. The dim illumination didn't do him any justice either, serving only to amplify his sagging skin and the shading over every wrinkle.

Galewind traced horizontal circles for him in the air with her finger. "When… when the hill spins around to just the proper angle, I can see a replay of exactly what I saw moments before Amot's dancing sword went missing."

Lord Ralador honed his hawkish gaze on Eriff. "Is that true, Champion Haulik?"

Eriff narrowed his eyes, gauging as he waited for the cycle to repeat itself. When it did, he winced. "Truly a mess. I can hardly see a bloody thing."

The queensman couldn't quite place where he'd been when his shield shattered, or exactly in which direction the bastard sword had been flung following his successful disarm maneuver. *It all happened so fast,* he thought, *and these aren't necessarily the sorts of details one stows away during a battle.* What he did remember was the surge of adrenalin that'd coursed through his body as he fought back against the Kith's aggressive blade, the frustration and anger of having the white metal coming at him relentlessly, out of nowhere, again and again, and the humiliating notion that flashed in his mind for an instant—that he might have to yield after all. Eriff also remembered the feeling of relief that washed over him when the fight was finally over, when he was victorious. But not glory. Only exhaustion, while pondering whether or not he could have lasted another ten seconds. After a long moment of silence, Eriff grimaced, shook his head.

"Mmm… The first flash might be the correct position of Amot's desperate strike relative to the scenario hill, but I cannot speak for the second flash, if it even is a flash."

"It's a flash," the knightmaiden stated, bluntly.

Lord Ralador scowled the way he always did when referring to members of the other Quarters that he considered incompetent. "Only the Kith scout can answer to the second flash. He's the one who lost control of his weapon and let it fling off the face of… whatever you call this place."

Eriff grasped his sword belt. "Yes, I held on to *my* priceless sword." He regarded the one-eyed Kith commander. "Where in bloody hell is your scout?"

Before Commander Garondi could answer, Eriff turned to the Jhin Masters to translate the exchange for them. Out of the corner of his eye, he noted Garondi clenching his jaw and grinding. Eriff was sure the lead ranger didn't trust the account the Jhin Masters were hearing. The queensman paused, glanced Garondi's way. *And rightly so,* he thought, with a smirk. *You want to give your version of events, Kith? —then go ahead, learn to speak Djinxarai and all the power to you.* Eriff turned his gaze back to the masters and continued with his jaded translation.

They'll never find the striker, thought Amot, massaging his temples where he sat, eyes to his boots. Muffled voices filtered in from the Red Room. He took a deep breath, tilted his head up and let his eyes fixate on something… anything. It didn't matter what. Lumen Hadamard's lab was the most comfortable place he'd found on Seventh Kaeda, apart from the Gardens of Light. It was a familiar sort of mess: the old furnishings, the odds and ends, the sorts of things you never see out in the open… it reminded him of the attic in his grandfather's cabin, above the workshop. *Always a good place to hide or get away from people,* he thought. And somehow, the clutter helped him think straight.

How did this happen?

Amot recalled the sense of displacement, the aggression, the surge of energy that overtook him. After that…

Did I lose control? His commander had warned him about control and presence of mind in combat; warned him many times. *I just can't seem to… something just happens to me.* Amot began to wonder if his memory of the events was even complete. An empty feeling settled in the pit of his stomach. *This won't play out well with my probation,* he thought. No one had said anything of the sort yet, but the Overseer's patience had to be wearing thin. *And if he catches wind of another problem…*

Amot could count on his uncle at least—his father's good friend— to stick up for him. *Will that be enough?* He didn't know the answer.

After the scout's father went missing, never to return, the grig had spent countless hours of his own time coaching Amot in the ways of the Kith. Not that Amot's own commander, Berendt Garondi, hadn't put in his share of effort as well. But as mentors the two had very different ways about them. Feleg was pure Wilder while Berendt was a fort man through and through, one of the few rangers without an ounce of Wilder blood in him. As a Kith commander, he stuck to the rules. Not necessarily in a military sense—his rules applied out in the wild. Feleg, on the other hand, came off as laid back, easy going and practical, as long as you were on his good side. He seemed satisfied with a solid effort that didn't end in disaster, chalking up mistakes—even big ones—to life's lessons learned.

What's the lesson this time? I've lost a dancing sword—the finest weapon ever fashioned. In the wrong hands it could slay the Queen of Gan, or anyone, for that matter.

The door to the lab swung open. In walked his commander. Berendt eyed Amot solemnly. "It's time," he said, quickly shutting the door behind him. "The officers have a few questions for you. Remain calm and don't answer anything you're not sure of."

Amot pushed himself to his feet from the low table he'd been sitting on, faced his commander squarely. "What did I do wrong? Should I have obeyed your order to stand down?"

Berendt sighed. "No," he said, staring back with a troubled gaze.

Amot detected a hint of regret in his voice.

"I was wrong to tell you that," Berendt continued. "You did everything right, Amot. Don't let them tell you otherwise. A bit reckless maybe—I've come to expect that from you. But you proved a fierce opponent and that's exactly what the situation set you up to be. You brought pride to the Brotherhood, no matter how this pans out. Great pride."

Hadamard heard the door to his lab open. He watched as Berendt stepped out, and then Amot. Straightaway, the Kith commander marched his subordinate to the main assembler. The two faced the crowd. For a long moment, an uneasy silence filled the control room.

And then came the whispers and murmurs among the officers. With cutting loudness, Berendt cleared his throat. He gruffed out an introduction of Amot to all those present.

In short order, Ralador, Feleg and Eriff proceeded to grill the scout about the striker incident. And after Amot finished explaining that he knew nothing of the colored flashpoints on the assembler display, and after forthrightly describing what he'd felt before the incident occurred, and after indicating the hill reminded him of a place he'd been to before, one of the Jhin Masters spoke. Eriff translated her words.

"What we are about to show you cannot leave this room. It is sensitive, Djinxarai…" Eriff's voice trailed off, eyes narrowed as he struggled to decipher a term. "Umm… magic?"

Nekenezitter cut in, "Thaumaturgy."

"Ah, yes," Eriff said, "thank you." The queensman continued. "Does everyone accept the responsibility of guarding what you are about to witness at all costs? If not, you must exit the building."

Hadamard scanned the faces of those present from Theia. Each one of his own, he trusted. And he trusted the rangers at his side: Berendt, Hallman, Amot—they could keep a secret. The queensmen, well, the luminary didn't know for sure, but they nodded compliance just the same. The knightmaiden—surely. In the end, all in attendance responded in the affirmative.

Hadamard regarded the Jhin Masters. "We accept," he said. They nodded their understanding. A second Jhin Master spoke.

Eriff's voice followed. "He just issued a command to his projectionists: 'Run the trace.'"

Before he'd even relayed the Djinxarai's words, the late-coming projectionists heightened their actions at their stations, manipulating thin air with their hands. The main assembler's display volume changed dramatically.

Blue particles rose and swirled to form a spinning column of sand. At the next series of colored bursts above the scenario hill, a narrow stream connected the column to the blue flash. Like a blue dust devil, the column whirled faster and spread out, whipping up the other colors into the mix. New vortices formed. The hill that had been visible became shrouded in the churning chaos, like a miniature version of Kaeda's Temper.

Lord Ralador scowled again. "Another mess," he grumbled.

As though to contradict, the circular motions ceased at once. The particles slowly lost their momentum and drifted downward, leaving behind solid forms. And the view changed, reminiscent of the lensing effect from farseeing with strikers. A hill again appeared in that fractured view, but not quite the same hill. The tilted display showed the hill to be situated in a wide field. Farther out, a wispy tree line—real looking trees whose tops swayed in the wind. The grounds resembled the scenario terrain, but the dimensional scales were all off.

Hadamard glanced to Anya, then looked to Amot. "The map Smat gave her…"

"I don't need a map," the scout replied. "That's Dead Gnarl's Knoll, which is what I saw… for real… right before everything went black."

Gesturing to the assembler stations, the Kith commander barked an order, "Hallman. Get back there and find that map. And don't disturb the projectionists."

"Yes, Sir," Hallman said. Without delay, the tall ranger hastened to the stations area and began his search.

Hadamard called after the kithblade, "Look for a drawer stuffed full of old parchment."

Feleg turned to address Lord Ralador. "That 'mess' depicts a location near Turnsby."

CHAPTER XXXIX

FELLOWSHIP

(Hadamard, Berendt, Amot)

THE SIX DJINXARAI projectionists, cogitating in tandem, locked onto the trace. The fractured terrain tilted, spun, and zoomed in and out six different ways as they homed in on the source. A more detailed, cohesive picture began to materialize. Separate fragments merged, displaced images overlapped, and blurry borders combined and sharpened. The result, after all their efforts, was completely common-place in appearances—a close-up of a windblown, grassy field.

Hadamard's skin tingled as he watched. "Unbelievable," he whispered to his old friend, in his mind sorting through the countless hours he'd spent pouring over forbidden tomes. He shook his head slowly. "The ancients never had anything like this. It isn't even covered by the treaty."

The grig responded under his breath so only Hadamard could hear. "If the Djinxarai can trace dancing swords…"

"I know," Hadamard replied, voice hushed. The thought had already crossed his mind. "That means the legends about the Jhinyari being able to do the same with their swords are probably true."

The luminary's only solace was that he'd never invoked the Jhinyari brightblade. He'd only studied the qualities of its white metal to pass on to the striker forgers at Ironeagle.

Lord Ralador raised his voice, addressed the luminary and the grig.

"By the will of Aelish, speak up you two, so we can all hear. Are you saying the lost sword is in Turnsby? Among the Glebe Stouts?"

Eriff scoffed. "I say it is impossible to project that far. If this is a trace operation then there is something wrong with our Djinxarai. They are not tracing where the bastard sword went, they are simply showing us what we already know—where it started."

Feleg looked to Hadamard for an explanation. The luminary shrugged, at a loss for words, then swept his gaze over the smooth-as-sand display. He contemplated the evidence. *Something doesn't look right,* he thought, but he couldn't put a finger on exactly what.

An introductory trill reverberated through the air as Nekenezitter weighed in. "Perhaps <click> Amot can <tic> illuminate the situation."

"Really?" Eriff swung his gaze from the assembler to the scout. "Well, Amot?" he said, as smug as can be. "Indeed, illuminate us."

Amot glanced to his commander for permission to speak. Berendt responded with a grunt and a short nod. The scout turned to address the room, eyes shifting from one officer to the next.

"During the fight, I had trouble keeping track of the Queen's Guard commander," he admitted. "I became… immersed in the projection. I imagined the other side of the hill as vividly as I possibly could."

"Of course," huffed Eriff. "That is precisely the sort of thing we were instructed to do. That is how the strikers function."

Amot continued, ignoring the interruption. "But the fragments came together in a weird way to form the image, like pieces from two different puzzles."

Lord Ralador furrowed his brow. "How so?"

Before Amot could answer, Nekenezitter trilled in. "I believe <click> Amot recalled <tic> the true form of the <clack> hill, not the one before him in the scenario, <chirr> likely because he has ties to Turnsby."

"Hmph." Lord Ralador regarded Amot. "Is that true, Scout? Do you know of this place?"

Amot nodded. "Yes, Your Lordship. My grandfather trapped in the Turnsby area when I was very young, along the small streams on the edge of Whisperwood. I tagged along. The actual hill that was replicated in the scenario lies between the north gate of Turnsby and the forest—"

"You have your confirmation, Crown Advisor," Lord Ralador broke in. His stern gaze redirected to the Gloom's large, bespectacled eyes. "Now get on with it. *Advise.*"

Hadamard raised a staying hand to Nekenezitter. "Hold on," he started. "Are you saying Amot imagined the other side of a similar looking hill in his head, one that he was familiar with, and took a swing at Eriff?"

The Gloom narrowed his eyes, tilted his head to and fro. "More like <click> he imagined some combination of both <tic-tic> hills, superimposed, and he swung at the portion of Eriff that he saw."

He connected the two locations. A fog lifted from the luminary's mind. A fog of uncertainty. "Of course." The room stirred with Hadamard's unshared realization; confirmation of the Gloom's insight. All eyes fell upon him. "But something went wrong, didn't it?"

"<click> I believe you know <clack>."

Hadamard shifted his gaze to the queensman commander. "You, Eriff, were here in the dome the whole time, but Amot's mind was focused elsewhere." Then he met the March Lord's hawkish stare. "In the heat of the moment, Amot stretched his thoughts beyond the confines of the dome and sharpened them far afield to fill in the missing pieces… that is the essence of farseeing, but in the extreme. Somehow, that mental picture he was trying to form brought the two worlds together—far and near, here and there… the hill he knew in Turnsby became one with the scenario hill constructed in its likeness."

With a soft chirr, Nekenezitter acknowledged that he and Hadamard were on the same page.

Feleg narrowed his eyes, holding to an even, evaluating expression. "Amot swung the dancing sword many times before though, without incident."

"And that doesn't explain why he dropped his sword," remarked a March officer, a hint of disdain in his voice. He was medium-built and, by the insignia on his chain armor, a duelist in rank.

Nekenezitter chirred in, "<click> The forces at play <clack> were not what he expected. There is a pull <tic> into the Void, a suction, that cannot be helped. With such a faraway target…"

"It would be overwhelming," finished Hadamard.

"That's what it felt like," Amot said.

"I still say it is impossible to project that far," Eriff countered. "We have no proof—" Nekenezitter interrupted with a trill.

"Apparently <tic>, it is not impossible <clack>. Not for Amot, anyway. Perhaps for you <click>, because you are not as talented <tic-tic>."

Hadamard smirked to himself at the Gloom's blunt words.

The queensman commander was taken aback—flabbergasted—by the crown advisor's suggestion. He raised his voice. "Who do… How could…" He scowled. "What do you know of talent? How dare you suggest such utter nonsense."

"You'll have to keep your voice down," Hadamard scolded, worried the projectionists would lose focus. In firm but hushed tones, the luminary addressed all in attendance. "Keep your voices down, everyone. The projectionists need to concentrate. They're deep into some extremely delicate farseeing now. They cannot be disturbed by loud, random babble."

Eriff's pinched expression made plain his distaste. He went on to translate the exchange for the Jhin Masters, taking an abundance of time and words to do so.

The duelist March officer spoke up. He was older than Eriff, with thinning blond hair, white at the sides. He rubbed his weak chin, pondering. "So, can the scout pinpoint the weapon's location then?"

The luminary paused to regard Amot, then turned his attention to the duelist. "The answer to your question is 'not really.' Our best hope is the assembler."

Lord Ralador prompted Berendt. "Kith Commander Garondi?"

Berendt rubbed his beard with one hand, staring at the display. After a slow nod, he turned to address the Djinxarai manning their stations. "Projectionists, I know this is asking a lot, but can you get a more refined fix on the lost weapon. We don't have a lot of time before nightfall out there."

Hadamard glanced at the assembler. Fine particles had become airborne in it, slightly blurring the view.

Tall Hallman approached Hadamard, a rolled-up scroll in hand. "I found the map," he said, "Tri-towns area." He began to unfurl the parchment in front of the luminary. "This is exactly what Amot described and it looks about right from what I can tell."

"Where exactly? Show me," Hadamard said.

The ranger held the map in full view of everyone around him. It showed the territory west from Webfoot to the Bearded Hills and south to Doncaster, with Turnsby dead center between the Dim and Upper Malevuin rivers. Along the page border, a series of small insets had been skillfully drawn in, styled like magnifying glasses and depicting close-up views of local landmarks in the region: a gate, a market square, an old tower, the two river crossings…

Ralador shifted his gaze from the display to the map, back to the display, and then back to the map again. He drew his eyebrows together, pondering the two. "Well, where is this place on the map? And exactly where is the striker?"

Hadamard spotted a small, peanut-shaped loop towards its top edge. "That might be the hill," he said, pointing, "North of Turnsby."

"Looks about right," Amot said.

"This map's too small to be of use though," Feleg said. "Not enough detail."

"What's the scale?" Berendt asked. "That looks awfully close to Harrow."

"I don't see a scale," Feleg replied. "But you're right. Maybe a dozen miles from Harrow's Gate."

"Oh," Hallman interjected. He lifted his thumb from the edge of the map. "Sorry," he said, wagging it over the close-up underneath. "The projectionists must've used this for reference."

Sure enough, the insert depicted a magnified version of the scenario hill, complete with topographic curves.

"He's right," Hadamard said. "Are there still rangers in that area? "

Berendt puffed. "We haven't had border patrol forces stationed there for at least a decade. I don't think the Tri-towns monitor it either."

Galewind leaned in to have a closer look at the map. "The Aerie overflies the Whisperwood Line on a weekly basis," she said, pointing to the forest's northern boundary. "There's never much happening that way, just the usual traffic along the Dim River."

"Let's hope it stays that way," said the duelist. "If the sword falls into the wrong hands…"

"May I?" Berendt asked, gesturing to the map. Hallman handed it over and the Kith commander walked it to the wall. He held the map in the red glow of the sconce there. After studying the parchment for a long minute, he addressed Feleg, quietly. "Could you get the projectionists to put a person or some familiar object up on the assembler display, for comparison? I need a better sense of scale."

As he spoke, the only Reg Force officer in the room approached the assembler. She had short-cropped hair and a medium build. "Lieutenant Prithman, Logistics," she announced casually, to no one in particular. Eyes squinting, she pointed to the base of the hill. "Isn't this what you're looking for?"

Officers slowly gathered around her. Hadamard struggled to discern the shape she was referring to. It lay on the ground, long and thin, possibly coming to a point…

"Difficult to tell," Feleg said. "But it's definitely something. Not necessarily a sword though—could be a stick, or rocks maybe."

Lord Ralador's hand jerked up, pointing at the image.

"There, what is that?"

Prithman responded, "Something's moving in the projection."

Berendt's mouth fell open. "What the…"

"I see it too," Galewind nodded. "No. Wait. More than one."

Hadamard also caught sight of the distinct shapes, floating and unattached in the growing haze of the display. Two, or perhaps three blurred figures prowled the area around the hill on all fours. *Dogs*, he thought, at first glance. The image rippled.

"Wolves?" Feleg said.

But there was something wrong with the way they moved. One stood upright.

"Wulvers," Berendt gruffed. "They come out to prowl at dusk."

"Man-wolves," Hallman added.

"There's your reference," Hadamard told Berendt.

Prithman asked, "Do they have the striker? I don't see it anymore."

Berendt moved in, squinted. "I can't tell. Too fuzzy." He leaned in for a closer look and pointed to the lighter-toned figure in the image. "That one shines brighter than the rest." He turned his gaze to Prithman. "The others are dark—almost impossible to make out."

The sands of the assembler wavered. A shock wave propagated from the display's center.

"What was that?" Eriff said.

Suddenly, the sands scattered, as though to the winds. Then they collapsed, blanketing the slab table and sending up a cloud of fine dust. The observers broke away, sputtering and flapping their hands in front of their faces.

Behind the table, Anya stumbled, but caught her own fall. Hands atop her knees, she braced herself. A heartbeat later, Crusher's crutch slid along the rock floor. He began to topple. Feleg—moving surprisingly fast—dashed to Crusher's side, caught him before he hit the ground.

The Jhin Masters, the diviner from the Chamber of Aelish and Hadamard quickly made their way to the stations behind the main assembler. The luminary supported Anya, while the masters and the clergyman spread out to tend to the other projectionists.

Ralador grimaced, one hand still waving at the dust. "What is wrong with your assembler? Get the picture back."

Galewind enlightened the assuming March Lord. "I believe our projectionists need a break, Loraith."

Between heavy breaths, Crusher spoke. "We kept the trace active as long as we could. Jhin's gift is but a glimpse that dampens with time, and time has run out."

⋰

The Kith commander surveyed the officers in his midst—a casual grouping of high-ranking officials from each of the military orders. They'd congregated near the entrance to the Red Room while the luminaries, Jhin Masters, and others occupied the assembler station zone.

Perfect, Berendt thought, *no civilians*. The time was ripe to carve out a rough course of action and divvy out responsibilities. He waved his fellow officers in.

"I don't know about you," Berendt started, eyes scanning one to the next, "but I've seen all I need to see. We need to send a recovery team to Turnsby. *Immediately.*"

The knightmaiden was the first to respond. "The Aerie's gryphons can get there the swiftest, but if the Wulvers have the dancing sword…"

An older March officer in their midst let out a quick, disgusted snort. "They are beasts. Absolute beasts."

"Queensmen will accompany the valkyries," Eriff stated, "to provide protection, recover the lost sword, and secure its return to Gan."

Berendt grunted. "Oh no you don't."

Galewind interjected, "Valkyries are quite capable of protecting themselves, thank you. It's the recovery I'm concerned about."

Still annoyed at being snubbed by Eriff, Berendt continued. "My rangers are trained exactly for this type of recovery mission. I can send a section of our finest out on horseback. They'll be on location by morning."

Eriff squinted hard, jerked his head back. "Kith? Are you mad?"

Lord Ralador opened his mouth to speak but coughed instead. He wiped the dust from his lips, then cleared his throat. "This is already <ahem> a *Kith catastrophe,*" he sputtered.

I bet you like the sound of that, thought Berendt. He glanced at Tall Hallman, who was clenching his jaw to contain himself. *I hear you,* he thought. The commander closed his eyes for a moment, inhaled deeply. He let the slight pass.

"Respectfully, Your Lordship," he explained, "the Kith are best equipped to execute this mission. We conduct searches all the time for missing people, valuable items lost or stolen, forbidden books, hidden tech… you name it. We have expert trackers among us. On top of that, Amot needs to be a part of this mission. You saw what he's capable of. He can use one striker to home in on the other when he gets there, and he can do it better than anyone."

"I saw what he is capable of all right," Lord Ralador retorted. "I don't need two dancing swords lost. Champion Eriff Haulik is just as capable at farseeing."

"Then send them both," Berendt said. "This is clearly a ranger op, though. My scouts can enter Whisperwood on the sly. That piece of terrain is dangerous, and not only because of the Line of Control with Harrow..."

The duelist March officer spoke up. "How bad can it be? A few man-wolves are no match for—" Ralador raised his hand to silence the man.

"How are you going to find them?" Berendt countered, addressing the duelist. "Shroud's Well, there isn't a queensman in the dome that can track worth beans."

The queensman shrugged. "We'll spot them from the air, on the backs of gryphons."

Berendt grumbled back, "Never mind that Wulvers live underground in burrows." He shook his head. "What's more, they're clever hunters and fierce fighters. Extremely territorial. Worst of all, they live among the *ghost pines.*"

Eriff breathed out a tolerating sigh. "Humor me, Kith Commander. What are ghost pines and why do they matter?"

"It's a long story," Berendt replied.

"I insist," Lord Ralador told him, "but keep it high level."

Berendt's bad eye began to itch something fierce. "Pardon me a moment," he said, before turning his back to the officers to face the wall. He lifted his eyepatch and gave the wound underneath a gentle rub. That only made the skin burn, so he scratched at it until it was raw. Finally, still unsatisfied, he replaced the patch, turned back to face his peers. *Just give it to them straight,* he told himself, then gruffed out a response.

"I'll start by saying our sources are sketchy and the intelligence is plagued with contradictions, but by most accounts ghost pines were once Hurlorns, until they went rotten to the core and became something else. Something dark and foul—tormented souls, twisted. They infested Wilder territory with their malevolence." He paused to adjust his eyepatch. The raw skin stung underneath. "'Some sort of disease,' claim the sages of the 9th, a disease that drives them mad. It's always the pine-like variety that gets it. Not all pines, mind you, just a rare few." Berendt grunted, rubbed his beard. "Long before my time, Spirit Hurlorns drove them away to the triangle of land between the rivers Malevuin and Dim, isolated from everything. Deepweald Hurlorns never go there, and sensible Stouts from Turnsby know enough to stay the hell away. Only the Wulvers walk freely among the ghost pines."

The March Lord paused, eyes digging into the lead ranger like a judge's stare on the accused. He sighed heavily. "Very well," Ralador said, "Send your rangers."

For a moment, Berendt was pleasantly surprised, until Ralador continued.

"But not Amot," he said. "Amot is to be detained."

Berendt grimaced, fell silent. He remained silent in that long moment reserved for him and him alone. No one else spoke.

At hearing his name raised, Amot left his uncle's side and approached Lord Ralador. The man seemed surprised at the intrusion.

"I have to go on this mission," he told the March Lord, straight up.

Eriff's retort was just as blunt. "You shouldn't be here," he told the scout. "High-ranking officers only." With a hand gesture, he drew the door guards' attention.

Amot didn't budge.

Hallman stepped to his Kith brother's side. He faced Eriff squarely, arms folded in defiance. "Amot isn't going anywhere until the March Lord hears him out."

"Speaking as the Overseer's representative," Berendt added, "I'm telling you that leaving Amot behind would be a mistake."

Lord Ralador scoffed at the three rangers. Eriff took the liberty of responding on his superior's behalf.

"Very well, indulge us," Eriff said to all, then singled Amot out. His tone shifted to derisive. "So, Kith-boy, exactly why is that? Tell us exactly why you have to go along with the valkyries and the queensmen, and all the grown-up rangers?"

Amot could have stated any one of fifty good reasons why he should go. But he stated none. Something inside the scout told him that no reason would suffice. Not here, not now, not for Eriff. Something inside told him that silence was the best answer. And so that was the answer Amot provided. He stood still and silent with Eriff glaring at him. The scout could feel the queensman's discriminating gaze struggling to interpret his ink markings, while he himself tried not to give his emotions away.

Eriff egged him on. "What, nothing?"

Amot maintained steady eye contact with Eriff as the door guards approached. Hallman blocked the guards' path, widening his stance to brace himself. He stood stiff as a mountain.

Berendt bit his lip hard, then spoke up. "I'll assume full responsibility for Amot on this mission," he told Ralador.

The March Lord didn't respond.

Amot had the overwhelming feeling that his presence in this conversation had become self-defeating, and that his commander would be better placed to argue his case without him. *Berendt will find a way,* he decided. With a single nod and a slight pat on the shoulder, Amot signaled to his Kith brother defender. The tall ranger swallowed hard, then stepped aside. But before the scout allowed himself to be escorted out of the chamber, Lumen Hadamard hastened over from the assembler stations, face flushed and red under the collar.

"Bring Amot to my study," he said in a huff, addressing the guards. Then he turned to Amot. "We need to talk before you go—on a separate matter." Hadamard's eyes darted to Lord Ralador and then back, an obvious hint that whatever the luminary had to say could not be stated in front of the March Lord.

Amot agreed and the two guards led him away. At a safe distance from the officers, the expression on one of the guard's faces softened. He addressed Amot in a low voice. "Eriff can be a real pain," the man said. "Especially with Lord Ralador present—family connections, you understand. He's not so bad really, when you get to know him." The second guard hardened his own expression, pursed his lips slightly, but said nothing.

"Thanks," Amot replied when they reached the study.

The guard responded with a bitter smile. "I suggest you bar the door from the inside."

Amot nodded, entered, then shut the door behind him. Sliding the bar down, he locked himself away in Hadamard's crowded chamber.

CHAPTER XL
JAKKA
(Vey, Akrylla, Hersh)

THE JOURNEY FROM Deepweald was a blur in Vey's mind. She readily drank Milla's tea whenever the old woman offered it. The bitter brew numbed her pain. It made her forget. But its effects were not the same as the purple powder. This blend didn't play with her mind so much. Ang and Riddik drank a different tea, one that made them stronger every day. Milla wouldn't give them the recipe, not until their bargain was fulfilled.

Vey's feet hurt like blisters. Her ankles were coated in mud. Everywhere she was forced to walk smelled like rot, algae, and dead things. The air was sticky and so was her tattered, red dress. The special assistant's moccasins squished with every step over the spongy ground she hiked upon—the best ground she could hope for amidst the small assortment of well-rounded hills that spread out for miles around them. The low-lying areas between the hills were choked with rotting vegetation and blotted with scummy water. Blackened trees hung over the still waters like stooping skeletons, branches draped in moss and lichens. Now and again, edges and corners of large, buried structures poked out of the earth. Relics of the forgotten past.

Another dark evening had set in, and Vey waved off yet another cloud of gnats in her path. She didn't care anymore if they flew into her hair or stung her face. And although Milla's scented water helped to keep them off, still, her limbs were left welted and itching. *I can't bear another night out here,* she thought. The idea of reaching the city before nightfall is what kept her feet moving, even though she knew not what to expect. Only Milla's signs and everyone else's inability to resist her whims directed them there. *Whatever awaits though,* she surmised, *can't be worse than the cruelty suffered under Riddik… Can it?* Vey moaned a dull moan to herself. *I want out of this hideous place.* She wanted to scream it aloud at the top of her lungs, but if she was too vocal about her complaints someone would make her pay—Riddik, Milla, she didn't know which. She almost did it anyway.

None of Vey's current discomforts mattered to her though, compared to how she was treated when Riddik was in charge. And she knew the recent lull in unbearable hardships that had descended upon her wouldn't last: Hersh was still at her side, but he wouldn't be for long because he'd soon be auctioned off to the highest bidder. Ang was almost pleasant, and that couldn't last long either. Riddik was too weak to cause trouble, but only until his antidote kicked in. And Milla, well… Milla was neither here nor there, almost as bad as Hersh. She mumbled a lot to herself in strange tongues—Nali, Jhin and a desert dialect that Vey could recognize, and another that could only be leviathan in origin. And she kept staring off the trail, searching for things that weren't there.

Only Ang the Bitch knew the path through the swampy terrain to Jakka. The special assistant, the half-giant, the hag, and the Cutter followed her blindly. After Milla's successful hunt for medicinal herbs, Ang had steered the travelers clear of the Lord of Scales Stronghold, as promised, and snuck the party past Gargun's Hate without notice—a fort captured by the Elderkin from the resident Baruush. Se'shehan Hill required a bribe for passage, which Riddik paid reluctantly. It was the first time Vey had laid eyes upon a full-blooded Nali—a reptilian-based form of Outlander. If she wasn't half out of her mind, she might have been afraid. Its skin was scaly and its eyes cold and black.

Ang had gotten stronger more rapidly than Riddik, who still relied on his staff for support. The old woman kept saying he was sick because he was a glutton: "You stuffed yourself more than the half-giant could've, twice your size," she'd told the Cutter. Riddik didn't like that talk and only scowled at Milla in response. He accused her of giving him less of the antidote, somehow. Actually, he got more. Ang snuck him her share.

Hersh had regained some of his strength under Milla's watchful gaze. Vey heard Milla mumbling once, the same way she always did when administering a dose to the half-giant. She'd heard her say softly: "Just enough, in case I need you." That made Vey wonder.

The vice-regent had attempted to talk to Vey many times on the journey, and she'd tried to talk back. But she had trouble understanding the things he was saying and he had trouble saying them to her. It was a mess. He was quiet now. "Trancing," was the word she'd come up with to describe the far-off look he bore.

The special assistant looked ahead to Ang. The demoness' skin seemed a darker shade of crimson since they'd entered her home territory. She stood taller, straighter, and she held her head slightly higher. Riddik followed her closely, struggling to keep pace. He'd hobbled past Vey and the others to catch up, as though he had something to say. But Ang did all the talking even when he got there. Her voice rang low with measured enthusiasm—quite unlike Ang. And the way the demoness spoke to Riddik—bragged even—of the despicable region's sites and history made Vey think she actually liked the swamp. *She never really opposed coming here,* thought Vey. Ang spoke also of her House in Jakka, on Hasstik Hill. Hers was not a reputable house, apparently, but was well-connected to the underworld. "Esfelas" was its name, set among the foothills of the city proper in the thick of the mired ruins. In Nali, the word meant "half-blood."

And she hasn't been mean-spirited lately either. I wouldn't even say she's a bitch right now.

Vey caught fragments of the Outlander's conversation. "A nest of holes with access to a hanging city," Ang told Riddik of the Jakka Hills. Something in her voice sounded like grim pride. "Ruins from a lost civilization," she also said, "now buried with all its secrets." That was supposed to impress the Taint. But Riddik replied that the swamp was only home now to snakes, bats, and rats. He said the Baruush owned half of it since Bitterhelm's invasion years ago—the better half—and that they'd discovered all the secrets. That got the two of them arguing, then blaming each other for Kori's death, then blaming each other for getting poisoned, then for losing profits… the list went on and Ang won every argument, twisting her stinging words into the Taint like a dagger into his worthless flesh.

Still a bitch, thought Vey, *and good at it.*

Riddik only became more frustrated. He threw his arms into the air, cursing Shroud. Milla just let them quarrel.

Vey squeezed her eyes shut, walked blind for a long minute, puffing out air as she stepped. *The Bitch might be back, but at least Gutless Kori's gone. Dead now. Dead as glass.* The Wulver's death was the one small thing she'd hoped for that had come true. Vey didn't miss the beast's low growls, its prowling about, or the way the creature salivated over her. *If only Riddik could be next.* She imagined the mean little Taint as a crystal statue. *He'd make a good one,* she thought, *standing squat, snarling and brandishing his stupid curved blade.* It was a pleasant daydream, with a certain fitting stillness to it. Vey felt her lips curl into a slight grin. She stumbled, then opened her eyes to reality, to the path ahead. But all she saw was the image of a frozen Riddik, so vivid in her imagination it refused to depart. Over a few seconds, the image faded from the back of her mind and the world came into view again.

Ahead, a sense of doom loomed over the mountain they approached. Tall and stark against the surrounding marsh, the main peak's black tip punctured the low-hanging clouds. The City of Snakes, according to Ang, lay amidst the hills and the mire at the mountain's base. Vey lowered her eyes to her feet, tried not to think about what might happen next.

~Schemers

Akrylla knew something was amiss. *I should have poisoned those two Outlanders outright when I had the chance, and put them in a brew.* It wasn't their constant bickering—that was normal. But what wasn't normal was how the pair had suddenly brought their argument down to hushed tones. *Whispering secrets,* Akrylla suspected. Riddik's wheezing as he struggled to keep pace with Ang had become louder than his sawed-out words, while Ang's angry voice, which normally rang like bells in Akrylla's ears, had softened to a hiss. *Those two are scheming against me, they are.* She'd heard the name "Blackdagger" amongst their whispers.

~Fiend

Not to be trusted. Akrylla knew the name and she knew its many faces over the years, the decades. The current Blackdagger was a vile and well-connected Baruush, the master of a brutal trafficking operation that bore the same name. Back home, the Blackdaggers roved the Scarsands as smugglers, thieves, and assassins, running jobs from the Bloodspill to the Mystic Dunes, and through to Kel Samu. Here in the East, Jakka and Bitterhelm were the organization's main hubs of activity.

~No more

Akrylla called ahead.

"Enough," she scolded. "Riddik, get back where you belong, bringing up the rear. Or no cure for you." Between the hobbling and the heavy breathing, the sadistic Taint looked nearly as bad as when she'd first poisoned him.

"Go to hell, Witch," he retorted. He grimaced in pain, all bent out of shape. "I don't want any more of your venom. I've had plenty and it isn't doing me any good."

"I mean it," Akrylla shot back, not willing to be messed with. "We're nearly at the gates and I don't need you anymore. Why give you the final dose? Why deny myself the pleasure of watching you squirm in agony without it?"

Riddik halted, scowling, and turned to face Akrylla square on. He raised his walking stick and waved it at her, threatening. "Maybe *I* don't need *you* anymore, Witch. Maybe I should bash your ugly skin."

But you don't bash, do you Riddik? We all know you cut, and that cutting is what you do.

Ang slowed slightly, but kept walking, eyes ever forward. Obviously, she wanted to stay out of this spat.

In a huff, Akrylla stormed straight past Riddik. "That's it, you sadistic little Taint," she spat as she went by, "you've ruined it. I'm tired of keeping you alive. No cure for you." She shot a discreet glance at his free hand. It rested on the grip of his curved blade.

~Guard

Stay calm, Akrylla told herself. *Only one more hour and we're there. If I can hold him off until then...* The shaman remembered her claw dagger, which held her deadliest poison—for emergencies. *The tiniest scratch, lethal.* With subtle movements, she slid the weapon from her satchel, undid the safety latch and held the dagger hidden in the wide sleeve of her robe. She craned her neck around, shot the Cutter a nasty look.

Riddik heaved heavy breaths as he stood glaring. His eyes, crazed wide and dark as coal, burned into her skin.

~Pleasure

Yes... Akrylla knew the look. *He sees pleasure coming. Pleasure in causing me pain. He thinks I deserve it. He thinks it is his right.* Her pulse quickened. But instead of pumping fast and light, her heart drummed steady and strong in her chest. As steady and strong as an old woman's heart could drum. She wrapped her fingers around the hidden dagger's grip, ready to strike. First, if necessary.

Show no fear, she told herself. *He feeds on fear.*

Ang's voice chimed in. "Look, the *Mruthlissk*," she called, elongating the "s" sound. She'd gotten far ahead. "The road to Jakka." The Bitch glanced over her shoulder and saw what Riddik was doing. She stopped, let out an exaggerated huff.

"Let the hag be, Riddik," she demanded. "I want to live, and so should you."

"I don't need you either, Bitch," he responded.

Ang raised her voice, sharpened her tone. "Do as she says, Riddik, and take up the rear. Take up the rear or Blackdagger himself will hear of your continuous chain of screw-ups."

The Taint grumbled another curse, spat, and fell back as instructed.

Akrylla fixed her eyes dead ahead. Through the brush and the stunted trees, she glimpsed the stony path that Ang had announced. The mosaic of flat stones reminded her of a turtle's back. She sighed a quiet sigh of relief, having gotten through another showdown with Riddik. The shaman slipped her weapon back into her satchel as she hiked.

Talking voices sounded from the road, along with a "yaw" and the crack of a whip, like someone driving draft animals to pull a cart. Akrylla called ahead to Ang.

"Should we lay hidden until whoever is near passes?"

The demoness shook her head. "Just look like you know what you're doing," she told her, as she stepped out onto the road.

Akrylla hesitated, glanced back to confirm Riddik's taking up of the rear position, then followed warily. With slow steps, she ventured into the open and made her way to Ang, waiting for her. The shaman took in her surroundings.

The road to Jakka city cut a meandering path through the marshes before bending around the base of the mountainside and out of sight. Small groups of Nali and Baruush walked the stony surface in both directions, while their beasts of burden hauled carts. Whip in hand, a wiry-looking slave trafficker on horseback headed towards them and the city, cursing at his bound and struggling thralls, driving them on. Heads of passersby turned to gaze at the newcomers.

Akrylla spoke to Ang in a low voice. "But are they used to seeing… outsiders who are not bound… not slaves?"

"Trust me, they've seen everything," Ang replied. She tracked the shaman's gaze to the trafficker. "He won't bother us, not with a half-giant among us. Might make us an offer though. In his mind, we're just the competition—reeling in a half-giant would raise his status."

"Ah yes," said the shaman. She double-checked her satchel for smelling salts in case she needed to fully revive Hersh. *Still there.* Her hold on the half-giant had lasted well, all things considered. He'd been more than willing to take his doses. More than willing, but less than eager. Reduced as they'd been, she still had no trouble keeping him in line. *A man of his word… I should have spared more.*

As the slave caravan neared, the moans and groans of the captives filled the air. A gaunt, malnourished woman collapsed among them. After a short halt and a crack of the trafficker's whip, she failed to rise. Dead or exhausted, Akrylla had no way of knowing which. Nonetheless, after a second crack of the whip, the caravan proceeded. Bound as they were, the fallen woman was dragged along by the half-dozen or so other slaves. The whip-cracker took a long look at the half-giant as he passed, barely sparing a glance for anyone else. *Knows to mind his business… Ang was right.*

Ang and Akrylla waited for the others to catch up, then they all set off together on the final leg of the journey that would bring them to the city gates. Ang stuck close to Akrylla's side this time. *Clingy, all of a sudden,* thought the shaman.

~She seeks

"What is it you want?" Akrylla asked. "Another vial? Why? Riddik's ready and willing."

Ang made a face like she'd swallowed acid.

Akrylla pressed her. Not because she believed what she had to say next. More, to work in some advice. Ang was not one to be generous with her body, the way a shaman should be. "The half-giant, maybe?" Ang did not respond in any capacity. "You have to learn to take what you can get, sometimes," Akrylla told her. "You have to learn to lower your standards. In a drought, you take what water you need to sustain yourself, even if it's tainted."

Ang spat back, "I'm not a dried-up old hag, like you."

"Not yet… I was young like you, once, you know." *And like you in other ways too.* The pair walked in silence for a time, broken only by their footsteps and the rush of the winds blowing down from the mountain. As her thoughts drifted, Akrylla's own young reflection flashed in her mind, the way she'd once looked as she sat peering into her favorite mirror, the one on the dresser in her room. The one in Kel Fariz.

~Pretty

So many years… so many possibilities. The young Akrylla could angle that mirror just so to reflect her soft image in another, full-length mirror behind her, and then back again, and so on, until the never-ending chain of reflections pinched out of sight. A reflection for each blessing: *Happy. Carefree. Loved…*

Ang interrupted her train of thoughts.

"We can help each other."

"Why would I help you, Ang the Bitch?" *I know you conspired with Riddik.*

Ang grimaced. "Because you see potential in me." Ang gestured to Vey, keeping step behind them. "Like you see in her."

~Apprentice

Yes… she's smart. Good instincts. "Convince me," Akrylla told Ang, her voice flat. *I could save this one too, from what is to come.* "Why should I take you on?"

"My brothers schemed against me in my own House," Ang began. "They made everyone hate me. I'm not sure if you know this, but by the will of Gorganna, the eldest woman should rule a family. I did, for a short time, but my brothers are indulgent. When I stopped them from wasting everything we had on stupidity… from ruining everything… they…"

"They turned on you," Akrylla finished.

Ang nodded. "Yes. They made up lies and destroyed my name. I had to join the Blackdaggers—no one else would take me. Then Grewl sent me to rotten, stinking Bitterhelm as a slave catcher, only because no one else would have anything to do with me in Jakka."

"Your brothers, they labeled you 'the Bitch'?"

"Everyone calls me that now and I don't care. I don't care because that's exactly what I'm going to be when I get my house back. I will cast them out the way they cast me out. To the Baruush hordes."

"How many brothers do you have?"

"Nine."

"How many sisters?"

"None. I once had three. My father poisoned them, along with my mother and I, so he could rule the house. I was resistant—my mother saw it coming and made me that way. She gave me small doses."

A deadly game, thought the shaman. *She's lucky her mother didn't kill her trying to save her.*

Akrylla furrowed her brow at Ang. Her voice was flat. "What exactly did you do to him," she asked.

A malevolent smirk spread across the demoness's face, proud and dark. "Well," Ang replied, "I couldn't count on the House poison…"

"Obviously."

"I discovered my father wasn't resistant to acid in the least."

Akrylla chuckled. "I like the way you think. Bitch indeed. Aunts and uncles?"

"Hate me. At first, I thought I could bring you to my House, Milla, and that you could use your witchcraft somehow… that's what Riddik and I were arguing about."

"But?"

"No. My brothers will never yield. They are stupid and you are ugly—that's all they will see. But I say you are valuable, Milla, for you are wise and traveled and know of poisons. Not like a slave. I must present you to Gorganna, to gain her favor and plead my case—that's what you want anyway isn't it? To serve Gorganna? That's why you brought us to Jakka." Ang looked to Akrylla for confirmation.

The shaman nodded. "The signs are clear," she said. "I have Ekkon's blessing, not a surprise given his many snake-like tentacles."

Ang continued. "The Mother of All Snakes will appreciate that I brought a valuable servant to her. I will ask her to restore my House, with me as its head and you as my shaman. Together, we will spread her name and her will. I will ask her to cast out my brothers."

~Opportunity

"Do you really believe what you say is possible?"

Ang nodded a confident nod. "We'll have to convince the Clergy first…"

Akrylla hesitated, considered Ang's offer. "Ekkon's Wheel, the signs were genuine."

~Accept

"We shall present ourselves to your Mother of All Snakes. But what of my Vey?"

"Vey is not ready for Gorganna, not yet. She could be devoured. She must remain behind."

Akrylla sighed. *The Bitch is right, sensible.*

"Vey must be kept safe," the shaman insisted.

"I know just the place," Ang replied. She halted, reached under her vest and produced a bone tube tucked away there. She spoke low enough that the others couldn't hear. "Give everyone a short rest. I have some handwritings to do before we get to Jakka. Grewl—the slave keeper—has cells and he has lodgings. He's a businessman. I'll cut him in on the half-giant profits to buy a room and protection."

"Riddik won't allow that."

Ang grimaced. "Out in the wild, Riddik has power over us all. But we're in Jakka now. Here, Riddik is nothing more than a second-rate flesh peddler, with a reputation for bringing in damaged merchandise because he doesn't have the discipline to keep his damn knife in his belt or his dick in his pants."

"And you?"

"I'm not just a slave catcher. I help keep the books for all of Bitter-helm and I oversee one of the operations there. Blackdagger tells me I have potential."

"Indeed, you do," Akrylla said. "Strange, isn't it? How everyone always seems to want the same person? There are too few of your kind in the world, my dear, and too many Riddiks."

Ang smirked in agreement, left to find a dry place to do her work.

~Access

Yes… she will prove valuable. Everything is falling into place as it should. The signs were right…

❧

In the early moments of freefall, a colossal arm lashed out from the mountainside. Strong fingers, grey as stone, gripped the flesh of Hersh's upper arm. A rush of wild acceleration flooded his mind, as his body swung from certain death. The huge grey hand let go, shunting him into a deep, tall fissure in the bluff. Time stopped as he glided into its darkness, unknowing. That precious moment, Hersh braced himself mentally. Eyes squeezed shut. Expecting. Protecting. Waiting.

The half-giant slammed into rock and ice; his shoulder erupted in pain. He glanced off the rock wall and hit another. Time accelerated to a dizzying pace.

Uncontrolled, tumbling and skidding, the vice-regent plunged down the length of the fissure to where it narrowed. Finally, his body stopped at the pinch point, wedged between converging walls. One leg dangling beneath him, he felt the open air against his bare skin. As debris bounced past him, ricocheting off the bluff to a deadly plummet, Hersh found a foothold to stabilize his position. He brought one bloodied hand to the rock above his head, felt out a hand hold and crimped his fingers over it. Gripping for dear life, he hoisted himself to his feet. Then he tilted his gaze to what loomed above.

The fissure was occupied. Deep in its shadows, a dark and hooded figure lurked. Legs braced against two walls in perfect balance, the figure stood in a twisted fighting stance, tall and imposing, poised to strike in six different ways. Taller than any giant he'd ever seen.

Hersh glimpsed a purple, reflective sheen to the material of the robe worn by the giant. *The purple-robed wayfarer—the original Faceless— except five times its size!* He knew instantly what the encounter meant.

Hersh caught his breath, swallowed, then spoke up. "Master Wayfarer Kemgi," he said.

"It is I," the giant responded.

"Must we?"

The giant shuffled partially out of the shadows, no longer faceless. Stone-grey limbs jutted out of the purple robe. Her face resembled roughly-hewn stone.

In answer to Hersh's question, Kemgi nodded slowly, then shifted her balance. With lightning speed, the giant's rear leg shot out of the darkness. It struck Hersh square in the chest. Ribs crunched with the blow that sent him flying backwards. He landed sideways in the crack at the bottom of the fissure, and nearly slid through.

Lying there, Hersh gasped for breath, the wind completely knocked out of him. A cool sensation tickled the small of his back. *Another plummet beneath me?*

Kemgi did not relent. She pulled back her leg, shifted her balance again, then drove her huge fist at him.

All Hersh could do in response was to cringe. A cringe and a slight wriggle—a minor re-angling of his body against the sides of the fissure. In doing so, he released the pressure holding him in place. As the fist was about to impact, he dropped through.

The fist smashed above him. The rock wall splintered and shattered. The half-giant fell sharply away, broke his fall on a bed of ice and landed on his back. A painful, sonorous cry sounded from above. It echoed through the mountaintops.

A long pause ensued, followed by muffled grunts and gasps from above, and moving about. Hersh just lay there, reveling in the numb of cold ice against his body. It dulled his pain. Finally, the Master Wayfarer spoke.

"We are done. Come, you and I must speak." Kemgi's huge, grey hand worked its way through the gap in the rock above him.

Hersh hesitated, then grasped it. *If I can't trust her, who can I trust?* She hauled him straight up and out.

⚘

Vey's animal-hide footwear afforded little protection to her feet from the cobbled road to Jakka, rough and uneven. The Mruthlissk wound its way between the worn foothills of Blacktip Mountain and the chunky ruins strewn about the swamp. As light rain pattered their faces, the travelers passed a handful of soggy hamlets along the way. The local Nali residents lived in mud holes, several to each mound, equipped with stick fences and woven decks. Rickety walkways split the reedbeds between dwellings.

I hope the lodgings Milla mentioned are better than that. Vey wasn't expecting the Seaside Rendezvous in a place like Jakka, but hoped they had something at least as good as the Wolf'N Stein. *Anything would be better than what I have been through these past few days,* she thought. The special assistant wasn't exactly sure what Milla had in store for her. *I'll just have to play it out, gain her trust, and then disappear at the first opportunity. I'll go through the swamp again, if have to, to reach the Lord of Scales, and I'll send help for Hersh the moment I arrive.* It wasn't a great plan, she knew, but it was a plan that gave her hope, and hope was all she needed to keep her going.

After passing seven giant warrior-monks cut from the steep, rising rockface, and after rounding a bend at the base of the mountain, Vey caught her first glimpse of Jakka city. Smoke billowed up behind a pair of wooden, squarish towers, straight ahead. A scattering of monolithic hills, blackened as though scorched, rose above the city's partially-rubbled walls. According to Ang, they hosted the nineteen prominent houses of Jakka. From a distance, each had a natural fortress-like appearance. With dusk upon the city scape, they flared up one-by-one, alight with bonfires.

Ang had gone on to explain that House Esfelas was built into the seventh hill in from the gates. The first nine houses were Nali, and the next two mixed guilds. The last eight were held by Baruush warlords that had invaded Jakka a dozen years ago. Half of those properties were now in ruins, due to infighting. The occupiers' combined horde ranged for miles outside the city in camps scattered throughout the mountain's roots—a constant reminder of Bitterhelm's grip on Jakka, and a constant threat to stability.

Following the demoness' advice, Vey kept her head down as she passed through the leviathan-bone gates of Jakka. Even so, Baruush guards at the gatehouse hooted and hollered at her, shouting out "new whore" to her back. Riddik grinned to them as though it were true, and he called on them to bet on his giant in the fighting pits. Vey just kept walking as city noises began to well up, all around. She sidestepped to move closer to Hersh, clung to his arm. She tugged on it, but he still didn't respond. "I need you, Hersh," she implored. He hadn't responded in hours.

Beyond the gates, the cacophony of grunts, harsh voices, and wails grew louder. The stone path opened up into a busy market square. Beyond that, narrow streets ran between ruined buildings, choked with rubble. The market was packed with makeshift stands, bartering Nali, and sparring Baruush. The place smelled like smoke, burnt hair, urine and feces. Vey's ears rang with the noise of it all.

The grounds were rocky, moldy, and full of decay—soiled produce, stinking meat, and… some dead thing set against a crumbled wall with flies buzzing around it. *Hopefully not a person.* As they pushed through the masses, all manner of beast-men crowded around her, with strange, monstrous features.

The thick crowds. The sights. The sounds. The bustling about…

So confusing.

Vertigo.

Blood rushed to Vey's head. Heat washed over her. Her vision blurred. *What's… what's…* She brought a shaky palm to her temple. Beads of sweat seeded her forehead. Vey moaned, then stumbled.

Blackness overtook her.

⧉

"Master Wayfarer." Hersh found his footing and bowed respectfully.

The giantess gestured to a narrow ledge at the mouth of the fissure they'd been fighting in. They both took their seats, casually sprawling out to let the mountain winds cool their battered bodies.

Kemgi gazed to the west, where the afterglow of the sun's passing still lit the clouds in soft shades of mauve, just above the horizon. Her voice was one of compassion, laced with pity. "Wanderer of Mountain Paths, you have come far, but again you have failed. Three remaining skills you must demonstrate. And you must do so in combat."

Hersh's heart sank in his chest. *How can that be? I lasted nine rounds?* He wanted to ask these things of her, but he knew that doing so would be disrespectful.

"Will you tell me the first of the three?" he said.

"Yes. Empty Vessel," Kemgi replied, still avoiding his gaze.

390

Hersh was aghast. "I have emptied my heart, my being, and filled it with the Order. You know I am dedicated. What more could you ask?"

The giantess frowned at the dying light of the day. "How can something which is full be filled? You must cast off all that burdens you, and all that is preconceived. You must unlearn all that should not be known."

"I do not understand the last part."

"When the giantess Invrin defeated Helnum of the Star Sands in combat, she did not know how to be unkind. Helnum's followers were spared."

Hersh nodded. "I know the story. I understand. Will you tell me the second?"

"Yes. Still Mind. Only when the waters are still, do they reflect what is true."

"This is easy to see."

"But difficult in practice, when the storm rages."

"And the third? Will you tell me the third?"

"Yes. At One."

"What does it mean to be 'At One'?"

"That is the wrong question."

Out of respect, Hersh did not push the issue further. "Master Kemgi Wayfarer, will you tell me, how must I demonstrate these three things?"

"No. There is only one path. The wayfaring is not easy, nor should it be."

"Please, Master Wayfarer…"

"No, you must not be told. You must discover this within yourself. Telling you would be of no consequence anyway, for you will soon lose memory of the world you know. This much I will say: You must forget all and fight anew from your core being. Abide by the values you seek to embellish. Let them rise from within."

Kemgi turned her gaze from the sunset to Hersh. The giantess looked deep into his eyes, into his mind. She raised the palm of her unbroken hand to his forehead. "Forget, my Wanderer of Mountain Paths," was all she said.

A second later, an unfamiliar face faded from the half-giant's vision, replaced with darkness. He realized his eyes were closed. *A dream,* he thought. *What was this dream?* He could still smell the mountain air, but the memory wouldn't form. A sudden chill seeped into the half-giant's body—the chill of cold stone.

꙰

When Vey came to, she was in a cool, dark place. Her clothes were damp. She lay suspended on a bed of… *wicker?* She could still smell the swamp in her hair.

Something scurried in the dark. Vey jerked up. The wicker bed creaked as she shifted her weight, looking about. There was light. Dim light. A torch. Her head started to spin. The image in her mind confused her.

Bars. Are those bars? The torch was on the other side of them. *Why does my room have bars?*

When the world's tilt straightened out, Vey's eyes darted about the room. There wasn't much to see—it was squarish and of roughly hewn stone. No windows, no chairs… *what kind of inn is this?* She spotted a grating in the floor and she could hear running water beneath.

Vey stood up, rushed to the bars. There was a door, a lock… she rattled the door. It wouldn't open.

"Hello," Vey called into the hall. She saw other cells. Prisoners.

"Hello?" she repeated. "I think there's been a mistake."

An abrasive grunt sounded from a flight of stairs down the hall. It was followed by an unexpectedly cynical voice, with a much higher tone.

"No mistake," came the reply.

"Is this a brothel?" Vey asked.

"I wish," the voice said.

Vey spotted a bone scroll tube on the floor, leaning against the stone wall outside her cell as though carefully placed there. She fell to her knees, reached through the bars. Stretching her fingers to their fullest, she grasped the scroll tube. The special assistant tapped out the parchment and unfurled it. She rose and angled the document to the torch light. The script was a mix of Nali and Baruush, mostly the latter.

Her chest tightened as she translated the words. She gasped, then stopped breathing entirely. Vey brought a hand up to rest just beneath her neck.

Three high-quality slaves for Blackdagger, courtesy of his most loyal servant, Ang of House Esfelas. Instructions are:

~ Fight the half-giant once or twice before auctioning him off. He'll fetch a better price that way.

"No," Vey cried, as she read on, tears welling up behind her eyes.

~ Allow the redheaded maiden to heal up for one week. Outfit her with Western clothing of the highest quality and have her skin inked artfully around the unfortunate scar on her chest. She is otherwise untouched and will fetch a high price. Riddik the Cutter, who played a minor role in her capture, humbly requests the deal to include one free visit from him.

Vey broke down, crying. Vision blurred by tears, she read on.

~ The hag is a snake deadener for Gorganna to judge and likely devour. I shall report back on the high favors granted to the hag's Blackdagger captors.

The Special Assistant to the Grey Clerk swallowed her second gasp, collapsed to the bed. The flimsy structure snapped beneath her and crashed to the floor. As she lay there, sobbing, a picture unfolded in her mind: the meaning of belonging to a brothel in Jakka. *Brutality. Rape... Drugged out of my mind... Monstrous children...*

"I want to die," she moaned, wondering if the world might end any time soon. *Not soon enough,* she decided. Vey cried herself to sleep.

CHAPTER XLI
GREY WOODS OF MIND
(Hadamard)

HADAMARD MADE HIS way towards the study, Feleg at his side. He'd brought the grig along for two reasons: to lighten the conversation he was about to have with the scout and to scope out the plan going forward. A plan not just for Order Lumen, or the Kith Quarter, or Seventh Kaeda, or even the Queen of the Hidden City. A plan for everyone personally involved in this mess.

We're sunk if we don't work together, Hadamard thought. Each one for their own separate reasons; each one subject to Lord Ralador's broad influences. The March Lord had only named Amot to suffer a tribunal, so far. But what of the creators of the powerful weapons? What of the masterminds behind the exercise? Ralador could argue this was the plan all along and that the likes of rangers and Djinxarai can't be trusted. There was no telling where he'd stop.

"Where's the snitch?" Feleg asked.

"I left Nek chirring with the March Lord and company, on their way out to the dome." Hadamard paused. "Actually, the little imp is growing on me."

Feleg's head jerked back. "Really?" Then he snickered. "I loved how he dug into Eriff. Wasn't expecting that, not from him."

"He has his moments." Hadamard felt a pang of guilt for having judged Nekenezitter so harshly. "Besides, there's no need to drag him into this." But there was more to the luminary's decision to leave Nekenezitter behind than he'd let on. The Gloom didn't have stakes in the game afoot and Hadamard could use an unsullied ally on the inside of the royal circuit, a voice of reason in the queen's ear.

The Red Room had nearly cleared out behind them, the officers having all but departed. When the two friends reached the study, Hadamard tugged on the door. When it didn't budge, he rapped on it.

Moments later, the bar lock on the inside grated along the rough-woven vinewood. The door creaked half open and Amot peered out through the crack. He stepped back, swung the door wide open.

As the grig limped through, he addressed the scout, sarcasm tainting his voice. "Funny how no one noticed you were locked away all this time with the entire remaining arsenal of dancing swords."

"Ralador would have a fit if he found out." Hadamard smirked as he strode in, then regarded Amot. "You didn't lose any more, did you?"

"I had no idea the strikers were even here," Amot replied.

"Some scout you are," Feleg quipped.

The luminary shut the door behind them, then bar-locked it. He re-angled the old crate he'd sat on previously and made himself a comfortable seat. His feet were sore after hours of being drilled by Ralador, standing in front of the assembler. Feleg's could only be worse.

The grig planted himself down on the same low table he'd sat on earlier.

Amot remained standing, casually leaning against a cluttered shelf. "Can I see the other dancing swords?" he asked.

The question caught the luminary off-guard. "Of course," he said, defaulting to his accommodating self. "Yes, I should show you. Remind me before you go."

Feleg addressed Amot. "You're in, by the way," he said. "Tentative noon departure, but confirm with your commander. Mission details to follow."

"Ekkon's Wheel," Amot uttered under his breath. A slow smile formed on his lips.

Feleg went on, "You're not out of the woods yet, Amot. A military tribunal awaits."

"Tribunal?" Amot said. "What's the charge?"

Feleg answered, "I don't want to get into that, but I guarantee the Kith will stand behind you no matter what the charge is. Let's just say it'll be whatever the March Lord decides best suits his purposes." He leaned back and got comfortable. "Finding the lost sword would go a long way towards clearing you, Amot." Feleg paused to look the scout straight in the eye. "What I mean to say is that you, personally, need to be the one to find it. We could argue your co-operation was instrumental to the recovery due to your special ability to connect with the sword."

Hadamard raised his eyebrows to his friend, shot him his best "don't bullshit me" look.

"What?" Feleg shrugged, then pleaded his case. "The judge won't know any better. Just make the whole thing sound mystical, throw in a leviathan or two and you're done."

Hadamard puffed out air. "Ralador can be ruthless," he countered, "and he's not one to be underestimated. We're going to have to work harder than that to keep our heads off the chopping blocks and to keep the sword and others like it from falling into enemy hands."

"Hmph." Feleg crossed his arms over his chest. "On that point, the Queen's Guard should never get their hands on these weapons. Not with that kind of range. This weapon isn't for the open battlefield. This weapon is—"

"I know," Hadamard broke in. A feeling of heaviness came over him. "The exercise proved that much. With two strikers captured by the opposing force and another lost to unknown hands, I was forced to think of the other side of the equation: how can we defend against this capability, once we put it out there?"

"The archives would be especially vulnerable," Feleg said. "King Taradin's long dead, but he still has cultish followers in Harrow with designs on technology. They'll never stop trying to gain access to old-world secrets. Look what happened in the Scarsands."

Hadamard nodded in agreement. "Until we get a better handle on how to control the strikers, limit their use, they need to be locked away. Otherwise, no one is safe."

Amot interjected, "Can't we just tell all of that to Lord Ralador, make him see your points?"

The luminary glanced to his old friend. They both scoffed. Then Feleg regarded Amot.

"You have much to learn about how the worlds work, Scout."

Hadamard cut to the heart of the matter at hand, the real reason he'd gathered Amot and Feleg in the study. "We don't have much time. Here's what we need to do." He shifted his gaze to the grig. "Feleg, I need you to liaise with the 4th Division director."

Feleg's eyes widened. "The Silencer?"

"Yes, Feleg. The 4th may need to be activated. Not to bump anyone off, but for security—their knowledge could help defend against the worst-case scenario."

The grig paused. "The Blue Tower also has the most secure facility—the very core of a volcanic plug."

"Not to mention the Aerie on top—defended by gryphons," Hadamard added.

"Throw away the key."

"For now."

Feleg leaned forward in his seat, folded his hands together. "I'll do my best to convince him," he said, head slowly nodding, eyes to the floor. "It is not a trivial matter. Harrow will take notice."

Hadamard pushed for more. He knew he was asking a lot of his friend. "And I need you to track what people are saying in the Hidden City."

"Again, I'll do my best," Feleg said. This time he winced. "I don't have regular access to Royal Quarter circles, that's all."

"You'll come up with some bullshit," Hadamard said.

Feleg smirked. "You know you can count on me for that."

"And try drumming up a conversation with Nek every so often."

The grig met Hadamard's gaze. "Where will you be?"

"My place is here, for now," Hadamard replied. "I need to run more experiments and train my prospects—we'll need the brain power. That brings me to my next request."

The luminary rose from his seat, made his way to Amot. The scout straightened his stance; Hadamard faced him squarely. A solemnness lurked within the Wilder's wide-eyed stare, and something forlorn permeated his expression.

Hadamard raised a hand, placed it on Amot's shoulder. "Amot, I need you to return with your uncle. Like he just said, you absolutely must be the one to recover the striker. When you have it, safeguard it—from everyone, including the Queen's Guard." Hadamard paused. "And I have to ask one more task of you. It won't be easy."

Amot drew in a long breath, exhaled. "Anything to help."

"This is precisely why I wanted to speak with you before you left. It is very important—extremely important—that I understand the origins of this phenomenon we're dealing with; how it all began. I can't find the words to describe how important it is. I suspect it connects to the same anomaly that led our people from the old world to Theia in the first place, beginning eons ago."

"You're shittin' me," Feleg responded.

"I've never said this out loud and I don't have any real proof. But the more I see, the more I'm convinced that the answer lies in the wake of humanity's passage to this world. Hurlorns—through their collective consciousness—are the only beings who can make the connections for us; the only beings with access to thousands of years of living history. Even the greatest Jhin thaumaturgist's knowledge surely pales in comparison."

Amot grimaced. "I'm not sure I'm the one for that… I don't understand how it all works… elemental stones… fractured dimensions… cutting through space and all that. And I don't know exactly what it is you need to find out."

Don't try to explain everything, Hadamard told himself. He held back and kept it simple. "I'm looking more for the essence than the technicalities. You have unique family connections that give you the kind of access us luminaries can only dream of."

"You mean to a Spirit Hurlorn."

Hadamard nodded.

Amot's eyes widened in self-reflection. "I do owe one a visit…"

"Exactly," Hadamard replied. He glanced to Feleg.

The grig winked back, then regarded the scout. "You have it in you, Amot, to do what needs to be done. I know that." He turned his gaze to Hadamard. "He's ready."

Heavy with caveats, the luminary spent the next half hour explaining the bare minimum of what Amot needed to know about Hurlorn and Jhin thaumaturgy, as he once had to Feleg. Amot was keen to understand. He listened intently and had many questions, especially regarding the special rules that applied to the Otherworldly Realm. Feleg, seeing that the conversation no longer involved him, quietly made his exit early on. In the end, after much discussion, Amot pledged to leave for Deepweald's sacred grove the next day, early morning before the coming recovery mission. He would ask a certain Hurlorn he once knew for some answers to Hadamard's most important questions. A Hurlorn his grandfather knew well, as a man, before the transcendence.

After the scout's pledge, Hadamard breathed a deep sigh of relief. Feleg had already attested that Amot's word was as solid as rock, like his father's and grandfather's before him. And after Amot bade farewell and exited the study, Hadamard sat back down on his crate, pondered the moment.

Exactly the kind of access I need, he assured himself. *But will it be enough?* No human or colossus could possibly know.

DIAMONDBACK

(Galewind)

I WILL HAVE TO *pay an early morning visit to the Aerie,* thought Galewind. *Lady Apsarla and Order Valkyrie need to be briefed.* The knightmaiden's visits to the Aerie had been few and far between since her posting to the palace more than a decade ago. As she waited for her glideboat's departure from Tetherport, Galewind read over the final entry in her notes.

The recovery mission was discussed in Scout Amot Rixin's absence:

- A March officer (duelist - name unknown) suggested that a Djinxarai projectionist be sent in place of Rixin, but a Jhin Master objected, stating that their talents are extremely limited outside the Otherworldly Realm.

- Kith Commander Berendt Garondi's adamant opposition to Rixin being excluded from the mission probably destroyed his prospects for joining the Queen's Guard, a personal goal of his for some time.

– Lord of the March, Loraith Ralador, wanted to send a company of queensmen, but the grig and ex-ranger identified only as Feleg pointed out that such an action was sure to alert Harrow, and that King Taeglin of Dim Lake would react by sending greater forces to the Line of Control in Whisperwood Forest. Such forces surely would complicate recovery, especially if the mission required penetration into Harrowian territory. All agreed secrecy was the best policy.

– In the end, it was decided that two detachments of horse riders will be sent, with ***valkyries*** to provide overwatch. Garondi will lead three ranger trackers into the forest to recover the lost dancing sword, while Champion Eriff Haulik will take three Queen's Guards to block the northern passage to Harrow's Gate and thereby prevent the sword from crossing into enemy territory.

– Scout Amot Rixin will join Garondi's detachment, but under severe restrictions. He is not to bear arms. He is not to invoke a striker, should one be made available, except under extreme circumstances and even then, only for farseeing.

– On Lord Ralador's insistence, upon Rixin's return, the scout is to be tried in a military tribunal for 'overly aggressive actions towards a member of the Queen's Guard during an exercise.'

Risks / opportunities going forward:

* Tension between the Kith Ranger's and the Queen's Guard could jeopardize the mission's success.

* The mission will be entering Wulver territory. Little is known about the nature and capabilities of the ' man-wolves' that dwell there.

* Securing a striker could prove to be a valuable move for Order Valkyrie.

Mission parameters:

Last-minute details to be coordinated between the Queen's Guard, the Aerie, and the Kith Rangers by pen and raven. I recommend we rendezvous at Elgar's Pocket.

Mission code name:' Operation Diamondback.' (secret)

ABOUT THE AUTHOR

Everyone has quirks. Everyone has patterns they fall into again and again. Everyone has conditions they like to see satisfied.

My research supervisor wrote both poetry and particle physics. He once told me that he listened to blaring opera for the particle physics. I'm not sure how he wrote poetry. I doubt the recipe was any different.

I would like to say that the words just pour out of me when I'm writing, that the blank pages fill with pixels before my very eyes like magic. It doesn't happen that way though, not usually, not for me. Rarely, perhaps, but the typical process is much different and depends on many things, most notably my state of mind. I have to become lost in my own inner workings. Another precondition seems to be that some idea has to have been rolling around in my head for so long that I just have to get it out before it drives me mad. I may have a few notes scribbled on an envelope to help me out, or typed into my cellphone, rolled into a mnemonic, or otherwise recorded using whatever medium was available at the time.

The biggest obstacle to writing: there is no time.

For anything.

Life is busy, and so almost all of my writing happens during the minutes, the tens of minutes, and if I'm lucky, an hour or two in between everything else. It happens when I am up in the middle of the night, sleepless, and when I am waiting alone in my vehicle. It happens when I don't expect it. It happens after dinner when, with a glass of red wine in hand, I might be able to sneak away into our back room. The "Great Room" I call it. And it is a great room, with a red hardwood floor and a high ceiling that slopes down parallel to the roof. It has a phonograph behind the bar and a milk crate of vinyl to go with it. Everything in that room is interesting to look at, from fantasy art to brightly colored metal bugs to resin casts of dinosaur bones and even a saber-toothed tiger skull. A ceiling fan with a tree-stump for a base and antlers cupping light bulbs keeps the air from getting stale. A 400-year-old table from Mexico holds my laptop and candelabra. There are big windows looking out onto farmland.

And there is a sword hanging above the fireplace that I found buried in a construction site when I was ten years old. Yes, a sword. It was encased in cement, and all the kids in the neighborhood tried to pull it free, but couldn't. When I tried, it slid out easily. I knew then that I would be king of the block from that day forward (OK… just kidding about the last part, but I did find one).

That's another thing: letting yourself get carried away. You can always go back later and make better sense of what you wrote while chasing some elusive thought. You need that raw material. The raw material comes when you forget that you are typing, when you forget who is in the house or even who is in the room talking to you, when you forget all that is happening in the world except for the one thought you are chasing, the one idea that is so hard to catch you think it might not be worth the chase, that it might just slip away. But it is worth it. And it will slip away if you don't catch it right then and there.

In essence, I just keep chasing.

Where was I again?

- Kevin

❧

K.B. Sprague is a Canadian epic fantasy writer and physicist.

Born in small-town Northern Ontario, he developed a curious mind and a true appreciation of the natural world during his youngest years. K.B. Sprague went on to attend universities in Southern Ontario, earning a doctorate in theoretical physics. Summer work terms still kept him grounded in the North though, spent working in a uranium mine and mineral prospecting camps. After graduating, he took on research projects in the natural resources, defense, and security sectors, with excursions into nuclear and particle physics, medical imaging, directed energy, geomodelling, complex systems, war games, quantum technologies, and artificial intelligence.

K.B. Sprague lives on a hobby farm on the outskirts of Ottawa, Ontario with his wife and three children. He recently wrapped up *Reforged*, the second book of the *Luminary* series, and is writing the third.

❧

I hope you enjoyed the read! If so, a review on amazon.com would be great! Thank you for your support.

Ingram Content Group UK Ltd.
Milton Keynes UK
UKHW051804090323
418254UK00001B/17